THE DEVINE DEVILS

JEREMY SPILLMAN

ACKNOWLEDGMENTS

A special thanks to my wife, Melissa, without whom none of my creative endeavors would be possible.

To my sons, Nathan, Edwin, Bennett and Jed who have to put up with their crazy dad trying to make stuff up all the time.

A heartfelt thanks to my editor Alice Sullivan, who made this book infinitely better than it would have been without her.

To Eric Church for being giving enough to write a foreword for *The DeVine Devils*. It means the world to have your words about creativity in this book.

To Dave Barnes, Travis Meadows, Brad Allen, Scott Spillman, Clint Ingersoll, Sarah Ingersoll, Jenn Schott, Ken Johnson, Randy Montana, Eric Church, Jon Green, Tyler Dial, Mary Steenburgen, Ted Danson, Brandon Lancaster, John Osbourne, Bill Buntyn, Bill Gallaher, Erica Cole, David Lee, Trent Willmon and Dean Dillon for being the first people to read *The DeVine Devils*.

FOREWORD

Writing songs with someone is a creatively intimate process. You get to know someone at an inspirationally cellular level—what their fears are, their hopes, shortcomings, failures, triumphs, and dreams. The most important thing you get a glimpse at, though, is a person's imaginative soul.

I've written amazing songs with Jeremy Spillman—some you've heard, some you haven't—but all are equally unique and special in their own way. That's just the kind of writer Jeremy is.

We have written things together that people have felt enough passion for to tattoo their bodies with the lyrics or the titles. I've had the good fortune to stand on innumerable stages for countless masses of people, and had them sing those lyrics in deafening, unified harmony. So to say I've seen the power of what a person can come up with in the silent solitude of a half-lit morning, would be entirely accurate.

However, I was admittedly unprepared for the moment when, somewhat out of the blue, Jeremy handed me a manuscript and said, "Hey man, I've written a book." Full disclosure here, I'm an avid reader, maybe 50-60 books a year. I'm even what academia would call a *book snob*. Selfishly, I'm quite proud of that pugnacious self-evaluation. So as I stared at a simple white sheet of paper with a foreboding title in faded black letters, I wondered aloud, "What in the hell are DeVine Devils?"

I learned the breathless tale of these brothers, Audie and Shane, reminded me a lot of my relationship with my brother. Sure, we may have not done the same sensational things as the DeVines, but we did deal with our humanity in an entirely primal and musical way. A bond that people share over music, and specifically making music, is among the strongest connections life provides.

Jeremy does an amazing job of using that bond as a backbone to a dizzying adventure—one that deals with life, death, humor, loss, prejudices, love, and of course music. I very simply loved it.

I always judge a book on how much I think of it, and miss reading it, after I finish it. I still think of *The DeVine Devils* often. I miss their characters and the conclusion of the time I spent getting to know them. I miss the relationship the brothers share with each other, and yes, when I think of them, I miss my brother also.

I'm thankful Jeremy wrote it, and I'm thankful he shared it with me and with the world. We are all better off for it.

Eric Church

PROLOGUE

Arizona Territory
1863

"The white man and the Indian should live as brothers."

The general's tone came off rehearsed. He pulled the glove off of his right hand and offered it to the Apache chief to shake.

Chief Cochise held his gaze for a moment, then looked away to peaks of the blood red, striped plateaus. They rose like would-be tombstones in the desert around them.

The Arizona territory was still jagged and bullying to a man without the guts for it, and western America had earned the name "The Wild West."

But to the Apache, it was home.

Cochise met his eyes again.

"We will let the white men coming from the east pass in peace," he said as he took General Capstock's hand.

The strength in the Indian's grip surprised the soldier.

It pained Chief Cochise to make this vow, but he knew that for his people it was the only hope of evading total slaughter. They could defeat the Americans in small numbers, but the troops' forces grew every time. Cochise knew he needed to make this deal to protect his people.

General Capstock smiled.

"Good. Let's break bread."

Cochise didn't trust Capstock's toothy smile. There was something calculated in it.

Even though these *Magáani* had promised his people could hold this land—this land his ancestors had held sacred for millennia—he knew their hearts still desired it. And he knew they thought a few redskins were a small price to pay for it.

"You break your bread. I'd rather eat meat."

Chief Cochise matched the deception of the soldier's smile with mystery in his own. He could feel the general trying to sum him up. He'd be damned if he'd make it easy.

CHAPTER 1

Azariah DeVine was born in 1835, a farmer's son in Eminence, Missouri. He stood a head taller than most men at six feet and three inches. His unlined face mostly hid behind a pepper-black beard, manicured to a sharp point at the end. The patch of hair just underneath his prominent lips was white and equally sharp. It gave him a look of hardness that didn't match the kindness in his river-green eyes. Azariah was teased for being too skinny in his youth, but working with his father, hauling hay and driving fence posts, had broadened his shoulders and chiseled his arms enough to make him intimidating to anyone who didn't know him. He wore a coal-black, wide-brimmed hat like his father before him that shaded his eyes in such a way that people wanted to get close enough to solve the mystery in them.

He heard the call to preach at fifteen years old, and with the help of the Eminence Church of Christ congregation, he attended Eden Theological Seminary in St. Louis. His family had been too proud to ask for help but too poor to carry the burden alone. Sending a child into ministry was one of the few things the DeVines would have accepted handout money for.

Azariah carried his father's old cracked, leather-bound King James Bible at his side everywhere he went. In those days when men drew pistols to settle their disputes, he drew scripture.

Much to his family's displeasure, though, he felt the call leading him to the Apache Indians. His star of Bethlehem hung over the west, and he believed his purpose in this world was to be a missionary to the red man.

He'd held curiosity about the Indians ever since he was old enough to look at picture books. The DeVine farm was a little less than a mile away from Mac Carson's place, who had been an early agent to the Apache in the Indian wars, and Azariah would steal away from his chores every chance he got to hear Mr. Carson speak of his time with the Jicarilla Apache. Mac was one of the few white men the Indians called friend, and he spoke of them as such to Azariah.

Those around him tormented him with tales of scalping, gruesome rants of wild beasts of men whose savagery would strike terror in even the Vikings or the Mongols, but their fear-dipped arrows only deepened his resolve.

"Shadrach walked down in the fiery furnace, and God met him there," he'd say to justify his desire to minister to the Apaches. "He'll go with me, too."

The only fear Azariah knew was of failure, and to him that meant not following where he was led.

After his time in seminary, Azariah pursued and married a native flower of Missouri, Adalina Carson, the daughter of Mac and Sadie Carson. They had grown up together and bickered as children, but as they matured, so did their feelings for one another.

She was a thoughtful girl, untaken by the trivial cares that the young usually possess. Her raven hair curled like ocean waves folding in on themselves, and she witnessed the world through shy, caring eyes the same color as the bluebell poppies that bloomed in the spring. An hourglass figure hid in the blue dresses her thin elegant fingers had made for herself.

She had not been without more than a handful of suitors in her time, but Azariah had won her heart. He had pursued her with courage in his words and an honest intent. Adalina was moved by his passion for life, both for her and his calling.

She didn't love the idea of him going west for months at a time, but she had grown up with a father who'd done the same, so it was familiar, and she loved Azariah enough to take the good with the bad.

Adalina was Mac's only child. He had known Azariah was cut from good stock since he was a boy. He respected his bravery and understood the allure of the redskins, so Azariah easily had Mac's favor.

Like most couples, Adalina and Azariah started having children shortly after they were married. Within the first three years they had two sons, Audie first, and then Shane.

Azariah had been making trips west since before they were married but stayed home the first five years of their marriage to look after Adalina while she was pregnant and raising their infant children.

Her mother, Sadie, had passed while giving birth to Adalina. Adalina took to motherhood with a gratitude that came from never having a mother of her own.

She was content with her lot in life. With the exception of her husband's treks to Indian territory, she considered her life one to be favored. Her big dreams only traveled about three hundred miles to the City of Kansas. A trip to a fine tailor or a ride in a rail car suited her fancy just fine.

Azariah's family had a plot of farmland just outside of Eminence that was given to him after his parents' passing. Forty-seven acres of slow-rising hills populated by birch, beech, and elm trees. The fields of fescue blanketed the ground and sparkled like precious jade stone under the weight of the morning dew.

The land was as fertile and abundant in wildlife as any in the state of Missouri. In the summer, the sunset would light the western sky on fire, and in the winter, even when it shone white in the noon of the day, the sun offered no warmth at all.

Azariah's parents had died three years apart from each other. Zeek DeVine, Azariah's father, had passed from what everyone assumed was a heat stroke. Ada DeVine, Azariah's mother, had found him dead in a cotton field late one hot August afternoon. They laid him in the ground in his white wool work shirt stained with dusty sweat and cotton work pants worn through in the knees. Ada had refused to shave the silver beard that flowed down to his waistline, stating that God and she loved the man the way he was. She said she knew Zeek wouldn't want to meet Saint Peter unbearded and in some suit he never would have worn in this life.

Ada passed away only a few months after Azariah wed Adalina from what all who knew her judged a broken heart. She was delighted her son had married and was pleased with his choice, but without Zeek there to share it with, she just didn't have much will to stay around after that.

Zeek had cleared ten acres for cattle to graze and built a home there. Azariah had added a bedroom onto it when their second child came. Adalina thought of the room as a luxury, but Azariah wanted the best he could offer for his family.

It was a country home. Beech logs that Azariah's father had cut were the shelter against the outside world for the DeVine family. The wood had settled and weathered to a darker brown over the years, with the exception of the addition Azariah had built. The tin roof that topped the building had small patches of rust on it and little patches of new tin covered where a leak had worked its way in through a rogue nail hole or two. The persistent chant of a summer shower was soothing enough to lull any DeVine to sleep.

There was cotton and corn to tend in the summer and a few pigs, cattle, and chickens to tend to year-round. Kitch and Mabel Tandey, a black family who lived just down the road a half a mile, helped out with the crops when Azariah was away. The DeVines gave them a quarter share of the crops and half of the bull calves for their work.

Azariah got a small stipend from the church congregation for his missionary work. While it wasn't much, it was enough to buy some thread or material they needed every so often from the mercantile.

The blue-eyed Mary flowers Adalina planted around their porch sweetened her view in the warmer months, while a giant bur oak gently swayed Azariah to contentment in a summer breeze. It was a simple place. A place of work and play and laughter and lessons. A place where a good man and woman could live and die in peace.

~

After twelve years of marriage, Adalina had become used to the uncertainty of Azariah's return. She fought her anxiety with her hands. There was always a piece of clothing that needed mending, meals to cook, garden to tend, and a host of other chores a woman raising two boys needed to do. She navigated their lives with grace, but her prayers were humble.

Adalina never complained, but the boys knew she was never at peace when their father was gone, and he was gone about half of every year. Azariah's faith scattered their family west; her faith held it together in Missouri.

Azariah would spend months in Arizona territory. Each time it seemed his homecomings grew further apart.

He had grown to understand the Apache and appreciate their ways. When he was home, he preached of their unselfishness and their regard for each other in impassioned rants at his local church.

"It is an abomination how our people are ravishing the Indians!" Azariah delivered from the cross carved pulpit. "And all in the name of God and progress! I have ministered to these so-called savages, and I tell you they are capable of peace with peaceful men. They've welcomed me into their camp and offered heart to my words. I beg you, do not be deceived by the dime store novels that speak of the evil and debauchery of these people! Yes, they are sinners just as you and I are, but they are in need of and capable of receiving the love of Christ! Do not fall prey to the deceit of the printing press. Help me in welcoming these sheep into heaven's fold!"

Few people saw things the way he did. He was preaching to the choir, but the choir didn't like the preaching. Most people in

Eminence, Missouri had never even met an Apache, and it's easier to fear a person than love them.

Unknown things make easy monsters.

It was the year 1868. Azariah was thirty-three now, and he had become as passionate about proselytizing for the Indian as he was in ministering to them. It was an obsession, one no one shared with him. Even Adalina's father, Mac, had withdrawn his consoling shoulder.

Mac, withered and weathered from an adventurous seventy-four years of life, had let the comforts of home far outweigh the call of the wild. He wanted Azariah to stay home to tend to his daughter and grandsons.

"Your life is in Missouri now, Azariah," Mac said as he pointed a crooked cane at his son-in-law. "There comes a time when every man needs to settle down and meet all his days from the same doorway. I gave up my wayfaring ways. Your family needs you. Lay aside the wild abandon of youth and take up a man's yolk."

They'd been having these word wars for the last year now.

"How can you say these things? You know full well the dangers the red man faces! I will not turn a blind eye to their affliction!" Azariah's face heated crimson at the hypocrisy he heard in Mac's words.

"Can the red man offer you the assurance of your adoring wife in the dark of night? Or the strength of a well-raised son when you are on in years?"

"I will not cower from the path God has set me on! If it is a choice of my family or calling it will break me, but I WILL CHOOSE GOD!"

Azariah was pacing the porch outside Mac's house as he spoke. He had stopped to deliver the last sentence right in front of where Mac sat on a rocking chair.

"You have so much to learn of life, Azariah." Mac shook his head as he scolded. "Some things in this world aren't supposed to come with a choice. A man's family is a hand full of aces. It should win every time."

"I'm not a man who gambles with those things," Azariah shot back.

Sometimes the last word doesn't win the argument. It's just the last word.

~

"Honeysuckle, I want to talk to you."

Adalina hesitated then went back to hanging clothes on the line.

Twelve years of loving a person brings with it a familiarity. She knew Azariah wanted to speak on things she didn't want to hear. She could hear him trying to hide it in his voice.

"Why do I feel I won't be comforted by this conversation?"

"I want to take you and our sons with me the next time I visit the Apache."

Her dress flared as she turned quickly to face him. She held her hands up in disbelief and stood there looking shocked for a few seconds before she spoke.

"You have lost your wits, Azariah! You would lead your family into the godforsaken unknown of the West? Even from your tales I know it is no place for women and children!" she protested.

Azariah stepped to her and stroked her arms as he spoke.

"God has protected me at every turn, and he will protect my family. I have never faced mortal danger. The Indians are my friends, Adalina. They would welcome you and the boys with respect."

"Azariah, I love you, but I cannot go with you. My heart has no bounds, but my feet do. Please put this notion from your mind!"

"Adalina, my heart is set on it. How can I convince these blinded people of the worth of the red man without help? I need them to know peace-loving people can coexist without contention with the Apache. What better way than to bring back a family safe and full of wonderful tales of the Indian way of life? The people need to see that our government is the evil one here! Not the Apache!"

"You would risk your family to bring this revelation to Missouri?" It was more an accusation than a question.

"There is no risk, Adalina. Have I ever come home with injury? Even a scratch?"

Adalina clenched her fists and planted them on her hips.

"A man going out to the wilderness is not the same as a boy. Or a lady! How could you ask such a thing of me?"

"I beg you to consider it. Have faith, woman! God has always brought me back. Why would he not do the same for you and the boys?" he asked.

"I will not!" Adalina exploded. "I abide your calling because it has always been the sun rising to you, Azariah. But it is not my calling, nor our sons'. You may very well prove your point to the masses, but you will do it without endangering your family!" She pounded her fists on some unseen thing at her sides as she spoke.

"I'm taking my sons, Adalina. They are nine and eleven now. That's older than your father was when he set out to trap the first time. With or without you, I'm taking Audie and Shane," Azariah said as firm as he could without losing the gentle he was aiming for.

He turned from her and made his way up the porch steps to walk inside their house.

"You will not!" she declared as she ran after him. "You cannot take my sons from me! You take the comfort of you being here, and I have learned to live without that when you are gone, but you will not take being a mother from me, too!"

"I have decided. They'll go with me when I leave in two days. I beg you to reconsider and come along." He walked back to her and rested his hands on her waist. "I desire your companionship in this. You're the woman I love, Adalina. The only one I ever will. Nothing would make me happier than having you on this journey."

She pulled away quickly and gave a sigh of defeat before she returned back to the sagging clothesline. She had no more words in her. She frantically hung a pair of Shane's pants and didn't bother to wipe the tears Azariah had inspired streaming down her face.

Azariah had no violence in him, but when he set his mind to something, he moved to it with might. Few men who walk this earth have ever had that combination. He hadn't come across the force yet that could stop him. He saw the latter quality in his sons, especially in Audie, and it troubled him some, mostly because Audie could never be accused of not being violent. He had blackened more than one eye at school, and he and Shane swapped blows at least once a day. But that's the way with brothers. A wrestling match could just as easily be a show of affection as it was a contest of strength. Much of the time it was both.

Audie and Shane were fine sons. Each had their own strengths and struggles, but Azariah and Adalina loved them with everything they had.

Audie had his own way of seeing the world. He was quiet at times, even pensive, taking in the life around him like it was research. Still, there was no doubt that he was all boy. He welcomed his challenges with the will of an untamed stallion, and like his father, he had no intentions of being broken. He was tall for his age and growing so fast that it seemed his pants were always a couple of inches too short or his shirt hugged him a little tighter than it should. Audie's wavy locks were from his mother, but the leanness of his face left no doubt who his father was.

Like his brother, Shane was all boy, through and through. He was a little more easygoing than Audie, but would let his fists fly when pushed to his limit. There was more of a playful spirit about him. He enjoyed the fouler things that most boys do. Spitting, farting, snakes, frogs—anything with a modicum of gross to it. His mother detested this quality. His father was entertained by it.

He showed affection much easier, maybe because he was the youngest. And despite all the bickering and fists that came between him and his brother, he looked to Audie like the moon does the sun. He preferred to shine with him rather than against him.

Even though the two were at odds most of the time, Audie would have gone toe to toe with any one of God's creatures to protect his brother. In his mind, he was the only one who had the right to pick on Shane.

Shane had more of Adalina's look. You could see her most in his eyes. Azariah liked to claim that was the reason she doted on him, but Adalina would laugh and say that was ridiculous.

Azariah loved to sit and watch his sons play around the bur oak in the yard. It gave his heart rest from the world that set upon it. The battle in his soul stopped raging for a small stretch of time when he studied them being rambunctious.

He had a cedar wood guitar that had been payment to him for some farm work he did for one of the ministers at Eden Theological. It was an odd way to get paid, but he loved music and accepted it with a "Thank you, sir."

He would strum on that guitar and take in the scene before him like it was a Shakespeare play in St. Louis. But soon reality would set in, and his mind would give way to less pleasant matters.

"Audie, Shane, come over here. Tomorrow at first light you'll ride west with me. Have your ponies saddled and ready. I'm taking you to meet my Apache friends."

"Really, Daddy? Real Indians?" Audie's eyes widened.

"Yes, real Indians. Shane, does this make you happy?"

"Will Mama come?" Shane asked.

"Son, your mother doesn't want to come on this trip. Maybe the next one."

"Don't worry, little brother. They'll be plenty of bears and coyotes to tuck you in at night."

Audie pushed Shane and knocked him a couple of unsteady steps to the side before he came back with a fist to Audie's shoulder. Audie laughed and pushed him again.

"I'm not afraid of coyotes!" Shane said with a tiny quiver in his voice.

"Boys, stop arguing and get your things ready for the ride tomorrow. It's gonna be a long one. I want you well rested, so no staying up telling ghost stories like last night."

"We thought you were asleep, Daddy!" Audie was stunned his father had heard them.

"Son, the Indians taught me to hear when I'm asleep and see with my eyes closed. Maybe they'll teach you, too. If the bears and coyotes don't get you first."

Azariah formed his hands into claws and stomped toward his sons as they ran off laughing.

"Now, get going."

The boys bounded away to prepare for the next morning.

"Well, you've got them riled up." Adalina walked up, wiping her hands on a dish towel and smiling to hide the worry she had welling up inside of her stomach. She'd heard the conversation from the kitchen window.

"They want their mother to come along. I beg you, Adalina, to at least entertain the idea."

"Who would take care of this place, Azariah?" Her fists were clenched and on her hips. "It's going to be hard enough with you taking them, but if I went, too? Do you want your home in shambles when you return? It infuriates me the way you are incapable of reason when your mind is set to something!"

She lifted one hand off of her hip to poke a finger in his chest. "They are nine and eleven! I don't care how old my father was the first time he ventured out. These are my sons! You steal half my sleep when you're gone and now the other half will be taken as well! Do you ever think about the cost of your calling to me? Do you ever take account of my sacrifice? What if you save your precious Indians and lose your family, Azariah? Is that a price you're willing to pay?"

"I do not believe that is what God has for us, honeysuckle. I wish I could show you my heart and the confidence God has given me that my family will be safe."

Azariah spoke softly to try and calm his wife.

"Well, God has spoken no such words of encouragement to me."

"I love you, Adalina. You and you alone."

"I love you, too. Damn you, Azariah DeVine." A tear strolled down the left side of her face against her will. She turned to face him with despair filling up her eyes.

"Please make sure my boys come back unscathed. And I wouldn't mind it if you did the same."

"I'd die before I let harm come to them."

"That's what I fear, Azariah."

Adalina closed her eyes and lowered her head. She prayed for her family.

The next morning rolled in like faraway thunder. Azariah welcomed it like rain in the summer. Adalina dreaded it like a bad winter storm.

"Mama, why won't you come?" Shane asked.

"Mama has to stay and tend to the place, baby, but I'll think of you every day. Will you pray for me before you go to sleep at night?"

Adalina was fighting the tears with a smile, but the tears had more ammunition.

"I'll take care of him, Mama. I'm the toughest bastard to ever walk out of Missouri!" declared Audie with his chest puffed out.

"Audie DeVine! Where did you hear that word? Young man, I'm of a mind to send you away with the taste of soap in your mouth. I don't ever want to hear that kind of talk from you again!" She glared at him with rebuking eyes.

"Yes, ma'am. Sorry, Mama."

She certainly didn't like hearing her son use that kind of language, but it helped to break the tension. She was grateful for that. That was probably all that saved his mouth from a bar of lye soap.

"You boys hug your mother and say your goodbyes. We need to get moving."

"Bye, Mama. I love you. We'll be back soon."

Audie hugged his mother and quickly mounted the golden-maned horse. He had his mind on leaving. He loved his mother, but right now all he could think about was adventures out west.

"I love you too, Audie. You mind your father."

She reached up and took his hand in both of hers. Adalina's voice broke as she spoke.

Shane pressed his head against the ruffles on her navy dress. Her long fingers stroked his unkempt hair as he squeezed her tightly. "I love you, Mama. I promise I'll pray for you every night."

That won the battle for the tears. Adalina let go of him and turned around in a failed attempt not to let her sons see the sadness leaking from her eyes.

"I love you, Shane. I'll miss you," she said, still turned away.

"You boys ride on up ahead. I'll catch up in a bit."

Azariah felt the curve of his wife's body as he paced his hands on her hips.

"I love you, Adalina. I'm sorry this is so hard on you. I never want to hurt you."

"I know. You are what you are. I hate it, but I love you. Sometimes I hate you because I love you."

Adalina's pretty face was distorted and tear soaked now.

"That's a little confusing, honeysuckle."

It was a small attempt at humor. It had no effect on her.

Azariah kissed her forehead and then her crimson lips and held on tight to her slender waist for a while. He loved her spring morning scent. The familiar of her velvet skin. These were the times he felt the pull toward staying. It slowed him down but never stopped him.

"When will you be back?" Adalina tried to smile again.

"I'm not sure. Maybe three months."

"Take care of Audie and Shane. Don't let Audie pick on his brother too much."

"They'll be too busy to be ornery. I love you, honeysuckle."

"I love you, too."

He mounted his gelding and rode off in a trot down the wagon-wide path. Azariah looked back, but Adalina had her eyes closed again in prayer.

No matter how many times he left, neither one of them ever got comfortable with that part.

~

Shane and Audie felt like grown men on the trail out west with Azariah. Even little things like gathering kindling for an evening fire or skinning the gray and brown fur off of a rabbit to cook made them feel like they were ready to walk in a man's shoes.

"How much longer till we reach the Verde Valley, Daddy?" Shane was busting at the seams to meet the Indians.

It had been almost two weeks since they'd left home.

"About a week and a half, son. Not too long."

Azariah had found a little clearing about three yards in either direction, thirty paces off the trail. There was brush almost all around it, so any intruder would have to move like a ghost to get in unannounced.

"Daddy, will you show me something new on the guitar tonight?" Audie asked.

"Pretty soon you'll be showing me, Audie! You've got a touch with those strings that I don't have. I'd rather hear you play."

"Aw come on. Please, Daddy?"

Azariah chuckled. "Okay. After you play a while. I'm running out of things to teach you."

Audie got the guitar out and started strumming a mournful song while his father packed dark-brown tobacco leaves in a beechwood pipe he'd carved himself. Audie had a way of making the guitar sound different from anything he had heard before. Azariah could never put his finger on what was so compelling about it, but he got lost in the music when Audie played.

"What's that thing you're playing?"

"I don't know. Something I made up."

"Well, it sounds to me like a rain cloud opening up in the summer. I don't know how you do that, Audie. You have a gift."

"Sounds like a horse pissing to me," offered Shane, grinning from ear to ear.

"Well, you smell like horse turds!" Audie fired back.

Azariah chuckled.

"Boys, I don't think either one of you have much in common with horse excrement."

Audie went on playing into the night. Shane listened till his eyes were weighted too heavy with sleep, and Audie wasn't far behind him. Azariah stayed up much of the night praying and thinking. It was his usual evening.

It would be a week and a half before they reached the Indian territory.

CHAPTER 2

The ride from Eminence wasn't easy for any man, but Azariah had made it enough times that he knew a few secrets. There were shortcut paths off of other paths, places where the wild game nearly fell in your lap, and a bevy of other tricks that a well-seasoned traveler would make use of. Having his boys along for the journey added pleasure, but they also brought with them aggravation. It was well worth it to him, but he was more ready than usual to arrive in Verde Valley. He knew his sons would be fascinated with the Indian children. Their new friends would keep them busy for a while, and that was a good thing, because he was ready for a break.

A friend of his, Natan Lupen, which meant Grey Wolf, was the first to find him. Natan had heard them coming from inside the red-rock ravine where he had been hunting for small game and snuck up to see. He recognized Azariah's voice when he got close.

"Preacher makes so much noise even a raging river couldn't hide it."

Audie and Shane jumped and spun their heads around at the sound of Grey Wolf's words.

"Well, what kind of preacher would I be, Grey Wolf, if I didn't make a little racket?"

Azariah knew Grey Wolf's baritone voice well. It was comforting to hear.

"How are you, friend?"

"From your sound, more rested than you."

Azariah laughed.

"You are perceptive, Natan. It's good to be at the journey's end. Grey Wolf, these are my sons, Audie and Shane."

Grey Wolf looked at the awestruck boys. "You have a good father. You're welcome among our people."

"Thank you, sir. We're glad to be here." Audie sat up straight as he spoke.

"Good to meet you, Mr. Wolf," Shane said as he reached a hand out to shake.

Grey Wolf laughed heartily. "That is a white man's title, but I know you mean it as a sign of respect. It is good to meet you too, Mr. Shane."

They headed toward the camp. Azariah felt at peace here among the so-called heathen. The colorful way the people dressed, the domed grass-covered wickiups they lived in scattered all around, and the dirty-faced children so in awe of seeing a white man. Azariah loved it all.

The camp was truly a thing of wonder to Audie and Shane. All together it was around two hundred yards in every direction, spilling over with a look and a life they never could have imagined without seeing it firsthand. There were a little more than a hundred people walking around, and each one was more fascinating than the last to two boys from Missouri. They had only heard their father's tales of this place. Their previous visions didn't do it justice. The tanned buffalo skin tents, the women with beads hanging from their leather clothing, the men with mohawks and red and yellow sashes around their midnight-colored hair—everything held some curiosity about it. The boys were storing up a thousand questions for their father.

Grey Wolf and the others dismounted and tied their horses to a tree limb. Audie's and Shane's feet touched earth in the camp for the first time. Azariah looked around and walked over to an elderly looking Indian and shook his hand.

"Boys, come here. I want you to meet someone. This is Chief Cochise."

Audie and Shane almost tripped over each other trying to get to him first.

"Dad, is this really Chief Cochise?" Shane asked.

"Yes, boy. I am Chief Cochise. I am a friend of your father, and I welcome you to our land. We are honored that your father brought you on his journey."

"Thank you, sir. I can't believe it's really you!" Audie spoke, but it was Shane's sentiment as well.

Chief Cochise chuckled. "Preacher, your son thinks I am a dream!"

"They've heard a lot about you, Chief. They're honored to meet you."

"Enough of this talk. Let us eat." Chief Cochise didn't love flattery. He grimaced and motioned the visitors toward a table where a few women were bringing out food.

The next few weeks would be some of the best of Audie and Shane's lives. They would make friends and learn things like how to make a bow. They'd learn how to kill their dinner with no more than a knife. They would see a world that most folks from Missouri would never get to see. They would learn what the buffalo provided and how the Apache saw the land as sacred. They'd learn that their father's words about these people were true.

They'd learn that sometimes the best things come to an end.

❧

Two months later

Audie and Shane took to the Indian way of life like it had always been their own. Maybe because they were still young. Maybe because of Azariah's affection for the Apache. Either way, the boys greeted their days there as openhearted as they did in Missouri.

Much like back home in Eminence, days were spent doing chores, such as gathering firewood or hunting small game with the other children and swimming in the river. But the nights were different. They were passed around a campfire with Azariah's guitar strumming along to the music the Apache drummers were making. Audie and Shane would sit around the fire, watching the odd dances the people would do and listening to the unfamiliar tunes. They were learning Jicarilla Apache words such as *chelee*, which meant horse and *ba'iitso*, meaning wolf. Water was *kóh*, and one they used most often was *iyą*. It meant eat.

Natan was teaching Shane how to play drums. He had grown to love Shane, and he enjoyed being able to show the boy something he knew. Maybe Natan loved him because Shane let people in his world a little easier than Audie did, or it could have just been because he was the youngest. Maybe it was because Natan had lost his only son in one of the Indian wars almost eight years earlier.

Azariah knew they had to leave soon, and it pained him and comforted him at the same time. But school would be starting, and Adalina would not be happy at all if he caused the boys to miss it. But more than that, he longed for the scent of Adalina's hair, the softness of her lips. Still, God walked with him in this place. It was no small torture to choose between the two.

He continued the boys' education while they were there. A couple of hours a day they would read from the well-used pages of Azariah's Bible or do simple math problems with a stick in the dirt or with stones. His sons hated it, but he insisted. Some of the other Indian children would join them at times. Azariah loved being able to read the Bible to them.

Pretty quickly after they had arrived in the camp, Shane had become close with a girl from the tribe named Lozen. She was rough enough to hang with Audie and Shane. At times she would get the best of Shane in a wrestling match, which would earn him some ridicule from the other children. Lozen would, in turn, challenge the hecklers, and most of the time defeat them, too.

She had hazel eyes that seemed more the color of the Gila River when she was near it. Her high cheekbones gave her a strong look, and the bow ever ready on her back was as precise in her hands as any in the camp. She wore a buffalo-skin shirt and pants as opposed to the dresses that were custom for Apache women.

Lozen was a year younger than Shane, but she had eyes that looked like they'd seen more than eight years' worth of life. She was determined to be a warrior. Her father had been a mighty warrior for the Apache, but she had lost him to a battle against the U.S. Army when she was five years old, when their camps were still in fertile lands, before they had been driven this far west.

In the same battle, her mother had been captured by the soldiers who killed her father. Lozen had watched the whole thing from her hiding place in the brush. She was nearly dead from dehydration when the elders found her unconscious there days after the fight. They nursed her back to health, and from the moment she was well, she swore she would be a warrior herself.

Against much persuasion and pleading from others in the camp, Lozen lived by herself. She had her own tent and provided all her own food and necessities. An older lady, Onawa, was the closest thing she had to a mother, but Lozen would never speak of her as such.

Some met her claims of being a warrior with scoffing while others encouraged her. To Shane, she was a friend. They were too young for love, but Azariah could sense Shane held her in tender regard, even with all the roughhousing.

"Boys, these people have taught me much of the ways of God. Some see them as heathen and savage, but I see a people who would protect their own with their lives. Greater love has no man than this, that a man lay down his life for his friends."

The sun had two hours before it reached its peak in the sky, and all Audie and Shane could think about was everything they'd rather be doing that morning instead of learning. The boys hated reading time, but they knew their dad well enough to know he loved speaking on these things, and because they loved their father, they listened. Some of those words would sink into their hearts like seeds on newly broken ground. Most children don't realize how much the things they're told early in life affect them, but those first roots of wisdom run deep. A man may spend his whole life trying not to hear those voices, but they never stop whispering.

"Daddy, why do so many people want to hurt the Indians?" Shane inquired one morning.

"I would kill anyone who tried to hurt my friends!" Audie boasted as he brandished his knife and sliced through unseen enemies in the air.

"Audie, killing is not the answer." Azariah's voice was steel and fire as he spoke. "Our way is through the power of God. He will provide salvation for these people. I believe it's our job to introduce the Indians to Him. Practice faith, not vengeance."

He stared at Audie for a moment to make sure he felt the weight of his words.

Audie heard the words but kept his fists clenched.

Azariah turned back to where Shane still lay on the other side of him.

"Shane, the Indians are the rightful owners of this land. Many men from the east want to take it from them. Some men will kill and steal to get what they want. It's been that way since the beginning. The Apache are doing the only thing they know to do in the face of evil."

"Daddy, if they hurt Lozen, I'm gonna have to help Audie!" Shane insisted.

Azariah chuckled.

"I understand how you feel, son. You like Lozen. I'm glad you want to protect her. But I'd be fearful for the man who tangled up with her! She's pretty handy with her fists. He might wish he hadn't picked a fight after she was done with him!"

Just then Audie jumped on Shane and they began to wrestle around on the floor, Audie fighting with all his strength but acting like he wasn't, and Shane fighting with all his strength but not hiding it.

"Alright, boys, run along and play. You've got all day left to see how much dust you can stir up."

"Can we go swimming, Daddy?" asked Shane.

"You mean you and Lozen?" Azariah asked with a smile.

"Uh, yes, sir."

"Yes. Be back by noon."

They were gone in a flash.

That night was like most nights had been since their arrival, a joyful gathering around the fire. A hunting party was leaving the next day, and tonight was a celebration. Shane was playing the drum in time, and Natan was glad to see it. Shane had learned the swagger of the beat and how to rise and fall in energy with the mood of the people. Azariah's face glowed seeing his son take such an interest in something.

Audie was strumming the guitar to Shane's rhythm. Azariah was a proud father.

"That's your guitar now, Audie. You play it better than I do."

"Really, Daddy? It brings you comfort. I don't know if I should take it."

"I want you to have it, son. You make that thing sound like . . . I don't know, like a storm is coming. It sings all by itself in your hands. It belongs to you now. I hope you'll let me play it every now and then, though." Azariah gave him a smile.

"We'll see," Audie toyed with him.

Azariah grabbed him and gave his hair a good tousling.

Audie laughed and continued playing.

CHAPTER 3

"Sir, the Indians have left for a hunt. Headed north," the scout reported to his lieutenant.

"How many bucks left behind, Corporal?"

"I believe only eight, sir. That's how many I counted till the Injun relieving the one on guard came around."

"How many in the camp in all?" Lieutenant Briggs asked, but he knew the scout wouldn't have been able to determine that.

"I'd be afraid to say, sir. I never got too close to the camp. Didn't want to alert the other braves of my being there."

"You're dismissed, Corporal."

"Yes, sir."

Lieutenant Frederick Briggs was cut from rough stock, just the kind of man the government would trust to slaughter a camp of unsuspecting women and children. His dark, narrow eyes were hard to meet for most, and the slowness of his manner belied the fact that he was as dangerous as a stick of dynamite. He was a barrel-chested man, not necessarily of good physique, but he carried the strength of a bear. He was vicious to his troops at times and deadly to his enemy. Killing didn't cost him a second of sleep. His conscience was only weighted by the thoroughness of the job. He never knew his mother, and there was a rumor that his father had killed her. That same drunkard father had beat him mercilessly, and he carried that rage with him like rations of food. When he was hungry, he always had enough to feast on.

~

"When do we attack the camp, Lieutenant Briggs?"

Corporal Stephen Waters had been Briggs's right-hand man for years now. If he needed something bloody done, Waters had no qualms about getting his dirty hands dirtier. He lived for it.

"Tomorrow afternoon. The Injuns always rest after lunch. Lazy bastards. We'll hit them when they're weak. Save the best-looking squaw for entertainment after. We'll take her with us."

Waters laughed and ran his thumb and a finger in opposite directions across his auburn mustache. "Hell, maybe I'll keep two or three. The boys wouldn't mind a little variety."

"I like how you think, Waters." The lieutenant spoke with a lack of emotion that could chill bones.

"Tomorrow then." Waters left.

Some of the other soldiers would drink tonight. Briggs didn't mind, but he himself never partook the day before a fight. It wasn't so much about keeping his senses sharp as it was that he felt the whiskey numbed him to the pleasure of it. He liked to feel the havoc he was delivering.

~

A day had passed, and the camp settled into life without most of the men. There were thirty-eight in all who had left. Azariah had been on a hunt before, so Grey Wolf had urged him to stay since his sons were with him. He obliged.

Azariah sat with the elders and swapped knowledge of his God for theirs. It wasn't so much of a debate as it was a subtle persuasion. The Indians were becoming more open to his beliefs. Azariah didn't preach to the Indians from a soapbox. He got on the same level as them. They talked. They didn't argue. Azariah wanted to show his Apache friends his God, and he knew the way to do that was not from a hellfire-and-brimstone pulpit.

On this day, as he was sitting with some of the elders, he'd insisted Audie and Shane join them. He wanted them to see how peaceful the conversations were between him and the Apache, even though they might disagree on some things. And since Shane was there, Lozen came, too. They fidgeted with boredom but didn't dare speak of it. They all knew to be quiet in that place, that tent where the elderly and the men considered wisest sat and smoked and listened and reasoned. Some of the most important decisions were made there.

The talk had started after the midday meal and lasted a couple of hours.

It was the last peace anyone in the camp would ever know.

"On my command, escort these reds to the gates of hell." Lieutenant Briggs could almost taste the blood that was about to be spilled.

"Any prisoners? Besides a squaw or two for pleasure, of course." Waters laughed. He was hoping for a no.

"Rumor has it there's a preacher here with his two sons. It was asked that their lives be spared, but in the confusion of battle, casualties are inevitable, right?"

Waters cackled again. That was the answer he was looking for.

In a matter of minutes, dozens of souls would pass from this life to the next. The blade and the bullet would tear down the veil that hung in between.

Back in Missouri, Adalina balanced her heavy days with work and whatever else she could find to keep her mind from standing still long enough to focus on the possibilities of what could be happening out west. There wasn't nearly as much to do without two little mess-makers running around, so, after her own chores, she would help her father and anyone else in the area she could spend some time with.

"How long till Azariah's return?" Mac asked his daughter.

"Azariah said three months, which means four. It's been two. So an eternity from now."

"He never should have left you to fend for yourself! How reckless of a husband!" Mac coughed, worked up after speaking.

Adalina went over and patted him gently on the back.

"Father, you left me with Mabel Tandey plenty when I was a child. I wouldn't be so quick to judge Azariah. He's a good man with unselfish and pure intentions. You know this."

"Still, I wanted better for my daughter."

"I married the man I love. I have no regrets. And you more than approved of my choice at the time. The troublesome parts may worry me into an early grave, but that's part of who we are. It's a good practice of faith, even if it's a painful one."

"Faith can be found without such aggravation," Mac said, clearing his throat.

"Not for Azariah."

Adalina finished straightening up around her father's house and mounted her horse to ride back to her home.

She left feeling worse than when she came.

The soldiers had surrounded the camp. There were forty-three men in all; twenty-two on horseback and the rest on foot. The air before the attack felt heavy and hot, like the devil was sweeping the land with fire to hurry the hands of violence. Most soldiers felt an anxiety before the battle, but Waters felt calm. The task at hand weighed on the soul of most, but he felt no gravity of conviction for the deed about to be done. Killing was a sport to him, not a task.

Briggs was seconds away from the signal when a young man next to him said,

"Sir, I can't kill a child."

The baby-faced soldier quivered as he spoke.

"Private, those little bastards will grow into full-grown bucks. You will kill all those in your path or face my wrath. Save another man the trouble, boy! Be rid of them while the ridding is easy."

"Yes, sir, Lieutenant Briggs. I just thought—"

"I don't give a coyote shit what you think, Private. Do your job, or I'll leave your sorry ass lying in this camp with the squaws. If you act like a woman, you can die like one."

This exchange entertained Waters. He noted the private's reservation. If the boy lived through the day, he'd make sure to toughen him up a little.

"Soldiers, ATTACK!"

It was late afternoon now, and the meeting of elders had ended. They were sitting crossed-legged outside watching the children play. The women were cooking in fire-heated pots outside of tents and watching infants and toddlers crawl and walk and fall, and the older children were scattered, playing games or doing various chores. There was one Indian brave who had been on guard, but Waters had laid waste to him with stealth and a knife.

Azariah was in his tent with Audie, Shane, and Lozen.

"Boys, we head back in three weeks. I want you to remember this place. I want you to tell everyone of the peaceful way of life of our friends. I want you to speak of the friends you've made here and of swimming in the shallow of the river and the things you've learned from these people. Can you do that for me?"

"Yes, Father. Can Lozen come with us?" Shane asked.

"I'd love that, son, but Lozen belongs here. This is her home. She's to be a warrior. She's needed to protect her camp."

Lozen pursed her lips and tried not to smile, but her pride got the better of her. She liked Azariah's words.

They all heard a gunshot and a scream. Azariah felt the hair on the back of his neck stand up.

Audie went to the tent flap to look out.

"GET BACK!" Azariah demanded as he grabbed Audie and threw him away from the entry.

Azariah went back to the flap, careful to make sure no one saw him peer out.

A feeble grey-haired woman with blood running down her face was struggling to get up off her knees and crying with the sound of death sorrow. Two beautiful young Indian maidens were being dragged away, screaming like banshees, fighting to face any fate but the one they were being forced into. Everywhere there was death and malice and evil. A young mother with a bloodied face moaned and clung to a silent baby. There were stone-still bodies with bullet holes lying awkwardly on the ground and young boys gut-stuck by their own knives, likely so soldiers could save bullets. Shallow pools of blood fed by rivers that flowed out of the dead and the dying collected the dust from all the commotion.

The demons of war were so present they were almost visible, and they were feasting. Azariah felt his heart go out of him.

He looked back to his sons and Lozen and mustered all of the strength he had in him. In a frantic voice, he said, "Shane! Audie! Grab those canteens. We've got to head for the river! Lozen, stick close to the boys!"

"GO! NOW!" Azariah yelled.

They ran out of the flap with Azariah leading and saw a young brave fifty yards from the tent screaming and trying to dodge a fist. He swung an ax with everything he had but was knocked unconscious with the butt of a soldier's rifle.

"Jesus, get my children to safety. Don't let this be their end," Azariah pleaded as the four of them ran hellbent for the Gila River. He had motioned his children up ahead of him so he could be between them and any soldier who might give chase.

They were halfway to the safety of the brush when a soldier spotted them. Lozen saw him first. The soldier took a knee to steady his aim. Azariah saw him and turned. He fell down on his knees, spreading his hands out and waving at him in an effort to distract the soldier and shield the children from the death ticket he knew was coming.

"NO!" Azariah demanded.

For a second, there was no sound, as though the land held its breath. The bullet and the arrow passed in the air. Lozen had taken aim at the soldier.

Her arrow found its mark.

So did the soldier's bullet.

It was Lozen's first kill.

It was the soldier's last.

"NO!" Audie screamed.

"DADDY!" Shane echoed.

The boys began to run back toward Azariah, but Lozen urged them to keep going.

"More soldiers are here! We have to go! We will die, too!"

The boys froze in indecision for a second, but reluctantly took off in a sprint after Lozen.

The battle raged on for another hour. The devil painted the day in red.

Azariah was barely clinging to life when Waters stumbled on him.

"Well! Ain't you the white speck in the chicken shit. A man who beds with redskins ain't no better than one himself."

"I would never claim to be a better man."

Azariah gurgled blood as he spoke. He held the hole in his side where the bullet had lodged in his liver.

"Tell me, did a squaw whore dick-drag you here or are you just low enough to like living amongst these heathens?"

Azariah mustered up all the defiance he could.

"God brought me here!" His words came with dark-red blood

trickling out of the side of his mouth. Waters knelt down and stared at Azariah with a smirk on his stubble-ridden face.

"Well, I'd tell Him what a raw deal He gave you when you see Him."

He ran a well-worn knife through Azariah's throat. He kept it there for a few seconds just to feel the energy of it. Waters felt a tingling as he watched the life go out of Azariah.

He pulled the knife out, splattering blood all over himself, and leaned in close enough to kiss Azariah. "I think you're right, Preacher. You ain't no better than a red. Don't feel no different killing you."

CHAPTER 4

The camp lay in ruin. Night had fallen, and the ghosts of war had taken up residence where unhaunted ground used to be. Now it was soaked in blood.

Lozen and the brothers had hidden under an overhang on the eastern bank of the Gila River until they only heard silence coming from the direction of the camp. The moon hung high by the time they started heading back.

Audie was the first to find his father. He couldn't speak as his eyes took in Azariah's lifelessness. His ashen face had the look of a scream, but no sound moved from his lips. It was too much to bear for a boy his age. It was too much to bear for a full-grown man.

Lozen and Shane came up behind him. Shane hid his face in his hands and moaned a sound that should never come from a boy as he fell to his knees.

Lozen was stone-faced as she took in the scene. She walked around, saying silent goodbyes to the people she had known who lay there dead. She never cried, and she never spoke a word. This wasn't her first encounter with death.

Natan and the hunting party soon came back. The only other person to survive the attack, Onawa, had escaped and ridden to get them. They arrived to find the horror that the union soldiers had left behind.

Horses with their tongues hanging out of the side of their mouths lay with cut throats. Buzzards were beginning to circle.

The hunters were looking for their women and children. There was wailing when they found them. There were screams when they didn't.

Two braves whose older daughters were missing were shouting war cries as they mounted up in hopes of taking them back from the soldiers.

Onawa went to Lozen and stroked her dark hair for a second, but Lozen pushed her hand away. She went to stand by Shane.

Natan came upon the boys and Lozen standing over his friend's bloody lifeless body.

"It should not be so. Azariah had no man's blood on his hands."

The words were kind but offered no comfort to Audie and Shane.

Natan saw the heat in Audie's countenance. His face was untensed and red in the moonlight, but his eyes had narrowed with a focus on Azariah. The boy had the look of a man who had a reckoning to bring. Audie had his father's eyes, but there was a fire in them that he hadn't seen in the preacher's.

Natan reached down and gently took the blood-stained crucifix from around Azariah's neck. He slowly put it around Audie's.

Then Natan reached down and dipped three fingers in the blood that had half-dried on Azariah's throat.

He ran his fingers down Audie's face, forming three straight lines on his right cheek. Audie never took his eyes off of his father. A tear rolled over his father's blood and dropped red on the ground. Audie shed his last tear in a long while that night.

Azariah's death would cause an ocean of blood in the end.

~

Audie and Shane buried their father in that harsh ground the next day, working till late in the afternoon to dig his grave. They chose a spot close to the river where Azariah used to watch them swim. Natan offered to help, but Audie insisted he and his brother do it alone. They covered up the life they should have lived when they filled that hole with their father and dirt.

Folks grew up faster in those times, but Audie and Shane took up a man's burden long before they should have. They said goodbye to all things childish and marked their father's grave with a cross they made out of oak limbs and leather. They knew that was what he would have wanted.

Over the next few days, the brothers joined the Indians as they dealt with the despair of the camp. The Apache, as according to their custom, buried the dead and burned all of their possessions. It was their belief that the dead resented the living and would come back to haunt them, so those who remained would destroy anything connected to the deceased and move the camp. Audie and Shane didn't understand this, but they didn't question it.

Natan spoke to the brothers while who was left of the tribe was packing to leave. "I will take you back to your mother at first light. She will want to know of the death of Azariah."

Shane and Audie were silent for a long time.

"No. We will stay with you." Audie's words held no trace of room for negotiation, but Natan argued against it.

"Your place is not here. Your mother will need you."

Shane spoke next. "Our mother is strong, and she has her father to look after her. I won't go back without Daddy."

"You are not supposed to stay in this pla—"

"Our father wasn't supposed to stay in this place either!" Audie shouted.

Grey Wolf could see the hearts of Audie and Shane were fixed on staying. He never would have allowed a child to speak to him in such a tone, but he was wise enough to know the hell in Audie's words was not intended for him.

"Come here," Natan commanded.

The boys walked over to him.

"Hold out your hands."

They did as they were told. Natan took his knife from the buffalo skin sheath that hung at his waist, grabbed Audie's right hand, and cut a two-inch gash across the palm. He did the same to Shane. They winced when the blade broke skin but never tried to pull back.

"From this day you will be known as the sons of Grey Wolf. I will not take the names your good father gave you, but I will mingle our blood to make it so."

He ran the blade slowly down the palm of his own hand and joined the cut first to Shane's and then to Audie's sliced palms, as if he were giving them a handshake. He held it there each time for a while.

"My son, *Itza-chu,* died bravely in the battle of Apache Pass. It weighted my heart with a great sadness, but now I have new sons. I respected your father, and I will look after you as my own."

The DeVine brothers felt a strength in the joining of their blood with Natan's. He loved them, and they loved him. Grey Wolf was a net that kept them from crashing into hard ground after a long fall.

It had been one year since Azariah and the boys had left, and Adalina all but lost hope of their return. She begged her father to send someone to search for them, but Mac would not. Years passed before she felt any spark of life again.

CHAPTER 5

The brothers became as one with the Apache. Their days were filled with work. They learned to hunt. They learned which plants were edible and which were used for healing. But mostly, they learned to fight.

Grey Wolf trained them in the ways of a warrior, and they became deadly under his tutelage.

Shane and Lozen grew even closer, the bond made even tighter by the fact that Lozen had killed the man who shot his father. In time, the affection turned to romance. Lozen loved Shane, but in her mind, she could never fully devote herself to him, or anyone. A woman warrior didn't have that luxury. They shared their first touch, their first kiss, their first everything, but Lozen was determined to remain untethered by marital bonds. Shane had asked her the first time when he was sixteen and she was fifteen, but she had declined the invitation, explaining her reasoning. He would ask many times after that, but even though she had a heart for only him, she would be bound to no man.

The brothers stayed with their adopted family for the better part of ten years. They fought battles with them, bled with them, and mourned with them. They loved those people as anyone loves their own family, and the Apache held them as their own.

They forgot much of their old life in Missouri, but they would make music at night around the campfire and sing songs their father had taught them. At times, it was like pulling the scabs off of wounds of old memories. Audie would make up songs of his own, and Shane would sing harmony and play along on the drums. It became their favorite pastime, and they became very good at it. On days where they weren't hunting or training or out fighting alongside Grey Wolf, singing was how they passed the time.

The brothers created a fierce and haunting sound together. They sang with the heartache and brutality that their lives had been given. They sang with an artfulness that can only be gifted to the broken. They sang because they had no other way to poke a hole in their festering hearts and let the poison out. The others in their tribe would listen in an almost trance-like state, sometimes nodding their head in rhythm and sometimes dancing in the light of the fire.

The songs Azariah had shown them took on a new character with Audie's odd chording and sense of melody. The music they made was very unique, but they had no way to know that at the time.

The only thing they had kept from their former existence was Azariah's Bible, a copy of a British weekly literary magazine titled *All the Year Round* that somehow had made it to the states, the guitar Azariah had given to Audie, and the crucifix he wore around his neck.

They had read the books cover to cover countless times. Sometimes out of respect to their father, sometimes out of boredom, and sometimes truly searching for answers to their questions.

Audie and Shane missed their mother but seldom spoke of her.

Every man needs some battle to fight. Whether their weapon is a rifle, a plow, or a pen, they need some struggle to feel alive. Some men search this life endlessly for that struggle or plead with the world for their own war, but the DeVine brothers didn't have to ask for theirs.

CHAPTER 6

The year was 1877, and the landscape had changed in the west. Audie and Shane were twenty-one and nineteen now, and no longer the naive boys who had traveled from Missouri with their father.

The Apache population had been whittled away by attrition, leaving them less threatening to the ambitions of the east, so more of the government's focus had turned to the Sioux and the Cheyenne. Many of the Apache had been put on reservations or killed, but there were still a few dozen bands of a hundred or so that were cunning enough to evade the U.S. Army's grip. The soldiers still came, just not as often.

Natan was older now and in bad health. He had contracted smallpox, a disease that the Europeans brought with them and one that had wreaked havoc on the Native peoples.

Smallpox-infested blankets were given to the Apache by the government as yet another way to dwindle their numbers. Natan's pride wouldn't let him touch one, but not every Apache he encountered had the same conviction. Another native had contracted the disease, and unknowingly passed it to Natan. Smallpox is contagious and airborne, and it didn't take much for an Apache to be infected.

Natan had dwindled to a wisp of himself over the past six months. The skin on his arms and midsection was mostly covered in a rash, and he hadn't been able to keep food down in over a week. He wouldn't speak of the pain, but the boys could see it on his sunken face. He was not long for this world, and they knew it.

He had lost his wife to an unknown illness over twenty years earlier, and his son had died in battle. Audie and Shane were the only family he had left, and they stayed by him.

The Jicarilla went to great lengths to make sure no child of the tribe came in contact with the dying, or even contact with those comforting the dying, out of fear that the aura of death would mark a child in their weakness. The brothers had moved Natan's tent a half a mile south of the camp, and food for them was left in a brush pile halfway between every day. They would not see those in the camp until after Natan's passing.

Grey Wolf lay in his tent holding to the last few strands of life he had.

"My time has come to shed this body and join my people in the Land of Ever Summer. I have been brave and kind to my people. They will welcome me there."

Shane and Audie listened but didn't know how to respond. They had never quite latched on to the Indian way of thinking about the afterlife, but they weren't certain if they believed Azariah's version either. They tried to understand both, but there were still shadows in their minds over these things.

"I had a son who was brave and went before me, and I will see him there. But I have two sons who will still walk this world after I'm gone. Will they be brave when I leave this place?"

"Yes, Grey Wolf. We will be what you taught us to be. And we'll always be honored and grateful to be called your sons." Shane fought the quiver in his voice as he spoke. He tried not to let sadness strangle the words from him.

Grey Wolf summoned a smile. It was small and painful to make, but he wanted to take the sting out of his previous question.

"I know you will. But an old man wants to hear it when he sees his end. You have made me proud like good sons should. I will die with a full heart."

"We'll remember everything you have shown us, Grey Wolf. We will live the way you taught us, and we'll fight against your enemies. We'll fight against those who killed Azariah." The softness in Audie's voice didn't match the fury in his words, but Natan knew he meant it.

Azariah wasn't spoken of much, but he was thought of often. The boys had missed him and their mother fiercely over the years they had been with the Jicarilla, but it felt disrespectful somehow to speak of them. Natan had raised them as his own sons, and the others in the camp had treated them as such. Some, only out of fear of Natan if they didn't, but either way, Audie and Shane felt accepted there.

"Azariah. He was a good man. One who should not be forgotten. I thought of him like a brother. His courage was not on the battlefield but in his battle for his God. I think if he had lived, he might have convinced me of this Jesus he spoke of so often." Grey Wolf forced another smile, but this one was even weaker than the last.

"You must be wiser in your fight than I was, than our people have been. The white man's numbers are too many. You have to fight with your wits now. They will never be defeated by force alone. I fear they may never be defeated at all."

"What do you mean?" Audie asked.

"I don't know by what means you must fight, but I know you have a white man's way of thinking. You understand their thoughts better than any Apache can. That may be the only way to beat the white man."

Natan let out a sudden and violent cough that lasted far too long. Shane laid a hand on his chest, and Grey Wolf grabbed it in both of his. They sat beside his bed and waited. There wasn't much they could do for him but offer comfort.

"You should rest now, Grey Wolf. That's enough talk for the night." Shane was worried they were upsetting him and making his condition worse.

"The next time I sleep, I will not wake. The choice is mine now, and I am ready to go."

Audie and Shane sat there without words between them for a long time. They had already had one father pass from this world. They didn't want to see another one go. They loved the old man, and they knew he loved them back.

"I'll miss you, Grey Wolf. You have been a good father to us." The words stumbled over the lump in Shane's throat.

Grey Wolf grabbed a hand from each brother and squeezed. There was a strength in his old hands the boys didn't expect. Then he let go and crossed his arms over his broad chest.

And he fell asleep.

Audie and Shane buried him in the custom according to the Apache. They found soft ground and put his body down into the same earth that Natan had fought for his whole life.

They watched in silence as the smoke rose from the pile of leather, bone, and wood that belonged to Natan.

And they said goodbye to another person they loved.

CHAPTER 7

"We should go and visit Mother. That's as good of a place as any to decide what we should do next."

Audie had thought about going home during the last days of caring for Grey Wolf. It wasn't that it was his best idea; it was just the only idea in his mind about where to go. To Audie, it seemed there was nothing left for them where they were. And after losing two fathers, his heart yearned to see the only parent he had left on this earth.

"Audie, we can't just show up on Mother's doorstep! It's been ten years! She's got to think we're dead. It should stay that way."

"Do you have a better idea about where to go?"

Shane was quiet.

"Do you remember the way?" Shane asked.

"Maybe. We can find our way east easily enough."

"Damn, Audie. You want to ride a month's journey east on a maybe? That doesn't seem like the soundest plan."

Audie gave Shane a look to show him he had enough confidence for the both of them.

"I don't even know if Mama would recognize us," Shane added.

Mama. The word felt uncomfortable and comforting at the same time on Shane's lips. That's what he and Audie had always called her, but it had been a while since he had spoken that name. It would take some getting used to again.

Adalina had been a good mother. The brothers carried guilt for never going back, but their will for vengeance ate away at it enough to make them stay. Still, there was sweetness in their hearts at the thought of seeing her.

"Take care of anything you need to over the next few days. We'll leave when the mallows start to bloom. Shouldn't be long."

Audie would have left that night, but he knew Shane had things he wanted to do before they set out.

There was only one affair Shane needed to take care of before they left: a beautiful Apache warrior named Lozen. He loved the woman without reserve, but her dedication to the Apache cause kept her from taking a husband, at least in her mind. Her lover was all he would ever be, and he was the only lover she had had. Most Braves wanted nothing to do with a woman as hard as her, but the men bold enough to pursue her left wishing they hadn't.

He found her practicing her bow a stone's throw from the river.

"Hell, Lozen. How much better can you get?"

"Bullets are faster than arrows. My bow needs to find its man first."

"Well, stop killing trees and come over here," Shane beckoned.

"It's too early in the day for love, Shane. Wait till tonight. The moon will be full." Her full lips turned upward in a seductive smile, but she never stopped shooting.

"I only want to talk."

"Ha! You lie to me! I know your tricks."

"Audie and I are leaving soon."

Lozen gently released the bow's tension and let it fall to her side. She turned to him and searched his handsome face for some further explanation to the words he spoke and saw a mixture of longing and suffering.

"Where to?" she said as she walked toward him.

"First to our mother's house. Then I don't know."

She was quiet for a moment. The thought of him leaving had never gathered in her mind. He had been so many things to her for so long.

"I . . . I don't know if that's a good thing for you, Shane. You have lived here since . . ." Her words trailed off at the thought of Shane's father. "Will there be anything for you in Misery?"

Lozen had become somewhat knowledgeable of English since Shane had been with her, but some words were still out of reach.

"*Mi-zur-ee*, Lozen. Not Misery. And we'll make our way fine. We intend to fight for the Apache. To find the men who killed our father. Natan told us to be wiser than he was. He said we have a white man's mind and that is how we could defeat them. We are set on doing that. We just don't know how yet."

"Oh."

In that *oh* was so much. Hurt, understanding, yearning, and the inexplicable essence that makes a woman a woman.

Lozen may have been as tough as a man, but she was still a woman. And Shane was the only man who ever got to catch a glimpse of that.

"I could stay. If you'd marry me, I would stay." He pulled her to him slowly and stroked her long black hair.

Lozen was silent again. She rested her head on his shoulder. He knew she wouldn't before he let the words go, but he still wanted them to land on her. For her to feel their weight.

"Shane, I . . . I can't do that. You know why. But I thought . . . I thought you would be here. With me."

He stepped away from her a little and gently tilted her chin up so she would look at him when he spoke. There was a brokenness in her eyes that stung him to know he couldn't fix.

"I need you as a wife, Lozen. Not just . . . whatever we are. Your bow will leave you lonely someday. I won't."

The words were a fall wind hitting her skin, comforting after the heat of the summer, but bringing the chill of the winter ahead.

"Neither one of us has a choice." They weren't the right words, but they were the only ones Lozen could conjure up at the moment.

Shane wanted to plead his case further but knew there was no use. She was who she was. It wasn't in his power to change that. This wasn't their first time having this conversation. He had tried every angle he could think of to convince her—motherhood, continuing the Jicarilla line, loneliness—to no avail.

Lozen kissed him like she knew he was forbidden. He met her lips with the same passion.

Shane wrapped his arms around her tighter as he spoke.

"I love you, Lozen."

"I love you, too, Shane."

She hid her face in his chest for a moment out of fear that tears were coming.

The wind brushed her hair against him. They stayed that way for a long while.

CHAPTER 8

A *month later...*

The brothers had been on the trail headed east for three weeks now. It had taken Azariah three and a half weeks to get them in Verde Valley almost ten years ago, so they knew they were making good time. They could tell they were well into Kansas by the landscape.

The Rocky Mountains had been out of view for days, and they'd left the level fields of western Kansas yesterday. The flatlands had surrendered their hold on the territory to jagged green hills scattered with wild onions and buttercups. Sugar maple branches held hands with the buckeye trees and sang a peaceful song that the boys hadn't thought of in a long time.

They slept when they had to, usually every couple of days or so. Meals were rabbits and squirrels since it was too early in the spring for berries or wild corn.

It had been an uneventful journey, except for a few strangers they had met along the way. Mostly buffalo hunters and a few stragglers looking to find work on the railroad or just searching for any of the promise the West had been painted with. There were a few hard characters but mostly friendly people on their journey, not looking for trouble.

The brothers had taken clothes off of two men they had killed three years ago when they were out hunting with Natan. Scalpers. Men who made a living selling the scalps of the Apache. It hadn't been a hard decision to kill them. They'd washed the blood out of the clothes in the river and acquired a new wardrobe. Audie and Shane had also gotten the two Rose Texas saddles they were riding on from those scalpers. The brothers figured it best to appear as "white" as possible when entering back into their old life.

Both Audie and Shane wore tan cotton pants. Audie had a long-sleeve red shirt with snaps instead of buttons, while Shane wore a blue denim shirt with a dark-brown leather vest. Audie's weathered brown boots had spurs attached, and Shane's boots were lighter in color and made of softer leather, making the shafts sag a little.

Audie wore an oil-rubbed duster that hung a couple of inches below his knee. The amber leather had darkened to a shade or two shy of black. Shane wore a black coat made out of grizzly fur.

Audie rode with his guitar on a strap, slung across his back. Shane had tied two drums together and had them strapped across his horse behind the saddle.

They'd packed very little otherwise. Their books, moccasins, a little money they'd found when they took the clothes, some healing herbs, peyote—they didn't have much else to take.

There was no trace of boy left in them, at least not in their appearance. Audie stood about four inches over six feet now and Shane was couple of inches shorter. Audie was the more muscled of the two, but Shane was stout enough that the word skinny never came to mind.

Audie had grown a beard over the last three weeks, and by Shane's estimate, it added five years to his appearance. He had tried to convince his brother to grow one as well, but Shane's vanity wouldn't allow it. Both men had long dark hair, but Audie's was the wavier of the two.

They didn't look like two men you would want to throw fists with unless you had to. Audie's hazel eyes were sharp and deep, making them hard to stare into for a stranger. Shane's July-blue-sky eyes seemed just a shade darker than was natural.

The brothers had spoken little since they set out. Their goodbyes to their Indian friends had been hard. Some didn't understand why they were leaving. Audie and Shane had tried to explain it the best they could, but their explanation had left some who heard it wanting.

Shane and Lozen had spent the last week together soaking up as much of each other as they could. It had been a wonderful and torturous time for both of them.

"Was she mad at you?" Audie inquired out of the blue as they rode along.

I don't think so," Shane responded, knowing exactly who Audie was referring to. "She made her choice too."

"Would you have stayed if she had married you?" The question hung in the air like the feeling of heavy rain before it falls.

"Yeah." The answer sounded off like a flood coming down.

Audie and Shane let the conversation end there. Audie didn't like the answer he heard but didn't feel like he should make his dissatisfaction known. He knew it had wounded his brother to leave the woman he loved, and he also knew his brother provided a strength for him that no other man could. Still, Audie believed vengeance for their father's murder should hold precedence over everything else. Even love. Audie had put being a warrior above it. It was hard sometimes for him to know Shane didn't. The irony was the woman Shane loved did.

Shane stopped on the path, his senses alerting him to something happening in the distance. Audie detected his sudden alarm and stopped alongside him.

They heard shouting. More than one voice. One seemed to be in pain and the others sounded mocking, but they couldn't make out the words. They could tell the voices were coming from ahead and to the north, probably just off the trail.

They dismounted their horses and tied them to a low-hanging buckeye limb. Audie hung his guitar on the horn of his saddle.

"I can't hear what they're saying," Audie whispered.

Shane felt around his waistline out of habit for his knives.

They headed softly in the direction of the commotion. One of the many skills they had mastered was stealth. Whoever it was would never hear them coming.

"Shit, Jessie. I wish we had us another nigger to kill, too! One just whets my appetite!" A man laughed out as he whipped a man tied to a tree.

"Too bad we can't kill him twice! You got nine lives, boy? Like an ole tomcat? Naw. You're more like a mangy ole mutt. Ain't worth the bullet it would take to end your sorry life," the other man, Jessie, reasoned.

The beaten man let out screams and whimpers. They were sickening sounds. He was shirtless, and his back was glistening with blood and sweat. The dark red ran down, staining the tan pants he wore.

"Now, don't you go getting too worked up, boy. We ain't gonna kill you. We're gonna take you back for that reward and let that rich bastard's brother you killed do it. He's been wantin' for your blood awhile now. That sumbitch oughta be primed to give you a proper send off!"

The brothers had come up to the left side of the men about fifteen yards away. Audie gave Shane a motion to go around to the back of them. Without a sound, both brothers moved into position.

Audie walked out slowly into plain sight of the men, careful to look as nonthreatening as possible. He held up his hands as he entered their camp.

The man with the whip quickly dropped it and turned toward him, drawing a Colt army revolver in one fluid motion. The other grabbed a Slant Breech Sharps carbine rifle out of his saddle and had it pointed toward Audie in less than two seconds.

These men ain't tenderfoots, Audie thought.

"Hello," Audie said. "No need for the peacemakers. I'm just a traveler headed back east and heard the ruckus. Came to see what it was about."

"This ain't no concern of yours, mister. I'd head back the way you came if you like keepin' blood in your veins." The man with the rifle spit.

"I mean you no harm, sir. What's this man's crime?"

"Hell, he don't need no crime! You see that night skin crawling on his stinkin' carcass? But if you gotta know, he killed a man in South Carolina. Been on the run for might near fifteen years."

"Hell, you can't count your fingers and toes, Jessie!" the other man ridiculed. "Been 'bout near twenty years."

Jessie gave his partner a nasty look. "Well, it don't matter how long it's been. He's slicked by ever' bounty hunter from here to the bottom of Dixie. We've got this sumbitch now, though." He kicked the whimpering man's calf, buckling his leg.

"I killed the man who done killed my wife and baby! What man wouldn't do that?" the black man moaned.

"Well, you ain't no man, nigger! You a nigger! Don't make no difference who kills your people," Jessie retorted.

"Well, I'd say he has a point. What man wouldn't kill for his own?" Audie reasoned.

"Boy, you lookin' to see your guts on the ground? You hear me? He ain't no man! He's a sorry-ass nigger! Now, get outta here before I string you up with him!"

Jessie cocked the revolver to show he wasn't bluffing.

"Shane." Audie spoke the word gently, so as not to startle the two men. Before they had time to process what was happening, Shane appeared out of nowhere and sank a throwing knife in Jessie's throat and another one in the other man's chest.

Thunk! Thromp! Audie grabbed the pistol before Jessie could get off a shot. The man with the rifle managed one, but it was high and to the right of Shane, who was at his side in an instant and had the rifle.

Jessie's throat erupted in spasms of blood, pumping his life through clutched hands and onto the ground. He made a sound somewhere between a choke and a gag, like his mind couldn't make up which one to do. He hit his knees and then went down face-first, planting his face hard in the grass and driving the knife in his throat to the hilt.

The other man bled out slower but lost sight of this world just as quick. Shane's blade had split bone to find the man's heart. He writhed around for a torturous few seconds before he lost consciousness.

Both men were dead in moments.

That was something the Apache had given Audie and Shane. Killing came easy now. It was natural.

The man tied to the tree was beaten badly. Audie walked over to him.

"What's your name?"

The man continued to stare at the ground without speaking.

"Friend, I mean you no harm. What's your name?"

"That's the same thang you say ta those two inbreds right before yo man sank a blade in 'em."

Shane had been watching the exchange, but after a short while he went to retrieve his knives from the two dead men, wiping the blades on their shirts.

Audie walked closer to the man tied to the tree. He reached out slow and easy with his knife and cut the ropes that had bound him. He inserted the blade back in his belt and took three steps back.

"Sir, I can assure you we have no interest in making you our captive. I'm Audie DeVine, and the other man with me is my brother, Shane. You should let me see to those wounds of yours. They look pretty angry." Audie tried to lay his words out like an invitation.

"Moses Cofey," he managed to get out as he slumped to his knees. Audie knelt down to steady him.

"Well, Moses, I'd like to clean those wounds sooner than later, if you'd oblige."

Moses was still for a moment, then gave a slight nod. Audie studied him for a few seconds, then went to his own saddle to get some sagebrush and arnica he had brought with him. He walked over to Jessie's limp body and cut off a piece of the sleeve of his shirt that wasn't blood soaked. He then found a canteen in the wagon the two men had been riding in, soaked the cloth with water, and went to work cleaning the eviscerated flesh of Moses' back.

Moses winced but didn't have the strength to do much else. Audie rinsed the cloth out several times and rewet it to clean all the man's wounds. He noticed the scars of previous lashes crisscrossing each other and the new wounds looked like plowed up, crooked rows in a field. When he finished cleaning him, he packed the healing herbs inside the man's cuts. He took Jessie's pants off and tore them into strips to tie around Moses to keep the sagebrush and arnica inside the wounds.

When he was done, he offered the man a drink of his own canteen. Moses quickly took it and drank half, water spilling out of his mouth as he felt the cool go down his throat.

"Shane, go get something to cook for supper. This man needs to eat."

Shane had come back with the horses.

Moses slumped over, face down in total exhaustion. Audie went to the wagon and found a blanket to cover Moses with.

Moses fell asleep before he could eat. Shane and Audie made camp. They would stay there for the night.

"We need to bury them," Shane reckoned as two rabbits on a stick cooked over the fire.

"Yeah, I figure we drag them about five hundred paces north to keep anyone near the trail from finding the bodies."

They ate while Moses slept. Shane had cooked enough for all of them, but Moses' weary won out over his hunger.

Under the darkness, the brothers made their way through the thick patch of woods with the bodies and dug a wide, shallow grave. They threw the men in and covered it back up with the loose soil. When they felt satisfied with the job, they headed back to the camp.

"You think he's saint or sinner?" Shane quizzed Audie on the walk back to Moses.

"I don't know. Maybe both, maybe neither."

"Well, hell, Audie. You can't be both."

"Those two bastards didn't deny his story. Hell, that would make anybody want to kill. A man don't deserve to die for that kind of killing," Audie reasoned.

"Let's hope not," Shane said.

The brothers checked on Moses periodically to make sure he was still breathing, but Moses slept until the next morning. When he woke, he drank water from the canteen but still didn't have the stomach for much food.

Audie and Shane had only stopped to rest when absolutely necessary on the journey. This was the first time the had stopped for more than one evening. They took turns at watch again that night.

Audie dreamed of the giant bur oak that he used to play under as a child.

Shane dreamed of Lozen.

CHAPTER 9

Moses woke the next morning with a little more strength and an appetite. Audie had shot two squirrels and gathered some herbs to season. Moses ate like it was manna. Shane was the first to speak.

"How'd they take you?"

Moses looked at him and Audie for a few seconds. Something in their eyes seemed cold, but he detected no deception there. He hadn't met many friendly people in his travels. Trust wasn't something he gave out on the cheap.

"They tracked me fo' a week. I been all over this here part of the country fo' quite a spell. Thought I knew it betta than I did. They cornered me in a holla 'bout half a day from here. Don't carry no pistol. Woulda kept runnin' but they had me on both sides."

"And the man they said you killed?" Audie's question came off more matter of fact than he meant for it to.

Moses studied them a little longer, trying to figure out if there was any harm in answering these questions. He settled on the notion that he couldn't change whatever they were going to do.

"He was my massuh. Back before Abraham Lincoln do what he did. My woman, Phibe, was pregnant with our baby. Massuh was ornery as a dickens, but we's happy. She believe it was gonna be a son. I always wanted me a son. Massuh'd go on a drunk an' get the devil in him an' starve us out for a number a days. I knew that baby wasn't gonna make it without some food in 'em, so I snuck in Massuh's house one night an' stole some. Not even much. I didn't eat none for myself. Gave it to Phibe fo' the baby."

Moses soft features didn't match his history. He looked to be in his forties or fifties from the gray in his hair, with a face that only showed gentleness and fear.

Moses stopped the story here, shut his kind eyes, and shook his head like he was trying to will away some thought he had.

"Anyway, Massuh found the food where I hid it in our room. He put me in chains right out in the heat. Then he . . . he killed Phibe. Use a hoe ta bash in her head. With our baby inside her! She was screamin' . . . callin' for me . . . but them chains . . . he made me watch 'em do it. Told me it'd learn me not to steal from 'im."

Moses sighed and put his hands on his knees. It'd been a long while since he turned through those painful pages. He kept his eyes on the dirt the whole time he was recollecting his woes, as if there were a movie of those events playing right there in the earth beneath their feet. He'd close his eyes occasionally like there were scenes too hurtful to watch. His voice exposed a weariness from years of shouldering a burden too big for a soft soul.

Audie and Shane had both weighed his mannerisms and spirit and separately concluded that he was a good man with a rocky road behind him. They sympathized with him. They were all too familiar with the hellhounds that come howling after you lose someone you love to evil.

"He didn't kill me 'cause he say I's a good worker. Tried to beat the mad outta me. I tried to let it go. The Good Book say you s'pose to. But I just ain't that strong a man. I waited for a good long while afta he took those chains off. I let him think I didn't have no more fight in me. One night when he'd got on that rotgut and passed out, I took me a pitchfork an' . . . did what I did. Didn't want to. It was like I had to do it. It's been a torture ta my soul ever since, knowin' I took a man from this here world. I try to take my comfort in an eye for an eye an all that, but ain't no comfort in that. Just a wish that they'd never been an eye to reckon for in the first place. Anyway, I ran as far an' fast as I could. Ain't found no peace a mind nor body ever since. Been running ever since."

Moses didn't cry any tears as he told the story, but Audie sensed he had cried a flood in days gone by.

"That's how I end up a wanted man."

There was a long silence. Moses hung his head as if telling the story was a defeat of some sort. The brothers studied the ground as well. Searching for something to take a little sting out of his pain. There was nothing. The stripes on Moses' back weren't the worst of the wounds given to this man.

"Well, take comfort in knowing you're safe here. You're not wanted by us."

Audie wanted to say something more consoling, but that was the length of his solace. Soothing words were not much found in his heart. He didn't crave them, so he didn't know them.

Moses was quiet after that. He still didn't trust Audie and Shane. The brothers knew this but didn't hold it against him or even blame him for it.

Audie and Shane had decided to take the wagon and use it as their own. They were busy sorting through the dead men's items to see what they could use.

"You think it's safe to take the wagon?" Audie questioned Shane as they were packing up.

"I thought about that. I wonder if we took this cover off and stained the wood if it would take the familiar out of it?"

"Yeah. That's a good idea. I'd hate to run into any of their friends along the way who might recognize it."

Audie grabbed a pail and went out in the woods looking for something to stain the wood with. There was a little stream about two hundred paces south of the camp site. He dug into mud on the edges of the creek and filled the bucket with the dark, wet soil.

"It ain't perfect, but it should do to darken these boards a bit," he informed Shane when he returned.

The brothers began rubbing the mud into the rugged wood of the wagon, making sure to embed it in the lumber as deeply as possible. They had to make a few trips back down to the creek for more mud. By the time they were done, it was a whole different shade of brown.

"Surely nobody knew this wagon well enough to tell the difference. We should be okay," Audie said.

Moses was still weak from the whipping he had taken but had gotten up and walked around a bit throughout the day. The boys had noticed his movements but let him be. They were trying to show him they trusted him, in hopes of earning his. Moses was very aware that they hadn't tried to restrict him in any way. He still hadn't figured them out, though.

That night Moses and the brothers sat around a fire and ate rabbit in silence for a long stretch of time. Finally, Audie broke the air.

"Moses, will you be able to travel in a couple days?"

Moses was surprised at the sudden sound of Audie's voice and the question.

"You intend ta take me with ya?"

"It's your choice. I don't feel good about leaving a man behind who's still nursing his wounds, but if you'd rather be on your own, I won't stop you." Audie tried to step lightly.

"It'd be good to have two men horseback with one on the wagon," Shane reasoned. "Are you a hand with a wagon, Moses?"

Moses still couldn't fully get a beat on these men. He felt no danger from them, but why would they offer to let him ride with them? Him, a wanted black man.

"I can manage a wagon," Moses offered.

"Well, that's good, because Audie ain't worth a horse shit with one."

Audie laughed and picked up a small limb and threw it at Shane's chest. Shane let it bounce off with a chuckle.

Moses liked the brothers. He hoped all of this wasn't too good to be true.

"You ain't worried 'bout me bein' wanted an' all?"

"I've been thinking about that," Audie told him. "I think we can do something about that."

Moses looked puzzled.

"You need to change your appearance. Shave your head. Grow a beard. Anything to throw them off." Audie knew that wouldn't be enough, but it was a bridge into the conversation.

Moses shook his head. "I can do that, but I don't think that'll get 'em off my trail."

Audie agreed. "You're probably right, but it might help. I knew a man once, an Apache Indian. In a battle he had fought, he received a gash across the cheek, starting at the edge of his eye down to his lip. He wore it as an honor, but it changed the way he looked."

"You . . . you wanna cut my face?" Moses stuttered.

"I don't *want* to do any such thing. It's an idea. The man they're looking for doesn't have a scar on his face."

Moses relaxed. Audie did have a point.

"Moses, we're on our own out here, too. And we don't blame a man for killing one who killed his wife and child. If you want to ride with us, you're an equal. If you don't, we're happy to give you a horse and some supplies. You're a free man," Audie said.

"Y'all sure ain't like no folks I ever knowed before."

Shane laughed out loud. "There's a reason for that."

Audie smiled. "Think on it, Moses. We'll stay here another couple days to let your wounds heal some more. When we leave, you can come with us, or not."

No one spoke much the rest of the evening. Audie and Shane took their usual shifts standing guard. Moses slept a little deeper that night.

The brothers were getting antsy sitting in one place for that long, but they knew Moses needed time to heal. Truth be told, he needed more than a couple days, but that was about all they felt they could handle.

The next day at first light, Audie announced he was going to kill a doe to eat. He came back about four hours later with the smallest deer any of them had ever seen.

"Damn, Audie," Shane teased. "That ought to be enough meat to feed us for five minutes."

Audie was cutting the backstrap out of the doe and reached down to grab a handful of intestines. He chucked it at Shane.

"Well, if you get hungry, there's more food in those," he said.

They cooked the meat over a fire, and afterward Audie got his guitar out and started strumming. Shane busied himself sharpening a knife on a piece of sandstone.

"I used to play the banjo when I's a young man," Moses offered up out of the blue.

The boys both stopped what they were doing and stared at Moses.

"What's a banjo?" Shane asked as he worked a blade out of a tree trunk.

"It's a lot like that guitar there but with five strings. It sound more . . . well, that guitar's like a blue jay. A banjo's a crow. If a crow could sang."

Shane and Audie looked confused.

"Our father used to say when Audie played it sounded like a storm coming."

Audie looked at Shane, surprised he remembered that.

"Guitars like rain hittin' the earth. A banjo is rain hittin' a roof."

The DeVine brothers understood. A little.

"I'd love ta hear y'all sang me a song." The boys didn't need much persuasion.

Shane got the two old Apache drums that Grey Wolf had given him off of his horse, and Audie checked the tuning on Azariah's old guitar. They hadn't sung and played together since they left the Jicarilla, and this was a welcome distraction.

The boys eased into a song called "Something Bad This Way

Come" that Audie had written. Moses lost himself for a while in the flow of it. The boys could tell he was enjoying the show.

"That was somethin' right," was all Moses could offer after the first song, but Audie and Shane knew it was high praise.

"Play more," Moses insisted.

So the DeVine brothers entertained Moses well into the night. It brought him a pleasure he had long forgotten existed. It brought them pleasure knowing they took this poor man away from his struggles for a while.

Around midnight they were sung out.

"Well, I need to stretch my legs," Shane said as he rose to his feet.

"Moses, have you decided whether you want to ride with us or not?" Audie asked.

Moses was silent for a bit.

"I'd like to. It's been a long spell since I had company'a any kind. You two ain't worried 'bout them that's afta me?"

"Well, it's not an ideal situation, but we'll take our chances. Have you thought about changing your appearance?" asked Audie.

"I have. I ain't cozy with the idea, but a scar might be the thang I need. I ain't in no hurry ta get a blade run 'cross my face, but I sure would love this runnin' ta be over. And I thank a good head shavin' might be worth the time, too."

"It's settled then. You'll be the wagon man," Shane said as he slapped his knee.

"Where's we headed?"

"Eminence, Missouri. Where our people are," Audie said.

"Moses, you a drinking man?"

Audie was glad Shane asked and not him. He wasn't looking forward to this man's face getting carved.

"Never was. Why you ask?"

"I found some whiskey in the wagon. If we're gonna give you a scar, I say we get it over with. It wouldn't be a bad thing if you slugged half of one of those pints before we do it."

Audie wished Shane would ease up a little, but still he was glad not to be the bearer of bad news.

"Alright." Moses was starting to trust Audie and Shane, but this was asking a lot.

Audie walked over to the wagon and got out one of the bottles. He gave it to Shane who uncorked it and took a long swig.

"I hate to see a man drink alone," Shane grunted through a grimace.

Moses took the bottle and chugged it as fast as he could. He pulled it away and spit a little out in a spray. It was obvious he wasn't a man given to strong drink. He put it back to his lips and took another long pull. This time when he took the bottle away, he put both hands on his knees like he was going to throw up. He breathed through it for a while and rose back up again.

"That oughta do it," he winced.

The boys could see his worried face start to untense from the alcohol. At least there was some comfort in that.

"Moses, you tell me when you're ready. I'll make it as quick as I can."

Shane drew his knife and held it to the fire.

"Why you heatin' that blade?"

The whiskey took some of the quiver in Moses' voice away.

"It purifies it and keeps infection from setting in the wound. It'll help it not to bleed so much, too."

"I'm gonna say a prayer 'fore you do whatcha gonna do."

Shane and Audie felt awkward. They bowed their heads.

"Good Lawd, I pray you turn Missa Shane here's knife into a blessin' for me. I pray this cut make me a new man in the eyes a dose who lookin' for me. Amen."

Moses paused. "I'm ready."

"Close your eyes, Moses," Shane coaxed.

Moses stared at him for a second, then closed his eyes.

Shane's knife moved slowly across Moses' face. He went from the top of his nose just under his left eye to the back of his cheek. The heated blade made the flesh sizzle as it dug in, and the smell of flesh burning filled their nostrils, making Audie and Shane wince and hold their breath. Shane left a cut about six inches across. He had gone deep. He knew the effect wouldn't be enough if he didn't.

Moses groaned, pulled back, then opened his eyes and stood stone-faced.

"Let me clean that up." Audie walked over to the wagon to find a cloth.

"I'm not gonna put healing herbs in this cut, Moses. We want it to heal, but not fast. The worse it looks the better off you are," Audie said as he wiped the blood away. He wrapped strands of a torn shirt around the top of Moses' head to his chin and back over a few times to cover the cheek.

"I'm gonna rest my eyes now."

Moses took one more pull from the whiskey bottle, stumbled a little, but made it to the place he'd been laying at night.

"This sho ain't no easy world you made for us down here, Lawd."

The brothers silently agreed.

"I am a poor wayfarin' stranga . . ."

Moses quietly sang a song Audie and Shane had never heard.

"Da DeVine brothers. Y'all might be DeVine. Y'all might be the devil. The DeVine devils. That's what y'all is."

Moses said it as if he were amused. The liquor was making him talk.

"While travelin' thru dis world below . . . ," he kept singing.

"I kinda like it," Audie smiled and said.

"What?"

"The name. The DeVine Devils."

Shane just stared at Moses, a little amused at his rambling.

"The DeVine Devils." Moses was still muttering. He was chuckling now.

"I'll take first watch," Shane said as he walked a little way from the camp.

"The DeVine Devils," Moses mumbled one last time. He put the stress on the *De* and not the *Vine*, giving it a more soulful overtone.

Those were the last words spoken that night.

The next morning they packed up and made their way east.

It was three more days till the band of misfits reached Eminence. The boys hadn't offered Moses much history about themselves yet, and he hadn't pried too deeply. But when they knew they were close, Audie felt he had to explain a little about the odd reunion Moses was about to witness.

"We haven't seen our mother in about ten years, Moses. We're fairly certain she thinks we're dead. I just wanted to give you fair warning before we get there."

"You boys had ta be pups then when that po' woman seen you last. How'd that come about?"

"That's too long of a tale to tell you before we get there. Someday I'll shed light on it, but for now I just didn't want you to be caught off guard." Audie didn't know how he felt about telling their story to anyone, but he had to give Moses something to chew on before this whole thing went down.

"Heh-heh. I'm ridin' with ghosts. You boys is full a' surprises."

Audie gave Moses a friendly smile. He wondered how this man would react if he knew the truth.

The new scar on Moses' face was nowhere near healed, but they could all tell it was going to do the trick. He had a droop in his left eye now, and the cut took away all symmetry from his face. He wasn't hideous, but the scar would make people turn away quickly, which would be advantageous.

"Thunder Ridge Road." The wooden sign with the name carved in was a new addition since they'd left, but they both remembered the two massive weeping willow trees at either side of the entrance.

It was the road that led to their childhood.

Audie reigned his horse to a stop when he saw it. The other two men stopped with him. They stared for a while.

"She's your mama. She gonna be overjoyed ta see her babies. Y'all don't need ta be scared."

The brothers turned their stares to Moses. Those were the right words to hear at this moment, and it surprised them that he could read their hesitation so easily.

Shane nodded his head at him in a thank-you. "We've probably got another four or five miles. Won't be long now."

"Well, let's don't sit here and rust." Audie gave his horse a firm kick.

They headed off in the direction of . . . they didn't know what. Home? Their hearts were confused and tender. The thought of a hug from their mother felt like it could bust a dam full of tears somewhere inside them both.

They rode for two more hours in silence. Shane and Audie had a thousand thoughts and memories coursing through their minds.

Moses silently prayed for his two new friends. Even hard men love their mothers.

They reached their childhood stomping grounds about an hour before sunset. It was familiar, but time had inevitably made some changes. Someone had painted the house white. The tree swing was gone. Azariah's rocking chair was gone as well. The boards on the porch had been replaced with new ones that looked more like they were put there by machinery than a man.

Adalina came out of the house wiping her hands on a dishrag. The years had left their stamp around her eyes and lips, but she was still the same beautiful woman they remembered. She was in her early forties now, and there were strands of gray in her dark hair, but it suited her somehow. She had a navy-blue dress on, just like the ones they remembered her wearing.

"Can I help you?"

They were in her front yard about ten yards from the porch.

Staring silently seemed to be the theme of the day for the DeVine brothers. They couldn't speak. It went on for an uncomfortable amount of time.

"There's feed and water for your horses in the barn if you need it," Adalina said nervously.

"Mama," Shane spoke first.

Adalina turned pale. Her mouth dropped open. She tried to speak, but no sound would manifest.

Shane and Audie dismounted and took off their hats. They had grown into fine young men, striking even. Audie had the look of his father. Shane was a blend of Azariah and Adalina.

Adalina ran to them and hugged Shane first, then pulled Audie toward them. She sobbed. Still there were no words.

Her tears were a catalyst for the brothers. Neither one had cried since the day they'd buried their father.

"I thought . . . I tried so hard not to give up hope . . . I . . ."

The boys understood her tear-drenched ramblings.

They hugged and cried for another ten minutes or so. Moses just smiled at the situation. It had been a long while since the man had seen something good in this world. He felt blessed in the moment.

It was a glorious and awkward homecoming, all the same. Nobody knew where to start or what to say.

Adalina pulled away just a bit to study the faces of her sons. She took in every feature. The sternness Azariah's blood gave them, the dark of their long hair, the thickness of Audie's beard, everything. She studied their eyes and could see that they had missed her. There was a steel in them that she didn't recognize. She could still see the boys she watched ride away so many years ago. She was crying when they left. She was crying now at their return.

"I thought you were . . . I prayed so hard for this. I thought God had forgotten me. I'm so . . ." Adalina searched for words, but there weren't any powerful enough.

She held on to them for a little longer. As if she was scared that, if she let go, it wouldn't be real. Audie and Shane felt something they hadn't felt since they were children.

She pulled away a bit more, still hanging on to a shoulder of each son. "You boys are so big! And handsome!" she said, half laughing and half crying.

"You stayed beautiful, Mama." Audie spoke just above a whisper.

"Oh, I look like an ole ragged Missouri farm girl, but thank you, sweet boy, for saying that. Come in! You look like you need rest. You all look weary." Adalina turned her gaze to Moses. He took his hat off in respect.

The boys smiled at their mother. Still a mother in every sense.

"Mama, this is our friend Moses. We met him on our travels, and he's with us now. He's a God-fearing man. You'll be happy to know we're keeping good company," Audie explained.

"Well, thank the Good Lord for that." She smiled at Moses, trying not to react to his fresh wound. "Moses, are you hungry? Would you like a meal?"

"Why, yes, ma'am, if'n it ain't too much trouble."

"Well, come in!"

"Mama, you don't have to go to any fuss. We can make do on just about anything," Audie said.

"You hush up and let your mama cook for you. I haven't got to cook for my sons since . . . Well, I'm gonna cook you something special."

"I'm gonna take the horses out ta that barn. They could use a refresha." Moses felt like the boys wanted time alone with their mother.

"Okay, but you hurry back. I'm gonna have a feast prepared for you in no time."

Moses tipped his hat and led the horses toward the barn. The rest of them stepped inside the kitchen.

"Are you all by yourself, Mother? Is there no one to help you around the place?"

Adalina hesitated. "Don't worry about that right now, Audie. I want to know, where is Azariah?"

Now it was Audie and Shane's turn to be quiet.

"He's . . . he hasn't been with us in a while, Mama," Shane confessed after a long pause.

Adalina held her hand over her mouth and teared up again.

"It happened ten years ago, Mama. He was murdered by a bunch of Billy Yanks in a raid on the Apaches."

Adalina felt a deep sadness, but at the same time, a relief. She had tortured herself for years with questions about her family. Had Azariah stayed gone because he wasn't happy? Did he love the Apache more than her? Had he been killed? Had he fallen in love with an Indian woman or someone he met in his travels? She knew most of these were ridiculous, but not knowing will make someone think ridiculous things.

At least she was finally getting some answers, even if they were brutal ones.

"The Apache took us in as their own. A great man named Grey Wolf raised us. We were taken care of, Mama."

"Those damn Indians! They stole your father away and then you!" she said as she clenched her fists and stomped her foot.

"Mama, our father was murdered by the U.S. Army. The Indians were his friends," Audie softly defended.

"That may be, but if Azariah had not been so drawn to those cursed Apache, I would have kept my family!" Adalina burst into sobs again, agonizing tears that had built up for a decade. Audie and Shane both ran to their mother to hold her.

"I understand, Mama. We're here now. I'm sorry you've been alone for all these years. We're to blame for that, not Father," Audie offered in a comforting voice.

Adalina still cried but softer now. The embrace of her sons was a comfort she had longed for, for so long. It helped to heal an old wound that had laid open for what seemed like eternity.

"Was . . . was Azariah planning on returning here?" There was fear in Adalina's voice.

"Of course, Mama! We were to leave just a few days after the raid happened. He missed you, Mama. His home was here."

Adalina's sobs ramped up, and she hid her eyes in Shane's shirt. It consoled her beyond words to know Azariah intended to come home. That question had festered in her heart for a decade. She felt selfish for asking in this moment but was relieved as well.

She stepped back from Shane and wiped her eyes.

"I . . . I remarried three years ago. I lost all hope of ever seeing you and your father again."

The brothers pulled away to look at her.

Audie felt anger but realized quickly he had no right. He was glad someone was there to look after his mother.

"That's good, Mama. I'm glad you're not alone," Shane said with a loving smile.

This made Adalina cry a little harder. Her sons loved her. It was good to see that after so long.

They stayed this way for a while. The ties between a loving mother and her children are something sacred and unbreakable. It may have been years since they had connected, but there was not an ounce less of love between them.

Moses peeked in the door to see what was going on and thought it best if he remained outside. He decided to lay underneath the bur oak in the front yard and nap.

CHAPTER 10

I t was an evening of sorrow mingled with joy. In this broken world we live in, it is almost impossible to completely separate the two. Audie and Shane told of their father's death, their years spent with the Indians, Lozen, and everything they could think of that was fit for their mother's ears. Adalina told about the man she married, a Pinkerton agent named Thomas Thorntree. He was off with his work right now.

"Evidently, I'm incapable of marrying a man who wants to stay at home with me." Adalina chuckled, eyes still damp with tears.

Thomas was a man who had started out as passionate about justice as Azariah had been about the Apache. There was a time when he would have hunted his current target down through hell if he had to, but he was getting older now, and the thought of settling down with Adalina nudged at him to hand in his badge. Still, it stood to reason that Adalina would be attracted to him. True passion in a man was a magnet to her heart.

"Why did you not come back to Missouri after Azariah's death?" Adalina asked, mixing hurt with anger. The question cut through the room like one of Shane's knives before it landed.

Shane looked to Audie to speak the answer.

"We were young, Mama. Our father had been murdered, and we wanted to avenge him somehow. We thought the Apache could give us that. I'm sorry we left you hanging in the balance all these years. It felt wrong somehow to come back here after Daddy's death. He loved the Indians so much, and we grew to love them, too."

"Why would you not want to be with your mother? Why would you choose those cursed Apache over me? I hate the Indians! They stole my whole family!"

Audie and Shane let her vent. They could offer little condolence.

"I'm sorry, Mama. It wasn't exactly like that. It didn't seem like a choice at the time," Shane tried to reason.

There was more silence, then Adalina's face softened.

"Your friend, Moses. That cut does not match the tenderness I see in his eyes. Did he live with the Indians, too?"

"No. He was a traveler we picked up along the way. And yes, I believe he's a good man. Some men had taken a whip to him when we found him. He's had a hard journey up till now." Audie spoke in half truths about Moses. It wouldn't have been prudent to tell her the whole story.

Against much protest, Moses had decided to take his supper outside that night. He did it as a kindness. He knew Adalina and her sons would want time together and he would be a distraction. He was snoozing again as soon as he had downed the pork shoulder, new potatoes and bread that Adalina had cooked.

"Well, please go and get that man and tell him he's not allowed to sleep outside at my house. I'll spread a pallet for him on the floor. It would be a sin to let him stay out there in the elements."

Shane went to wake Moses and tell him to come in.

Adalina reached out to Audie and felt the crucifix and feather he wore on a leather strap under his shirt. She pulled it out.

"Azariah's." She ran her finger along the length of it, remembering the man who it originally belonged to. "And the feather?"

"It's from the Apache. It's for luck."

"I hope they didn't make you believe in that nonsense, Audie. Your father loved them, but he wouldn't have stood for that." She still had a lion in her voice when she spoke of the Indians.

"It's just a feather, Mama," Audie said.

Moses and Shane came back in. "Ma'am, there ain't no need ta make a fuss over me. I'm jus' fine outside."

"Not at my house, you're not. You'll sleep inside like any decent child of God. Audie, fetch me some blankets from the chest in my bedroom."

Audie walked into Adalina's bedroom. So many memories of his childhood flooded his mind. He'd hid from Shane in this very room plenty of times when they were younger. He remembered the lectures from his father in here, and sometimes Azariah's hand on his backside when he had disobeyed. He remembered feeling loved in here.

Audie grabbed the blankets from the chest and headed back toward the others.

"Audie, you and Shane can sleep in your old room. Moses, will this room be suitable for you?"

"Why, yes'm, this room will suit me jus' fine. Thank you, Ms. Adalina. I'm in your debt."

"I'm in your debt, Moses, for bringing my sons back safe and sound."

She made a pallet on the floor, complete with a pillow and two blankets. To Moses, it looked like a slice of heaven. It was the first time he'd slept in a house in over twenty years.

"Good night, Moses. You make yourself at home. If you need anything at all, just help yourself," Adalina offered.

The boys followed their mother back to their old bedroom. Again, memories flooded Audie's head. They were in Shane's mind, too. The nights staying up telling ghost stories. The mornings being awakened by their parents. The games of hide-and-seek they played so long ago in this very room. Before the world changed.

"It's your old room. I'd say the bed is a bit small for you two, but it'll have to do."

The bed was only about six feet long and four feet wide. Someone was sleeping on the floor.

"You can have the bed, Audie. We ain't both fitting on there."

Adalina smiled. Shane had always looked up to his brother. Some things hadn't changed.

CHAPTER 11

It was an odd feeling, waking up in a house, for all three of the wanderers who had drifted into Adalina's home. Sleep had been uneasy for Audie. He'd dreamed, like so many nights before, of soldiers marching in to do their worst. It was a pleasant awakening to find he was safe and sound in his mother's home.

The coffee from Azariah's old blue metal cup washed away the fretful scenes from last night, and Adalina's fried eggs laid waste to any lingering thoughts of danger.

"I want you boys to go with me today to see your grandfather. He'll be joyed to see you. He's been sick with tuberculosis for two years now."

"Of course, Mama. How bad is he?" Shane asked.

"I'm afraid he's at the end of his strength. I don't know how long he has. There is a nurse who stays with him, but he's ornery in his old age. He prefers me caring for him, though he would never give me the compliment of saying so. I have tried to get him to move in here with Thomas and me, but he'll have none of it."

Mac Carson and his daughter had grown apart since the disappearance of Azariah and the boys. She never could quite wrap her mind around the reason.

"Miss Adalina, I'd be happy ta mend that fence out there by the road if'n that's somethin' you want done," Moses offered.

"Why, Moses! That'd be wonderful! Thomas keeps trying to get around to it, but his work keeps him away so much. I'd be glad to pay you for your trouble."

"No need for that, Miss Adalina. Yo' hospitality is enough."

Adalina smiled at Moses and cleaned up the breakfast table before she got ready for the trip. Moses went to work on the fence. Shane and Audie went outside to wait for their mother.

"We need to watch what we say, Shane."

"Why do you say that?"

"Mama married a Pinkerton agent. She said he hunts down criminals for a living. I don't know what we're gonna get up to, but whatever it is, we don't need a damn Pinkerton knowing our business."

Shane mulled it over without replying.

Audie walked over to Moses. "You okay to stay here while we head to see our grandfather?"

"Sure am." Moses smiled.

The boys got the wagon ready for the trip.

It was an hour to Mac's house. The ride was spent summoning up old scenes from the brothers' youth. It felt good to Audie and Shane to remember innocence.

When they arrived at Mac's, the place didn't look as they'd remembered it, though they hadn't thought of this house since they could recall.

Mac's home looked unkempt and void of any welcoming. The three knotty pine columns on the front porch seemed to be bars to keep the world out. There were overgrown thistles and weeds all around, most certainly hiding king snakes like guards on the path to the door. A weather vane creaked obnoxiously at the side of the house as if to say, "No peace will be found here."

When they got there, he was sleeping. The nurse, Ellie, had let them in, asking them to be quiet.

"How is he doing?" Adalina inquired of the nurse.

"He's not well at all today. The coughing has progressed and there's blood in it. He mumbles about things I can't understand at all."

Adalina looked worried.

Shane put his hand on Adalina's back to comfort her. They heard a stirring from Mac's room.

"Let me check on him." Ellie left.

"Mr. Carson, you have visitors today." Ellie said it as cheerfully as possible, but it did little to lighten the dark feel of the place.

Adalina entered first, then Audie and Shane.

The boys walked up to either side of his bed and leaned in. Mac squinted until he recognized them. Silent tears made their way down to white beard.

Adalina went over to Mac to comfort him. "You know your grandsons. That's good, Daddy."

Mac beckoned the boys closer to him. There were still no words. He reached up toward Audie to hug him. Audie bent down in an awkward embrace. After a long minute, Mac did the same to Shane. Mac had never been this affectionate when they were children. It was odd to see him this way now.

"You're alive!" Mac whispered.

"Yes, Grandpa, we are. And you are, too, thankfully," Shane said.

"Where . . . have you been? And what of . . . your father?" Mac struggled to get the words out.

"We've been living with the Apache all these years. Soldiers killed Father in a raid on our camp. A great warrior named Grey Wolf took care of us," Audie said. There was pain and pride mingled in his words.

Mac cried a little harder now and covered his face with his hands.

"We should leave Mr. Carson for a bit and let him collect himself," Ellie told them.

Adalina reached down and kissed Mac's forehead gently.

They all left the room, except Ellie, and went into the sitting room.

After a few minutes Ellie came out and reluctantly announced that Mac wasn't up for any more visiting today.

"We can come back tomorrow," Adalina said confused.

"I'm sorry, Adalina. He said he doesn't want to talk to anyone right now. He's just a little overwhelmed with everyone here, I think." Ellie seemed embarrassed to be telling a daughter her father said he didn't want to see her.

Adalina and her sons walked out of the door to go back home.

When they returned, Moses was closing in on the fence repair. He had found some trees that made perfect stakes for the worm fence.

Adalina smiled at him. "Moses, that fence looks brand new. Thank you so much. You must have worked up an appetite with all that fence mending. Come in in a bit and let me make you a bite to eat for your troubles."

"Thank ya, Miss Adalina. That'd be right welcome 'bout now."

Adalina went in the house and began cutting up potatoes. Shane and Audie went to help Moses finish up.

"Thank you for this, Moses. I appreciate your kindness toward Mama," Audie told him.

"Oh, I got ta have something ta do with myself. Besides, it's a peace in it. It feel good ta work with my hands again."

They worked on the fence for the couple of hours that were left in the afternoon, till Adalina yelled for them to come in for supper. It was a good night. There was no talk of sadness or past pains. They chatted well into the evening about Eminence gossip, Thomas, or anything that made their mama smile, till weariness beckoned them to sleep.

CHAPTER 12

The next morning over breakfast, Adalina informed everyone they would be heading back to Mac's, in hopes he was in better spirits. After they ate, Adalina cleaned up the dishes while the three men went outside.

Shane filled the canteens and put them on the wagon for the journey. Audie and Moses sat on the front porch staring at the new day.

"Is everyone ready?" Adalina walked onto the porch and asked.

"Yes, Mama. Moses, are you coming along?" Shane inquired as he climbed in the wagon.

"No, thank ya. I'm gonna make myself useful 'round here."

"Suit yourself," Shane said.

They left for Mac's house. Shane manned the reins. Moses went to digging up thistle weeds with a hoe around the place.

They arrived at Mac's around ten, in just enough time to beat what heat the day had to offer. Ellie greeted them at the door.

"He's doing better today. He's been asking for y'all."

Adalina and her two sons entered the bedroom where Mac was.

His face darkened with sadness again, but there were no tears. He beckoned Adalina over for a hug. He hadn't done that in years. Afterward, he asked Shane and Audie to come over so he could have a good look at them.

"I had given up hope of ever seeing you two again. My sickness came from this worry. The sight of you is healing to this old carcass."

Adalina hadn't heard him speak of these things till now. She was surprised to hear her daddy talk like this.

"It's good to see you, too, Grandpa," Audie said.

Mac hid his eyes in the palms of his hands and cried softly. Adalina sat on the bed beside him and put one arm around his shoulder.

"Hush now, Daddy. Your grandsons are here. We can be thankful for that," she offered.

After a few minutes, Mac grabbed a handkerchief on his nightstand and wiped his eyes.

"I am grateful you boys are here. More than you know," Mac said. "How are things out west?"

The brothers spoke of the Apache to the old man. These were things he understood from his days as an agent to the Indians. They talked of buffalo hunts and the Indian saddles, wild corn and cactus. Mac enjoyed rehashing these things. It had been a while since he'd had the chance to.

Adalina excused herself from the conversation. It was clear by the scowl on her pretty face that she had a river of anger flowing through her toward the people who saw her children grow up in her place.

Ellie had made a lunch of pinto beans and cornbread for everyone and brought the food into Mac's bedroom so he could enjoy their company with the meal. When they'd finished eating, everyone walked outside except for Audie. Mac held him back for conversation.

"I need to speak on some things to you, Audie. An old man needs to clear his conscience before he leaves this world."

Audie pulled his chair closer to Mac's bed.

"I'm not like my father, Grandpa. I'm far from a man of the cloth."

"No, boy. I'm not looking for a priest. Just forgiveness. I've offered my soul to Jesus." Audie was lost on Mac's intent.

"I called for the raid on that camp."

Mac saw the confusion on Audie's face.

"It's been a damnation to my soul ever since! I was enraged with Azariah for taking you and your brother and leaving Adalina. He should have been home with his family, taking care of my daughter and my grandsons!"

Audie felt a darkness creep over him. Like the sun had just set in his soul. His fists clenched and unclenched, and he worked to keep his breathing even and slow.

"I . . . I don't understand. How did you order the raid?"

"I sent a letter to a friend in the army. Actually, not a friend, an old acquaintance. I told him the location. You have to understand, I told him not to harm you or your brother or Azariah! He wrote me afterward that he had not seen Azariah or you and Shane in the raid. I knew the bastard was lying! He always was a despicable man."

"What was this man's name?" Audie asked coldly.

"Briggs. Frederick Briggs. The name feels like a blister on my tongue now."

Audie burned the name in his mind like a red-hot brand.

"He's the reason my father is dead."

"I know, boy. I know. I'm asking forgiveness for these sins before I leave this world. I don't want this noose around my neck when I meet my maker!"

Mac began to sob softly. The pitiful cry of a worn-down man.

"Shhhh. It's alright," Audie comforted.

He got up and checked outside to see if anyone heard Mac crying. No one was close, so he quietly closed the bedroom door and walked back to Mac's side.

"So you want absolution from your sins from me before you die? For the murder of my father? And all the innocent Apache who were slaughtered that day? You want me to send you to Jesus in a snow-white gown?" Audie's eyes were all that gave away the freight train of rage rolling through his soul.

"Yes, son. Forgive an old man his trespasses so he can pass in peace."

Audie stroked Mac's thin white hair on the side of his wrinkled head and stared into his grandfather's pleading eyes. The time hung heavy and slow like the still before a tornado.

"There is no forgiveness in me." Audie grabbed a pillow beside Mac and placed it firmly over Mac's face. The movement was so fast that Mac hadn't had time to protest before it covered him. Audie pushed down on the sides of the pillow with all he had, holding his breath and grunting as silently as he could. He smothered him for his father. He did it for the Apache. For himself.

The old man struggled with his chubby, sun-spotted hands to remove the pillow, but he was weak from age and sickness, and he was no match for Audie. Audie hoped Mac's muffled screams wouldn't be heard. The more he screamed, the harder Audie pushed. The resolve Azariah had passed down to him was too strong to be overtaken by any other virtue. It was that strength that held the pillow in place.

After a short eternity, the old man gave up the ghost. Audie pulled his weapon of choice away from Mac's head and stared at him for a moment longer. He didn't know why, but he wept softly. He felt the hole inside himself grow even larger.

When his wits were about him again, he wiped his eyes and straightened the mess Mac had made of the sheets. He folded his grandfather's hands across his chest and fixed his gown, trying to make him look as peaceful as possible.

When he was satisfied with the state of things, he collected himself and walked out where the others were sitting. His emotions still raged, but he kept them hidden.

"Mama, I need talk to you."

Everyone stared at Audie, but no one could read the look on his face.

"Grandpa has passed away. I'm sorry, Mama."

"No! He was fine just a half hour ago," Ellie cried.

"He's gone? Audie, is Daddy gone?" Adalina was on the verge of becoming hysterical.

"Yes, Mama."

She ran to Mac's bedroom and stopped at the door. There was no life in the room. Ellie ran past her and frantically checked his pulse and breathing. There was none.

Shane walked in from outside to see what all the fuss was about. Adalina and Ellie were crying. Audie was not.

CHAPTER 13

They buried Mac out behind his house, in the shade of the tallest beech tree on his property. Shane and Audie could add gravedigger to their list of master skills at this point. Shane could sense something was wrong with Audie, but he held his tongue. Adalina was just glad to have her sons there and was too distracted with the passing of her father to notice.

They stayed with Adalina for four more days. On the third day, Audie announced they'd be leaving, to the surprise of both Shane and Moses.

Out on the porch, Shane tried to make a case against it.

"But, Audie, I don't know that now is the best time to go. Mama needs us here. She's just lost Grandpa, and Thomas isn't back yet. Besides, we haven't even met him."

"I don't care to meet Thomas. He'll be back soon enough to look after Mama, and there's not a damn thing here for us. We leave tomorrow at first light."

"You know, Audie, you're not God. It's not a sin for me not to do your every bidding."

Shane fired off the words like bullets.

"Then stay here. Rot in Eminence like all of the other sore-asses around this godforsaken place."

Audie spoke nonchalantly, but it unsettled him more than a little to think of life without his brother.

Shane walked away, afraid he might punch Audie if he stayed any longer. He knew there was no reasoning with his brother when he was like this.

~

Later that afternoon, Adalina came outside and found Audie sitting under the bur oak where he used to play as a child.

She sat beside him and rubbed his back.

"I think you're even more like your father than I thought," she said softly.

Audie didn't want to bite, but her bait was too tempting.

"How so?"

"You have leaving in your bones. Just like him."

"He was a better man than me."

"How do you measure such a thing, Audie? I'm unable to," she asked.

Audie gazed out into the fescue field, trying to find answers to questions he couldn't speak.

"Will you return?"

"Someday."

"You've only just got here, Audie. After so long away from me. Is life here such an intolerable thing?"

"No, Mama. Not at all. It's just. . . I'm different now. Father's death, it changed me. Made me. . . restless."

Adalina was wise enough to know that with men there were things to be reckoned that a mother could have no part in. She spoke no words in combat of his.

"Well, it's a sin to let a mother wither away without at least a visit now and then." She smiled at Audie. It was laced with heartache, enough to make Audie feel it.

"I'm sorry about Mac, Mama."

"Well, that was no fault of yours, Audie." She stopped rubbing Audie's back. "And since when do you call your grandfather by his Christian name?"

Audie rose and walked away, leaving Adalina perplexed.

The next morning when everyone else woke, Audie was already dressed and road ready. He told Adalina goodbye with a quick hug before he mounted his horse. He rode up ahead before the others said their goodbyes.

Adalina was trying not to cry but was wiping away tears at the same time.

Moses thanked her for the hospitality. She informed him he was welcome back anytime.

"I wish you could have met Thomas," she said to Shane, holding his face in her hands.

"I know, Mama. We will someday. We'll be back. Audie . . . he just doesn't know where he belongs. And honestly, I don't either."

"Well, you know where I think you both belong, and this place will always be waiting for you."

Shane hugged Adalina for a moment, then kissed the top of her head and said goodbye.

And they were gone.

CHAPTER 14

There wasn't much in the way of conversation as they left Adalina's. Audie had decided the City of Kansas was as good a place as any to go at this point. Shane had no better suggestion, so the City of Kansas it was.

Moses had shaved his head, and the beginnings of a beard were starting to appear. The scar was beginning to heal but still had scabs, and the droop in his face wasn't going away. He definitely looked like a different man from the one Audie and Shane first met on the trail east.

"Whatcha two plannin' fo' when we get ta the City of Kansas?"

"I plan on bending an elbow till I get slurring drunk," Shane said, only half joking.

Shane had taken to the whiskey since his first taste, around the time he was fifteen. It was part of the DeVine brothers' ritual to drink whatever spirits they found on men they warred with while they were still with the Apache, but Shane had done most of the drinking.

"I'm not sure. Maybe we can sing for our supper somewhere."

It was turning out to be a warm day, but Audie had cold in his bones. He still heard his grandfather's muffled moaning in the sounds of the trees around them. Half of him hated himself for the killing. The other half wished he could kill Mac again.

"Moses, what do you want to do when we get there?" Shane asked.

"All's I wanna do is not get my ass strung up." He said it with humor, but the boys knew there was serious in there as well. Still, it was good to see the man at ease enough to joke. He was loosening up around them.

Not many other thoughts made it past their lips till they reached the city.

The City of Kansas was stunning to the three men. There were women wearing lacy dresses of every color with big bustles below the waist, walking like pretty flowers blowing on a breeze through the streets. Wool-suited businessmen with expensive-looking timepieces attached to their sides and hard-faced cowboys in brown leather chaps and hats arguing for the upper hand in whatever deal was going down. There were rambunctious cattle auctions and overrun taverns that teased and tempted with their offerings. This place had a heartbeat that made a man want to move in rhythm to it. They overheard talk of a prohibition on alcohol, but talk was all it was at this point. This city was a celebration.

"We've got some coin. Let's go try one of these City of Kansas steaks." Shane's appetite was awakened by all the advertisement around him.

They tied off in front of the first restaurant they came to.

"I'll stay out here an watch da wagon," Moses offered.

"Like hell. That wagon will be fine. Come in and eat a steak." Audie didn't want to treat Moses like a slave.

"I thank ya, but maybe y'all could just bring me somethin' back. I don't wanna be causin' no trouble first thing when we get here."

Moses was looking at the sign creaking in the wind on the hitching post that said "No Coloreds." He'd learned enough about the DeVine brothers to know they'd be willing to throw down just out of principle. He knew they weren't the kind of men who saw color as a divider, but he didn't want to have to make them prove it.

Shane looked at the sign.

"To hell with that, Moses."

"I'm thankful y'all feel that way, but I don't need nobody payin' me too much attention. Ya know?"

"He's right, Shane. We'll bring you back something, Moses," Audie reasoned.

"Thank ya," Moses said.

Audie and Shane stepped into the Kansas Cattle Cookery and ordered three steaks and two beers and tried their best to look like this wasn't the first time they'd been in a public place since they were in their single digits.

"Remember that book we used to read, *All Around the World?*" Audie quizzed.

"I think you mean *All the Year Round.* Yes, I remember it."

"Whatever it was. There was a tale in there about singers who would play on the streets and people would stop and listen and throw a little coin in a hat for them. I think they called it busking. Remember that?"

"Yes." Shane smiled, knowing where Audie was going with this.

"What if we set up right on the edge of town and gave these folks a show? See if we're more than just campfire entertainment?"

"I like what you're thinking."

Shane thought for a moment.

"We'll call ourselves the Singing Warriors. That's a good name."

"That's a terrible name, Shane."

"Eat shit, Audie."

"I think Moses had a better name."

"What's that?"

"The DeVine Devils."

Shane pondered it. "That'll rattle the good folks around here. I don't know."

"It'll make them pay attention, that's for sure."

"I mean, I like it, but it's . . . stout."

"Ain't a damn thing wrong with stout."

They finished their meal and wrapped up the steak for Moses. He was leaned up against the wagon when they came back.

"That's a fine piece of meat there," Audie told Moses. "Chow down."

"Thank ya."

"We're gonna head to the edge of town and see if we can't attract an audience with a song or two. What do you think about that, Moses?" Shane asked.

"I think if'n y'all sang anything like what y'all did fo' me, y'all might be famous." Moses grinned while chewing on a bite of his beef.

"Well then! Let's see what we're made of."

Both brothers were excited and nervous to test themselves.

They all mounted up and rode down to the south end of town. Audie and Shane felt a tingling in their hands as they anticipated the show.

"This looks like a good place."

Audie dismounted and grabbed his guitar off of the wagon. Shane grabbed his drums.

"You ready?" Shane asked Audie.

"Hell no."

And so it began.

"Let us pause in life's pleasure and count her many tears,
*   While we all sup sorrow with the poor,*
*   There's a song that will linger forever in our ears;*
*   Oh! Hard times come again no more."*

Audie sang the first verse a cappella. The nervousness created a tension in his voice that gave the words emotion. People were staring but no one ventured over yet.

. . .

"'Tis the song, the sigh of the weary,
Hard times, hard times, come again no more,
Many days you have lingered around my cabin door;
Oh! Hard times come again no more."

Audie began to strum his guitar, and Shane joined in on harmony and beat out a rhythm on the drums. It was a song people knew by a writer named Stephen Foster, but these people had never heard it like this. No one but a few Apache Indians and Moses had ever heard it like this.

A few people walked their way.

"While we seek mirth and beauty and music light and gay
There are frail forms fainting at the door
Though their voices are silent, their pleading looks will say
Oh hard times come again no more"

Dozens were gathering around them now. The brothers' nerves were in sort of a crescendo as they noticed the people noticing them.

"'Tis the song, the sigh of the weary,
Hard Times, hard times, come again no more,
Many days you have lingered around my cabin door;
Oh! Hard times come again no more."

They sang another verse and chorus. As the last note faded, they could tell that the hustle and bustle around them had stopped. The crowd stood there looking dumbfounded at the two men singing. A couple of seconds passed with no sound.

Then the crowd erupted.

Shane and Audie stood there, openmouthed. They didn't know how to receive the applause. As the cheering died down, they recovered, though. Audie threw down his hat for tips and they started singing again. They sang for almost an hour straight. By the time they had finished, there was such a crowd that those in the back couldn't see. There were almost a couple of fights from people trying to push their way toward the front.

Moses stood by watching. He was glad to see the boys shine.

Grey Wolf taught them the way of the warrior. They learned the discipline of the knife throw, the motion of the axe swing, the power of the fist and foot, and the deadliness of the gun.

But the DeVine brothers had another skill. Audie had the spirit of the Wild West in his guitar, and Shane thundered the beat of a savage in his drums. They had bled their way into a sound all their own.

CHAPTER 15

"**W**e made four dollars and change. That's more money than I've ever seen in my life," Shane declared.

Audie was still caught up in the moment.

"Well, you boys stirred 'em up. I thought they might lynch ya fo' stoppin'."

"Moses, this money's yours, too."

Audie felt the need to clarify Moses' status with them.

"I 'preciate that, Audie, but wasn't me makin' those folks put they money down."

"It's yours, too. We ain't gonna argue with you about that," Shane insisted. "Right now, I need whiskey from one of those places Daddy used to call a devil's den. Being as I'm a devil now, I ought to fit in nicely. I'll see you two dandelions later."

Shane walked off in the direction of the closest saloon.

"Well, Moses, what do you think you and me ought to do? Go chase loose women around somewhere?" Audie joked.

"No, sir. Not me. That's your bidness if you wanna do that, and I ain't the man who gonna stand in your way," Moses said laughing.

"Ah, I wouldn't even know where to look. Let's go check on a place to stay for the night."

They walked into a saloon that boasted "Rooms to Let 5 Cents."

"Give us three rooms," Audie told the barkeep.

The man behind the bar smirked and had a surly disposition that instantly agitated something in Audie.

"That'll be fifteen cents, unless you're planning on your nigger staying in one."

Audie fixed his eyes on the man for an awkward length of time before answering.

"My colored friend here will be staying, yes."

The barkeep snickered like a teenager who just farted in church.

"Whatever you wanna call him is fine. That'll be two cents extra. For the cleaning fee, of course."

Audie gave the man a look that revealed hellfire behind his eyes. The barkeep's condescending manner was replaced with a coward's paleness in his face.

"I . . . I'll get your keys."

Audie gave the man fifteen cents and they went to find their rooms.

~

Shane was more than liver deep when Audie found him.

"Don't soak up too much, Shane. This ain't a time to be off guard in a new place like this."

"Well, hell, Audie. I'm just thirsty. It ain't my fault how drunk this bottle gets me."

"Here's a key to your room, Room 3, written right there on it. Banyon's Saloon, six storefronts down. Can you remember that?"

"I got a memory like a steel trap. Ain't nothing gets past here." Shane tapped his temple.

"Don't get yourself in trouble," Audie scolded as he left.

~

The next morning showed up earlier than Shane had expected. Audie's banging on the door felt like horses stomping on his head.

He unwrapped himself from the curvy blonde-haired prostitute he'd paid to spend the night with him and stumbled to the door, naked.

"What the hell, Audie? Can't a man sleep?"

"It's ten in the morning. A man's slept half the day away."

"Shit. Alright. Let me get my duds on." The girl stirred a little but never got up as he gathered his things. He left and went to find Audie and Moses by the wagon in front of the building.

"How much did you spend last night?" Audie more accused than asked.

"I don't know. I've still got some left."

"We're not out here just so you can drain a tavern and fill up some whore every night. Get it out of your system," Audie spat.

"Alright! Damn! Stop shouting."

"I'm not shouting. Go get you some food to kill that headache."

Shane went and got some grub while Audie talked to Moses.

"You just gettin' your feet wet. Give it some time. An' give your brother some, too. This all new for ev'ry one. You ain't a man seems like he gets off his path too easy. Jus' give it time."

Audie thought on Moses' wisdom till Shane came back. He was grateful for this man.

"Whew. I gotta possum in my gut this morning!" Shane announced, trying to lighten the mood.

"Well, you ain't far from a boot in your ass. You up for singing again today? Maybe on the other side of town?"

"Yeah. Let's wait till this afternoon when all the people are heading home. I think we'll do even better with that traffic," Shane said, secretly hoping his hangover would be gone by that time.

"Alright. You best not even smell a bottle before then."

Shane laughed. Audie didn't.

They spent the day checking out the rest of the city.

The DeVine Devils played again that afternoon to a crowd that only wanted more when they were done.

"We made five dollars and thirty cents today! We could live half a year on that much money!" Shane said.

"Not if you spend it all on whiskey and whores."

Shane gave Audie a sarcastic look in retort.

"Good afternoon, gentlemen! A hell of a show you boys put on. What was your names again? The divine something or other?" A man in a top hat and black suit spoke to them like he was campaigning.

"The DeVine Devils. And who might you be?"

"LC Banyon. Owner of a number of fine establishments here in our great city. I would like to speak to you gentlemen about a business proposition."

"What sort of proposition would that be?" Shane asked.

"Well, one in which we all make a lot of money, of course!" LC lacked no confidence.

"Well, speak on it, Mr. Banyon. We're listening." Audie tried to seem even keeled to keep the odds in his favor. Growing up with the Apache, he was no stranger to negotiations.

"I've noticed the people your musical offerings have attracted these last couple of days. I'd like to offer you a job at my saloon here. I want you boys to be the house band. I'll pay you two dollars a night. Free room and board for all three of you, and you can keep any tips you might get from the patrons in appreciation of your music. In return, you'll play for me six nights a week, from nine till midnight, and of course, it would be an exclusive agreement. Meaning you wouldn't be allowed to play for anyone else here in this town, even on the streets out here as you have been."

"Does the offer include drink?" Shane inquired.

Audie gave him a daggered glare.

"Well, son, that depends on how much you plan on drinking," LC half joked.

"Just enough," Shane answered.

Audie kept his gaze on Shane a moment longer and then focused on Mr. Banyon.

"Four dollars a night. And make it ten till midnight. Two hours of song is plenty for an evening." Audie smiled at him.

"I don't know if I can pay four. But I can do two and a half hours."

"I think a man such as yourself sees the value in having our talents all to himself. I believe four is a fair number."

LC studied Audie's eyes. He didn't see the give he was hoping to find.

"Then four it is. Not only do you bring a crowd, but you drive a hard bargain, too. I can respect that. So, do we have deal?"

"Yes, sir. We have a deal. Do we start tonight?" Audie asked.

"By all means. I've got some boys in the saloon building a stage as we speak."

Audie laughed. "You were that sure we would say yes?"

"Young man, you strike me as someone who doesn't take no for an answer very often. I hope you can appreciate that same quality in me."

"Yes sir, I can."

"We'll see you boys this evening?" LC asked as he ungloved his hand and offered it to Audie.

"Tonight." Audie shook on it.

LC tipped his hat and walked away. He turned again to speak to them. "The DeVine Devils. Where'd you fellows acquire a crazy title like that?"

"Our friend Moses here gave us that name."

"Well, at least it's a name that won't soon be forgotten, I reckon." He chuckled as he left.

"I like that man," Audie offered when Mr. Banyon was out of earshot.

It was a typical saloon of those days. There were the poker-faced gamblers looking for a lucky hand, hard luck drunks siphoning off whatever drink they could squander, lonely soldiers on leave hoping to find a willing woman, and the ladies of the night looking for lonesome men. This would be the kind of place you would find the brothers from now on. They never felt at home away from the Apache, but there among misfits they felt a little closer to it.

There would be ladies who were mesmerized by the swagger of the music. They would be enticed by the beat and sway in time to it, curious as to what kind of men could conjure up such provocative sounds. The men would watch the brothers quizzically for a while, but in the end Audie and Shane would win their favor as well.

The brothers didn't realize how much power their music had until those first few shows. For them, it was second nature. To the crowd, they were a welcome distraction. It was an appropriate backdrop to the dreary places where the lost and lonely gathered. Their music was a great chaser for the whiskey, captivating enough to woo you away from your worries for a while. It felt like a church for the wayward. After all, they were the sons of a preacher . . .

Banyon's Saloon was the proving ground the DeVine Devils needed. They learned what they were made of there. Each night they climbed into the music a little easier. The nervous became friend instead of foe. They learned control. They learned the nuances of the crowd. They learned themselves.

And their fame spread. People were coming from miles to hear this new music spoken of by travelers.

They played Mr. Banyon's bar for the better part of nine months. Shane settled into the life. Having his choice of women every night made the transition less difficult. Moses took care of any errands that needed doing. He kept the horses in shape, collected payment, and managed all of their affairs.

But Audie was growing ever restless. He thought of Grey Wolf often and remembered his promise to fight against those who murdered his father. He had no intention of breaking it. He longed for a fight. The music was a release, but not enough to free him of the pull toward a battle.

Other than onstage, Shane had been keeping his distance from him the last few days. Audie had become increasingly unpleasant to be around.

Audie had asked Moses to saddle his horse. It was Sunday, their day off, and he wanted to ride hard and fast to nowhere.

"You sho seem low for a man sitting on top'a the world," Moses said as Audie approached.

"What the hell are we doing, Moses? We're no more than a time passer for drunks and whores. There's no purpose in it. It just puts easy money in our pocket. I'm a warrior! I don't want to rust away in some whiskey trough!" Audie punched the wall of the stable, shaking the structure and spooking the horses.

Moses worked to get Audie's horse under control. "You need ta calm down, Audie! Go take yo'self a ride an' have a think on things. I can't tell ya what ta do. But gettin' riled up like this ain't doin' nobody any good. You gonna find your way. An' you boys got somthin' sho nuff special in your singin'. Don't go draggin' it around jus' 'cause ya down."

Moses couldn't understand all of Audie's frustrations. There was a lot of backstory he didn't know. Still, he didn't ask. He figured it best to wait till Audie or Shane wanted to tell him.

Audie mounted his horse and rode off with a swift kick and a "haya!"

He returned around sundown. They were in the winter months now and the days were shorter. His horse was weary and in need of water when he arrived at the stables.

Moses was waiting.

Audie dismounted and handed over the reins.

"Where's Shane?"

Moses started tending to the horse and didn't even look up when he spoke. "It's nightfall. You know where he be."

Audie found Shane in Banyon's Saloon and sat down on a stool next to him. "Barkeep, pour me an elbow bender."

"Well! Audie DeVine is gonna partake tonight. What's the occasion?"

"It's been a while since we drank together. I figured it'd do us good," Audie reckoned as he lifted his whiskey.

"You wanna leave the city, don't you?"

Audie smiled. "You know me, brother. And I know you, too. You don't."

"I like it here. You have to admit, it's a good life."

"That's just it, Shane. It's too good. We're getting too comfortable. Remember our promise to Grey Wolf?"

Shane stared at the floor. "Yes, I remember."

"I need to keep that promise, Shane. If it kills me. And you do, too."

"I know, Audie. I know. I want to. I guess it just felt good for a while to take the burden off of our shoulders. Didn't it?"

"It felt easy. But easy never did a damn thing worth doing. Don't you miss fighting?"

"Yes. I miss a lot of things."

Lozen. Audie hadn't thought of her in while. Evidently that wasn't true of Shane. "Then why do you dirty your sheets with a new whore every night?"

"It keeps away the lonely."

Audie felt for his brother in that moment. "Look, we'll keep playing. We have to earn a living. But let's take our show on the road. Find a new town. I don't know. Maybe along the way we can . . . do something." Audie lowered his voice. "There's bound to be some Billy Yanks heading west we could slow down or some scalpers we could rid the land of or maybe someday we'll run across those responsible for the raid or . . . anything but nothing."

Frederick Briggs. The name crossed Audie's mind like an arrow. Audie needed the man's death like he needed air.

"Okay, Audie. You're right. This isn't what we set out to do."

Audie ordered another round from a handlebar-mustached bartender cleaning a glass. "We'll give Mr. Banyon a couple of weeks' notice. He's been good to us. I don't want to leave him without some warning."

The brothers enjoyed the evening together, recounting stories and getting drunk. It was a much-needed night for them.

Audie told Mr. Banyon they would be leaving. He didn't love the idea, by any means, but he wished the brothers well and told them they'd always have a place to play if they needed it. Not everyone was a snake in this world. It was good for Audie to see that.

The boys did their farewell show a couple of weeks later. It was standing room only. There were dozens of angry people out in the streets who couldn't even get in. Banyon's Saloon sold out of whiskey and beer, something that had never happened in the history of the place. It was a good night for all.

"Where we headed, boys?" Moses asked as they started the journey the next morning.

"West. Let's see what Wichita's like."

The DeVine Devils and Moses rode out of town like a slow-moving train. People waved and cheered in hopes they'd come back around again.

CHAPTER 16

The trip west was a quiet one. It was January. Not the best time to travel, but Audie had no reservations about it. There had been some snow, but not enough to cause any delays.

Audie mulled over the future while Shane tried not to think about the past. Moses sang songs of the slaves to Audie and Shane on the journey. They enjoyed being entertained for a change. They had stopped in Emporia for some supplies and actually heard mention of themselves at a restaurant where they'd had lunch. Folks were talking about the DeVine Devils as if they were famous.

Much to Shane's disappointment, Audie didn't want to let on that they were who they were. "Best to keep a low profile," he said.

Wichita was just as fascinating to the boys as the City of Kansas. They did their best not to appear wide-eyed. The beautiful women, the storefronts, and the saloons were still things of amazement to them. Moses, who had grown a full beard now and kept his head shaven, was very watchful of the crowd around him, always looking out for someone eyeing him.

They arrived around eleven in the morning.

"Let's get settled. Moses, will you go find a good price on a stable?

I'll get us some rooms. Shane, do what you do best and go check out the saloons to see which one we need to offer our services to."

Shane's mouth was practically watering.

After Audie secured their accommodations for the night, he went to check out the city.

~

Shane met Audie by the wagon that evening at suppertime, staggering a little and smelling like a whiskey barrel.

"That didn't take long," Audie said, referring to Shane's lack of sobriety.

"Well, I had to fit in, Audie. How would it look if I went into a saloon without drinking?"

"What'd you find with all your fitting in?"

"Well, recently, right over there at the Buckhorn Tavern, there was a shooting incident that involved a music box and a man named Jack Ledford. Evidently Jack won, leaving Mr. Vigus, the proprietor of the tavern, without a source of entertainment. I hear it's much affected the level of patronage."

Audie laughed. "Sounds like a perfect place for us."

"Yep," Shane slurred.

Audie went to find Moses and get a bite to eat. Shane meandered back to the bar.

~

The next day Audie found Mr. Henry Vigus at his establishment having breakfast.

Vigus was a plump, bald, little man who brought to mind images of a ringmaster at a circus. He wore a striped brown suit, and his handlebar mustache was just a touch too big for his small, chubby head.

Audie ordered a plate of pork, hotcakes, and eggs and sat down at the table with the owner.

"This is a private table, young man. Unless we have business, I'd suggest you take your nourishments someplace else."

"We do have business. You need entertainment in your saloon. I need a place for my brother and me to play."

Henry studied Audie. This man didn't look like any minstrel he'd laid eyes on before. Too strong of a disposition. "And who might you be?"

"Audie DeVine of the DeVine Devils."

"Ha! Horseshit. That's the boys that play in the City of Kansas. Word is that dumbass Banyon pays those boys two and a half dollars a night. They ain't going nowhere. Go away, young man. I ain't one to be taken in by imposters."

"I *am* Audie DeVine, and it was four dollars a night. Plus tips from the drunks. My brother and I needed a change of scenery. That's how we wound up here. Of course, if you're not interested, I'm sure we could find employment at one of these other fine saloons in this city."

Audie got up to go. Vigus changed his tune.

"Now, hold on a minute, young man. If you are who you say you are, then I'd love to see if this conversation could have some positive effect for the both of us."

"It can, provided you're willing to do a little better than our old employer, Mr. Banyon, did."

"Well, hell, son. Calm down. We ain't even courted yet, and you already want a ring. You youngsters. Always wantin' to dip your wick before the wax is even melted. Y'all need to learn the art of the dance. It makes the afters more satisfying."

"That's a disturbing comparison."

"It's just talk, Mr. DeVine. Something I'm guilty of too much sometimes. How about a show tomorrow night here? So I can make sure you're who you say you are. If that goes as you lead me to believe it will, we'll be able to talk about an arrangement that would be beneficial to the both of us."

Audie liked him but didn't fully trust him. "Fair enough. What time should my brother and I be ready to play tomorrow night?"

"Eight should do well. Before the drunkards get too drunk and there's still some money in the elbow benders' pockets."

"You have a way with words, Mr. Vigus. We'll see you at eight tomorrow night."

"Pleasure conversatin' with you. Help yourself to a drink or two if you need one. On the house." Henry made a gesture to the bartender and pointed to Audie.

"A little early for that, but thank you all the same." Audie had a look around the place. It wasn't as welcoming as Mr. Banyon's saloon, but it would do if it paid.

They passed the day away getting acquainted with the layout of the city. A couple of hours after dinner, Audie and Moses were standing out by the wagon when they saw Shane.

"At least your brother picks pretty girls." Moses laughed as he spoke to Audie. They were leaning on the wagon watching the traffic and listening to the night unfold when Shane walked by with a rather voluptuous brunette. He never noticed his brother or Moses.

Audie smiled and rolled his eyes. "I'm headed to bed. I've had a little too much rotgut this evening myself."

"I'll see ya in the mornin', Audie."

Audie tipped his hat. Too much whiskey to Audie was just enough to feel it slowing him down. A world of difference from too much for Shane.

Audie went to bed, and Moses followed suit soon after.

CHAPTER 17

The next day, like most before it, came in a haze for Shane. Audie was slightly fuzzy, but nothing a cup of coffee wouldn't fix. Audie heard commotion from his window.

"You sure are an uppity nigger. If I want to look in this wagon, I will. It reminds me of one I've seen before. How do I know you didn't steal it?"

Audie dressed and ran downstairs and out the door as fast as he could. He didn't need the coffee to stir him awake. He was electric in the wake of danger. "That's my wagon, mister. You got any questions about it, you can ask me," he said as he walked through the door outside.

"Well, I was enjoying talking to your nigger here. Where'd ya get it? The wagon, not the nigger."

The man speaking was rather large in stature. He wore a black leather vest and a black short-brimmed hat bent up on the sides. His face was hard and stubbled with dark whiskers, and his narrow, focused eyes held no hint of fear. It was obvious from his stance that he was confident in his physical ability. Confidence was as good of a weakness as fear when you knew how to use it against somebody.

Audie walked up to the man calmly and quicker than the man

expected. He punched him in the base of his throat. The man grabbed at his neck while Audie gave him a punch to the gut, followed by a kick to the knee. The man was instantly on all fours, gasping for air, and trying to figure out if his knee or his innards hurt worse.

Folks in the street stopped to watch the altercation.

Audie leaned over him slowly so as not to alarm him any further. "This man's name is Moses. He's a friend. I don't particularly like seeing a friend disrespected. Now, if you want to ask me some questions about this wagon, I'd be happy to answer." Audie picked him up by the collar. The man was still gasping. "No? Alright then. Sorry for the misunderstanding."

He slammed the man back down on the ground.

Moses was grateful, but he was worried that the man had recognized the wagon. He gave Audie a look that told him as much.

"Easy, Moses," Audie said out of earshot of the gasper. "He's either too afraid now to ask any more questions, or he's hellbent on teaching me a lesson for the beating I just gave him. Either way, we're okay. Don't worry. We'll sell the wagon off for a new one in a few days."

They looked back to see the man stumble trying to get up. Audie took note that no one tried to help him.

Moses felt an old knot tighten up in his stomach.

"Let's get some grub. We'll eat across the street where we can see the wagon."

Moses followed Audie to a restaurant called Beef & Beer. The owner wasn't much on creativity. They chose a table toward the door and by the window that looked out on the street. Moses was the only black man in the place.

A meek server walked up to the table. "Sir, it's our policy not to serve colored folks in here. I'm sorry for the inconvenience. Understand, it's the restaurant's policy, n-not my own." The stuttering waiter had obviously seen Audie take down the big man a few minutes ago.

Audie just stared at the fearful man. Moses got up to leave.

"Moses, sit dow—"

"No, Audie. I'll be by the wagon. It ain't worth another fight."

"My apologies again," the server stammered, trying to ease any ill will his request may have caused.

Audie shook his head. "Just give me two steaks and potatoes wrapped up. I'll eat outside."

"Yes, sir." The waiter walked to the kitchen a lot faster than he had walked to the table. Audie gave the man a crinkled-up banknote for the steaks and went outside to be with Moses.

"Bring them to me outside when they're ready."

A half an hour later, the two were eating in quiet on the back of the wagon when a boy of about ten walked up and stared at Audie. "Hello, young man. Can I help you with something?" Audie asked the lad.

"Nobody ever beat up Mr. Siringo before, mister. He's pretty mad about it, I bet. I'd watch my back if I was you. He's mean. The meanest man in this town. Maybe the meanest one in Kansas. I heard he killed a man with his bare fists in a fight before. I seen him send two men to Doc Hagle."

"His name's Siringo, huh? What's this Mr. Siringo do for a living?"

"He's a bounty hunter. He's famous for it."

Moses' heart sank.

"Run along now, kid," Audie told the boy. The young man bolted down the street grinning from ear to ear with pride that he'd talked to the man who had bested Siringo.

"That ain't no good, Audie."

"Relax, Moses. He thought he recognized the wagon, not you. And his beef is with me. If he thought anything about you, he would have said so. He was too sure of himself not to."

Audie went to wake Shane up around noon. He had to bang on the door for a long while before his brother raised from his stupor.

"Get your ass out of bed, Shane! It's dinnertime already. We got a show tonight."

Shane opened the door buck naked, smiling at Audie.

"You're still drunk."

"Nah."

"You smell like a puked-up bottle of corn liquor," Audie accused.

"Well, you look like the south end of an ass-shot possum."

"Get your drunk ass some coffee and chow and get ready for a show! If we don't deliver tonight, we don't get the job!"

Shane retreated and started clumsily pulling clothes on. Audie left shaking his head.

The brothers were ready by showtime. They had rehearsed a little in Audie's room, drawing a crowd outside the door to get a closer ear on the music.

By the time they got to Mr. Vigus's place, it was almost eight o'clock. They got into position and led off with their traditional opener, "Hard Times Come Again No More."

As usual, it didn't take the crowd long to get into the music. The women took notice first, so the men followed suit. A half an hour into their first set, they had earned a permanent spot at the Buckhorn Tavern.

"Well, Mr. DeVine, you weren't lying. You boys are pistols." Vigus walked up and said.

"Let's discuss pay," Shane led.

"Well, I'm happy to pay you two dollars and a half a night like that dumbass Banyon was."

"It was four," Audie corrected for the second time.

"Well, that's a pile of money for just singing."

"How big of a pile of money are you gonna make off the crowds we pull in? Four and a half," Audie bartered.

"And free whiskey," Shane added.

"Shit, boys. That's putting your hand pretty far up the skirt. How about four? And free whiskey. You won't be taking a pay cut that way, and I can still feed my family."

"How big's your family?" Shane inquired.

"Well, it's just me at the moment, but you never know when old Cupid is gonna send an arrow!"

"Four and a half." Audie wasn't asking.

"And free whiskey," Shane reminded him.

Audie gave Shane a hard look.

Mr. Vigus studied them for a moment. "Alright. You've twisted my titty long enough."

"You have an odd way of talking, sir," Shane said.

Vigus sipped his coffee and wiped the ends of his drooping mustache.

"We're settled, then?" Audie asked as he stuck out his hand.

"It's a deal." Mr. Vigus and Audie shook on it.

"I don't need you boys on Sunday, though. All the townspeople get religion, so we're slow on those days."

"Fair enough." Audie and Shane climbed back on stage to play the last set.

CHAPTER 18

Clay Siringo was just as the boy had described him. Mean. He was the bounty hunter known for his nerves of steel and ability to put down any man in a fight, be it fist or pistols. He was the man who had taken down the Butch Cassidy gang a couple years back. He wasn't liked by many, but he was respected by all. Well, not so much him, but his ability was respected. He was known for using questionable methods when capturing his targets. He had lied at one point to get hired on at the Pinkerton Agency, telling them his name was Paddy Garrett to ensure he'd get the job. To the people, he was as much villain as hero. To those brave enough to ask him about his tactics, he would just say, "If you wanna catch a criminal, you gotta think like a criminal."

He was as crooked as half the crooks he put away.

Siringo had inquired around to see who the man was who had laid him out yesterday. He was amazed to find out it was a musician. *Am I getting weak?* he thought. *There's no way that man or any should have been able to take me down like that.*

There would be a rematch. He didn't have a choice. His pride was hurt a lot more than his body. He wanted to feel this Audie DeVine's bones crush beneath his boot heel, and he determined he would.

More than a month had passed well for all involved at the Buckhorn. Their music made the perfect atmosphere for any saloon to thrive. Vigus was happy, Shane was drinking too much, and Audie was longing for any chance to wreak havoc on someone he judged deserving.

Moses' nerves calmed. He went about his tasks of taking care of the brothers' money and dealings unbothered. There had been no sign of retribution since he and Audie had had their run in with that Siringo character.

Shane had his pick of the ladies each night. Audie could have had his pick of women, and now and then he did, but mostly he chose to abstain. It wasn't on any moral basis. He just believed women clouded his mind. Truth is, he desired a woman as much as Shane did, but he feared becoming attached. Shane found a lover most every night in hopes it would kill his longing for Lozen. It numbed him, but Lozen was still there. In the moments after he made love to someone else, he'd pull away thinking of her. He had never pulled away from Lozen.

There was a barmaid, an Indian woman named Lomasi, whom the boys had become friends with. She was a few years their senior and quickly became like an older sister. Lomasi was Cherokee, but Audie and Shane felt a kinship to her nonetheless. They never told her their history, but she sensed their fondness for her and had her questions why. She would scold Shane like a big sister about his debauchery, and she would try to make Audie drink a little more to loosen him up. Lomasi was good for the boys.

Audie and Shane had been playing at Vigus's place a month and a half now. It was a Saturday night, the rowdiest night of the week, when a band of soldiers came in. They were a motley-looking bunch. All wanting to get baptized in the whiskey and hoping for some woman to be impressed by their uniforms. All would find the former and some would find both.

The place was packed. All in all, there were probably two hundred and fifty patrons.

Shane saw them first. He counted ten soldiers. He knew tonight wasn't going to be business as usual. "Lomasi, give me a beer instead of whiskey. I might need my wits tonight."

"Ha! You have no wits," she teased and gave him the beer.

Audie registered the room's occupants as he walked on the stage for the first set. He felt his face get hot. It was a welcome feeling.

Audie looked at Shane with eyes he knew well. Shane knew tonight would carry something different with it.

The band finished the last song of the first set and the crowd surrendered a drunken cheer. The two of them stepped off the stage for a breather and a drink.

"Dance with me, squaw!"

A soldier with beer dripping off of his beard grabbed at Lomasi's dress as she was wiping a table. He groped her ass with no hint of decorum whatsoever.

Lomasi pushed him away and headed back behind the bar.

Audie's blood boiled as he stared at the soldier with hell in his glare. He controlled his anger, but just barely.

"Play us some 'Camp Town Races'!" Another soldier had walked up and slapped Audie on the back. He was drunk and jolly, with a strand of hair from his balding head falling over his face. He didn't have the discernment to see the war in Audie's eyes.

"Bring some of that over here, Sanders! I know you ain't got the cod to use it all up!" the slovenly soldier yelled to his brother in arms who had been fondling Lomasi.

"Keep level, Audie." Shane spoke low. "This ain't the place. We'll take them somewhere else."

Shane was trying to lure Audie away with a carrot.

Audie turned his gaze away from the whiskey-bent soldiers. "We would be honored to play a song for the men who so chivalrously protect the oppressed of our nation!" Audie said to the jolly soldier.

"Lieutenant Baker, at your service!" The lieutenant stuck out his hand to shake Audie's, missing the sarcasm.

Audie drank his shot of whiskey and slammed the glass down. Then he shook the drunk's hand. "I hear you boys are having hell with the Indian uprising. Those Apache are a savvy breed," Audie pried.

"Savvy? The only thing those red nigger heads are good for are holding feathers. And besides, savvy ain't worth tits on a boar hog when a new Winchester has their red ass in its sights." The soldier had disgust on his tongue when he spoke about the Indians. Audie kept thinking about how he'd love to cut that tongue out.

"New Winchesters?" Audie asked, trying to cover his rage with the sound of curiosity.

"Got a half a wagon full of them, and enough ammunition to blow every Apache in that godforsaken land a new asshole," the soldier slurred proudly.

"Can I buy you boys a drink? Lomasi, bring these fellows a bottle of the oh be joyful. On my coin," Audie said. *The drunker the better*, he thought.

"Well, I've got to go earn my whiskey." Audie handed the Indian woman his money.

"Let them drink all they want. They'll get too drunk and small to be of harm to you," he whispered to her.

Audie gave Lomasi a comforting look, and she let him know she understood. Then he walked on stage and picked up his guitar. He started strumming loudly, and Shane picked up the beat behind him. They played the last set. Audie's rage owned the music for the rest of the night.

"Thank you, fellow travelers. We're the DeVine Devils. Remember us well!"

The saloon crowd cheered one last enthusiastic applause, and almost instantly it was back to business.

"Man, I was on fire tonight!" Shane shouted as a sultry-lipped lady caught his eye from below the stage. "And that redhead right there looks like she could use some warming up."

"Keep your prick in your britches tonight, Shane. We've got other things to do."

Audie and Shane walked out to the wagon and stowed away their guitar and drums. "I numbered ten gray coats in and out of the saloon tonight. None looked like he had much sand in him, but still that's quite a few to take on." Audie spoke and half thought out loud.

"I say we go check out that wagon. See what we're really getting ourselves into," Shane offered.

They both took off their boots and slipped on the moccasins they had stashed in their own wagon. They had learned to be silent as the dead. The moccasins helped. You could always hear boots coming if you were listening for them.

Audie crawled back into their wagon and started fumbling around for something. Shane asked him what he was looking for, but he had no answer for him.

A couple of minutes later Audie climbed out with a small leather pouch.

"What the hell, Audie? Now isn't the time for peyote! You won't be back in your right head till tomorrow night!"

"It's not for me," was all he said. Audie ran back into the saloon. There were still a few straggling drunks, and Lomasi was cleaning off spilled beer from the bar. It was almost one o'clock in the morning, and Moses had turned in for the evening hours earlier.

"Lomasi, do you have any water boiling back there? Could you spare a cup for me?" he asked his friend.

Lomasi walked to the kitchen and came back with a steaming cup of water. She handed it to Audie.

"Thank you."

"Thank you for your kindness tonight with those soldiers," she said, a little embarrassed.

"Do soldiers aggravate you often in here? In that way?"

"If I could run from here fast enough, there have been many times I would have separated those Billy Yanks from their lily-white balls!" She had enough conviction in her eyes to make Audie believe her.

He stayed there for a second to feel the full force of her words.

"Thank you, again."

And he was gone.

~

They found the army wagon just at the edge of town, by the last building and next to the first patches of brush.

When Audie and Shane got close to the wagon full of munitions, they could tell right away there were two soldiers on guard. Mostly because those two soldiers were drunk enough not to be worried about their duty to guard the guns. They were more interested in the no-doubt stretched stories they were entertaining the other one with.

"I asked her, how the hell does a sixteen-year-old girl know how to do things like that?" The soldier laughed violently as he recounted a tale of a whore he had paid for a night in Tombstone. "Next thing I knew, her daddy, the sheriff, busted in the room and told me I was defiling his unpicked flower!" He was coughing now, he was laughing so hard.

"I looked him square in his beady eyes and said, 'Defiled her, my ass! Hell, she knows more about a cock than any woman in this den of whores!'" The soldier was doubled over in laughter now, gasping for breath.

The other soldier on duty was thoroughly entertained, as well. He was cackling like someone was tickling him with a feather.

The story got more unbelievable from there. Shane rolled his eyes at Audie, and they had to wait for the man to spin his yarn until they had the opening they were looking for.

"Hell, Westers. You do beat all. You're lucky that sheriff didn't put your stones in a sling," the second soldier spouted in between the last of his laughs.

"I need to go piss some of this fire water out," Westers offered, and with that he walked away in the brush.

The second soldier felt the need to stretch his legs. He walked around the other side of the wagon.

That was the break Audie had been waiting on. He snuck up to the wagon where the soldiers had been and slowly opened the leather covering on the back. The left half of the wagon was filled with brand-new '76 Winchesters. Probably about two hundred and fifty to three hundred in all. Other than a few provisions and a water barrel, the rest was filled with boxes of ammunition. Audie had a moment of terror thinking about where that many rifles might be routed to. And why. Every gun would coat a bullet with Apache blood if he didn't stop them.

Audie had sprinkled the cup of water Lomasi had given him with the finely ground peyote. He unscrewed the opening on top of the soldiers' water barrel and dumped his concoction inside. He'd put enough in there to send twenty men to another world for a good seven or eight hours, a world you didn't want to go to unless you were prepared for it. He screwed the cap back on the barrel, slowly let the leather cover down, and made his way back to Shane.

The soldiers were never the wiser.

Shane and Audie headed back to their own wagon. "Be ready to ride at first light. I bet those drunken gray coats won't be leaving till after that whiskey is sweat out a little, but either way, we'll be there."

Shane and Audie went back inside the saloon and up to their rooms for some rest.

CHAPTER 19

The next morning at first light, Audie was the first to wake, as usual. He roused Shane. Shane knew his brother well enough to get up and get moving fast.

"Go check on the soldiers' wagon."

Shane was off, but this time he wasn't trying to be stealthy. It was easier to assess the situation while on a morning stroll than to sneak and do it.

When he got there, he saw eleven soldiers milling around still whiskey soaked and looking dazed. A colonel on horseback was eyeing his troops as if they disgusted him.

"Collins! Sanders! Look alive! We'll get scalped for sure if you two sore livers are on lookout!" the man in charge barked.

"Yes, sir, Colonel," the two said with lackluster. The soldiers filled their canteens with water from the peyote-laced barrel before mounting.

"Don't empty our water before the trip, you dim-witted daisies! Lord! Did you boys drown ever last bit of sense you had last night?"

"Sorry, Colonel. I'll replenish it before we make west," said one low-energy private.

The colonel walked over and filled his canteen as well, to the surprise of the soldiers he had just told not to.

"You have to fill it up anyway!" he barked to those studying him.

Shane tipped his hat and walked past. *This might be easier than I thought.*

After a while, the band of soldiers slowly headed west out of town. There were twelve in all.

There was at least a half-mile between the troops and the DeVine brothers. They were keeping enough distance between them so as not to alert the soldiers of their presence. Audie knew the peyote wouldn't take effect for a couple of hours. "You know what to look for," Audie said to Shane.

Moses asked what that was.

"Vomit," Shane offered, with no explanation why.

The sun was almost at high noon when they saw the first signs. They'd been riding for four hours now.

"Look there, Audie." Shane pointed to a spot in the road. There were three different dried piles of vomit. A stray dog was at one of the piles feasting.

"We'll give them another half hour to make sure they're good and in the wind."

Another few minutes passed, and Audie motioned to Shane. "Hang back here for a bit, Moses. We'll come back to meet you after."

"What you boys gettin' yourselves into?"

"Just hang back," Audie said harshly.

Audie hadn't wanted to bring Moses, but with the business with Siringo, he didn't think it wise to leave him behind.

Shane and Audie rode off south and west, away from the trail. They were going past the Flint Hills where there was more than enough foliage and rocks to allow them to come in from the side of the soldiers unnoticed until they were just about upon them.

Colonel Bruce was a little pride-smitten about his assignment to accompany these arms to other men who would have the privilege of using them, but he was a soldier, and he didn't question his superiors. He rode out in front of the wagon leading his troops. There wasn't glory in this mission, but he would conduct himself according to his training.

A few hours into this leg of the journey, the colonel was beginning to worry that this Kansas weather was getting to his Virginia constitution. For the last little while, he felt as if the sky were changing from blue to violet to a yellowish-brown color and over again. He was doing his best to shake it off, but the visions seemed to be coming more rapidly. He took another big drink from his canteen and wiped the sweat off his brow. Why was he sweating? It was freezing out here.

He breathed hard, and the air came out in vapored designs. All at once, he felt a sudden uncontrollable urge to regurgitate. And he did, never stopping his horse.

"What is wrong with you, Colonel?" he hissed to himself under his breath.

One soldier on horseback was looking around bewilderingly at the terrain, as if it were an enchanted land he was traveling through. Another had just vomited and had his hands in the air, studying them intently as if he'd never seen them before.

All the soldiers seemed in a trance. There was the sound of men throwing up intermittently between moans and laughs. If someone didn't know what they were looking at, they would have thought all twelve men were possessed by some mischievous demon.

There was no order given from the colonel, but everyone had come to a stop. There were two men inside the wagon who had both stumbled out clumsily, one laughing wildly and the other with a knife drawn, turning this way and that, slashing at some foe no one else had knowledge of. No one paid him any mind.

The colonel had become extremely unsettled now. He was aware of the strange behavior of his men, but more pressing was the sun that was pulsing as if it were trying to reach down and touch him with its deadly heat. Even through the February freeze, the sun seemed like it was wrapping him in fingers of fire. He fought the urge to put an arm up to shield himself. "This damn heat," he said half dreamily, half disturbed.

One soldier on horseback had passed out and fallen out of his saddle. The horse, sensing that something was out of sorts, ran off into the brush. Another man on his horse saw this and started screaming hysterically.

The colonel saw an Indian riding toward him on a pale stallion with an axe in the air as if ready to strike. The sun was still pulsing, but it seemed to be pulsing through the Indian, doing no damage to the savage riding hell-bent in his direction. He closed his eyes and shook his head, but the vision persisted. He was in another place now. The psychedelic ravagings of peyote were not for the faint of heart. He had no idea it was that that was coursing through his veins.

"Damn, injuns! They've bewitched us!" he mumbled, fumbling for his pistol to no avail. The other soldiers were preoccupied with imaginary friends and enemies.

The whole world slowed down and became deathly silent for the colonel. The Indian was fifty paces away now but seemed to be moving at a snail's pace. The colonel managed to unholster his gun, but in his state of confusion, he dropped it. Just then his vision changed, and the Indian was a white man with long dark hair riding right up to him on a black horse with an axe held high. Time sped up, as if making up for the seconds lost when it had slowed down.

Audie slammed the blunt end of his axe down, glancing it off the side of the colonel's head. The man was knocked out cold. He fell off of his horse, and the horse fled out of fear.

Audie dismounted his horse and sent it running.

Shane ran into the battle on foot, poised and ready, from the side of the caravan with a knife in each hand and one in his mouth. He took out two of the remaining five soldiers on horseback. The man who had been screaming violently caught a knife in his gut. *Thunk!*

You could hear the flesh rip as the blade entered his body. He fell off of his horse, still screaming, with blood gushing from his midsection.

The other knife found its target in a soldier's throat. He hit the ground with no sound but flesh landing on dry earth.

Shane took the knife from his mouth and landed it in the heart of another soldier on horseback. The soldier slid off of his gelding, groaning with an otherworldly-like spew of blood, spit, and noise and came to rest right beside where Audie was fighting another unfortunate traveler. He recognized the fallen man as the one who was harassing the Indian barmaid the night before. He planted his axe in the soldier's privates.

Audie looked up to see the soldier who had been fighting the invisible enemy coming for him. He ran to meet him. The soldier swung his knife at Audie, who easily side-stepped it. He brought the blunt end of his axe down on the soldier's knife hand, crushing it and spinning them both around.

When he had come full circle, he planted the sharp end of the axe in the back of the soldier's head. The man spun and grabbed at Audie's shirt as he fell. Audie felt a small snap, but the sound of iron splitting bone was brutal enough to keep Audie's focus. He didn't know it, but the soldiers had ripped his father's necklace from around his neck. The cross and feather fell and ended up underneath a soldier covered in blood.

Shane suddenly noticed a soldier trying to run away. He pulled a knife he had in his belt and sent it to rest in the soldier's back. He quickly retrieved two of his knives from the others he had previously brought to an end.

The two soldiers manning the wagon reins had been shocked and staring for most of this encounter, but they finally came to and were pulling their rifles, drawing down on Audie. Shane took out the first with a knife to the chest. The second had opened his mouth to scream when Shane's knife landed in it. He got off a shot, but it was far to the left.

The soldier who was hysterically laughing was still unaware they were being attacked. Shane took the final knife from his belt and made two slashes across the man's throat. The blood sprayed out on Shane and the ground like a red spring. The man still had a smile on his face as he collapsed.

Audie finished off the soldier he was fighting with an axe blow to the head and a knife under the man's chin, up through his brain. The motions were so swift they were barely discernible.

The DeVine brothers delivered death as easy as black clouds deliver rain. Azariah's resolve that flowed in their blood mingled with the darkness his terrible passing had given them, made them relentless and unforgiving killers. Grey Wolf's great Apache warrior training had given them the vehicle to carry out their destruction.

The brothers examined the area to see if there were any other contenders to reckon with. They noticed a man, the one who'd passed out before the fight, was unconscious but still breathing. He was lying beside the soldier with the knife in his midsection. The gutted soldier was still trying to scream, but his screams sounded like terrified whisperings now.

Audie and Shane each took a pistol from the two soldiers. They sent both men to their maker with bullets in their heads.

Shane heard a man whimpering. He found a soldier cowering under the wagon and pulled him out by his hair. The man winced from the pain, grasping at Shane.

"What's your name?" Audie asked with little emotion.

"Luke Collins. Please, spare me, mister. I ain't ever harmed a soul on this earth. Honest!" The man sobbed.

"Then take comfort in knowing you'll leave this world with only your own blood on your hands."

Audie pointed the pistol at him. Luke tried to shield his face from the shot with a quivering hand. The bullet passed through his hand and then his skull.

He shook no more.

Audie and Shane were coated in blood, but very little of it was their own. It was this blood that Audie had been craving for a while. It was this blood that made Shane remember how much he loved the taste of it.

They lit a fire underneath the wagon and moved away quickly. They knew the fire would send the boxed ammunition spewing in all directions.

It was a hard decision, but they knew it wasn't worth the risk of getting caught with stolen army Winchesters, especially when the weapons had cost the government twelve soldiers as well.

They washed up in a small stream they found about a quarter mile off the

trail. They had a change of clothes in the wagon. These would be burned.

Shane dragged the still-unconscious colonel underneath an oak tree well off the trail. Audie took his knife and dug deep underneath a rock ledge till he found what he was looking for.

It was late afternoon when the colonel finally came to. He had his hands bound behind his back and was tied to the oak tree. Audie had been patiently waiting for him to wake.

Audie was standing over him when he finally opened his eyes.

"You're . . . you're that crooner from the saloon. Who the hell are you?" the colonel quizzed.

"You tell me your name, soldier, and I'll oblige," Audie said, holding a sack with something rattling inside.

"Colonel Tom Bruce, decorated Union soldier."

"Decorated doesn't impress us much, mister, nor does Union soldier." Shane spoke with disdain in his words. "Where were these guns to be taken to, Colonel?" he asked.

"I'm already a dead man. Why would I give you that information?" the man asked, still groggy from the peyote.

"Death can come as a kindness, sir, or it can come with malice. Your words will decide which," Audie said.

The colonel studied Audie for a few seconds. It didn't take long to realize his words didn't have a smidge of bluff in them.

"We were to meet up with a regiment just north of Sierra De San

Maleo one week from today. How did you bewitch my troops and me?"

"Peyote," Shane spoke.

"Indian devilment! What kind of a man are you?" shouted the colonel.

Audie emptied the contents of his bag. He didn't have to look to see the terror on the colonel's face as he reached down to catch the rattlesnake right behind the neck. He knew it was there.

Audie walked the couple of steps to where Bruce was sitting. He knelt down so he was eye level with him. With the deadly viper in hand, he took pleasure in watching the emotion on the soldier's face as he realized what was about to happen. Audie waited there silently for what seemed like an eternity, eyeing the man tied to the tree. He squeezed the rattlesnake's head until the jaws pried open, exposing the horrific fangs and provoking it to rattle even more defiantly. He stabbed the snake's head at the colonel, forcing the fangs firmly into the man's neck. Colonel Bruce shrieked in horror.

"We are the adopted sons of a sacred land! We are the avengers of a murdered father and the slain Apache, bathed in our father's blood and washed in the sins of your slaughter! Bloodthirsty savages who howl in the night, and your kind will know our wrath!" Audie shouted.

"Kill me! This is not kindness!" the colonel screeched as the venom trickled through his veins.

Audie broke the tension with a gunshot to the colonel's head. He stared at the man slumped over for a long while. The colonel still had his eyes open. He met the next life with fear still on him.

Moses felt nauseous on the ride back and was at a loss for words. He hadn't seen the fight, but he had seen the aftermath.

Audie could sense his distress, so he spoke up.

"Moses, that thing back there, it didn't have anything to do with you. Your hands are clean. What Shane and I do is on our account, not yours. We promised someone we would fight against those who seek to kill the Apache. I know it's hard to understand. That wagon was full of rifles to kill Indians. We just saved many lives with the few we took."

Moses still didn't speak, so Audie changed the subject. "We should be back well before nightfall. Shane, I want you to go into town and see if you can purchase us a new wagon. Moses and I will sit a mile or so out of town and wait for you. We'll burn this one."

"Alright, Audie. That's a decent idea."

The sky was painted in sundown colors when Shane returned with the brand new Conestoga wagon. The boys and Moses switched the contents into the new vehicle and moved the old one a good ways off the trail before setting the second wagon on fire that day. They were still a couple of miles out, so they hurried back to the trail and headed into town.

"I don't know why God put me with you boys, but he did. But I don't like what ya do. I ain't havin' no part of it."

Audie and Shane listened to his words. They had none to offer in return.

"But y'all been a friend ta me, an' I ain't had too many'a them. The blood you spill. It's wrong. It's dead wrong. I'm gonna pray fo' your souls. I'm with ya till the Good Lawd say otherwise or y'all don't need me no more, but they won't be no blessin' from me on this violence."

"Well, Moses, I'm not opposed to anyone's prayers. Maybe you're like Moses in the Bible—here to lead us through our own Red Sea."

Audie smiled at Shane's musing. Maybe he was right.

"We don't expect you to do anything you don't feel good about, Moses. Our father was a preacher. How you feel is how he would have felt, too," said Audie.

"I'm starving. We need some nourishment right about now. Who wants to grace the Beef & Beer with me?" asked Shane.

Audie knew Shane was leaning a little more toward the beer than the beef. "A steak sounds good. Moses? You hungry?" Audie asked.

"I think I'm jus' gonna head up ta my room tonight."

They were coming up on the outskirts of the town.

"Well, Moses, we'll see you after the rooster crows," Shane said.

"Ha! You ain't heard a rooster crow since we left Mama's. A rooster couldn't wake your drunk ass up if he was sitting on your bed."

"Eat shit, Audie."

Moses was still troubled. The boys' banter usually entertained him, but not tonight. He was soul sick at what he'd witnessed today.

Moses tipped his hat and headed toward his room.

None of them saw the towering figure standing just to the side of the town's entrance. He was leaned behind a lumber wall waiting for their return.

Siringo.

He just happened to be in the same whereabouts when Shane purchased the wagon. Siringo knew the DeVine brothers' old wagon belonged to a couple of bounty hunters he hadn't seen in a while, and now they'd gotten rid of it.

That night when Audie undressed for bed, he realized he'd lost his necklace. He tried to put the thought from his mind. He couldn't do anything about it now.

CHAPTER 20

The news of the raid on the soldiers had spread through town, and all assumed it was Indians. After a couple of weeks passed, the excitement died down a bit.

The adventure with the soldiers settled Audie's mind for a little. He fell into a routine. Most days he would ride out of town just for the scenery, or maybe stop and practice with the axe or a pistol for a while. Some days when the muse would call on him, he would stay in his room and write new songs for the band to play, always sharpening his edges. Sitting still wasn't something he was capable of for very long.

Sometimes Shane would hang with Audie, but most days were slept away. He had become a creature of the night. Audie worried about his brother, as did Moses, but other than a scolding now and then, they let him be.

But in the evening the brothers played. All was right in their world when they did.

Moses got a little more leniency around town. It didn't take long for the folks to realize he was with the DeVine brothers and that the DeVine brothers didn't tolerate the usual treatment of a black man in those days. Moses was grateful, but at times he felt guilty because of it. He saw how other black people were treated. It weighed on him.

It was Thursday afternoon, and Audie was eating his supper with Moses on the bench outside of the Beef & Beer when Siringo came up and leaned on the hitching post just across from them. He stared at Audie a while before he spoke, looking for some give to the man in his eyes or at the corner of his lips. Audie held his glance.

Siringo couldn't find what he was hoping to. "Noticed you boys got you a new wagon. Nice one, too. Wouldn't think a minstrel could scrounge up enough for a fine vehicle like that. Shit, lots of people who make an *honest living* don't make coin that good."

"I don't know how our income is any of your business, Siringo." Audie hoped the fact that he knew the man's name would unsettle him a bit.

"Well, it ain't. Just curious, that's all."

Audie kept his eyes leveled on Siringo for an uncomfortable amount of time. "Is that all you wanted to talk about? My friend and I are trying to eat."

Siringo hesitated for effect. "Hmm? Oh, don't mind me. Go ahead with your meal. I'm sure you need it to do all that minstreling." Siringo smiled at Audie as if he was proud of the little jab he had just given him.

"Oh, one more thing I was wondering about. What did you gentlemen do with that old wagon you had? I haven't seen that thing around here. Figured somebody would have it. Saw one like it torched to hell a piece outside of town. You wouldn't know anything about that, would ya?"

Siringo saw the tell he was looking for. Just for a second, Audie's eyes flashed a hint of worry. He knew he'd hit a nerve.

Audie was trying to figure out how much the man knew. If he knew about the wagon, he could know about the soldiers, but why would he have waited two weeks to bring it up? He must have tried to dig up dirt and found nothing. Word of the "Indian" attack on the men carrying the artillery had been on the street for over a week now. Somehow he'd stumbled on the wagon. That was all.

"We sold it to a man passing through. What happened to it after that, I don't have any idea. Maybe he did burn it. Just for the hell of it. Sometimes it feels good to do something just for the hell of it." Audie made sure his eyes told Siringo he wasn't afraid to put him on the ground again. Just for the hell of it.

"What was his name?"

"He was a private man. Didn't want his name known."

Siringo smiled. "Well, alright then. Far be it from me to impose on a man's business when he wants it private. You know, Mr. DeVine, I been meaning to tell you. You throw a punch like a hammer when someone don't expect it. I wonder if you'd be worth a damn if a man knew it was coming."

"I've still got an hour before my show. We could find out real quick if you're curious about that, too."

Moses was getting more nervous by the second.

Siringo had tried to unnerve him with his last comment, but Audie didn't budge. He smiled at Audie again. "Ha-ha, I'm just talking, that's all. You go play your little show. Those drunks need their entertainment! Hell, I might come by some night and make a request."

"You do that."

Siringo tipped his hat and strolled away.

"That man know more than he lettin' on, Audie."

"He only knows about the wagon, Moses. He would have hinted at anything else he knew. This is between me and him now. You don't need to worry about anything."

"He don't seem like no man ta be messin' with."

"He's not. But neither am I."

Moses let the conversation die there. He didn't feel like eating the rest of his steak.

Audie found Shane at the back of the Buckhorn. He had decided to enjoy some smoking tobacco before the show. "I could use one of those."

Shane handed him the tobacco and the paper.

"We may have a problem with that damned bounty hunter I was telling you about." Audie filled him in on the conversation he'd just had.

"Shit, Audie. The last thing we need is someone rooting around looking for dirt on us."

"I know. Don't talk to Moses about it. He's worried sick as it is."

"What do you want to do about it?" Shane asked.

"I need to think on it."

They played the show that night a little on edge. And as usual, what they were feeling spilled over into the crowd. There were more fights in the bar that Thursday night than there had been in the last week combined.

CHAPTER 21

Thomas Thorntree was trail weary when he reached Eminence, Missouri. He had been assigned to a bank robbery case but hadn't had the slightest bit of luck with it. He knew the James-Younger Gang was responsible, but as to their whereabouts, he'd come up wanting.

Thomas was a good man. He was honest in his dealings and faithful to Adalina. He was dutiful in his work, and it pained him not to deliver. He had an easy spirit, but his work had given him a hardness. The older he got, the more you could see it in his eyes. It wasn't age creeping up on him as much as it was just the lessons of life teaching him things he didn't want to know.

He was thin but still had the look of a man not to be trifled with. Thomas had a thick, dark mustache speckled with gray, but there were no matching gray hairs in his well-trimmed hair parted to the side. He wore the suit of a Pinkerton agent, and for most that meant he was to be respected.

It was evening when he saw the glow from his own window. Adalina heard him coming and ran to meet him. She threw her arms around his neck and held on for a while. He kissed the lips he had thought of so many times in his travels. She smelled like home. Thomas loved her most in this world.

"I missed you. I have so much to tell you," she whispered.

He kissed her again. They retreated to the house and made love till their bodies were spent.

~

Later they sat in the kitchen drinking a midnight cup of coffee. Thomas could see a glow in her face that was foreign. She smiled at him like a little girl with a big secret.

"I have some wonderful news."

"I can tell! You look like you won the raffle for the prize pig. Come on, Adalina! Don't keep me in suspense."

"My sons are alive! They came to visit me while you were away! Can you believe it, Thomas? After all these years!" She went on to tell him every detail she'd learned from Audie and Shane about the missing years. She told him of Azariah's death, the Apache and Moses, and how handsome her sons had grown up to be. Every word was drenched in pure joy, sorrow or anger. Thomas listened intently to her story and was truly happy for his wife. It was a tale he might not believe if it hadn't been told by her.

"Well, when do I get to meet these fine young men?"

"I'm not sure. They promised they would return, but I don't know when. Audie seems like . . . like he has some things to figure out. I would have done anything if they had stayed, but they are grown men now."

"I'm sure they'll return, Adalina. This place is as much theirs as anyone's."

"There's something else, too, Thomas. Some news not as pleasing. My father passed away while you were gone, peacefully, thank the Good Lord. Audie was with him when he passed. He was delighted to see his grandsons. I think maybe he was waiting on them before he let go of this world. He was more loving in those last days than I have seen him in years, and he has no more pain now. I take comfort in that."

Thomas got up and walked over to where she was. He bent over and wrapped his arms around her shoulders and kissed the top of her head.

"I'm sorry to hear that, Adalina. He was a strong man. He'll be remembered well."

They talked a bit more, but Adalina could see that Thomas was weary from his travels and needed sleep. He fought her on it, but she made him go to bed.

They settled in and slept in peace. Adalina had her husband beside her and the knowledge that her sons were alive. She slept better that night than she had since the boys had left almost a decade ago.

The next morning, Thomas woke around seven thirty. Adalina had coffee ready for him and made him a huge breakfast. He hadn't feasted like that since he had been gone. He didn't take for granted the comforts of home.

"I'm gonna take you with me next time I leave. I don't know that I can do without your cooking that long again. That and a few other things," he flirted.

She smiled playfully and stroked the inside of his palm with her finger.

They heard hooves outside on the road leading to their house. Thomas could tell it was just one horse.

Adalina and Thomas went to see who it was.

A freckled-face, trail-dusted boy of about fourteen rode up and dismounted a little way from the house.

"Can I help you, young man?" Thomas more ordered than asked.

"Yes, sir. Are you Thomas Thorntree?"

"Yes, I am. Do we have business?"

"I have a telegraph for you, sir, from the Pinkerton Agency."

The boy handed him the paper. He tipped his hat to Adalina. "Ma'am."

"Hello, young man. What's your name?"

"Burch, ma'am. Cordell Burch, from the City of Kansas."

"Well, Cordell, you look hungry. Would you like a meal before you head out again? I just made breakfast a while ago."

The teenager patted his saddlebags.

"No, ma'am. I've got some fixins in here. Thank you, though."

"Well, I'm gonna wrap up some biscuits for you anyway. I can't imagine you won't need them on your long ride back. And please give that horse a feed and some water before you leave. He looks like he might need a meal worse than you." She smiled at Cordell.

"Yes, ma'am. Much obliged for your kindness."

Adalina went inside to fix the boy a travel bag.

Thomas read the wire. The boy could tell by his face it wasn't pleasing news. "Shit."

"I hope the wire ain't too bad of news for you, Mr. Thorntree."

Thomas just looked at the boy for a second. "You should go tend to your horse like my wife said, son. That's a good mare. Thank you for your service."

"Yes, sir."

Cordell went to the barn, and Thomas went back inside. Adalina was on her way out with biscuits and bacon wrapped in burlap for Cordell. She could tell by Thomas's face there wasn't too much happiness in that piece of paper he was holding. She gave the boy his gift, told him to take his time, and went back into the house to see about Thomas.

He was sitting at the table when she came in. She put her hands on his shoulders and gave him a gentle massage. "What villain has stolen your contentment this morning?" she asked.

"There's been a damned Indian raid on a band of soldiers just outside Wichita."

Adalina was not pleased with this information. "And they want Agent Thorntree to investigate."

"Yes. I'm sorry, Adalina. I can stall it a couple days, or maybe three.

Damned redskins! I wish the government would do their job and rid us of their savagery already."

Adalina couldn't help but see her sons' faces grow angry in her mind at Thomas's words.

"They are a troublesome bunch. More for some than others."

In Thomas's anger he had spoken absentmindedly.

"I'm sorry, sweetness. I shouldn't be speaking of Indians. I know how much they've carved at your heart."

"Let's not speak of it anymore today. At least let me have you for a couple of days without the distresses of this world," Adalina said with pleading in her voice.

He stood up and put his arms around her waist and kissed her as gently as he could.

CHAPTER 22

"Quit speeding up on the damn chorus!" Audie mouthed to Shane.

Shane gave him the evil eye for a second and tried to keep his tempo in line. Audie had been easily stirred since the business with Siringo.

"Stomp the ground, bang a drum
Something bad this way come,
Say a prayer, load the gun
Something bad this way come."

The song came to an end, and the brothers stepped off stage for a refresher while the people cheered their performance.

"Quit being such an ass up there, Audie. I ain't your damned mule to whip up on."

Audie started to tear into Shane but stopped himself. He turned around and ordered a double shot of whiskey. "I'm leaning too much on this rotgut these days."

"Shit. You get a feel good about once a month. Hell, as little as you drink, it might as well be water," Shane teased.

"Mind if I sit in with you boys? Maybe take some of the load off?" While they were talking, a stranger had walked up and laid a fiddle case on the bar. He was a young man, no older than twenty-one. He was tall and lanky but kept his shoulders back, which made him appear stouter than he actually was.

"Who are you?" Shane asked, surprised by the offering.

"Smyth Hoxie. The finest fiddler you've ever even heard of."

"That wouldn't be hard. I don't know any fiddlers," Audie rang in.

"And why would you? A bunch of high noses, except me. I'm the Billy the Kid of the bow." Smyth grinned ear to ear at his self-assigned title.

Audie and Shane both laughed. He was entertaining if nothing else. "How's that? You hold trains up with the threat of bad music?"

"Let me sit in with you, and you'll know what I mean," Smyth informed them with all the confidence in the world.

"We're a two-piece. I'm sure there's work for a fiddler somewhere else," Audie told him.

"Well, not the kind of work a man like me wants. Besides, y'all need some grease to glue those chords together. Don't get me wrong. Your rhythm is Sunday morning, but you need a little Saturday night."

Again, the brothers laughed. "Go on." Shane motioned away with his hand. "My brother told you, we're a two-piece."

"Alright, well, I can see where I'm not wanted. Y'all enjoy the rest of your show."

Shane looked at Audie, shook his head, and chuckled. The boys finished their drinks and climbed back up on stage. They opened up with another original song of Audie's.

For the third song of the set, Audie broke into "Hard Times Come Again No More." It always got the crowd going. It was familiar, but the brothers put a new spin on it. They had given it a darker feel than people were used to.

After the first verse, Audie heard something coming from the left that sounded almost like a train whistle. He looked to his left and saw the fiddler sawing away.

Shane yelled, "Get off the damn stage!"

If Smyth heard, he didn't let on. He played on with Audie and Shane, both of them caught somewhere between mad as hell and awestruck.

If Billy the Kid played fiddle, that was exactly how he would've sounded.

Audie and Shane played through the next verse without singing—mostly out of shock. Smyth had the crowd. He finished off his solo with a screeching note that made the air tense. The only thing you could hear was the music. The people were hanging on every note.

Audie came in singing like a lightning strike on the next verse. The crowd went wild. Audie and Shane had never felt energy like that while they were playing. They were both dumbfounded.

Smyth took one more solo at the end of the song. It was better than the first. He had watched Audie and Shane for a few nights now and knew their music well enough to play it like it was his own. He finished the night out with the DeVine brothers.

And what a night it was.

"Where the hell did you learn to play like that?" Audie inquired after the show. He slapped Smyth on the back so hard that Smyth coughed a little before he recovered from it.

"Self-taught. Well, I was trained by a pansy-ass girly-man named Francis, but I'm the one who taught me to play like *that*."

"I didn't know a fiddle could sound like that. I mean, I've only ever seen one other fiddle player, but he left me thinking the fiddle was . . . pretty or something. You make it sound like it has teeth," Shane reckoned.

"I like to think I give the fiddle a big ole cod sack, swinging low."

Smyth held out both hands like he was holding two watermelons as he spoke.

"That'll work, too," Audie said.

"So, what's to be my cut of the wages?"

Shane looked at Audie, curious to see what he'd say.

"Just drink your rotgut. It's on us tonight." Audie motioned to Lomasi that he'd take care of the tab.

Smyth slammed his drink and smiled. "Well, free whiskey will procure my services for a short piece of time. Don't dilly dally, though. I might find employment elsewhere."

"Nah. We're probably the only bastards bent enough for that bow of yours," Shane put in.

Smyth smiled and ordered another drink.

Siringo couldn't conjure up a speck of dirt on Audie and Shane. He'd gone down all his usual avenues, but the sheriff, the whorehouse, and his other informants gave him nothing. He knew Shane liked the whiskey and the women, but so did most of the other men in this town. He knew Audie had a temper. He'd seen that firsthand, and the story was corroborated by a few others who'd dealt with him, but as of yet, no history that would give him a reason to go after them in any legal way.

He knew their old wagon had belonged to a couple of lowlife, wannabe bounty hunters named Jessie and Jacob Halter. He had no trouble believing those halfwits had lost the wagon in a number of imaginable ways, but why hadn't Audie just told him the truth? There had to be something more to the story. Any way he sliced it, these boys seemed to appear out of thin air. He didn't need a reason to kill them other than his wounded ego, but it sure would make it easier if he had something to blame them for. If he didn't find something soon, he was going to have to kill Audie and Shane privately.

And it was so much more fun when he could do it with an audience.

Smyth rehearsed the songs with the boys every day for two weeks. Truth was, he loved playing on the fly, but he agreed to these rehearsals just to be in Audie's good graces.

Audie wanted the rehearsals to see what Smyth was made of, but he learned right away Smyth was a far better musician than he or Shane ever would be. He slashed his bow across the strings like he was squeezing the life out of them when Audie sang in angry tones. He made them weep when Audie was lamenting the world. Both Shane and Audie had to work hard to keep their jaws in their proper places when Smyth took a solo. The music they made owned Audie and Shane, but Smyth owned every note he coaxed out of his fiddle.

"You know my father used to get so mad when I called it a fiddle. No son of his was going to play the fiddle—only the violin," he told them as he stared at his instrument during a break. "The fiddle was for the heathen and the uneducated, he'd tell me. I guess he was right. Only a heathen would play with a couple of devils like you two." He laughed at his own joke.

"A lot of us become something that our mothers and fathers don't find very appealing," Audie more thought out loud than said.

"Well, this heathen life appeals to me! I can't get enough of it." Shane smiled at Audie as he chugged whiskey, just to annoy the older brother.

Audie shook his head at Shane. One day soon there would be a reckoning about his drinking. Audie knew most nights, if there was trouble, he wouldn't be able to count on Shane. Shane thought he was just as reliable when he was sauced, but Audie could tell his wits and his hands were slowed.

"Our father was a preacher," Audie said to Smyth. "Just think of what a joy we'd be to him."

"*Was* a preacher? Is he dead?"

"He passed away when we were young."

"Shit. If he was anything like mine, you got lucky."

"He wasn't," Shane interjected, feeling a slight tinge of guilt at the mention of his father.

"You boys want me ta go get ya some dinner? Y'all soundin' good, but I don't like sittin' round here like a knot on a log."

"Yeah, Moses, that'd be good. On me," Audie said.

Audie had been giving Moses most all of the money for keeping. He trusted the man, and he was always needing Moses to go get food or supplies or something that cost money. He might as well just let Moses manage it.

Moses wasn't quite sure what to think about the new addition to the band, but he didn't comment on it. Still, when Smyth had asked him for his cut of the wages, he told the fiddler to talk with Audie. Audie informed him the wages were to be split between the four of them.

Smyth had told them shortly after he joined the band that he was from a prominent South Carolina family. His parents had him trained by a classical violinist from an early age and had plans for him to play in the New York Symphony, but he wanted no part of it. He had left a life of wealth and luxury when he was sixteen to be able to play music the way he wanted. His family had disowned him when he decided not to follow the path they'd chosen. Smyth said that was fine. He had disowned them a long time ago.

"They sipped their mid-morning tea in their tailored clothes and fine apparel like the world owed them. They spoke of high culture and pedigrees and things that aren't worth the tits on a boar hog to me. I wanted to feel what made those drunk Irish weep with the music in the pubs, or what those black people felt when they were singing at their church. The music they make—it's alive! It came from their souls. I knew I had to go live outside of that velvet prison if I wanted to make music like that."

Audie was intrigued by his tale. Both brothers saw him as a fellow rogue.

"You're a rebel of the highest order. May you never have to drink mid-morning tea again." Audie nodded his respect and started playing his guitar. The other two musicians joined in.

CHAPTER 23

Thomas greeted this morning with dread. It wasn't for the journey or the job that awaited him. It was the goodbye he had to say.

"I packed you some biscuits and cured meat for your trip." Adalina had busied herself with as much as possible. It was her usual weapon against sorrow. Thomas watched her while she went about cleaning the kitchen. His horse was saddled and packed, ready for leaving. He had only been home a week.

"You look too pretty to leave, Adalina."

He came up behind her as she was drying a plate and put his arms around her waist. "You know I wouldn't stop you if you wanted to stay," she said.

"Someday soon I won't leave. Someday I'll be here so much you'll get tired of me."

Adalina had long since given up on hope of such things. "Not likely."

"I didn't get to go pay respect to your father's grave. I'm sorry, Adalina. We'll do that first thing when I return."

"I'm sure it'll be there when you get back. Besides, you weren't here long enough for me to share you with anyone else."

"You're a good woman. You deserve better than you have in this life."

"God gives us what he gives us. I'm grateful for the things I do have," she said as she stacked the plate on top of a similar one.

She spun around, and he kissed her forehead and pulled her close. They held onto each other for a moment. "I love you, sweet woman." He walked out to get his horse ready for the journey.

Adalina sat for a while and wondered why every man in her life had a wandering bone.

"A half silver eagle up front and another half eagle at the job's end."

Welks was a man with the lowest of reputations. There wasn't much he wouldn't do for a pay day. He was a criminal just because it suited his nature. The fact that he hadn't already been strung up by the neck was a mystery to all who knew him. He was a thief, a cheat, a destroyer of property—whatever put money in his pocket.

But he was also very good at getting away with it.

Siringo spit. He hadn't even wanted to be seen with Welks. He had told him to meet him at ten o'clock just outside the city entrance.

"No way in hell those DeVine boys ain't got some blood underneath their fingernails. I can smell it on them. You sneak around long enough, and you'll find some bones."

"If it's bones you want, then it's bones you'll get, Siringo. It ain't hard to find a man's secrets."

"You'd best watch it with Audie. He finds out someone's poking around, he's liable to hurt a man. The man has one of the finest punches I ever took. I'd imagine his fightin' skills don't end there either."

"Oh, you know me. I ain't looking for no fight."

Siringo looked at him with disgust. He was a gangly, filthy-looking bastard. He'd look dirty after a king's bath. His thin, scraggly hair hung in greasy patches over a face that looked like thin rawhide stretched over a skull.

"No, I don't know you, Welks. Let's get that straight right now. You breathe a word of this to anyone, and I'll split your noggin myself."

Welks laughed. "Understood."

"Just do your damn job, and don't be spilling the beans to anyone."

Siringo handed him the money.

Welks flipped a coin in the air and caught it. He tipped his hat and was off.

Siringo watched him leave before he walked back into town. He hoped he wasn't making a mistake.

Audie sat outside enjoying a smoke in between sets.

It was Friday night, and the crowd was rowdy. Smyth was definitely living up to his end of the workload. He'd been playing with them for three weeks now, and sometimes Audie and Shane felt like they were just part of the crowd when Smyth was sawing his fiddle. He had fire on his bow, and the more the folks in the bar cheered him on, the hotter it got. More than either DeVine brother, Smyth lived for the moments when he was in the spotlight. He felt like the crowd worshipped him when he was working the bow across the strings.

"Can I bum a match off ya, mister?"

Audie handed the stranger a match out of his vest pocket.

"You boys sure get that place riled up in there. I ain't ever seen the likes of it. Where you fellows from, anyway?"

"All over."

The stranger studied Audie for a second and nodded. "I hear that, man. I'm from gypsies myself. I've got winged feet just like you."

"My people weren't gypsies. Our father was a missionary."

The man laughed. "Well, the apple rolled pretty far from the damn tree, I guess. To each his own's what I always say."

Audie couldn't tell if the man was trying to figure him out or just making conversation. "What's your name?" Audie inquired.

"Welks. Burly Welks."

"Enjoy your smoke, Burly. I need to get back in there."

"Nice talking with ya. Sing one for me when ya get to it."

Audie tipped his hat and walked back inside.

The bar was rowdy and smelled like sweat and corn liquor. As Audie walked past the bar, he caught a whiff of women's perfume, but it was brief.

A potbellied man grabbed at Lomasi as she fought him off. "Come on, squaw! Give me some of that! I know you ain't been saving it! Injun cooch ain't worth a red cent. Come on!"

Audie was about to go after the agitator when he saw Shane coming in hot from the corner of his eye.

The man felt the back of his head hit the ground before he knew his legs were in the air. Shane was on top of him in an instant, bloodying the guy's face with one punch after another. The man never had a chance to fight back.

"You grubby son of bitch! You're not man enough to get your quim without taking it?"

The man's face was soaked in blood, and he was barely conscious. Shane reached in his vest for a knife.

Shocked that Shane had taken care of this one on his own, Audie grabbed Shane's hand just before he grabbed his knife. Without thinking, Shane swung with his free hand toward Audie, but saw who it was mid-swing. He stopped the blow just short of Audie's gut.

"Not here, little brother. A beating's one thing, but a knife's another." He spoke in a quiet voice right in Shane's ear.

Shane had a rage in his eyes Audie hadn't seen in a while. He liked it.

Shane got up off of the bloody stump of a man and stood over him for a while. The crowd had gathered around to see it. Lomasi had run to the back of the saloon in embarrassment.

Shane walked over to the bartender and put his nose about an inch from the man's face. "The next time a man treats her like that, and you stand by and watch, it's gonna be you laying on that floor. We clear?"

"Y-yes," stuttered the fear-struck man.

Shane stared another moment for good measure, then walked

away. A couple of cowboys dragged the broken man's body out to the street and went to get the doctor.

Audie and Shane walked up to the stage where Smyth was tuned and ready.

"Remind me to never piss you off! Whew!" Smyth joked, trying to lighten the mood.

Shane let out a howl like a coyote and began to play. The night was electric after that.

The show was over, and it was half-past midnight. The bar was mostly cleared out, with the exception of a couple of passed-out patrons. It smelled like the whole place needed bathing or burned down, Audie wasn't sure which.

He was eating a biscuit and washing it down with a beer when Lomasi came up and sat across from him.

"You have Apache blood. You and your brother. I can tell this," she said as she crossed her arms over her chest.

Audie was shocked. He laughed to cover it up.

"Our mother and father are from Missouri. We're as lily white as they come."

Lomasi smiled. "You lie. Apache blood is easy to know. It takes all fear from a man."

"Why do you say that? Because Shane and I look out for you? Hell, Lomasi. You take care of us, so we watch out for you. That's it."

"It's deeper than that, Audie DeVine. I'm grateful for it, but you do it for another reason. I see it."

Audie acted like she was crazy and dismissed her, but he was stunned that she'd picked up on their Apache influence.

He walked outside and found Moses.

"You're up late," Audie said to him.

Moses was outside sitting in a chair just staring out into the street. "You boys soundin' like you done called down the thunder in there tonight! Even from out here it'a hoot," Moses offered.

Audie smiled. "If I could do that, we wouldn't be playing these shit-stained watering holes."

"What's that business with the man they drug out half dead tonight? Is one of you that did it?"

"Shane. The man was bothering Lomasi. Shane couldn't tolerate it. I was glad to see some fire back in his belly again."

"That po' man was messed up pretty bad. Doc said the man's nose was caved in."

"Well, he won't be messing with Lomasi no more."

Moses shook his head. "I don't think he be messin' with *nobody* no mo'."

Nobody was around, so Audie spoke openly. "Speaking of messing with somebody, have you seen that bounty hunter around here anymore?" Audie asked.

"No. Not a peep, thank Jesus."

"Maybe he's cooled off," Audie said as he rolled up his smoke.

"I sure hope so. Say, is that Lomasi from the same people y'alls raised by?"

"No, she's Cherokee, but damned if she didn't just peg us being from the Apache. I guess it shouldn't shock me. The Indians have a way of knowing things like that."

They stood there in silence for a bit.

"If'n it's all the same ta you, Audie, I'm gonna call it a day."

"Yeah, me, too. I'm about ready for a little shut eye myself."

"Yo' brother with a redhead or dark-haired lady tonight?" Moses laughed as they walked toward their rooms.

"I didn't see him leave with one. He didn't drink much after the fight. I don't know where he went off to."

Shane had lit out as soon as the show was over. He hadn't felt the rage since Audie and he took out that band of soldiers a couple months ago. He had missed it.

He found the man he had beaten lying on a cot just inside the infirmary. The doc had cleaned up his battered face, or what was left of it.

No one else was around. The man was still unconscious, and his breathing sounded strange because of the rearranging Shane had done to the bones in his nose.

Shane stood over the man for a moment before he took out his knife. He listened to the awkward breathing and thought about how good it had felt to beat on that face. He still had rage plowing through his veins, so he finished the job he started. The knife found its way right through the center of the man's liver. Dark, thick blood poured out from his side.

The man gasped but didn't have the strength left for a scream.

Shane wiped his blade on the man's shirt and walked back to the tavern. He slept better that night than he had in many nights.

In the shadows just outside of the infirmary was a scraggly figure watching Shane as he entered and left the building. After Shane was well out of sight, the man struck a match off of the side of the building and cupped it inside his hand to guard against the wind.

Welks smiled and slowly pulled the match up to his face to light a cigarette.

CHAPTER 24

The next day the word spread of a murder that had taken place in the dark of last night. The man's name was Harold Setters. He had been a drifter given to the drink. He had no relatives that anyone knew and wouldn't be mourned by anyone in town. Still, there had been a murder, and the sheriff of Sedgwick county, Sheriff McNulty, had to do something about it.

Sheriff McNulty was an honest man the townsfolk trusted to deal with the criminal element around those parts. He was calm, even-tempered, and had taken down his share of evildoers. He wasn't one to act fast on much of anything, though. The sheriff always wanted a good think on it before he got into the doing of a matter.

McNulty was average height and fairly good looking, and the lady manning the bar downstairs smiled flirtatiously at him when he entered Vigus's rent house that afternoon. Shane had just had his lunch and was settling down to take a rest before he met up with Audie and Smyth for a couple hours of practice. He was dozing off when he heard a knock on the door.

When he saw the sheriff standing at the door, he tried to hide the nervous in his voice with irritation. "Can I help you, Sheriff?" he grunted.

"Hidee, Mr. DeVine. I just wanted to speak to you on a matter, if you had a spell. I didn't catch you at a bad time, did I?"

"You did catch me at a bad time. I was about to lay down for a little shut-eye before work tonight."

"Well, this won't take long, if you don't mind."

Shane opened the door to let McNulty pass through.

"I'm sure by now you've heard of the murder that happened last night. A Mr. Harold Setters. Drifter. Were you familiar with the man, Mr. DeVine?"

"No, and I haven't heard of any killings either. Why are you asking me about this?" Shane was trying to land his tone somewhere between irritated and ignorant.

"The way I understand it, it's the man you beat half to death last night at the Buckhorn."

They were both silent for a moment. Shane kept the irritation on his face.

"You remember the man I'm talking about, Mr. DeVine?"

"Yes, I do, but I didn't know his name. He was a man who needed to be beat, but I can assure you, I had nothing to do with his murder."

McNulty laughed. "Hold your reins a minute, son. Nobody's accusing you of anything. I'm just asking questions is all. Just doing my job."

There was another bout of quiet.

"What was the dispute over, Mr. DeVine? The one with you and the deceased."

"He made a very unwanted advance toward a lady friend of mine. I taught him a lesson in manners. That was the end of it."

"Well, I can't fault a man for defending a woman. Glad to see there's some men whose mama raised 'em right around here."

Another moment of pin-drop quiet.

"Well, I guess that's about all the jawin' I've got for ya, Mr. DeVine. If you remember anything you think might help us find the man's killer, please stop over at my office. Me or one of the deputies are usually around."

"I'll do that, Sheriff."

McNulty tipped his hat and showed himself out.

Shane closed the door behind him.

"Shit."

~

"I saw him go in and come out. He's the one that did the killin'."

"You sure about this? Absolutely positive it was him?" Siringo drilled Welks.

"Sure as Wyatt Earp's Colt .45."

"If you're crossing me, Welks, I'll have your ass in a sling. Couldn't have been anyone else?"

"I watched the man play drums all night long. It was him."

"Was his brother around anywhere? Or that nigger they keep company with?"

"Nope. Wasn't nobody but the one."

"Alright. Good job, Welks. Now, forget we ever did business."

Siringo reached in his pocket and pulled out a coin purse. He paid him the agreed upon rate. They parted ways as Siringo thought about how to make his next move against the brothers.

~

Thomas was ragged by the time he made it to Wichita. With the exception of a couple of stops for water or nature calling, he rode straight through. Thirty-two hours on the saddle.

He'd been here before. He'd been to lots of towns before. He carried none of the fascination that his wife's sons had had when they arrived at this place.

It was Tuesday evening when he made it into town. He smelled beer and horse shit on the wind. *What a welcome*, he thought.

He tied off his gelding and decided to go grab a meal somewhere. Thomas never worried about his belongings being stolen. The Pinkerton mark on his saddlebags warded away any would-be thieves.

"Whatever meat you got and potatoes. If you got anything tastier than horse piss to drink, I'd like a glass of that, too," he told a server at the Beef & Beer.

"Steak, taters, and high-grade horse piss. Coming right to ya," the server joked.

Thomas took the lay of the room. It was habit after years on the job. He didn't think there'd be any information regarding his assignment in here; he just liked to have his bearings on a place. He noticed a tall, lanky fellow sitting over in the corner eating grub like he never had a mama teach him any manners. He was trouble. Anyone could see that, but Thomas had a special eye for these things. He could tell this man had lived by no code but what his appetites dictated. And a man like that usually had an appetite for a lot of bad things.

It wasn't the first place he'd go for information, but men like him were a good place to look if an agent was only turning up dead ends. Weak-hearted crooks. You could always scare a little out of them without much trouble.

The waiter brought Thomas's food over and he dug in, keeping his composure as best he could while trying to have some semblance of manners. He was starved.

"Them DeVine Devils sure put the horny in the Buckhorn. Hell, every woman over there is just itching for it when they play. I ain't even had to pay for it in a month!" the customer said.

DeVine Devils? Thomas thought.

"Pardon me, who are the DeVine Devils you were talking about just now?"

"Shit, mister. What rock you been laying under? Them's the boys that been wetting the bar stools over at the Buckhorn every night. 'Cept Sunday. Not on the Lord's day."

Thomas smiled awkwardly at the man's reverence for the Sabbath after such a vulgar image.

"Sorry, I just got into town. Who are they?"

"It's a band of musicians. Two brothers and another man. Some of the strangest music you ever heard, but it'll make ya feel good. They're playing right now. Scarf down that slab and go see."

Thomas thanked them and did just that. He paid for his meal and followed the sound of the music over to the Buckhorn.

Welks was eyeing him from the corner as he was leaving. He'd spotted him the moment he walked in. He could almost smell a Pinkerton, even over his own stench.

It wasn't like a Pink to show up for a commoner's killing. He wondered what had brought the man to town and if he needed to worry. He smiled to himself. He had the dirt on the murder. That'd be an ace up his sleeve if he needed one. Hell, the Pink might even give him a reward.

Thomas made it over to the Buckhorn and ordered another beer. He was as weary as a bandit's horse, but he had to see who these DeVine boys were. That was Adalina's name before he married her.

It didn't take long to figure out they were her sons. The drummer looked just like his wife, and the singer looked a lot like the drummer. There was no mistaking. He was so caught off guard by this revelation that it took him a while to actually listen to the music, but when he did, he couldn't believe what he heard. It was savage and irreverent. Not the music he'd expect from the sons of Adalina and a missionary. He listened to one full set before he decided to go get a room and sleep. He wanted to meet Adalina's sons, but he thought that meeting would be best made on a good night's rest, and he was dog-tired.

CHAPTER 25

Audie noticed that Shane had been acting out of sorts lately. Ever since that night in the saloon with the Setters fellow, he'd been sober and short of temper.

Audie had suspected that Shane killed the man, but he hadn't said anything. He didn't know why he didn't ask Shane about it. Maybe it was his own secrets he kept that stopped him from asking.

"I'm ready, Audie. I'm ready for war. I don't know what I was doing before. Sowing wild oats or something, but either way, I'm ready." Shane spoke out of nowhere.

They were having a smoke by the wagon in the early morning. The town was bustling by.

Audie studied his brother for a while. "I'm ready, too, brother, but I don't know where the war is. I long for it like these drunks do their whiskey, but it ain't here. We'll find it. There's always someone who needs a good killing."

"I killed that son of a bitch who came at Lomasi. I gut-stuck him and watched the life go out of his eyes." Shane kept his voice low, but there was enough noise on the street to cover it from anyone's ears but Audie's.

Audie had a brief moment of sadness listening to his brother. He thought about the two innocent boys who had left Missouri on an adventure out West and the two vigilantes who had returned. He thought about how they would be different if they had stayed.

He missed his father in that moment.

"I have something I want to tell you, too," Audie said, keeping his voice barely above a whisper.

Shane blew out a wispy cloud of smoke and waited.

"Grandpa. He was the one who called for the attack on the Jicarilla village. He did it in hopes it would scare Father into going back to Missouri for good."

Shane dropped his cigarette. He was speechless. He stared at Audie for a moment with jaws clenched tight and then looked back toward the street.

A group of children ran by like a miniature tornado stirring up dust. When they passed, Audie spoke again.

"I killed him. I smothered him with his own pillow. He confessed to me, looking to ease his conscience before he left this world. I sent him away with the burden still on his bones."

"How. . .?"

"A man named Briggs, a lieutenant. Mac said he was a despicable man. He had told him not to kill Father, but this Briggs is a bastard."

"Do you regret it?" Shane asked, almost without emotion.

Audie paused for second. "No."

Shane stared at Audie for a long while, then bent over to pick up his cigarette. He raised up and took one last drag before flipping it into the street.

"Then may the son of a bitch burn in hell."

Thomas had slept till seven that first morning, a rarity for him when he was away from home. He awoke to the sound of the busying streets below. It was never a sound he welcomed.

He dressed and headed downstairs for a bite of breakfast. At least they had good meat here in the city. He sat down and ordered a full breakfast from the innkeeper on duty and began his usual routine of scoping out the place. He noticed the two gentlemen just outside the window smoking. It was the musicians from the night before.

He quickly thought about how he'd introduce himself, but he was nervous. These were the beloved sons of his beloved wife. He mustered up his nerve and walked outside to meet them.

"Excuse me, are you men the DeVine brothers who were playing at the Buckhorn last night?"

"The DeVine Devils. Who are you?" Shane asked before Audie had the chance.

Thomas chuckled nervously and removed his hat. "Ah . . . this is a strange meeting, if ever there was one. My name is Thomas Thorntree. I'm . . . I'm married to your mother. I just left there three days ago, and she shared with me the wonderful news that you two had returned home. It's an honor to meet you."

Shane and Audie both searched for words. Neither knew what to say or even how to feel. There was an awkward moment of silence until Audie reached out a hand to shake Thomas's.

"Mother told us about you, Mr. Thorntree. It's good to meet you, too. I'm Audie, and this is Shane." Shane stuck his hand out and shook Thomas's outstretched one.

"Please let me buy y'all some breakfast. I just ordered myself, but I'd love it if you two would come eat with me."

"Well, I haven't eaten yet. Have you, Audie?"

Shane looked to Audie to make a decision.

"Nope. We'd be happy to join you."

"Excellent. Come on."

They gave each other a surprised look and followed Thomas inside to the table where he was sitting, still a little shell-shocked at meeting the man who'd married their mother.

Thomas motioned for the waiter. "Please give these two gentlemen whatever they'd like on my coin," he said to the server.

"I'll have my usual," Audie said.

"Same," Shane echoed.

The waiter was off without another word.

"I realize this is unexpected, me being here and introducing myself." He leaned over the table toward them. "I got into town on assignment last night, and a fellow was talking about the DeVine brothers playing at the Buckhorn, so I went to have a gander." Thomas looked at Shane. "It was obvious by the look of you that you were Adalina's son."

"Why did you wait till this morning to introduce yourself?" Audie asked.

"Well, to be honest, I was pretty near wore out when I got into town. I rode hard from home to make it to Wichita."

"What did you think of the music?" Shane asked him.

Thomas smiled to try and hide the bit of nervous he felt at that question. "You boys sound like true originals. I've never heard music quite like that before. It was . . . harder than other tunes I've heard."

Audie and Shane laughed. "It's alright if you don't like our music, Mr. Thorntree. It ain't for everyone."

"Please, call me Thomas. It wasn't that I didn't like it. It just caught me off guard was all. Not what I expected from Adalina's sons." Thomas couldn't believe how nervous he was to meet his wife's sons. He was a champion at being even-keeled at his job, but he couldn't help wanting them to like him.

"Well, you should come by tonight. Maybe we'll grow on you. Our fiddle player is worth the trip alone."

Their breakfast arrived, and everyone dove in. Thomas had removed his hat when he sat down, but the brothers still wore theirs.

"How's Mama?" Shane asked.

"She's well. I haven't seen her that joyful since I've known her. You boys showing up did her heart a world of good."

After a few minutes of putting away their meals, Audie broke the silence. "You work in Wichita much, Thomas?"

"Nah. I've been here a few times. For a big place, it's not too bad. There are nastier towns on the trail, for sure."

"What kind of business brings you out here?" Shane asked.

Thomas remembered Adalina had told him of the boys' fondness for the Indians. He knew he had to watch his words here.

"There was a shipment of rifles bound west out of here that never made it to their location. The belief is that Indians attacked the soldiers transporting them. I'm to look into the matter and report my findings."

Shane and Audie kept their cool, but both brothers lost their appetites at the news. "Indians, you say?" Audie spoke.

"That's the theory now. It looks like more of the killing was done with knives than guns. Not many white men with that skill."

"Well, that sounds like a hell of a job. Trying to figure out who did what a couple of months after it happened," Shane said.

"Oh, so you've heard about it?"

Shane realized he'd said a little too much.

"Uh, yeah. I mean, we hear all the latest news at the Buckhorn. A lot of busy bees in there," Audie said, trying to sweep up Shane's mess.

"Well, if there's anything you know that might help me, I'd be much obliged for the information."

"We don't really know anything but the gossip," Shane said, doing a great job of hiding his nervous.

"Still, if you remember something interesting, let me know."

"Shane, I think we need to go find Moses and figure out what all we have to take care of today. Thank you for the breakfast, Thomas. I'm sure we'll be seeing more of each other."

"I'd love to come by and hear you play again tonight, if the invitation stands."

"Absolutely. We'll buy your drinks," Shane offered.

Thomas chuckled.

"I appreciate that. I assure you it'll be on the cheap, though. Not a big elbow bender."

Shane and Audie stood and tipped their hats to Thomas. He stood up in a hurry to be polite. They shook hands and left.

"Shit," Shane said when they were out of view.

"Of all the damn luck. Mama's husband is the man sent to cinch our asses up."

"Shit," Audie repeated.

~

Siringo had been plotting for days on what to make of the information he had acquired from Welks. He could arrest Shane easily enough, but there had to be a better use for it than that. Besides, Audie was the one he wanted.

If Shane would slay a man over a misunderstanding with a woman who wasn't even his . . . well, that kind of man wouldn't have much trouble with any sort of killing, Siringo reasoned to himself. And he could almost smell the death on Audie. He recognized those kinds of things in a man.

What Siringo wanted was a justifiable reason to kill them both. Out in the open in, in front of the town. If he called out Shane on the murder, then Audie would surely try to back his brother's play, giving him the reason he'd need to kill them both. But there were two problems. All he really had was the word of a notorious lowlife, and the dedicated lawman Sheriff McNulty would want things done by the book. He believed Welks because he'd seen it in Welks's eyes when he told him, but no one else in this town would believe a man like that. McNulty would want a trial and all that horseshit. So, if he did draw them out, he'd have to make sure McNulty wasn't around. Maybe he'd need Welks again after all. He figured Audie and Shane for pistoleers, even though they didn't go heels. He knew there was more to this story than he was privy to yet. He was determined to find the DeVine brothers out.

And kill them.

CHAPTER 26

Thomas felt like the breakfast with Audie and Shane had ended awkwardly. He wished he didn't care, but he couldn't help it. He had been dedicated only to his work until he met their mother. There had been the occasional woman in his life before her, but she was the only one who had made him want to settle down.

He wasn't used to caring what people think. In his line of work, a lot of folks he encountered didn't like him, and he was okay with that, but this was different.

Thomas set off to go talk to the sheriff about the soldiers who'd been murdered. Walking briskly, he tried to get his mind right for the sake of his job.

When he got there, he found the sheriff sitting behind a desk drinking coffee and reading the *Wichita Eagle Newspaper* behind a pair of thick eyeglasses. "Can I help you, mister?"

"Hello, Sheriff. My name is Thomas Thorntree, and I'm a Pinkerton agent here on assignment. Can I talk to you for a bit?"

McNulty stood and shook Thomas's hand.

"I'm McNulty. Pleased to meet ya. This about that Setters killing? I don't think we need a Pinkerton man for—"

"No, this is about the ambush that happened a couple hours out of town a few weeks ago. An incident where twelve soldiers were killed, and a wagonload of Winchesters and ammo was destroyed. You know anything about that?"

McNulty sat back down.

"Oh, yeah," McNulty said as he leaned forward. "That. I don't know if I have anything useful for ya on that matter, Mr. Thorntree, but there were some of your men here before you who left a package with me for safekeeping. Let me go get it out of the back."

McNulty grabbed a set of keys from a drawer, got back up, and walked to a narrow wooden door behind him. He tried a couple of keys until he managed to turn the third one in the lock.

"Those soldiers were a rowdy bunch. Pert near drank up the whiskey supply the night before," he said as he handed a dark-stained wooden box to Thomas. It was about a foot by eight inches by four inches deep and had *Pinkerton* written on the top of it.

"I hate to hear about what happened, but you'd think the government would send better than a band of horny lushes to protect a wagon full of guns. No offense toward you, sir." McNulty lifted his hands in sort of a mock surrender.

Thomas smiled. "None taken. The Pinkertons aren't actually affiliated with the government. It's a common misconception, though."

"Well, feel free to work the town over, Mr. Thorntree. I hope you find something. If someone is holding back on ya, come see me and I'll square it up. Who you thinking did it, anyway?"

"They think Indians are responsible. The scene I was told about would make you believe that for sure, but that's not making much sense to me. I don't know why a band of Indians would be that close to a town for one, and how would they have known the wagon was loaded with munitions? Furthermore, why were they destroyed and not stolen? It doesn't add up."

"I can tell you're a smart feller, sir," McNulty said.

"What was the murder you were talking about earlier? The Setters fellow?"

"Oh, just a drifter who pissed off the wrong guy. I think I know who done it, but I ain't got a lick of proof."

"Who you think did it?"

"Oddly enough, a minstrel. Boy named Shane DeVine. The drifter had been less than polite to a lady friend of his, and they'd got into a scuffle over it that same night. DeVine beat the guy within an inch of his life before someone pulled him off of Setters. Pretty sure he finished the job with a blade. Waiting him out is all."

Thomas's heart sank. He jumped to defend them without even thinking. "I know the DeVine brothers. I can't imagine one of them killing a man!"

"Well, maybe you're right. It's just a theory. How do you know them boys?"

"I'm married to their mother."

"Ha! You didn't say they were your sons! Music's an odd profession for a Pinkerton man's sons to take up."

Thomas cleared his throat. "They're my wife's sons from a previous marriage."

"Oh. Sorry, mister. Didn't mean to pry into your business."

"Thank you for your time." Thomas tipped his hat, tucked the wooden box under his arm, and walked out.

Thomas didn't know what to make of his conversation with the sheriff. Shane, a murderer? He couldn't believe Adalina's son would do such a thing. He couldn't or didn't want to. He wasn't sure which. His brain was still trying to process all he'd learned. First, he found out they played music for a living, the oddest music he'd ever heard, and in a saloon every night! Now Shane was suspected of murder. A hell of an introduction to his stepsons.

He returned to his room to examine the contents of the box McNulty had given him. There were three .45 caliber shell casings, a rope, and a blood-soaked leather strap—probably a necklace—with a cross and a feather tied to it.

This didn't feel like Indians.

Thomas read the report: *Few defensive wounds on the soldiers; bodies picked at by vultures.* He presumed the Pinkerton agent who visited the bloody scene deducted it had been a one-sided battle from looking at the soldiers' clean hands.

Thomas thought hard. *That means whoever took them, took them quickly. At least that sounded like Indians.*

He continued reading the report: *Twelve armed and trained soldiers dead, one colonel; most by knife; no other bodies found. Colonel was bound by rope to a tree out of visual range of the trail.*

His mind was racing. *No casualties on the attackers' side? Maybe they took their casualties with them, but a colonel tied to a tree? Sounds like they were interrogating him. But interrogation? That wasn't a method typically used by Indians.*

Something didn't add up.

He went about the rest of his day walking around town, asking questions about the soldiers. He questioned the people at the Buckhorn, including Lomasi, who didn't have a thing good to say about them. He questioned the man who owned the place and who'd let them the rooms they stayed in. He'd talked to the sheriff and a few other hopefuls as well, but all in all, it was a fruitless day. He knew he had to come up with something before he left town. Two unfinished assignments in a row would land you fired or on some duty no agent wants, like chasing after small-time horse thieves or pickpockets.

It'd been over two decades since he'd been on small duty. He didn't know if his pride could handle it now.

He finished the day worried and unsettled.

"I'm gonna draw 'em out. What I need from you is to tail their ever' last move and let me know when they're coming for me. They don't go heels so I can take them both with a pistol. I just need to know when they're coming," Siringo said.

"Well, that's just self-defense," Welks offered with a smile.

"Yes, it is."

"I can do that. Of course, that's a full-time job. I'll need two eagles up front and two on the backside. Plus expenses."

"What the hell kind of expenses? You trying to gouge me, Welks?"

"No, sir. Wouldn't ever do that. There's two of them. I need to employ another man for if they split up."

"You dumb shit son of a bitch. If they come, they'll come together. And the last thing I need is another soul privy to this little plan."

"Alright. Well, don't say I didn't warn ya."

"Just do your damn job, Welks!" Siringo spit at him.

"I always do." Welks smirked and disappeared into the night.

Moses went about his day doing what he usually did, taking care of any errands Audie or Shane had. Today he had taken their three horses out for a ride one by one to knock a little dust off of them. It wasn't the most exciting day, but Moses was grateful for any day now where he wasn't being hunted by someone.

Late that afternoon on the way back into town, he ran into an unwelcome face.

Siringo saw him and walked out in the street to block his way. Moses was at a slow trot on Audie's horse when Siringo came up and gently grabbed the reins.

"Well, if it ain't the singers' nigger," Siringo taunted Moses.

"Easy, fella," he coaxed the mare.

Moses scowled but held his tongue.

"What's them boys up to today? No good, I suspect. Why do you wanna nigger for those barrel scrapers anyway? Can't you find respectable work somewhere?"

"I ain't they nigga. I'm free ta come an' go as I please." Moses had a mouthful of other things he wanted to say to him, but he held the words like gravel in his teeth.

"Sure ya are," Siringo scoffed. "Say, you know anything about that man Shane beat the tar out of the other night? I believe his name was

Setters. He died, ya know. Somebody stabbed him. Kinda like they were finishin' off the job. You know anything about that?"

Moses had his suspicions, but he was honest when he said he didn't. "No, I don't know nothin' 'bout that."

Siringo laughed. "Well, I do . . ." He wanted to see how that sunk in on Moses's face.

Moses knew he was being sized up. He'd seen Siringo do this to Audie, and he held his nerves the best he could.

Siringo saw the nervous. He stepped closer and cocked his head sideways to study Moses' face.

"Say, where'd you get that scar from? That's a real humdinger. I'd love to hear the story behind it."

Moses continued his silence.

"You know the problem with a nigger? You never can tell if they're lying or not. They're just. That. Low."

Moses could feel a heat in the back of his neck that he hated. He wanted to cave this man's face in. "You have a good day, missa." Moses mustered up all the steel inside himself to say that without fire on his tongue.

He yanked the reins from Siringo and rode back to the stable.

After he boarded the horses, Moses found the brothers standing in the back of the Buckhorn.

"Mr. Shane, he thinks you killed that fella the other night. Told me he knew ya did it. That's a spiteful man, that Missa Siringo, and he ain't got nothin' but spite fo' you an' Audie."

Audie knew they had to do something about Siringo. The man was digging, and that's the last thing they needed. If he dug far enough, he'd find a graveyard.

"Alright, Moses. No need to worry about that." Shane tried to comfort him.

"Will you go see to the wagon and make sure he hadn't been sifting around in there?" Audie asked Moses.

Audie wasn't worried about the wagon. He just wanted Moses gone so he could talk to Shane freely.

"He's got to die." He had waited till Moses left, but Shane said it before Audie could.

"He's a bounty hunter. If he wanted to arrest us, he would. He's trying to make us come at him," Audie reasoned.

"So he's waiting."

"Then we don't go right now. We make him wait. Let him get uneasy before we go in."

Shane heard a noise around the corner of the building like a rustling foot. He looked at Audie and knew he'd heard it too.

Audie signaled to Shane without a word. They snuck over to the side of the building without a sound.

Welks was just beginning to realize the conversation had stopped when a fist came at him and knocked him to the ground.

Audie bent over to look at his handiwork. He'd clocked the man hard. Welks was trying to shake it off.

"What the hell, man! I was just coming back here to enjoy a smoke!"

Shane felt around in the man's pocket. No tobacco or matches. "What were you gonna smoke?"

"Well . . . I suppose I forgot my tobacco."

"I know you. I met you in this same place. You bummed a smoke off of me before," Audie said.

"Yeah, you know me. I was just gonna smoke."

The brothers' intuition told them he was lying.

"Who are you?" Audie interrogated.

"Name is Welks."

"Why were you listening to us?"

"I wasn't listening. I was just here to smoke."

Shane gave him a gut shot that knocked every ounce of wind he had out of him. "Why were you listening?" Shane demanded, keeping his voice low.

"You boys are loony!" Welks grunted with what little breath he had. "I wasn't listening!"

Audie hit him in the nose with an open palm. Blood immediately started pouring.

"Ahh! Alright!" Welks said, sounding like he had the worst head cold in the world. "Siringo sent me. I'm just a hired man to spy on y'all. I ain't got no skin in this spat."

Audie looked at Shane to let him know what he was about to do. He took his knife out and sliced the man's throat in one swift motion. Blood came out in spurts and spilled on the weeds the man was lying in.

Audie quickly wiped his blade on Welk's pants and sheathed it. The brothers were careful not to get any on their clothes.

"We've only got a few minutes before the show. Let's drag him as far out in that brush as we can," Audie said.

"Damn it, Audie! There could have been other eyes."

They looked around but saw no signs of a witness. They dragged him out about two hundred and fifty yards into the brush. There was a little stream nearby, and when they finished, they stopped to wash the blood off of their hands.

"Son of a bitch! He's sending spies for us! What the hell, Audie? We have to handle this now!"

"Let me think!" Audie said as he scrubbed his hands in the running water.

They walked back, watching out for any onlookers as they went. When they returned, Smyth was waiting for them in back of the Buckhorn.

"Where the hell have you two lollygaggers been?"

Audie and Shane brushed off Smyth's taunting as they entered the saloon. They had just walked on stage to play when Shane spotted Thomas at the bar. He pointed him out to Audie, and Audie gave him a look that told him he'd deal with it. He walked up to Thomas and shook his hand.

"Drinks are on us. We won't tell Mama." Audie humored him.

Thomas laughed. "Alright. We'll see."

Audie told Lomasi to give Thomas whatever he wanted on his

coin. Lomasi served Thomas up a shot and went about her business. The boys started the show and the crowd went wild, as always.

You could feel the brothers' troubles when they played. The tension of the kill came through in every note.

It made for a great show.

CHAPTER 27

T he next day came to Audie and Shane laced in worry. Thomas was investigating a crime they were responsible for, the sheriff suspected Shane of a murder, and Siringo was breathing down their necks. On top of all that, they'd killed another man last night and not in the best of circumstances. They were pretty certain no one saw them, but they couldn't be sure.

Moses, like usual, was up at the crack of dawn to meet the morning. He loved the time before the hustle and bustle of the city. It reminded him of his sweet Phibe.

It wasn't fall yet, but the mornings were starting to give little signs it was coming. Moses could just see his breath swirling in the air at this early hour.

Moses had made friends with an older lady named Beatrice who worked at the Beef & Beer. He usually went there for his breakfast and ate outside on a bench in front of the restaurant, and today he intended to do the same.

Beatrice was in her early fifties, just a bit older than Moses. She was slightly overweight and pretty, despite the signs of age creeping in. She always smiled when he came in.

"Well, good morning, Moses. You feel like some fried eggs and bacon this morning? I got a helping with your name on it."

Moses smiled at his friend. He looked menacing to the unknowing eye now, head shaved, and a beard fashioned into a point, not to mention the scar on his face that made people conjure up their own scary story about him. But somehow Beatrice could see people for who they were. She knew he was harmless.

"Why, yes, ma'am, Ms. Beatrice. How the day treatin' ya so far?"

"Same as it always does. 'Bout the same way I treat it."

She smiled at Moses and he chuckled.

Moses liked the woman's attitude. If you paid attention, she always had little bits of wisdom to chew on with the meals she served.

"You need any help with thangs today, ma'am? I'm sure Audie an' Shane won't be up for an hour or so."

"You're gonna have to start letting me pay you for your kindness, Moses. I ain't looking for no handouts. At least let me buy your breakfast."

"Ah, thank ya, ma'am. I jus' like ta stay busy is all. You helpin' me."

"I think you just pity an old woman," she said, only half playing.

"You ain't old yet. I see the way you whip them young'uns into shape back there. I wouldn't wanna tangle with ya."

Beatrice and Moses shared a good laugh. They always made each other's day a little brighter.

"I have some tablecloths drying out back on a line if you want to check and see if the dew's off them yet."

"Sounds like the perfect thang ta do while I wait on breakfast." Moses went out back to check on the laundry.

Thomas walked in about the same time Moses left. He sat down at a table and removed his hat, still a little fuzzy from last night but not bad. Three shots of whiskey were a lot for a man not given to the drink.

Beatrice came up and poured a cup of coffee. "What can I get for you, Mr. Thorntree?'

"Some eggs are fine, ma'am. And some bacon, please."

"Meal fit for a king, coming right up."

Moses came back in with the tablecloths folded up. "Just a tad damp but they's good."

"Thank you, Moses. Here's your plate." She handed Moses a plate piled high with twice as much food as she usually served a customer.

"You too kind, Ms. Beatrice. I thank ya for the meal."

He tipped his hat to her and walked toward the door.

"Excuse me."

Moses turned around to see a man he didn't know looking at him. "Yessuh?" Moses asked.

"Are you an acquaintance of the DeVine brothers? I think I've seen you talking to them."

Audie had told Moses that their mothers' new husband was in town. He figured instantly that's who this had to be.

"Yessuh. Are you Missa Thomas?"

"Yes. Thomas Thorntree. She spoke of a colored man who traveled with them, and I reasoned it was you. Would you like to have break-fast with me?"

"I usually eat outside on account of . . ."

"No, no, sit down! Please! Anybody who doesn't like it can deal with me."

Moses looked at Beatrice.

"Well, don't look at me, Moses. I ain't ever told you to eat outside. Sit your butt down like the man said," she added.

Moses grinned and took a seat at the table with Thomas.

"Seems like that woman's got your number." Thomas laughed. "I wouldn't mess with her if I were you."

"Believe me, I ain't," Moses said, still smiling.

"I hope I'm not imposing on you, Moses, is it?"

"Yes, suh. An' you ain't imposin'."

"Well, call me Thomas. And thank you for fixing the fence at our place. I've been meaning to get around to it."

"Happy ta do it. Ms. Adalina's a sweet lady."

"How'd you meet Audie and Shane?"

Moses paused. "We met out west a little piece."

Thomas wasn't trying to interrogate, but he noted the vagueness of Moses's answer.

"I jus' take care'a the day-ta-day things. They workin' on that music all the time, ya know. They's good boys. Of course, they'd have ta be comin' from a lady like Ms. Adalina."

Thomas smiled and nodded in agreement.

There was a stretch of uncomfortable quiet.

"I'm a Pinkerton agent out here on assignment. It was luck to run into them. Adalina will be pleased that I got to meet her sons."

"Whatcha out here workin' on? If'n ya don't mind me askin'."

"Not at all. Someone killed a dozen soldiers and burned a shipment of guns headed west. The man who inspected the scene thinks it was Indians, but I think he has it wrong. Too many things that Indians would never do."

Moses felt his stomach drop about six inches but tried to hold his emotion in check.

"That sound like complicated matters, Missa Thorntree."

"Call me Thomas. Yeah, it is, but I'll figure it. It wasn't ghosts out there doing the thieving, that's for sure."

Moses started choking down his breakfast like he was ravaged. He was ready not to be having this conversation.

"Well, I got to be gettin' my day started. Hope ta see ya around, Missa Thomas."

He got up and tipped his hat. Thomas stood, and the two shook hands.

"The heat's getting thick here, Audie. Maybe it's time we pack up and move on down the road," Shane said as he was throwing a knife up in the air. The blade point stuck in the floor, and he pulled it out to repeat the process.

It was about nine in the morning on a Thursday, and they were sitting in Audie's room.

"I'm all for it, but this kind of trouble will follow us. We have to take care of Siringo before we leave. Everything else will settle but not that."

"I know this is my fault. I . . . I lost it on that drifter. I don't know what came over me. He was all over Lomasi and I just lost it," Shane confessed.

"I know, brother. I know. My demons hit me like that, too. I know that . . . yearning. It's more powerful than me. I can hold it off for a while. Sometimes. But when a man deserves it . . ." Audie looked out the window of the room he had let. The room felt too familiar. He had done very little to make it feel like his own, but still he knew it by heart now. And knowing it made him want to leave it.

"Are we evil men, Audie?"

Audie took a deep breath and let the question soak into his soul for a while before answering. Shane knew he was mulling his answer over before giving it.

"Yes."

No one spoke for a couple of minutes. Then Audie turned to face his brother.

"Yes, we are bad men," Audie said. "But we fight men more evil than ourselves. We fight for something other than ourselves."

"Father would have wanted us to be another kind of man," Shane reckoned.

"And if Father weren't murdered in cold blood, we would have been. I loved him enough to follow . . . I would have been a man of the cloth, too," Audie admitted. He turned his face back toward the window out of fear that he might cry in front of his brother. The thought of his father rattled his heart.

Shane thought of Lozen in this moment. He felt her lips pull away from his in his mind. He didn't know why.

Audie broke the silence. "We've got to kill Siringo. Soon."

"Yes, but we have to make him try to kill us first. This one has to be done out in the open."

"He's got to be worried about Welks disappearing. Maybe we just feed that worry a bit."

"Yeah. He'll come running," Shane agreed.

Audie stared at the paper and quill sitting on a small table in his room.

"I think I know how to get his ass hairs up."

❧

Thomas had been here a few days now and hadn't found an ounce of hard evidence that would sway the case for him. He'd been out to where the ambush had taken place, but time had stolen anything that would hold knowledge of the doers. He had no options that he could see at the moment for further uncovering of the crime.

He bellied up to the bar at the Buckhorn that evening. The only good thing about this trip was meeting Audie and Shane. At least he could enjoy that and return with stories for Adalina.

He wasn't a drinking man, but tonight felt like a good night to be one. He was on his second shot before the boys started playing.

❧

Siringo noticed the note on the floor of his room as soon as he came back in from supper that night. He was a man given to detail. It was out of place.

"*250 paces behind the buckhorn,*" it read in scribbled handwriting.

"What the hell?" Siringo said out loud.

He was getting more nervous by the minute since Welks hadn't shown up. He wasn't a man who usually wrestled with nerves, but this was different. He was messing with a known criminal who could backstab him at any moment.

Siringo checked both his pistols to make sure they were fully loaded and headed out to the spot in the note.

❧

"I feel like a god tonight!"

Smyth was chomping at the bit to play by the time the boys got there. They were a tad antsy themselves, but Smyth thought the energy was on account of the stage they were walking on.

The brothers noticed Thomas at the bar and waved at him. Audie yelled to Lomasi that he'd pick up the tab.

They started the show off with a song Audie had written about a hanging tree. The lyrics to their songs were always esoteric. When the patrons heard it, they all made their own judgment as to what it was about, but none ever really got close to the truth. The emotion of the songs couldn't be mistaken, though. That was as clear as the sun at noon.

It's strange how the audience feeds off of the energy of a band. On nights like this there were more fights, arguments, and sex than on usual nights. The DeVine brothers had learned to channel their emotion into the music. It isn't a gift many are given. Most saw music as a set of prescribed chords or scales, but Audie and Shane saw it as a vehicle. And they steered that vehicle even when they didn't know they were.

Smyth had been trained classically but had long abandoned his education for something else. Something that couldn't be taught.

They were a band of outlaws.

They played that night with fire in their fingers and their voices.

They transcended. The energy they gave and got back from the audience was almost visible.

Siringo snuck out behind the Buckhorn, making sure no one caught a glimpse of him as he made his way. With pistol drawn, he cursed every twig that made a racket on his way to the spot.

It had been three days since Welks had gone missing.

Siringo smelled Welks before he saw him. When he heard the flies, he knew what he'd see next.

Welks's body was bloated and overrun with maggots. Some animal had gnawed away at the stomach but hadn't finished the job. The chest was swollen enough to have popped the buttons on his shirt. The face was almost unrecognizable.

But Siringo knew who it was.

He took off for the Buckhorn, pistols still drawn.

Smyth had taken to playing some of the more rambunctious solos on his knees as though it was a prayer to some god only he knew. The crowd ate it up. He ruled the night when he screeched his bow across the strings, horsehair flying like little bolts of lightning.

Audie was the first to see Siringo coming through the saloon door. The bounty hunter had his pistol drawn, pointed right at him.

Audie kept playing. Siringo wouldn't shoot him in front of a crowd unwarranted. He knew the man was smarter than that.

"I'm taking you two for the murder of Burly Welks and Harold Setters!" Siringo tried to shout over the crowd.

No one except the people right next to him heard what he was shouting. A few patrons he passed spotted the pistol, but the place was too loud for anyone to sound an alarm.

"You two bastards are goin' to jail or hell tonight! Get off that son of a bitchin' stage!"

Audie still kept playing.

Shane had spotted him now. Audie looked at Shane for a split second before he made his decision. He stopped playing guitar and reached behind him in his belt to pull out a knife.

Siringo suddenly dropped where he stood.

Audie still held the knife behind his back.

It was a bullet that stopped Siringo.

Thomas stood over the body with pistol in hand and looked up at the stage to Audie. He hadn't heard what Siringo was yelling. He just saw the man rushing toward Audie and Shane with a pistol.

Smyth was so enraptured in the moment he didn't realize the place had gone silent for a few seconds and continued playing. The notes finally faded into the quiet.

The saloon emptied, and the music was over for the night.

"He came through the door brandishing a .45. He appeared to be yelling something at the stage. I reacted in the manner I have been trained."

McNulty wasn't about to mess with a Pinkerton. If the man claimed he was stopping trouble before it started, then that's what happened in McNulty's book. End of story.

"Alright, Mr. Thorntree. I guess it's a good thing you were around to stop old Siringo here. He's a bounty hunter. Not the most likable one, either. I'm sure some around here will see it as a favor to the town."

A couple of deputies took Siringo's body down to the coroner. Jasper Dukes, the town coroner, was almost seventy years old and certainly in bed at this late hour. Pronouncing Siringo dead would have to wait till morning.

After McNulty left, Thomas had some questions for the brothers.

"Why was that man coming after you so hellbent?"

Audie explained, "I had a round with him a few weeks back. Laid him out pretty flat right out in the street. He was trying to push his weight around on our partner Moses, and it rubbed me the wrong way. He's been trying to pick another fight ever since, so he probably got too much rotgut in himself and thought he'd get that fight tonight."

Audie was stone faced the whole time he spoke.

"You two sure have a bad habit of losing your temper. I know about the Setters fellow you beat, Shane. You know that sheriff thinks you're the one who killed him, too?" Thomas said, keeping his voice low but stern.

"I ain't," Shane lied.

"Look, I'm not your father, and I know I have no right to act like it, but the way I understand it, your father was a very good man. And every one of us knows what a saint your mother is. I don't know what happened to y'all out there with the redskins, but you can't go around chopping down every man who gets your dander up. You'll end up dead or in a cell. And I don't want to have to carry Adalina to a funeral or a jail to visit her sons."

Shane started to tell Thomas they didn't need his advice when Audie interrupted.

"You're right, Thomas. Shane and I both need to bridle our temper, and we will."

Thomas searched his face to see if he was earnest.

All he saw was a hardness.

"Can I ask you a favor, Thomas? Can we keep all of this between us? I mean, can you not tell Mama about these matters? I don't want her worrying any more than she already does," Shane said.

"I wouldn't lay any more burden on that women if I had to. Just keep your hands clean. I know you love your mother. Don't cause her any more pain than she's already been through."

"We won't, Thomas. I guess we're just figuring our way out here. We'll take it easy from now on," Audie said.

They said their goodbyes and parted.

They didn't even have to discuss leaving. They knew it was time to move on.

Audie told Moses they'd be departing in two days' time. Moses went about getting their affairs in order.

Moses hated to see the trouble that was chasing the boys, but he was glad to get out of that place. Siringo had made the town feel unwelcome to him.

Mr. Vigus wasn't happy with their sudden departure, but there wasn't much he could do but cuss about it. He threatened to withhold their pay, but the look in the boys' eyes told him that probably wasn't a smart move.

Smyth had declared he was going with them.

"We spilt blood together on the stage. We're brothers now." Audie and Shane argued with him, but he persisted.

The next day the boys went to say their goodbyes to Lomasi.

"Who's going to scold you two when you act like children?" she teased them.

"Nobody as good as you, Lomasi," Shane said.

"You boys take care of yourselves. I will pray for a safe journey."

"I have something for you."

"No, Audie. I have no gift to give you in return."

"You already gave us one, Lomasi. You made us feel like family."

Audie worked one of his Apache blades and sheaths from inside his belt. He handed it to Lomasi.

"For any bastard who puts his hands on you unwanted."

Lomasi stared at the blade and then looked back up at Audie.

"You . . . you are Indian! This is Apache! I knew it!"

"Yes, but no one else needs to know that. Like I said, you made us feel like family."

She stared at Audie and then at Shane as if she could see the past in their chiseled faces. They let her read them. She touched Shane's face softly. She put her head on Audie's chest and began to cry gently.

Shane put his arms around her. "Hush now. We're alright."

He held her for a while longer. Then Audie hugged her, they bid her farewell, and headed out the door.

Moses had breakfast from Beatrice's kitchen one more time before they left. He didn't tell her he was leaving. He just wanted to see his friend before he went.

"You take care, Miss Beatrice. Doncha work them boys too hard back there."

"Hell, Moses. I'd be glad if they'd just work, let alone work too hard." She gave him a wink, and he tipped his hat and left.

"You boys are hauling out, huh? I might not know what to do with myself without y'all here stirring up shit."

The sheriff was taunting them. Audie and Shane just nodded and finished getting ready for the leaving.

"I know you killed that drifter, boy. I can't prove it, but I know it." He walked closer to Shane. "The man might have deserved half the beating you gave him for being ungentlemanly, but he didn't deserve a knife. You got out of this one by the skin of your teeth. You won't be so lucky next time. And that Pinkerton, your mama's husband, he's an honest man. Y'all might have him snowed right now, but he ain't gonna stay that way."

Shane stared at him a moment. He could see in the sheriff's eyes that he wanted him for the murder.

"You're mistaken, Sheriff. We don't have anyone fooled, and that drifter must have had other enemies."

McNulty spit on the ground.

"Y'all best be getting before the heat makes you change your mind."

The sheriff walked away without a goodbye.

Moses and Audie climbed up on the wagon while Shane and Smyth packed their saddles. No one spoke of the conversation with the sheriff.

The townspeople all stared curiously at the band of misfits about to depart.

"Why, you bugger! You were gonna sneak out of town without saying goodbye?" Mrs. Beatrice had spotted Moses and the boys, packed up and ready to leave. She was walking up to the wagon in a hurry.

"I jus' didn't want no fuss is all, Miss Beatrice."

She stopped beside the wagon with her hands on her hips looking up at Moses.

"Well, what if I want to fuss, Moses? Did you think about that?"

She smacked his leg hard enough to make the point that she wasn't happy about him taking off.

"I'm sorry, ma'am. I didn't mean no disres—"

"Moses, you ain't bound to these wild men. I've got plenty of work back at Beef & Beer if you wanted a more stable situation."

Her words took on a softer tone than Moses had heard from her. The years of slinging food for cowboys and soldiers had given her an armor, but she took it off for a minute.

"I . . . I can't, Miss Beatrice. My place is with Audie an' Shane. They been good ta me."

Audie had an urge to tell Moses he was free to do what he wanted, but he held his tongue. If Moses wanted to stay, he knew he could, and to be truthful, Audie leaned on Moses for a lot. The thought of being without him now seemed too much to deal with.

She stared up at Moses with her honey-brown eyes for a while, letting him see the misty in them. She would miss him.

"Well, you just ride along then. I don't know what to think about a man who'd pass up my cooking for campfire fixins." She tried to joke as her voice cracked a little.

Moses stepped off of the wagon and hugged her. She squeezed him tight for a few seconds, then quickly turned and walked away.

It wasn't proper for a white woman to hug a black man in those days, but Miss Beatrice would have quickly tongue-whipped anyone who had issue with it. No one did.

Audie was on the wagon waiting for Moses, acting like he was paying attention to anything else in the world but Moses and Miss Beatrice. Shane and Smyth had ridden ahead.

A preacher was walking up to Audie, making his disgust known for the DeVine Devils. "They chant to the sound of the viol and invent to themselves instruments of music. They drink wine in bowls, and anoint themselves with the chief ointments . . ."

"But they are not grieved for the affliction of Joseph. Amos 6: 5 and 6," Audie finished.

The preacher pointed his Bible up at Audie like it was a gun.

"You know the Bible, yet you play the music of heathens and pagans! May the Good Lord have mercy on your souls!"

"Too late for that. What was a man of the cloth doing in a devil's den, anyway?"

"Looking for lost sheep!"

"I ain't lost, and I ain't no sheep," Audie said.

His words had bite, but he couldn't look at the preacher when he spoke.

Audie knew his father would have felt the same.

"Go preach to the choir. You'll have better odds there," Audie said as he motioned Moses to go.

They rode slowly out of the west gate with the sheriff sitting on the front steps of his office watching them leave like he wanted them to commit a crime before they could get out. When they'd got a piece of distance outside the gate, Smyth rode back beside Audie on the wagon.

"What was that business with the preacher back there?" Smyth asked.

"He was just doing his job."

"What's that?"

"Running the devils out of town."

Moses snapped the reins, and the horses pulling the wagon gained a little speed.

CHAPTER 29

So they said goodbye to one more town with one more passenger in tow. Audie and Shane weren't sure whether or even how to share the other side of their lives with Smyth. Like everything else, they'd figure it out along the way. They were a band of misfits, for sure. No one in their party had anything resembling normality in their life thus far.

Everyone was mostly quiet on their journey to no one knew where except, of course, Smyth, a constant fountain of hilarious and useless commentary on the world. His banter ran the gamut of a good reprieve from their troubles to obnoxious and annoying.

"Moses, I need to know if something's true. I've heard from more than one source that men from Africa have a pecker the size of a forearm. Can you confirm this? I don't want to see it, mind you. I just want to know if it's true."

They all laughed, even Moses.

"Well, I don't know quite how ta answer that," Moses said, playing along. "I guess it depend on the forearm."

"Well, hell, a baby's forearm is bigger than mine. Or Shane's. Any forearm is pretty impressive."

More laughs. This time a little heartier.

"Speak for yourself, Smyth. You ain't ever seen mine. It'd give you nightmares, boy!" Shane defended himself.

"Ha! You ain't foolin' nobody, Shane. I know you're hung like a bull field mouse."

Audie almost fell off of his horse laughing.

When Shane regained composure from his cackling spell, he said, "What makes you an expert on a man's trouser snake? You seen a few in your day?"

"I've seen enough to know you shouldn't call that thing a snake. It's more like a worm."

Moses stopped the wagon he was laughing so hard.

After a while, once everyone recovered from Smyth's comedy routine, they started down the road again.

"Smyth, you might not be worth a shit other than the fiddle and a laugh, but I believe that's enough."

Smyth tipped his hat to Audie. They rode on a while west. Audie appreciated the break from thinking about what they would do next, but it didn't last long.

~

Audie was riding up ahead of the rest of the men on the westward trail, when Shane rode up to talk to him. "Where are we going next, brother?" It was a question Audie didn't want to be asked right now. He still had no idea.

"I don't know. Whatever town is next. We'll see."

"Well, I don't know if just wandering around toward the sunset is a good way to spend our time."

Audie gave Shane a sour look.

"You got any ideas on where to go?" Audie said, pestered.

Shane didn't speak for a bit.

"No."

They rode on for another long while.

~

After two days of travel, they found a place to bed down along a little creek just south of the trail they were on. There were two large weeping willow trees with short grass underneath and thick brush around the perimeter of the area. Any intruder, human or otherwise, would have a hard time getting in without making their presence known.

Smyth had quizzed the brothers about their conversation with the sheriff just before they left, but the brothers stuck to the version they had told McNulty. No need to let any cats out of the bag yet.

He was genuinely interested, but Smyth didn't focus on too many things outside of his own wants. It wasn't too hard to keep him in the dark.

"Damn law dogs. Anytime a man don't fit the mold they want to make him a villain. Get used to it, boys. We make outlaw music. Outlaw is what they'll call us," Smyth pontificated.

Moses listened and then excused himself to go get more firewood. Audie went off to find some food, and Smyth and Shane unloaded a few supplies they'd need for the night.

"An outlaw. Is that what you think of yourself, Smyth?" Shane asked.

"Why, hell yeah! What else would I be? They can have all their supposed-tos and oughtas. All those well-to-dos and the leather hands, too. They live in a jail, and they don't even know it. I wanna go out with my boots on. Not old and lying in some bed made for dying."

Moses and the brothers were always entertained when Smyth got up on his soapbox. There was a kindred spirit between them.

Shane stood watch that night as the rest of the party lay sleeping. The chill of fall was starting to make itself known when the sun sank at night.

He was thinking about Lozen. In these moments without distraction, it was impossible for him not to. Despite all the women he had shared a bed with these past few months, it was her his heart still wanted. He would have traded every lover for the girl he'd loved first.

Maybe it was the weariness in his bones that kept him from hearing the intruder. Maybe it was a memory he was chasing that dulled him to it, but either way he didn't hear the telltale signs until the knife was pressed against his throat.

Thomas was at a loss. He had enough circumstantial evidence to prove the raid on the soldiers wasn't Indians, but no hard-edged proof. In his mind, there was no way Indians would waste a wagon full of Winchesters and ammo. To them, that would have been a gift from the gods. No, this raid was more than just a lucky ambush.

He had sent word to the Pinkerton brass of his suspicions. They had sent word back to stay on the case.

Besides the frustration of the case, Thomas couldn't shake the feeling that things didn't add up with Adalina's sons. He didn't want to admit it, but he could smell blood on them. He wouldn't let himself sniff it out, because he was convinced if he did, he would find that Shane had killed that Setters fellow. And the way that bounty hunter was coming at them? There was more to that story than he wanted to know.

Now they had just up and left without so much as a howdy-do.

He tried to put them out of his mind. He wanted to focus on the job so he could get back to sweet Adalina.

Trouble was, he had run out of roads to go down.

Shane stayed deathly quiet. He knew at this moment if he opened his mouth, his apprehender would open his throat.

"Living in the white man's world has made you weak like one."

A hand turned his head and kissed him deeply.

Lozen.

Shane's adrenaline quickly turned to relief and then passion.

There were no words between them for the rest of the dark hours. None were needed. Their bodies spoke of the longing they had for each other since Shane's departure. They rocked and swayed in a rhythm that only belonged to them.

As the sun rose, their energy slowly gave way to conversation.

"How did you find us?" Shane asked.

Lozen laughed. "It wasn't hard."

"Why are you out here alone? It's dangerous for an Indian to go it solo in these parts."

She gave him a frown. She took his worry as unbelief in her skill, but let it go without words.

"Cochise has passed. I came to tell you and Audie."

"Cochise," Shane muttered.

The man had been larger than life to the brothers. They grew up with visits from the legend now and then. He had killed more enemies than any other Apache.

Shane couldn't believe he was dead.

"Yes. Age took him. His resting spot is in a secret place in the Dragoon Mountains."

Audie awoke to a woman's voice.

What the hell? he thought to himself.

Smyth heard him get up and followed him to investigate.

He came upon Lozen and Shane lying nude in the rising sun.

"Lozen! What are you doing here?" Audie exclaimed.

"Hello, Audie," she said as she pulled her pants on with no hint of embarrassment.

Audie looked away politely. Smyth didn't.

"Holy hell, Shane. You've got Indian whores finding you out here in the wild for a poke! What the hell kind of magic do you have in those pants of yours?"

Before Smyth knew what happened, Lozen was on her feet, bare-breasted and beautiful, and had busted Smyth's bottom lip open with the flat of her palm. He was laid out on the ground in an instant.

"Shit!" Smyth wailed out in pain.

Audie chuckled. He didn't have time to explain Lozen's distaste for disrespect.

Shane pulled on his pants and stood, handing Lozen her shirt. She pulled it on, never taking her eyes off of Smyth.

"Smyth meet Lozen. Audie and I grew up with her. Lozen, this is our companion, Smyth. He plays music with us."

Smyth pulled his fingers away from his mouth to reveal the blood that had coated them. He nodded his head at Lozen. There were foul words on his tongue for her, but the pain in his lip kept them there.

"Lozen, how did you find us?" Audie asked.

She smiled at him. "You and your brother have forgotten my skills. I found you the same way you would find me."

Audie studied Lozen for a second. He couldn't help but worry that she had changed her mind and was here to take Shane back as a husband.

Moses came up with a handful of firewood and spotted Lozen. He was shocked to see a woman had suddenly appeared in the camp but realized from the atmosphere there was no danger.

"Well, hidee, ma'am. I'm Moses Cofey. Nice ta meetcha."

Lozen saw the gentle in him immediately.

"I'm Lozen," she offered with a smile.

"Well, what a way to start the day," Audie said to cut the silence. "Let's get something on to eat."

"Audie, can I speak with you?" Shane asked.

Moses and Smyth took the hint and went to start breakfast. Smyth waited till Lozen was well out of eyesight and looked back to give her a go-to-hell glare as he was walking away.

"Chief Cochise died."

Audie was as stunned as his brother but somewhat relieved to know there was a reason for her visit other than just to see Shane.

"How?"

"It was his years that took him, not a fight," Shane said.

Audie pondered the situation silently.

"Did you meet any trouble on your way to us?" Shane inquired of Lozen.

"I killed two buffalo hunters three days back. But I wouldn't say it was trouble."

Shane tried to imagine Lozen as something other than fighter. A wife. A mother. Anything else but a fighter.

He could not.

"You came all the way out here just to tell us about Cochise?" Audie asked.

Lozen frowned.

"I would think that you would want to know about his passing! Or has being out here in this place stolen all of your respect?"

Audie hadn't meant it the way she had taken it. He was still hoping she wasn't there to offer Shane the married life he'd always asked her for.

"You're right. I didn't mean it like that. It's good to see you, Lozen," Audie said as he reached out a hand to shake hers. She ignored the hand and hugged him quickly. He awkwardly hugged her back.

She was never that affectionate before. The truth was, she missed him.

The three of them walked to meet the others for breakfast.

CHAPTER 30

Shane entertained the party for the next few hours with nostalgic tales of their childhood with Lozen and the others in the village. Moses listened with a smile on his face. Audie had spoken of this woman Shane loved to him before. He was glad to meet her.

Smyth was more interested in knowing how Shane had bedded a beautiful woman out here in the wild.

"Those are good stories. I sure don't have anything resembling that in my childhood. So, tell me again, Lozen, what made you come all the way out here to find us? Was it just for a go at Shane's pecker?"

She was almost to her feet in a second. Shane grabbed her around the torso to stop the wrath she was about to pour onto Smyth. She fought against him, but he held tight.

"Smyth, you can't talk like that to Lozen. She's to be treated with respect. She's an Indian warrior who could kill you quick as your next breath. Lozen won't tolerate being treated as any less than an equal. Make your peace with that now, or this will be a painful trip for you," Shane warned.

Smyth smiled snidely. "Fair enough. I'm just curious is all. Didn't mean any disrespect."

Lozen gave up the struggle so Shane loosened his grip. She gave Smyth a glare to serve as her own warning in case Shane's didn't sink in.

"That rabbit sho was good if'n I do say so myself," Moses interjected, breaking the tension. Everyone heartily agreed.

After breakfast, Audie took his rifle out to hunt for deer. They would feast tonight. Moses busied himself with little chores, gathering kindling for a fire and washing the cooking pot down at the stream. Smyth tuned up his fiddle and played a show for anyone who would listen. Shane and Lozen went for a walk in the woods.

Shane pushed Lozen up against a tree with his hand behind her head to guard it. He kissed her for no other reason than he loved her. He kissed her hungrily and then softly, and finally, with a fierceness that told her how much he'd missed her. She kissed him back for the same reasons.

After some time, Shane felt Lozen's fist knock the wind out of his gut mid-kiss.

"What in the hell, Lozen?" Shane asked through the pain.

"There have been other lips on your lips. Many. And other women in your bed. I can feel them when you kiss me, and I felt them when we were together last night."

Shane sighed. "You made your choice, Lozen. You have no right to get angry over who I sleep with if you won't commit to me!"

She smacked him across the face.

"Damn it, Lozen!" He pushed her down, and she landed hard on the ground. She stayed there staring at him and didn't attempt to get up.

"I have been with no other," Lozen confessed.

That softened Shane. He rubbed his cheek and sat beside her. Neither spoke for a bit.

Shane broke the silence. "I was lonely without you, Lozen. I know you don't understand, but I was with those other women because I thought it would kill the want in me that I keep for you."

Her dark-brown eyes stared at him for a while. Shane wouldn't meet her gaze. She finally looked away and spoke matter-of-factly.

"I fought. That's how I kept the thought of you away."

Shane lowered his head.

"I really did miss you," Shane said softly and in earnest.

"I know. I could feel that, too."

Lozen stood and offered a hand to help him up. He accepted. They made their way back to camp with the others.

By the time Lozen and Shane returned, Audie had a small doe hanging on a maple branch, and he and Moses were cutting out the back strap to cook that evening.

Shane heard Smyth's fiddle and went to get his drums out of the wagon. He put them next to Smyth and began playing along.

"Them boys make quite a racket when they get ta goin'. Most entertainin' thing I ever seen," Moses said to Lozen.

She didn't understand what he meant, but she gave him a kind smile in response.

"Audie! Hurry up and cut that bitch deer's ass and come play. We might as well be playing with our tallywhackers over here without you!" Smyth proclaimed.

"Why can't this one be more like this one?" Lozen said to Shane, pointing first to Smyth and then to Moses. Moses pretended not to hear out of modesty.

Smyth stopped playing.

"Well, hell, darling. I'll love you up, too, if that'll make you like m—"

A fist connected to the side of Smyth's face and interrupted his speech. Lozen had moved toward him, but Shane beat her to the punch. Smyth lay slumped on the ground. He cried out in agony.

"Shit, Shane! Awwww! Why do y'all keep hitting me?"

Shane reached down and grabbed his shirt collar and pulled him close to his own face.

"You're a hell of a fiddle player, Smyth. You're the most entertaining man in this group of misfits but get this through your damn head!"

Shane tapped at Smyth's forehead with two fingers as he spoke. Smyth tried to push his hand away and Shane smacked his fingers and kept tapping till he finished the sentence.

"You cannot speak to Lozen like that. I won't be able to save you from her blade if you do. I won't even try. That punch I landed on you just now, it would have been a full mauling from her if I hadn't beat her to it. So sheath your tongue, man! If you don't, she'll kill you, or I'll leave you out for the coyotes to hunt."

Smyth was thick-headed, but he got this message loud and clear.

That night the DeVine Devils entertained Lozen and Moses till the wee hours. They hadn't played in a few days, and it felt good to unleash for a while.

"Lawd! Y'all sho do a song right!" Moses exclaimed.

Shane walked over to Lozen.

"What do you think?"

"I think I see how you lure women to bed."

Shane prepared for another argument, but Lozen gave him a seductive smile. He realized her words had desire on them, not anger.

"Well, I'm dog-tired, y'all. I think I'm ready to call it day," Shane announced to everyone. He grabbed Lozen's hand and hurried her away.

"Shit, Moses. Looks like you and me and Audie are gonna have to love ourselves if we want any action tonight."

Moses and Audie laughed.

"Moses, do you mind taking watch tonight?" Audie inquired.

"Why sure, Audie. Whatever ya need."

"Wake Shane in a few hours and have him take a shift. I won't be back till morning."

"Where you goin'?" Moses asked.

"Not far. Nowhere you need to worry about."

Moses didn't like Audie's secrecy, but he let it go.

Audie dug around in the wagon for a small leather pouch. When he found it, he looked inside to see the ground-up peyote that he'd taken when they left the Indian village for Missouri. There was still more than enough for him to visit the other side.

He heated up water in the bowl they used for cooking and then filled a small cup three-quarters full. He added a couple of pinches of the dried-up, dark-green mushrooms and stirred the water around with his finger.

"Is that what I think it is?" Smyth had been watching him as he sat smoking a pipe.

"Depends on what you think it is."

"Is it peyote?"

"Yeah."

"Give me some of that Indian shit, Audie. I've heard that makes opium smoke feel like nothing."

"This *Indian shit* drives some mad," Audie said with a little venom. "It's not something you do just for a good time."

"Well, hell, I'm already crazy. It can't do any more harm," Smyth reasoned.

"It makes you sick. Then you'll talk to spirits you can't see on this side of things. You sure that's what you want?"

"Hell, yeah!"

Audie worried about Smyth's sanity, but he wasn't his father. If he wanted to see the spirit world, Audie wouldn't stop him.

"Alright. Come with me."

Audie led Smyth south of the camp about half a mile. They found a spruce tree with a clearing underneath it. Audie sat, leaning up against the rough trunk, and Smyth followed suit.

"Why'd you bring your fiddle?" Audie asked.

"I don't know. I like to play my fiddle when I'm drunk. Thought it might be fun on this shit, too."

Audie chuckled and shrugged his shoulders, took a decent-sized swig out of the cup he'd brought, and handed it to Smyth.

"Drink the rest."

Smyth took the cup and smelled it. He recoiled slightly from the stench of it.

"It don't seem too appetizing."

"Drink it or pour it out," Audie ordered.

Smyth held his nose and turned the cup up. He made a hissing sound after he swallowed it.

"Bad medicine," he choked out. "Now what?"

"Just wait. You'll know it when it comes."

They sat back and listened to the noises in the night.

Shane was lying beside Lozen and running his hand through her long, dark hair. He'd thought often the last few months of that beautiful, dark curtain that fell over her bare shoulders. He studied her face like he was memorizing it, but he already knew it by heart. He loved her as much as he had ever loved anything in this world.

She tenderly searched his eyes for the only love that ever warmed her. She found it there, where it had always been.

"You being here, it's a torture to me."

She slipped her hand down his pants.

"It doesn't seem like a torture."

"I love you, Lozen. I'd trade anything in this world for your hand in marriage. When you're gone, I can hold that feeling off with . . . When you're here, I can't."

She removed her hand and rolled over, turning her back to him.

Lozen murmured to Shane, "You make me want to stay. You make me want this every night. If I wasn't needed to fight, if I were someone else . . ."

"That's the problem, woman. If you were someone else, I wouldn't want you like I do." Shane pulled her close to him, and they laid in silence until sleep took them both.

The choice they had wasn't black and white. They did what they could in this life, not what they wanted.

CHAPTER 31

Smyth stood up after about an hour, held his stomach, and moaned.

"What the hell did you do to me, Audie?"

Audie laughed and rolled his head back and forth against the tree trunk. He felt a familiar high creeping up his back and into his head.

"Just wait. Relief's coming."

Audie's voice seemed to change pitch, higher and lower as he was talking. Smyth stared at him trying to make sense of it.

Just then Smyth threw up. It was a momentary but violent torrent of everything he had in his stomach from the day. He instantly felt better. The night seemed to go silent as the colors around him came alive. It was dark outside, but he could see everything now. The world looked like an art piece, like the ones hanging on the wall of the house he'd grown up in.

Audie had lost his nourishment, too, but it had gone unnoticed to Smyth. Audie was up walking, looking for—he didn't know what he was looking for.

Smyth began to feel hot in this new world he was in. He stripped down to nothing and became overjoyed with the feeling. It was as if the night were massaging every inch of his body. He grabbed his fiddle and began to play a funny little tune while doing a jester-like dance around the tree.

Audie had taken his boots off because he wanted to feel the earth beneath him. As he walked, vines came up from the earth to hold his feet, but he could break them easily with his steps. Every step felt like years to complete.

In the distance, Audie could hear a military drum tapping out a marching song. He heard the footsteps coming over a hill about half a mile in front of him. He reached for his knives, but they weren't on him. He tried to run to the camp, but he had stood in one place too long. The vines had his feet now and were crawling up his legs. He panicked.

The soldiers kept coming. They were marching, but their legs stayed straight and kicked high above their heads as they came toward him.

Audie saw Smyth playing his fiddle in the nude and screamed for him to come cut the vines. Smyth couldn't or wouldn't hear him. He just danced and played his instrument, having the time of his life.

The soldiers were coming closer. Everywhere he looked there were more. Thousands dressed in blue uniforms and black leather boots. The soldiers' faces looked like skin stretched over where ears, eyes, and mouths would be.

They were coming from the sky and from over the hill. They were coming from giant crevasses opening in the ground. They were climbing down from the trees and over fallen limbs in the forest. They were all marching toward him, but they looked past as if they couldn't see him. He screamed.

Suddenly everything froze, and the vines disappeared. Audie stood there, waiting.

"Gravedigger," he heard in a low, rumbling voice.

"Who speaks to me?" Audie asked.

He could move now but chose not to. The sky turned from night to day. The sun was black, but somehow a light emanated from it.

"Would you bring death to all these who stand before you?" A low, powerful voice spoke in an accent he'd never heard.

"And more," Audie answered as he focused his hate on the soldiers.

"When will your death lust be satisfied, gravedigger?"

"I . . . I don't know."

"Perhaps only when your bones lay in the grave, gravedigger."

Audie saw himself, Shane, and Smyth in the distance playing a show. The soldiers all turned to watch and cheer. Just then, fire came from Audie's and Shane's mouths and consumed the soldiers where they stood. Audie could smell the stench of burnt flesh. It was overwhelming. He knelt to the ground and vomited a river of blood. It flowed through the soldiers like a damn had burst and washed them back into the holes they emerged from. It thrust them back over the hill they had walked and up the trees they had scaled. It gathered around the feet of Shane, Smyth, and himself playing on the stage far away.

"What does this mean?!" Audie screamed.

Whatever was speaking to him was gone. He could feel it. He stood and wiped the blood off of his mouth, and it instantly vanished from his hand.

Smyth was playing with all his might now, but Audie could no longer see him. If Smyth slowed, he could see demons closing in on him. He played to keep them from killing him. His joy turned to fear, and the song went from playful to frantic.

Audie heard Smyth wail and looked up to see him crying, playing his fiddle like he'd never heard him. It was a tune from another world.

He saw Adalina in the distance. She was kneeling down in her bedroom in Missouri praying. She was holding something in her hand. He moved closer to the vision to see what it was.

It was his necklace with his father's cross and the feather from Grey Wolf. She clutched it while she mumbled words he couldn't make out.

"Mama! Mama!" he called out. She was oblivious to him. He tried to get closer, but his steps would not move him to her. He was ready for this vision to be over. He could hear Smyth crying and moaning in the distance.

He sat back down against the tree where he'd begun the night for what seemed like an eternity. When he opened his eyes, it was daylight. Shane was standing over him.

"Come get some food in your gut. It'll help bring you back."

Shane offered Audie his hand and pulled him up. He knew by looking at him what Audie had done last night.

"Smyth is still shivering like he saw his own ghost. Why would you give that idiot peyote? It's a wonder he came back at all."

Audie was quiet. The world was still not colored right, and he wasn't ready to speak to this side of it yet.

Shane sat Audie down and offered him some coffee and quail. Audie ate it timidly. Smyth sat to his left with a coat pulled over his nakedness. He was still whimpering but not hysterical like Audie remembered him last night.

Audie spent the morning silent. It was a couple of hours before he spoke. Moses was worried about him and Smyth, but Shane assured him they would be alright.

Lozen was packing up to head out.

~

"So this is it?" Shane asked, trying to masquerade the grief in his voice.

"I've spent enough time away. I don't want to get weak," Lozen said. She looked away from him to hide any trace of pain she feared might show.

Shane wanted to ask the same question he'd asked the last time they said goodbye, but he knew better. He saved both of them the disappointment.

He silently helped her cinch up her saddle.

"We're moving west, too. You could stay and ride a piece of the journey with us."

Lozen laughed. "I might be an old woman before we get anywhere with that tenderfoot."

Shane knew she referred to Smyth. She walked over to tell the others goodbye.

Audie and Moses bid her well. A still ragged-looking Smyth just tipped his hat. There was no love lost between him and Lozen.

Shane led her horse a few hundred feet from the camp to say his goodbye.

"Go back west, Lozen. Then find a reason to come see me again."

He kissed her and pulled back to stare at her a moment. She was as gorgeous as any woman on this earth to him. Her raven hair settled naturally around her high cheekbones. Her caramel skin showed no trace of the brutality she was capable of. The beauty made her power all the more enchanting. No one could imagine something that pretty being so deadly.

She smiled at him one last time, jumped on her horse, and rode off.

Audie and Smyth were mostly back to their senses by the time the sun started its descent that afternoon.

"Well, let's don't sit around here becoming old men, Audie. Let's move. Colorado probably needs a band or a battle," Shane said.

"Colorado is as good as anywhere. We'll leave at first light."

It was the first words Audie had spoken that day. He was still trying to make sense of last night. He had hoped to get some direction from his visit to the other side, but he walked away with more questions than he had before.

Smyth was back in the land of the living and trying to explain last night to Moses.

"I swear, Moses, there were a thousand devils nipping at me," Smyth said as he restrung his instrument with horsehair. Last night had laid waste to his strings.

"It was like my fiddle was blessed by some angel, and they couldn't get near as long as I played. I saw the music, Moses. Not just heard it, but saw it. I can't even tell you what it looked like, but I saw it, and it was a fear to the demons."

Moses shuddered. "A man ain't s'pose ta see them things, Smyth. Ain't s'pose to talk ta spirits."

"Well, hell, Moses. I didn't talk to them. I played to them."

Moses just shook his head and went looking for something to busy himself with.

The next morning came with a readiness to leave that place. Everyone was antsy to get moving. Even Moses didn't like sitting around.

They rode west for Colorado. Smyth had returned to his normal self and entertained them with comical and perverse ramblings on a number of things. He made the ride a bit more bearable, even if he did slow them down some.

CHAPTER 32

After a couple of weeks, they reached the city of Denver. It was November, and they'd barely beaten the first hard snow of the winter.

As they rode in through the eastern gate, they didn't feel as much awe as they had in Wichita or the City of Kansas. The ladies and the businessmen, the taverns and the shops, they had become commonplace in their everyday view of the world now.

They could feel the energy of it as soon as they arrived, though.

Denver in 1878 was booming. The gold rush had slowed down tremendously, but there was a new silver deposit discovered in Leadville, which promised to be the most profitable yet. Trains from Cheyenne and Kansas were now delivering residents, tourists, and supplies. Manufacturing in Denver was on the rise, bringing with it the makings of a true powerhouse city. The saloons and gambling houses attracted the roughhousers while the economy attracted the moneymakers. Wealth came easily to the city in those days.

They quickly found board for themselves and their horses. Audie had bargained for four rooms from a place called Carter House.

Nearby was a restaurant, Billy's. It advertised thick steaks and cold brew. They found a table in the back and settled in for a feast.

"Can I help you fine gentlemen?" a lanky waiter offered a few minutes later.

"Four steaks and fixings and four beers," Shane ordered.

"Alright. Simple enough." The waiter turned toward the kitchen.

"Me and Smyth will scope out places in need of our talents," Shane told the table.

"Why don't you do the scoping, Shane? I need to find me one of those houses of ill repute and get some willie worker to wet mine a little tonight," Smyth said.

Everyone at the table laughed.

"I imagine it ain't all that much work ta hear you tell 'bout your own willie," Moses joked.

"Moses Cofey! Poking fun! I like it. I imagine you'd have to pay double to get yours worked," Smyth reasoned.

They all laughed heartily.

"I don't need no part in that . . . ," Moses trailed off.

The steaks came, and they enjoyed their first full meal since they'd left Wichita.

After they ate, Shane went looking for work while Moses and Audie hung back at Carter House. They sat in the parlor, sinking into cushioned chairs and watching the flames dance in the fireplace.

"What's your plan here, Audie?"

"Don't have one yet."

"Well, I imagine this place is in need 'a some fine musicians like any other town we been to."

"Moses, you need to start going heels here." Audie spoke low. "I know you don't like guns, but just in case something happens. You carry all the coin. Somebody's bound to figure that out."

Moses shook his head.

"I can't do that, Audie."

"Moses, you don't have to use it. They just need to see it. It'll keep trouble at a distance."

"No, Audie. I won't be totin' no pistol."

"Damn it, Moses! Get out from behind your pulpit for once and act like a man. Even a preacher would go heels with a pocket full of silver."

"Would yo' daddy?" Moses spoke harsher than Audie had ever heard him. The question clocked him like a fist.

Audie looked at him with lightning in his eyes. Moses held his stare but without the fire.

"You're gonna get yourself killed. And me with you," Audie said as he looked away.

"I ain't killin' another man, Audie. What you do is between you an' the good Lawd, but I'll let my blood be spilt 'fore I spill some more."

"My father thought like that. He's dead."

Audie's anger eased a little.

"Yo' daddy died a good man with a clean conscience."

Audie was about to tell Moses he didn't give a shit about having a clean conscience when a very large, intimidating man walked into the room.

"You Audie DeVine?"

Audie looked at the man, trying to figure out what he might want.

"Who are you?" Audie quizzed.

The man continued like Audie had never asked a question.

"Come with me. The colored stays here."

"I think I'm fine right where I am," Audie said.

"Soapy Smith wants to talk to you about a business arrangement. He ain't a man you want to say no to."

Audie tried again to sum him up. All he saw was steel.

"You ain't in no danger and neither is your friend here, but that won't be the case if you don't get up off your ass and come with me. Now."

Audie sat there a moment longer for effect and then got up and stood close to the man to see his reaction. There wasn't one.

"After you," Audie directed. He looked at Moses to let him know it was alright.

The man led him down the street to a two-story building with no sign. They went through a small foyer where two men were standing like they were guarding the place. Next, they passed through a dark room full of card tables, men throwing money in the middle and calling each other's bluffs. Audie had never played poker, but he recognized the game right off.

They walked into a room with a big desk and a short, mildly overweight man hunkered behind it. On either side were men the same size as the one who'd led Audie here, dressed in suits and standing guard over him. Audie still couldn't suss out the situation. He didn't feel threatened, but he kept his guard up.

"Sit. Please." The smaller man motioned Audie to a rigid chair just in front of his desk.

Audie cautiously made his way to the seat.

"I'm Soapy Smith, owner of this establishment and many others in this fine city of ours here. You Audie DeVine?"

Audie hid his surprise.

"I am."

"You one of the DeVine brothers we keep hearing so much about? The minstrel?"

Audie just nodded his head. He was beginning to see where this was going.

"I thought so. You look just like the drawing."

"What drawing?"

Soapy motioned to the door, and one of his men stepped out of the room.

"You's looking for work here? You and your brother? I've got three saloons could use your skills a few nights a week."

"How do you know who I am?"

"You's a famous man. You and your brother."

Just then the guard came back holding a large piece of yellowed, crumpled paper. It was a rough drawing of Audie and Shane. It looked like a wanted poster, but there were no words on it.

The man held it up for Audie to see.

"Like I said, you's famous."

Soapy spoke with a New York accent that threw Audie off a bit. He'd never heard it before and had no idea where these men hailed from. Audie tried to hide his awe that someone this far west would know them.

"We're looking for work if the pay is right."

Soapy laughed. The three men working for him laughed with him.

"Well, friend, pay ain't a problem. I'm sure we can figure something out," Soapy assured him.

Audie kept staring at the drawing. He'd never seen himself on paper before. It looked like a sinister version of him and Shane. He didn't know what to think.

"You keep that. We'll call it a down payment."

The guard rolled up the poster and handed it to Audie.

"My brother is out there right now looking for saloons to play. What if he happens to find a better offer from someone else?"

Soapy and his men laughed again.

"You won't."

"Why's that?" Audie asked.

Soapy leaned forward over the desk and stared at Audie.

"'Cause I'll kill the cocksucker who tries to outbid me. I don't like competition."

Audie looked at him to see if his threat was just talk. He could tell by the man's eyes it wasn't.

"Look, you and your brother and those two other fellows get settled in for a couple of days. You need anything, you ask my man Alfonzo here."

Soapy pointed to the man who had led them into the office.

"He'll make sure you get what you need. We'll talk after that and come to an agreement on the terms."

Audie nodded. He wasn't quite sure how to handle this man yet.

"And another thing. Don't stay at the Carter House. Carter's a lowlife, and I wouldn't let my dog bed down in one of his rooms. Tell your crew to head over to the Tremont House. It's my establishment, and it's much finer than that shithole Carter charges people to stay in. You need a woman? We got that, too. Whatever you want." He spoke nonchalantly, as if anything were as easy as the asking for him to acquire.

Audie stood. Soapy stood in response. He stuck out his hand to shake Audie's.

"You'll find I'm a good man to know, Mr. DeVine, but I'm a bastard to be on the bad side of." He smiled a toothy smile. "Let me be your friend."

Audie shook his hand and turned to leave.

"Oh, Alfonzo. Make sure you get his money back from that Carter scum over there."

Alfonzo nodded and led Audie out.

Audie quickly found Moses and told him to pack everything, they were moving to Soapy's. He was still a little upset with Moses over their previous conversation.

"What was that all about?" Moses asked.

"Nothing to worry over," Audie offered coldly.

They spotted Smyth and Shane in a saloon on the way to their new accommodations. Neither had done anything but have a few drinks.

"We're moving over to a new place," Audie informed them. "It ain't final, but I may have found a place for us to play."

"Well, shit, Audie. I guess that means I'll have to sit here and get drunk instead of going out looking for work," Shane said.

"If drunk is what you want, drunk is what you'll get," Smyth announced. "Barkeep! Bring me and my partner here a whole damn bottle of elbow bender!"

"Get it out of your system, Shane. I ain't dealing with your ass being hungover again every day," Audie scolded.

"Go screw your horse, Audie," Shane replied.

Audie gave him a look that would have felt like a punch to anyone but his brother and left.

Moses told them where they could find their new place of lodging and followed Audie out. They went to unload their belongings while the other two finished what they started.

CHAPTER 33

Shane and Smyth spent the night drinking. Smyth bought the comfort of a woman and was gone just fifteen minutes before he returned to drink more with Shane.

"Hell, Smyth. You weren't gone long enough to get your pants off," Shane mused.

Smyth laughed. "It don't take long when you ain't had none in a month. And I ain't looking to pleasure no whore with half a night of pumping."

Shane smiled and shook his head. Smyth kept him laughing the rest of the night.

The next morning came to Shane like a hammer pounding on the inside of his head.

"Get up," was Audie's only greeting. He stood by Shane's bed waiting for him to come to his senses. Shane cracked open his eyes to a blurry room, then instantly closed them again.

"Get your ass up!" Audie demanded.

"Alright," Shane whispered. Just thinking made his head pound. He raised up to sit on the side of the bed. That small movement made Shane wince in pain.

It had been a while since he'd been drunk.

"We need to figure out who this Soapy is today. He's offering us a job. I'm gonna need you sharp, so get your ass up and let's get some coffee down your gullet."

"Alright, Audie, alright." Shane rose, stumbled, and started getting dressed.

"You said you weren't gonna do this anymore. I don't want to have to carry a drunk again," Audie scolded.

"Audie, calm yourself down. It was one night. I ain't gonna drink a river like I did back in Wichita. One night don't hurt. You oughta let yourself unhinge every now and then. You walk around half the time like you've got a wolf nipping at your hind end."

Audie drew back a fist to hit him, but Shane put his head in his hands to rub some of the hangover out of his eyes. He never saw Audie pull back to hit him or unclench his fist.

"Get dressed." And with that, Audie went and stood outside the door.

When Shane emerged, he had his clothes on. He looked like he'd had the hell beat out of him and he had everything but the bruises to prove it. Audie looked at him in disgust, and the two made their way to a restaurant for breakfast and coffee.

"Now, who's this Soapy again?" Shane asked as he dipped a biscuit in gravy.

"He's definitely a big deal around here. He owns a few saloons and other establishments and has men guarding him, to boot. Crooked but honest about it. He seemed like the kind of man who means business."

"And why are we getting in business with a guy like that? Sounds like a trouble we don't need," Shane reasoned.

"I don't know yet. Maybe we won't. I need to figure it out."

Audie pulled the drawing out of a pocket inside his vest and unrolled it.

The DeVine brothers in black and white on a twelve-by-twelve parchment.

"Hell's bells! That's us!" Shane exclaimed.

"Yep. He knew me just by sight. Evidently we're getting a little recognition for our singing."

"I wonder why Smyth ain't in it?" Shane asked.

"Maybe it was made before he came along."

They finished their breakfast without any more words. Shane couldn't stop looking at the picture.

"You the colored with those DeVine boys?"

Moses was out in front of Soapy's gambling house when a very small man in a finely tailored suit posed the question to him.

"Yessuh."

"Soapy Smith wants you to move your horses over to his stable. Said it's on the house."

"Well, I need ta talk ta Audie for I do anything like that."

"No, ya don't. It's Soapy's orders, so talkin' ain't necessary."

Moses hesitated to speak. Audie mentioned Soapy last night but said he wasn't sure about him yet.

"I need ta talk ta Audie."

"Now, lookie here, boy, I ain't got time for—"

"What's going on, Moses?" Just then Smyth walked up, staring at the other man.

Smyth didn't wait for Moses to answer.

"Hidee. I'm Smyth, Smyth Hoxie."

He stuck out his hand to shake the little man's.

"I's telling your friend here, Soapy Smith wants him to move his horses to Soapy's own personal stable, free o' charge. It's an honor, but this one wants to go have a committee about it."

"Well, that's because Moses here don't make any decisions. Me and the DeVine brothers do." Smyth knew the man wouldn't have respect for Moses, so he figured it was best to make himself the target.

The small man pointed a stubby finger up at Smyth's chest and started to talk.

"Now, you listen to me . . ."

"Where's this stable again? We'll be sure and head right over. I just need Moses here to help me with something first."

The man's composure relaxed, and he smiled.

"It's about three blocks down that a way."

He pointed down the row of buildings on Blake Street.

"Ya can't miss it. White stables with Soapy's name on the front."

"Well, I thank you and Soapy for your hospitality, friend. We'll be right along once we get a few things in order. What was your name again?" Smyth asked.

The man just kept smiling at Smyth.

"I never gave it to you the first time. It's Santino, Tommy Santino. Don't forget it."

"You can bet I won't. We'll be seeing you around."

Smyth stuck out his hand again to shake Tommy's.

Tommy waited just long enough for it to be awkward.

"Don't." He smirked as he finally shook Smyth's hand.

"Where's Audie?" Smyth asked Moses as they watched the little man walk away.

"Him and Shane gettin' a bite ta eat right over there."

Smyth headed in the direction Moses had pointed.

Smyth spotted the brothers and ran up to the table.

"That Soapy fellow you were talking about last night, he wants y'all to move the horses to his stable free of charge. One of his henchmen was about to light into Moses until I stepped in."

Smyth recited the conversation he'd had with Tommy.

"Alright," Audie said. "Come on, Shane. Smyth, go get Moses and wait in your room till we come back."

Smyth took off out the door.

Audie stood up to leave, and Shane chugged the rest of his cup of coffee and followed. They made their way over to the gambling house where Audie had met Soapy the night before.

"This guy's trying to corner us for some reason. You wearing your knives?"

"Always," Shane informed him.

"These boys ain't easy prey, so be on your guard. I would imagine they're wearing heat so look out for it."

Shane still had last night's fuzzy on his brain, but his adrenaline was quickly washing it away.

They burst in the doors of the building like two bats flying into hell. The two henchmen on guard in the foyer weren't there, maybe because it was still early in the day. Every gambler in the room stopped what they were doing and eyed the brothers. A giant of a man appeared from the left, hoping to escort Audie and Shane back outside, but Audie quickly broke his nose with an elbow to the face.

"Argh! You broke my nose, you raggedy bastard!" the man protested nasally.

The boys were almost to Soapy's door when another man tried to use a pistol to persuade the brothers to leave. Shane sent a blade right through his hand. The man looked at his hand and screamed, holding it in disbelief as if it were a diamond that had shattered. Shane retrieved the knife, wiping it off on the man's suit and they made their way into Soapy's office.

The two men guarding his desk had pistols drawn and pointed at Audie and Shane when they walked in. Soapy was sitting at the desk, calm and smoking a cigarette.

The brothers stopped. Audie never took his eyes off of Soapy. Shane watched the gunmen for any sign they were going to peel off a round.

"Why are you trying to put a leash on us?"

"Most people don't look a gift horse in the mouth." Soapy chuckled. "Then again, most people don't have the balls to crash into my office like a locomotive."

Audie just stared at him. Soapy didn't look away. Both men knew the other was not afraid.

"At ease, boys." Soapy called off his protectors. The men all slowly put down their pistols.

Soapy leaned back in his chair and put his feet up on his desk.

"I see something I want, I go after it. You boys carry quite the reputation as entertainers. I'm a man who likes to have the best. I do what I need to do to get it."

"Your man, Tommy. He was about to get rough with our partner this morning over where we board our horses. Not the right way to get on our good side," Audie informed him.

Soapy and his men all chuckled.

"What's so damn funny?" Shane demanded to know.

"Oh, we ain't laughing at you. Tommy, the one who was talking to your friend, he gets his ass hairs up easy is all. Mother Nature didn't bless him with any stature, so he tries to throw a little weight around. He just acts tough."

Audie and Shane softened just slightly at this explanation.

"Listen, I can sees you boys don't take no shit. I don't take no shit, either, so I respect that in a man. I want you working for me. You let me know what you want, and I'll make it happen."

Audie stood there a minute, then bent the front of his hat down in a parting gesture to Soapy. He looked at all the guards in the room and turned to go.

"Hey, I'm sure that yellow-assed Tabor is gonna come slithering around ya trying to get you in one of his saloons, but you's much better off working for me. He's a politician. That's the lowest form of human God created on this earth. You know that? It's in the Bible."

"Where at in the Bible?" Audie quizzed.

"I dunno. Proverbials or Deuteronomous or something."

Audie smiled. "And what are you?"

Soapy laughed. "I'm a criminal."

"At least you're honest," Shane said.

"We'll talk soon," Audie told them.

He and Shane left the office. The man who'd tried for his pistol was sitting in a chair, a lady washing the knife wound on his hand. The man who'd gotten an elbow from Audie was sitting beside him, head back to stop the bleeding. Most of the gamblers stared as they left, slack-jawed that these men had charged into Soapy's office and walked out alive, wondering who they might be.

"Well, that was fun," Shane said as they walked out the front door.

"You sure you wanna get in business with a man like that, Audie?" Shane asked. The brothers had walked across the street and were leaning against a building with a sign that read, "Denver Apothecary."

"No, but I'm sure I don't want to get in business with a politician."

"Yeah, but this man, he seems like he'd kill you as soon as look at you."

"He didn't kill us today," Audie pointed out.

Shane thought about it.

"Maybe we were lucky."

"No, he likes us. He's not used to dealing with someone he can't scare. We threw him for a loop."

"We ain't talked money with him yet," Shane said.

"Yeah, I'll do that. I think we've shown him he can't short us."

"Hell, Audie. I just want to get back to playing. I know Smyth does, too."

"Alright. I'll see if I can squeeze a fair amount of coin from him."

"Well, don't go talk to him now," Shane reasoned. "Let him sweat a little, wait on us to make up our minds."

Audie smiled and punched Shane in the arm.

"Shit, brother. I can't believe you still have any wits after all that whiskey last night," he joked.

"Eat shit," Shane said as he rubbed his arm.

CHAPTER 34

The boys spent the next couple of days rehearsing and getting into their rhythm again. They'd ride outside of town where they wouldn't attract a crowd and play for the better part of the day. Moses tried to make himself useful by getting lunch or doing any little errand he could think of. Smyth would drink his way through the nights, but Shane stayed true to his word. He'd bend an elbow for a bit but would head to his room before he got too far out in the ether.

Audie purchased a new set of catgut strings from the Due West General Store. It was the first new strings he'd put on his guitar since they began playing saloons a few months ago. He was amazed at how that small improvement made his guitar come to life.

Shane bought a new snare from the General Store. It was the first drum he used that hadn't been made by the Apache or himself. He loved that he could change the pitch of the instrument by stretching the skin with the tuning keys on the side of the drum. It was a massive change over buffalo skin stretched over a hollowed-out tree piece.

Everyone got the lay of the town and started feeling familiar with it. After three days of exploring and getting settled, Audie went to

215

Soapy Smith's office to talk pay. This time he entered without all the fanfare.

Just inside the door, a man stood guard with a bruised nose twice its normal size, a reminder of Audie's last visit. He let Audie see the malice in his face before he led him back to Soapy's office. Audie smiled and tipped his hat.

The guard knocked twice, then once. He heard Soapy bark, "Come in!" and opened the door for Audie.

"Glad to see you again, Mr. DeVine. Have a seat."

As usual, there were two men guarding the desk. They gave Audie a look to let him know there better not be any trouble. He just sat and smiled back.

"How does thirty-five dollars a week sound?" Audie offered.

"Whoa! You haven't even said hello, and you're already reaching in the till. Slow down, man."

"Forty dollars a week," Audie said.

Soapy studied Audie for a minute.

"Boys leave us. I want to talk to this man alone," Soapy demanded. The two men looked at him confused and began to protest.

"Leave," was all Soapy offered them. They gave Audie a menacing look and headed out the door.

"I feel like we got off on the wrong foot, Audie. Can I call you Audie?" Soapy questioned.

Audie nodded his head yes.

"Let me reintroduce myself to you. I'm Soapy Smith. I run this town. You need something done, I'm a man who can get it done. My friends are kings and princes here. I want you to be my friend, Audie. I like you and your brother. You've got balls, a thing in short supply in this world. What kind of bastard busts in my office with just a knife and lives to walk out? Shit! It scared me, and I liked it!"

Soapy stood up and walked around the room talking like a preacher working the congregation into a frenzy.

He sauntered around the front of the desk and leaned against it, inches from Audie. He took the lid off of a small metal case, pulled out two cigarettes, and offered one to Audie. Audie accepted. Soapy struck a match, lit his own cigarette, and then Audie's.

"I need men like you around, see. Weakness begets weakness. The scumbags in this town, the politicians, they look for any way to bring down this . . . thing of mine. This thing I built. They've got the law on their side, but I've got a fist!"

Soapy took a small glass sitting on his desk, drank the amber liquid it held, and smashed his fist with the glass inside it on the desk. He held the shards of glass tightly for a few moments, till the blood started oozing through his clenched fingers, then he shook the shattered pieces free from his palm and let the glass fall to the floor. Soapy calmly took a handkerchief from his pocket and wrapped his self-inflicted wounds.

Audie noticed the drops of blood that had landed on his own boots.

Soapy's shoes were clean.

Audie held himself in check. He wouldn't let Soapy see his astonishment.

"The law ain't nearly as strong as fear. You make a man afraid, and he'll throw his laws out the window."

"Everyone can't be made afraid," Audie informed.

Soapy smiled.

"Yeah, that's the man I want on my side."

"Why do you hate the politician so much, this Tabor?"

With renewed vigor, Soapy answered Audie.

"You want to know why? I'll tell you why. If I want something, I take it. I'll wring your damn neck till I get it! But I'm man enough to look you in the eye while I'm choking ya. I'm not a sneak thief looking to pick the pockets of the weak. I like the fight! It's more satisfying if some of the blood spilt's my own."

Soapy looked at his bloody hand and smiled as he was talking.

"Horace Tabor. He bought himself the mayorship so he could hide behind the law, but he's as crooked as any man on this earth. He'll drain a weak man of his last nickel all for the cause of the greater good!"

Soapy lifted his hands, palms up in the air for effect while he spoke.

"Oh, he's a public servant. Unselfish sacrifice for the betterment of this city. Horseshit! He lines his pockets just like I do. I hate him because he's chicken shit. I hate him because he's a hypocrite. I hate his liver and guts because so many blind folks here think he's a saint. I hate him because he hides his horns!"

Audie soaked in Soapy's sermon. He'd made a hell of an argument against Tabor.

"I have no love for government myself," Audie spoke.

Soapy took a step forward and slapped Audie hard on the back.

"Ha! I could tell you ain't no sheep!" Soapy took a drag off of his cigarette. "You and me, we're gonna make a good team."

"It's me and my brother and two other men. That's who you'll be paying."

"Of course. You take care of your own, like a real man," Soapy said as he blew out a cloud of smoke.

"Forty dollars, Soapy," Audie calmly demanded.

Soapy looked at him for a minute with a mischievous grin.

"Forty it is. Every week. But your music better be as good as they say it is."

"It is." Audie stood and stuck out his hand to shake Soapy's uninjured one.

"You's can start at my place the Chicago whenever you feel like getting your feet wet. It's on Front and Cherry. Go by and check it out tomorrow. It's a real nice room. I'll tell the boys you're coming."

He let go of Audie's hand.

"One more thing. If that snake Tabor comes crawling around trying to recruit you, I wanna know. He's tried to scalp my people before."

"Like I said, I don't like the government either. You don't have anything to worry about," Audie assured him.

He nodded and motioned toward the door and walked Audie out. On their way to the front door, Soapy noticed the guard with the swollen nose giving Audie the evil eye. Soapy walked up to him and squeezed his nose between two fingers, causing the man to howl in pain.

"Stop your sourpussing, Arny. He beat ya fair and square. Maybe I need to give him your job, you big dandelion."

Arny covered his nose and whimpered like a child.

Audie left and went to find the others.

"I like him. He's a bad man, but he makes no bones about it. I'll take a crook that tells me he's a crook over a self-proclaimed do-gooder any day," Audie told Shane, Moses, and Smyth.

"Well, hell yeah, boys. We're back in business. When do we start?" Smyth inquired.

"Tomorrow night at Soapy's saloon. We didn't talk time, but I say around eight is as good a time as any."

Moses was quiet as he and Audie walked to get dinner.

"You don't think we should work for this guy?" Audie asked, already knowing the answer.

Moses tried to dodge the question. "I's so hungry I could eat a horse."

"Come on, Moses. Answer me," Audie pushed.

"Ain't no bidness'a mine."

"But you don't."

Moses stopped and looked Audie in the eye.

"No, I don't."

"Why do you stay with us, Moses? Drunks, murderers, and heathens. It's got to be a torture to your soul."

"I stay 'cause you my friend." He held his eyes on Audie's.

That took Audie by surprise. He was quiet for a moment and let the weight of Moses' kindness sink in.

"One day we'll be wanted men, Moses. We can't keep this up

forever. You don't need that again. I went to the spirit world back a few days ago when we made camp down south. They told me . . . they told me some things. You should get away from us before the hammer comes down."

"So you still plan on killin' more folks?"

Audie started walking and went a few steps without answering. "Many more."

"It don't have ta be that way, Audie! A bullet can stay in the chamber as easy as it can leave it."

They came to the restaurant.

"Let's get a steak." Audie ended the conversation there.

CHAPTER 35

The first night on a new stage brought familiar nerves back to Audie and Shane. It had taken a while, but the brothers eventually learned how to use those nerves in their favor. The songs always had more energy when they were a little on edge. It felt like lightning running through them when the crowd was all in and they were locked into a groove. Those moments were like a drug.

Smyth, on the other hand, didn't have an ounce of nervous in him when he played. He coaxed the music out of his fiddle like it was a genie in a bottle.

They started the night off with a song Audie had written called "Last Train to Heaven." The crowd hushed about halfway through and all eyes were on them. When Smyth broke into a solo, everyone took a break from drinking and the saloon erupted in whistles, claps, and shouts.

The rest of the night was much of the same. Word spread around town that the famous DeVine Devils were at the Chicago, and all other saloons in the vicinity emptied. People turned away at the door were crowding outside in the streets for a listen.

Soapy sat in the back at his private table, flanked by a voluptuous blonde on his right and a petite brunette on his left. He had his two faithful guards standing watch. Soapy was ecstatic with the night's performance. He couldn't believe the sounds coming from the stage, and he'd never seen his saloon so alive.

Audie knew Soapy would be okay paying them whatever they wanted now.

They brought down the house until midnight. Audie could barely get out the door for men wanting to talk or women wanting to be with him. Shane and Smyth stayed behind to take advantage of their admirers.

Audie finally made his way through the crowd, down the street, and over to Soapy's gambling house where they'd been given rooms. He had no sooner taken his boots and shirt off when he heard a knock at the door.

When he opened the door, Soapy was standing there with the two women who'd been sitting with him at his table.

"I've got a present for you, friend. Call it a bonus for job well done," Soapy touted.

Audie always tried to keep his lust in check, but he was still electrified from the night's performance and these two women were gorgeous. He looked at them, trying to decide which one he wanted.

Soapy could see his indecision and jumped to relieve it.

"Oh, you don't have to decide between them! They're both yours. You earned it."

The blonde walked up close to Audie and put her mouth on his. The brunette followed suit and waited her turn for a kiss. Soapy laughed in joy at the scene and slowly closed the door.

It was dawn before Audie got any sleep.

"Shit fire and save matches, boys! We hit this town like a cannonball last night! I could've pecker-stabbed any girl in that whole damn saloon!" Smyth announced.

He and Shane had both enjoyed female companionship last night.

"Yep, Moses, you should have seen it. The place couldn't get enough last night. Especially the ladies."

"Oh, I heard. Y'all was tearin' it up, fo' sure."

It was noon and they were getting lunch at Soapy's restaurant across from where they had wowed everyone the night before. The sun was bright enough to hurt Smyth's whiskey-dimmed eyes as they made their way under it. It was their first meal of the day. Audie was the last to join the group.

"You just getting up? That ain't like you, Audie. You hit the rotgut too hard last night?" Smyth inquired.

"No." Audie offered no more information.

"Wait a minute! Did you play hide the meat stick with some lucky lady last night?" Smyth asked with such excitement that the table had to laugh.

Audie chuckled, too, but still didn't give up details.

"You did! You son of a bitch! Good for you! A man needs to get it out of his system once in a while."

Everyone continued laughing.

"You're next, Moses. I'm gonna get you pecker-pleasured even if I have to give it up myself one night!"

Moses just chuckled and shook his head.

Lozen wiped her mouth with the back of her hand and made her way slowly from behind the cactus back to her tent. She had snuck away for the third time in as many mornings, hiding the nausea and the emptying of her stomach, hoping no one would see her.

But Onawa, the woman who had always tried to look after Lozen, had noticed her stealing away every morning around the same time and had seen the pale in her face.

"Do you know why you are sick?" Onawa asked.

"I'm not sick!" Lozen defied.

"You are with child."

Lozen knew this inside but hadn't dared to speak the words out loud. It melted her defiance to hear them from Onawa. She had always been kind to Lozen. Almost like a mother, though Lozen would never speak that way.

"I know," Lozen admitted.

"Who is the father of this child?" Onawa intended to make sure whoever it was took responsibility.

"He is not here."

Onawa saw the tears coming before they rolled down Lozen's cheek. She put her wrinkled hand on Lozen's arm to comfort her. Lozen let herself fall into Onawa's arms and cried.

Lozen didn't like feeling weak, but at the moment, she was thankful for someone to lean on. She was glad not to carry the secret alone.

"I can't have a child. I'm a warrior! How am I to raise a child?"

"Hush, child," Onawa whispered. "You don't need to worry about that right now."

Lozen sobbed softly in her arms. It had been a month and half since she'd been with Shane. She wasn't showing yet with her shirt on, but she knew it wouldn't be long.

Thomas had left Wichita with little information regarding the case of the twelve dead soldiers. He had determined it wasn't Indians responsible for the attack but not much else. He'd spent two months digging for clues, and to have this little to show for his effort was torture for him. Until recently, he wasn't a man accustomed to coming up short on the job. It weighed on him tremendously as he rode the trail east, back to Adalina.

He arrived home, tired and frustrated. Adalina's sweet disposition would be enough to lure him away from the aggravation of work for a short while.

She was outside with a broom beating a rug on the front porch when he rode up. Thomas paused for a few moments, about fifty yards away, to take in the scene. She didn't yet see him. Her hair was swept up in a loose bun with tendrils that fell against her high cheekbones. There were streaks of gray that he hadn't noticed before creeping into the brown. He thought her more beautiful the longer they were together, and he never tired of coming home to her.

Adalina wasn't wearing the heavy wool coat he expected her to be in, and he could see she was cold. Winter was on the way out, but spring was still hiding in the gloomy skies of March. Nevertheless, Thomas was eager for them both to warm themselves by the fire inside their house.

Adalina looked up to see him watching her and let out a gleeful yell. He dismounted and met her on the porch. She greeted Thomas with a kiss that made his hard ride home instantly fade from his mind. They walked inside and settled into a chair in front of the fire with her sitting on his lap.

"How was the trip? Did Agent Thorntree remove yet another villain from the midst of the people?"

"Ugh, not exactly. Let's not talk about that."

She was surprised he had steered away from the conversation.

"What happened here while I was gone? Anything of note?"

"No, it's business as usual here in Eminence. Not much in the way of excitement, and that's how I like it."

"Good, good. I have some interesting news to tell you, Adalina. I had the pleasure of meeting your sons, Audie and Shane, while I was in Wichita."

"What? You met my boys?" Adalina responded, incredulous. She slapped him on the chest before she thought about what she was doing.

"They were playing music at a saloon there, and I have to say, it was some of the most interesting music I've ever heard."

Adalina was fixated, so Thomas continued excitedly. "And, Adalina, you'd be so proud of your sons. They were the talk of the town. Honestly, your sons are famous!"

She was shocked. It took a moment to take it all in.

She thought of how Azariah used to play his guitar and sing when her sons were small.

"What? Really? I can't believe that! I want to see them!"

"They have another fellow playing with them as well. Smyth Hoxie, I believe his name is. A fiddler. And I must say, he is a sight to behold. The whole thing is really . . . a new experience. I don't even know how to describe it."

"What do they call themselves?" Adalina asked.

Thomas hesitated. He knew she wouldn't like the name.

"DeVine Devils," he said with a chuckle to lighten the blow of it.

"DeVine Devils?" She held her hand over her mouth in shock.

"But why would they call themselves devils? That's. . . that's irreverent! Their father would roll over in his grave!"

Thomas agreed but tried to downplay it for her sake.

"Now, Adalina, I think you're overreacting a bit. I believe it's just for effect. There's nothing devilish about them. They were very pleasant," Thomas stretched.

Actually, he had more than a little worry about them himself, but he wasn't about to let on to Adalina. He saw no good that could come from burdening her with his concern.

Adalina kept on.

"Still, that's not a name any Christian should carry. It's those damn heathen Apache that did this! They killed Azariah and now they've tainted my sons! I hope the government wipes them off of the face of this land!"

She put her head down and shook it. Adalina felt guilty even before the words were uttered, but she couldn't stop herself. Azariah would have disapproved of the boys' musical name, but he would have been more livid and wounded at the words she spoke against his beloved people.

"I'm sorry you're upset, sweetness. Don't get too worked up about it. You would be proud of them if you saw them perform. They are masters at what they do. Why, I wouldn't be surprised if the name DeVine isn't spoken in every civilized household in these states in a few years!"

This did little to assuage her. She turned her gaze from Thomas to a small frame sitting above the fireplace. It was a yellowed photo of the boys about a year before they left with Azariah. There had been a photographer at the fair that year, and she remembered Audie begging his father to go. The boys had heard tales of the spectacles to behold at such a gathering, and Adalina and Azariah reluctantly took them one sunny Saturday afternoon. It ended up being one of her favorite memories of her family, and she treasured that photo.

Though she loved Thomas, she missed those days. She still felt the gaping hole in her chest that had grown from their absence for over ten years, a hole that even their return could never fill. It crossed her mind that they could be the devil himself and she would still care for them.

A mother's love knows no fences.

Adalina put her head on Thomas's shoulder and squeezed him a little tighter. He stroked her soft hair, and she softened as she settled into his embrace. He loved her deeply and wished he could guard her from all the worry this world had to offer.

But he knew he couldn't.

That night Thomas went to bed early. He was road-weary and could barely keep his eyes open. Adalina kissed him good night and remained by the fire to warm herself.

She noticed the box labeled *Pinkerton* on the table next to the chair she sat in and picked it up to examine it. She'd seen these boxes before, for other cases Thomas had worked on. He'd never forbidden her access to them, and he trusted her with even his most important possessions. Thomas often shared private details about a case in celebration or consternation, and it was curious that he hadn't done so tonight.

When she opened the box, she recognized the necklace immediately. She'd seen it on Audie just a few months back, and a lifetime couldn't erase the memory of the first man she'd loved who'd worn this talisman with such pride.

Adalina thought of the young boys who revered him and followed him despite her protests, and who were now men she hardly knew. A feeling of dread and then deep worry and sadness swelled in her body. She began to cry, weeping softly enough so Thomas wouldn't hear her.

Adalina held on to the necklace and prayed, but she didn't know what for.

The boys settled into a routine again in Denver. Nightly, they pushed the limits during the shows. There were nights that Soapy's men had to come in and start busting skulls to calm the crowd. The DeVine Devils' music had become more intense, and it could now pull the violence out of a crowd. It was hedonistic. No one had witnessed this kind of thing before, and it was a sensation.

Women would expose their breasts to the band and dance provocatively in front of the stage. This caused more than a handful of fights among the men. Smyth had taken to jumping off the three-foot-high stage and walking through the crowd playing his solos. He learned to hold out for a few songs and make the crowd beg for it before he did.

Soapy had his men expand the stage by six feet on either side. The boys had brought in four old whiskey barrels, and each night they lit fires in them, giving their faces an eerie glow when they were playing.

Audie, Shane, and Smyth fell into the trappings of being famous. The band couldn't walk the streets anymore without mobs of people gathering around them trying to get close. Audie didn't love all the attention, but it's impossible for that kind of adoration not to go to a man's head. He struggled with people loving him. He didn't even like himself.

Smyth, on the other hand, took to the attention like a fish to water. He'd longed for this his whole life. The women, the free drink, and the sheer worship from the people made him feel like the god he'd always wanted to be.

Shane fell somewhere in the middle. He took advantage of his status, but at times he had to pull away. He had stopped getting drunk during the shows and in saloons, but he would occasionally take a bottle up to his room by himself. He'd empty it as he lamented Lozen. He was with other women, but he never could get her words out of his head.

I have been with no other, he'd hear her say. He felt guilty and angry and lonely, and it was hard to tell which one would win most nights.

Moses kept himself busy taking care of the boys' errands. He worried about them. At night, while the boys played, he stayed in his room praying for their souls. He loved Audie and Shane. He didn't lecture them, but Audie and Shane knew he didn't approve of their lifestyles.

Sometimes he thought of his sweet Phibe and missed the child he never knew. He never spoke of these thoughts, but they held to him like the whip scars on his back.

He had started carrying a .45 pistol, much to his own displeasure. Audie and he had argued on more than one occasion about it. Audie had finally won him over by convincing him he needed Moses to go heels to protect him and his brother. He knew Moses wouldn't kill a man to defend himself, but he might to defend a friend. Audie felt guilty for using Moses' good-heartedness against him, but justified it for the sake of Moses being armed. He knew the pistol alone would scare more than half of the would-be attackers.

Soapy was making money hand over fist. He had cut new deals with the railroad to bring more liquor and beer. Former supply lines had failed to satisfy the masses of people who were flocking to see the DeVine Devils. He was thinking of expanding the bar. They could squeeze in roughly three hundred and fifty people, but he knew they'd pack twice that many if they had the room. There were people traveling to Denver from as far as Tennessee just to see the show. The demand for the boys far outweighed what he could provide in that space now.

Nights came and went, and months passed. On the surface, it seemed all was well in the world.

CHAPTER 36

"We could pass a curfew into law. Ten o'clock. That would cut out a chunk of his profits."

"You're a fool, Binkley. That would cut into our profit, too, which is already dwindled down to nothing, you small-witted twit!" Horace berated.

Horace Tabor's saloon had lost the majority of its business since Audie and Shane had come to town and set up shop at the Chicago. He was livid about it, and Binkley, his advisor, was coming up with nothing in the way of a solution.

It was a snowy Tuesday morning, and Horace was in his office with Binkley and his eldest son, James. The tension in the room caused a chill more uncomfortable than the one outside. Horace shifted in his polished leather chair and swung around to address his audience. The embroidered drapes were pulled open, but the sunlight did little to brighten the room.

"That twat Soapy has got me by the short hairs on this one. I want to cut his grubby little hand off!"

"Father, we could buy the DeVine Devils. Offer them more than Soapy. It would cost a pretty penny, but it would be like robbing his bank."

Horace stroked his pristinely manicured beard and thought about his son's words for a minute. Horace was a handsome enough fellow, and the years had failed to add the weight that so many others in their sixties had acquired. His gray hair laid as perfect as a toupee on his head.

"You know what your problem is, Binkley?" Horace asked.

"What's that, Mayor?"

"You came from weak seed. James can outthink you at any turn. Maybe I should just pay him double and throw your dainty ass out on the street," Horace threatened.

"But. . . I've always been loyal. . . that would be a mist—" He wrung his clammy hands like he was trying to rid them of some unwanted glue.

"Don't be such a pisspot, Binkley. It makes you seem even more like a girly man than you are," said Horace.

"Go to this Audie. I want a meeting with him. Tell him we can offer him anything he wants. Tell him he's working for a crook. We can give him legitimacy."

"Yes, Mayor. By myself?" Binkley asked.

"Yes, by yourself! What do you think's gonna happen? This man is gonna sing you death?"

Binkley didn't extend the conversation further. He hurried out the door.

"What's that little guy's name? The one who works for Soapy? The short one who acts ten feet tall?" Horace asked James.

"I'll find out. Why?" James asked.

"Let's hire him away, too. Appeal to his fragile ego. Tell him we see his potential, and we don't think Soapy is using him to his fullest. If we can get him, he may be able to give us some insight into Soapy's operation. I'm sick of Smith! Our pockets would be full, and our sleep would be sweeter if that son of a bitch wasn't here."

"Why don't we just kill the bastard?"

James was almost thirty and the spitting image of his father. All he lacked was the gray hair, the wisdom, and the power.

"It's not that simple for a public servant, James. Appearance is crucial."

James left. A young woman named Deirdre who worked as the mayor's secretary brought in that day's copy of *the Rocky Mountain News* and turned to leave.

The front-page story read, "DeVine Devils Raise Hell in Denver." Tabor scowled and flung the paper across the room.

"Deirdre!" he called her back in.

When she returned, he motioned for her to shut the door and stood to unbuckle his pants.

She reluctantly did as she was told.

"Audie DeVine?" a man asked timidly.

Audie looked up from his lunch to see an unthreatening man standing next to his table. He was at Colorado Cuts, a restaurant just outside of the heart of Denver. He loved the steak there.

"I'm eating, mister."

"If I could just have a moment of your time, sir. I have a business offer for you."

Audie studied the man and noticed he was dressed like the businessmen who walked around the city. He motioned for the man to sit next to him.

The man sat quickly and wasted no time telling Audie of the mayor's proposal. His weak disposition and nervousness almost made Audie scowl.

"My name is Chadwick Binkley, sir, and I work for the mayor of Denver, Mr. Horace Tabor. He's taken notice of the talent of you and your musical partners. He owns his own saloon here in Denver, and your draw at Soapy's has greatly diminished his business. Mr. Tabor would be willing to offer you double what Soapy Smith is paying you for your services."

Binkley waited for a response from Audie, but Audie only stared at him stone-faced, unwilling to show the stranger a response.

Binkley sat on his hands to hide the shake in them. "Sir, Soapy is a criminal," he continued. "Mr. Tabor is a politician and a legitimate business man. Working for him brings with it all the perks and amenities of the highest office in the city of Denver."

Audie waited a few more excruciating seconds to answer.

"Legitimate, huh? And what are the perks of working for the mayor?"

"Legality, Mr. DeVine, and unlimited access to any business here in our great city."

"Except Soapy's," Audie added.

"Soapy is a deviant, sir, with no other end than being locked away in a jail cell someday."

"I see." Audie paused and took a bite of his steak. When he finished chewing, he took a swig of his beer and looked Binkley in the eye.

"Well, you can tell Mayor Tabor that I'm worse than a deviant. I'm a devil. I'd rather bed down with the swine in the pens at the end of the street here than do business with him."

Binkley looked at Audie with surprise and took a moment to respond.

"Uh, s-sir, you're making a mistake. Soapy isn't long for freedom, and when he's locked up, Mr. Tabor's saloon will be the only one in this town. There's a great chance this offer to you will not stand once that happens."

Audie laughed.

"There's other towns, mister."

Binkley stood to leave. Audie's demeanor had made his usually timid spirit extremely nervous.

"Well, please, just think about it. I can be reached at the mayor's office any time of day." And with that, Binkley anxiously headed for the door.

As he was leaving, Deirdre was walking in to pick up lunch for Mr. Tabor. Binkley nervously tipped his hat to her and went on his way.

Audie noticed the woman from across the room. She was stunning. Her ink-black hair was up except for a strand she brushed away from her pouty lips as she spoke to the server, giving him her order. She was wearing a light-blue dress that was modest but showed the curve of her hips, clinging to them just enough to make a man imagine what was underneath. Deirdre looked to be of Italian heritage, her olive skin a smooth and silky shade.

Deirdre saw Audie staring at her from a table in the center of the dining room and blushed when she realized who he was. She took in his ruggedness, his long black hair, and his well-kept beard. The hazel of his eyes felt like a sunset sky she wanted to fly off into. She'd been to Soapy's a couple of times when they played and was as intrigued with them as anyone else, but she'd never seen him when he wasn't entertaining a room full of drunken fans.

Audie wasn't one to initiate conversation, but he couldn't help himself. She drew him in like a siren does a sailor. He stood up from his table and walked to where she was standing at the bar.

"Hello, I'm Audie—"

"DeVine." She smiled and said, "I've seen you sing. I know who you are."

He'd forgotten he was famous until she reminded him. They smiled a greeting.

"Would you like to have lunch with me? Could I buy you something to eat?" He shocked even himself with the invitation.

"Oh, I'd like to, but I'm on an errand to get lunch for my boss. I can't stay."

"Well, some other time. I hope to see you around here soon."

"I hope so, too, Mr. DeVine."

"Audie. Call me Audie."

"Audie. I'll call you Audie."

"What can I call you?" he asked.

She laughed, a warm trill that matched her demeanor.

"Oh! Where are my manners? I'm Deirdre, Deirdre Bellafonte."

"What a beautiful name. It suits you," Audie said with complete honesty.

Deirdre laughed and blushed again.

"I bet I'm not the first girl you've said that to," she flirted.

"Maybe not, but you might be the last."

Deirdre was surprised by his boldness. She wasn't expecting that reply, and she was more surprised to think he might actually mean it. Just then the food arrived for Mr. Tabor.

"On Mayor Tabor's tab, please," Deirdre said.

"Yes, ma'am," the server replied.

"You work for Tabor?" Audie had sour in his words when he spoke this time.

"Yes." She put her head down when she answered.

Audie tried to hide his disgust.

"You're the second person I've met today that works for him. A man named Binkley was just here interrupting my lunch."

"I'm sorry," she said.

"For what?"

"That you met Binkley. He's awful." Deirdre smiled to let him know she was being playful.

Audie chuckled. "Yes. Yes, he is."

He paused, entertained by the exchange. "Well, I'm sorry for you. You're the one who has to work with him."

She laughed.

"I'm sorry, I need to get Mr. Tabor's food back."

"You apologize a lot."

Deirdre laughed again.

"Goodbye, Mr. DeVine. Audie. Goodbye, Audie."

Audie tipped his hat and watched her leave. She swept the strand of hair away from her face again as she walked away, and Audie thought of pushing that strand aside himself to see her pretty face better.

She was beautiful.

"So, all I'm saying, Mr. Santino, is we think a man like you could hold a lot more sway in this town than an errand boy. Soapy doesn't see your worth. We can pay you more, and you'll work for the city. There's power in that."

Santino leaned back in the high-rise chair in James's office. He quickly realized that when he did so his feet didn't touch the ground, so he leaned forward again.

"What would the responsibilities of this new job be?"

"Well, first, we need a man who knows the inner workings of Soapy's organization. A man who helps us with that information could probably move up the ladder pretty quick in this administration. Who knows? Maybe even alderman someday. I think that just depends on how high you want to climb."

"I'd think you's would be in line to be alderman to your daddy," Santino deducted.

James folded his hands and smiled.

"I work better from the edges," he offered.

He was lying. The wheels were already in motion for him to become alderman next election cycle. This was just raw meat he was throwing to a mutt as a distraction.

"Soapy ain't gonna be happy if I switch sides like that. You know he hates your daddy. You're gonna have to make it worth it," Santino said.

"What would make it worth it to you?" James questioned.

"Fifteen a week. And I want to live in your daddy's hotel across the street there. For free."

James was shocked at how cheap Santino was. He didn't let it show.

"How about seventeen dollars a week and a room on the top floor?"

Santino lost his composure.

"I'm your man!" he declared.

The two shook on it, and James began peppering him with questions about Soapy.

"He called you a deviant, sir, but he said he was a devil. This man has a brutality in his soul. I don't know that you would want to have him in your employ. He seems a nasty fellow."

"Does he?" Tabor asked with distaste. Tabor leaned back and crossed his hands over his flat stomach.

"He talked of sleeping with pigs!" Binkley said as he shuddered at the thought.

"Well, he works for one. I guess sleeping with one isn't too far off."

Binkley looked appalled at the thought. He nervously fingered his thinning hair, smoothing it to one side.

"These DeVine Devils. We need to know what makes them tick. If this man is as vile as you make him sound, there's more to him than just singing in a whiskey well every night."

Tabor moved a piece of paper to his front and center and dipped a pen in ink to sign it. He glanced up to see Binkley staring at him expectantly.

"Now, get out of here so I don't have to see your impish face anymore!"

Binkley stumbled over himself getting up to leave.

Deirdre was eavesdropping just outside and barely made it back to her desk before Binkley came busting through the door.

CHAPTER 37

"When this baby comes, you must find the father and tell him he has a son," Onawa lectured Lozen. "He must know he has blood of his own on this earth."

"I'm hoping for a daughter," Lozen replied. She sat on the hard ground, eyes closed, face turned away.

"It's a son," Onawa said.

"How do you know it's not a girl? And anyway, the father is not the kind of man who wants a child."

"A child changes many things about a person. You yourself will have different feelings once you hold your son in your arms," Onawa wised.

Lozen sighed and raised her head to look at Onawa.

"A child in my arms. I cannot even see a vision of this when I close my eyes."

"You're a warrior, Lozen, a gifted one, but you are still a woman, so you also have the gift of bringing life into this world, not just taking it. You're not immune to nature. We are made a certain way and some things are natural."

Lozen returned to her tent to lie down. Settling into her mat, she rested her hands on her growing stomach. She was seven months along now, and there was no more hiding it.

239

Soapy had recently commandeered a house directly behind his saloon. He built a private fenced-in path for the boys to walk to and from the shows, if they preferred. It had become hard for them to move around the city without being accosted by a throng of folks wanting their time or attention. In the daylight hours, when it was mostly men and women conducting business and running errands, it wasn't as much of an issue, but at night it had become insufferable.

They were only playing five nights a week now and making one hundred dollars a week. Sunday and Monday were their days off. Soapy had fought to keep them on Monday nights, but the band won out. He was making so much money off of their performances that one less night he could live with.

It was Saturday night, usually their grandest of the week, and the three band members were walking the path to the saloon when Audie spotted Deirdre through the fence.

"Y'all start without me tonight. I'll be there in just a bit," Audie informed Smyth and Shane.

"What? That's crazy, Audie! Come on!" Shane said.

Shane had never played without his brother. It was a scary

thought.

Audie paid him no attention. He jumped up to grab the top of the fence, pulled himself up, and swung his body over in one swift move.

"Deirdre!" he called out across the crowd.

She spotted him walking toward her and smiled a little wider than she wanted to.

"Audie. Nice to see you again. I'm on my way to the saloon to see you sing."

"Wonderful! I'm headed there now. Would you like to walk with me?" Audie asked.

"Why, that would be delightful."

Audie offered her his arm and she accepted.

He led her through the crowd, away from the saloon and toward his house. Scores of people were calling his name as they walked, trying to get his attention, but he kept his eyes straight ahead. When they reached his house, he took out a key, unlocked the front door, and stood back, waiting for her to enter.

"Where are you taking me, Mr. DeVine?" she said playfully.

"Audie, please. To the show, of course," Audie teased back.

"This isn't the saloon."

"I know. But I have a secret way to the saloon only a privileged few get to travel."

Deirdre looked at the fence and smiled. She motioned to him to lean down with a beckoning finger. When he did, she pointed to the fence with people looking through the slats for signs of the band.

"It's not really a secret," she whispered.

Audie laughed and motioned her inside.

They walked through the front door, and he shut and locked it behind them. Audie was a little embarrassed, seeing the house as Deirdre must have. He felt like it was . . . showy. The nicest furniture money could buy sitting in the parlor, gleaming china in the cabinet, and a distinct air of abandonment, as if no one lived there and none of these expensive things had been touched.

Moses was sitting at a small table just inside the door.

"Hidee, ma'am," Moses said as he stood and took off his hat.

Audie was glad Moses was there to distract from the rest of the place.

"Deirdre, this is Moses. He's the boss of our whole outfit here. He keeps things running smooth."

Moses just chuckled and shook his head no.

"Well, I guess somebody got ta keep 'em in line."

"Hello, Moses. Nice to meet you," she said warmly.

"Now, if you'll follow me." Audie started walking through a sitting room and to the back door that lead to the path. He opened the door and waited for her to walk through, watching the curves that had first caught his eye. She paused outside, waiting for him. He shut the door and gently pushed her up against it.

Deirdre stared up at him, waiting for his next move. He was a good eight inches taller than she was. She noticed the perfect symmetry in his features, the square jaw, and a depth in his eyes she hadn't anticipated.

Audie put his hand under her soft chin and gently lifted her face up toward his. He leaned down and brushed his lips across hers. Deirdre hesitated for just a moment, then wrapped her arms around his neck. Involuntarily, she pressed the length of her body against his and felt an electricity that started at her mouth and pulsed downward. The world around them melted away as they fell into the rhythm of a kiss.

They paused, and Audie pulled back to look at her.

"I've been dying to do that since the second I laid my eyes on you," he confessed.

"Me, too."

"I don't want to go play my show. I want to stay here with you," he told her.

"Me too."

Audie smiled and leaned down to kiss her again.

They stayed that way longer than they had the first time. After some time, Audie pulled away. He felt a tense heat coursing all the way to his fingertips.

"I've got to go. Smyth and Shane are probably losing their minds right now."

"Okay," she said. She couldn't stop looking into those complicated eyes, wondering who this singer really was.

"Do you want to come with me? You can watch from the side of the stage. You don't have to go out in the crowd if you don't want to. I wouldn't fight my way through them just to see me," he joked.

Deirdre smiled.

"I think I'm just gonna go home," she said.

"Why do you want to do that?" Audie questioned.

"Because I'm not going to be able to think about anything but that kiss for the rest of the night," she confessed demurely.

He leaned down to kiss her again, this time with even more passion than before. She pulled away first, smiled her beautiful smile, and walked back through the house, tossing her silky hair over her shoulder as she disappeared.

~

"What in the hell were you doing, Audie? It's like we're up here playing with our own dicks or something!" Shane scolded.

They had played without him for almost twenty minutes.

Audie just grabbed his guitar and smiled at his brother. Shane was a little surprised at his manner. He hadn't seen his brother smile like that in. . . maybe ever.

"I hope it was worth it," Shane yelled over the crowd as Audie walked up to center stage.

"It was," was all Audie said back to him.

Shane had felt like he was flying blind playing drums without the rhythm of his brother's guitar, but not Smyth. No, quite the opposite. He loved any chance to be the main attraction. He gave the audience a show, and they rewarded him richly for it in shouts, claps, and drink offers.

Audie started playing rhythm, but let Smyth keep the spotlight for a while longer. He wanted to reflect for a moment on what had transpired earlier that evening.

The night was on fire after that. Audie, Shane, and Smyth were locked in as a band. They had begun to think with one mind while they were on stage. They could read each other's thoughts with a look. Their playing was a fluid conversation of melody and rhythm in a language only they understood.

They each played like they were the kings of their craft, and each for different reasons. Passion, fame, forgetting—all equal motivators. A magnetism joined them as one, and they fed off the hungry audience. The energy reached from wall to wall. Adoration, drunken anger, and lust pulsed from the patrons to the performers, and Audie, Shane, and Smyth reveled in it.

Had they known the names of two strangers who had slipped in the side door of the saloon that night, it would have been a much different show.

Thomas arose to the smell of breakfast and knew Adalina was already up. He walked into the kitchen and wrapped his arms around her slender waist, kissing her on the cheek. She had made bacon and biscuits, his favorite, with some apple preserves she had been saving for a while.

"Did you sleep well?" Adalina asked.

"Like a stone."

"Good."

She pulled away from Thomas, gently unwrapping his arms, and poured them both a cup of coffee.

"Come sit. Let's eat before it gets cold."

He was glad for her warmth, even though Adalina had seemed a little distant since his return over three months ago.

Truth was, she hadn't thought about much of anything but her sons' potential involvement in the case he was working on since

Thomas had been home. She hadn't asked about the case out of fear, but she had worked up her courage and was determined to today.

Thomas had done everything in his power not to think about it. He hadn't heard a peep from the agency, which he knew wasn't a good thing.

He busied himself around the farm and spent time with his sweet Adalina.

"God, these biscuits are delicious, Addy. I don't know why no one else can make these like you do."

"It's the buttermilk. Makes them fluffy."

"Whatever it is, it's heaven."

"So, what was that case about again? The one in Wichita?" she said out of the blue.

Thomas was surprised at her question. She never asked him about his work, at least not point-blank.

"Is everything okay, Adalina?"

"Yes. Of course. Why do you ask?"

He stared at her for a second trying to figure her out before he spoke.

"Well, someone—the consensus is Indians, but I disagree—ambushed a band of soldiers heading west out of Wichita. They were escorting a wagonload of new Winchester rifles for delivery to the army fighting in the Indian wars. Every single soldier was killed, and the wagon and rifles burned to ashes. It's the damnedest thing I've ever seen."

He paused, slipping into his thoughts.

"But I don't think it was an Indian attack, because they didn't take the guns. Since when would an Indian pass up a load of artillery?"

Adalina's heart sank. It wasn't what she was hoping to hear. The story she'd concocted in her mind was gradually becoming more of a reality as Thomas spoke.

"That seems . . . so brutal." Adalina tried to suppress the lump in her throat.

"It was. As savage a thing as I've seen. I couldn't even bear to tell you all the details."

Adalina wanted to weep but kept her composure. It was all too outrageous to believe.

She took a sip of her coffee and stared at Thomas.

"If Indians didn't do it, then who do you think did?"

"That's the misery of it, Addy. I don't have a clue. Whoever did it was damn good or a ghost. For now, the authorities will chalk it up to Indians to save face, but they're wrong. I just feel it."

"Oh. Well, you never know with those cursed redskins. They do all sorts of terrible things just for spite."

"No, I know it wasn't them. Indians don't waste anything. It would go against everything in their nature to leave those guns and provisions behind."

"Excuse me," Adalina abruptly dismissed herself.

She just made it outside before she broke down. She fell to the porch and wept, hardly feeling the wooden planks digging into her knees through her dress. She didn't even notice the early June rain falling heavily all around her.

She knew in her heart it had been Audie and Shane.

"All I'm saying is, we have it made here. Right now. We have a house. We're making money hand over fist. Women. Lord, the women! What else could we do and have this life?" Shane lectured his brother.

"I'm fine here, for now. I just don't want to get too fat and happy. We have more to do in this world than just sing for drunks. You know that," Audie shot back.

Smyth jumped in.

"What the hell are you two talking about? Y'all always got this mysterious shit going back and forth. What do I have to do to get in on y'all's little secret?"

It was noon on Sunday, and they all had a hangover of sorts from last night, though Smyth was the only one who'd gotten drunk. A great show will do that to a musician. Leave you feeling drained when you've given it all you've got.

Moses got up and went outside to walk for a while. He didn't want to be called on to answer Smyth's questions if there were any thrown his way.

The brothers ignored Smyth and continued their conversation.

"Well, I'm loving it. I don't plan on spitting in the face of fortune."

Audie just shook his head at his brother. Normally he would have continued to argue back, but today he had his mind on a soft-skinned, brown-eyed beauty. The fight in him was covered in kisses at the moment.

Lozen lay in her tent, nursing her newborn. Onawa pulled a blanket up over Lozen and the child to keep the chill away.

"What will you call the man child?" Onawa asked.

"I haven't decided yet."

"You have to find Shane and let him know of his son. This boy deserves to know his father."

Lozen sighed.

"I know I do."

"When you are able then? We will go."

"What if he doesn't want the child?"

"The child has you and the tribe to raise it."

Lozen turned her head away from Onawa. She appreciated the woman's concern, but it didn't change her feelings about the situation.

She couldn't commit to this child, just like she couldn't commit to his father. Long ago she'd made a vow to be a warrior, and mothering a son had no place in that.

She hated herself in that moment, but she would walk this world a warrior. Everything else be damned.

Keeping a promise can hurt as much as breaking one, even if the promise is only to ourselves.

CHAPTER 39

"What are you drinking, mister?" the bartender on duty at Soapy's asked the stranger.

"A whiskey for me and another for my partner here."

"Coming up."

The bartender turned, reached under the counter, and grabbed two small glasses in one hand and a bottle of corn liquor in another. He poured the whiskey into both, never interrupting the pour as he went from one glass to the other.

The two men were clearly cut from rough stock. The man who ordered was average build and not particularly distinguishable from the other men in this bar except for the hardness in his face. He had the chiseled lines around his mouth developed by hatred in a man and dark eyes that were impossible to look at for any length of time. Staring at them felt like it tainted your soul.

The other man was of a bigger build than most, but not what you would call fit, and carried a similar disposition, but life hadn't cut the same lines in his countenance. His face was emotionless. He had nothing but a look of cold and empty. His expression changed so little that time hadn't been able to carve much into him.

Both men wore a soldier's coat, but neither wore any other part of a uniform. They were roughshod and intimidating, like looking at a pair of hangman's ropes with thirteen loops a piece.

It was the fourth day in a row that the bartender had seen them in the saloon.

"You two gentlemen new to Denver? You looking to settle or just passing through?"

"What's it to you, barmaid? You looking for company tonight?" the man who hadn't spoken yet said.

The bartender, whose name was Roger, narrowed his eyes at the stranger and spit on the floor.

"Just making conversation is all. That'll be ten cents."

There was a pause of about fifteen tense seconds where no one spoke and neither of the two customers made a move to pay.

The man who had ordered the drinks burst out laughing.

"My friend here's just messin' with ya, is all. Don't take no offense to it. The name's Waters and this joker here's Briggs. We're just passin' through."

Waters slammed his whiskey. Briggs sipped his slowly and deliberately. Waters winced from the burn and reached in his pocket for a handful of bills. He rolled off a one-dollar greenback and laid it on the bar.

"Just leave that bottle here and save yourself some trouble."

Roger pulled the whiskey bottle back out, slammed it on the dollar, and walked away without a word.

Audie went out for a walk around town, something he wouldn't normally do. In truth, he was hoping for an encounter with Deirdre. Lost in all the stardust between them last night, he hadn't thought to ask where she lived.

He walked around Denver, nonchalantly peering into the windows of shops and restaurants. He heard the excitement and whispers of nearby pedestrians as he roamed, but he ignored it. He hated all the eyes on him when he wasn't on stage. He figured he could tolerate it today in hopes of finding what he was looking for.

Audie finally spotted her window-shopping outside of a fine dress store on the western end of town. The thought crossed his mind that he'd buy her anything in there if she asked him.

He walked toward her and called out her name. When she saw him, she ran to him and kissed him. When she pulled away, she was embarrassed at the people staring at her.

"I was thinking I'd like to take you for a horseback ride today if you'd oblige me," Audie said.

"I think I could oblige you," Deirdre said to him.

They turned from the shop windows, and he led her down the way to Soapy's stable, where they kept their horses. Admiring eyes followed them the whole way, but the couple was too absorbed in each other to notice.

They also didn't notice the short man in the new suit watching them walk the other direction. Santino couldn't believe his eyes. He turned and strolled back to James's office, tossing a five-cent piece in the air and catching it as he went.

He couldn't wait to tell James that his father's plaything was keeping company with one of the DeVine Devils.

Audie saddled a Palomino stallion that Moses had recently purchased, and they rode out of town about a mile. Deirdre sat behind him, shielding herself from the wind by holding him tightly around the waist, putting her hands inside his coat and her face against his back. Audie soon spotted a clearing right next to a few blue spruce trees and stopped. He dismounted and helped Deirdre down.

She crossed her arms tightly across her chest to fight the wind. It was summer, but the wind had a slight chill since they'd ridden up the mountain a piece.

He took his duster off and wrapped it around her. The bottom touched the ground when she wore it.

He gathered some kindling and pine brush and used two matches to start a fire. Before long, they were leaned into each other, both warming themselves by the flames.

"I'm surprised a musician is so handy out here in the wild."

Audie chuckled. He wouldn't consider this the wild.

"I was a fire starter before I learned the guitar," he teased.

She smiled.

"What's it like, being famous? It seems . . . lonely. Like you could never really get to know someone."

Audie was surprised at her insight. It unnerved him a little.

"You get used to it," was all Audie offered.

She searched Audie's eyes. She could see she was right about the lonely.

"What do you do for Tabor?" Audie quizzed, trying to change the subject.

"Oh, just errands . . . whatever he needs."

Audie could tell she wasn't eager to elaborate.

"He seems like an ass of a man. Surely there's better work out there for a woman such as yourself."

"Tell me about where you come from," she said.

Now she was changing the subject.

"That's a long story. We started out in Missouri, and ended up in Arizona territory."

Audie stopped there. After a moment, Deirdre laughed.

"Well, that's not a very long story! There has to be more to it than that!" she said, waiting for him to continue.

Audie hesitated. He'd never shared his story with anyone before except Moses, and even that was in bits and pieces.

"Our father was a missionary to the Apache Indians out west. We were born in Missouri, but when I was eleven years old, he took us with him to minister to an Indian village he'd become friendly with. We'd been there for a few months when soldiers raided the camp and killed my father. We stayed and were adopted by the Apache. That was our home until a few years ago."

Her eyes told him she felt every word he spoke. Audie found

himself sharing with Deirdre things he hadn't thought of in years. His father teaching him to play guitar, the nights around the fire sharing the gospel, and carefree days spent in the river by the Indian settlement. He shared things even further back, like playing in the creek across the field from their house and his mothers' sweet demeanor when he was a child.

He recalled these things with feigned nonchalance, but Deirdre could see the pain on his face.

"I'm sorry about that, Audie. This world isn't a kind place." She grabbed his hand in both of hers as she spoke.

"I learned not to be kind back," Audie said.

"I ran away from home when I was thirteen. My father was a drunkard. The street was a safer place than a house with him when he got too deep in a bottle."

"How did you survive?"

"I did what I had to." Deirdre turned away from him.

Audie gently grabbed her face and turned it back toward his.

"Hey, it's okay," he comforted. He leaned in and kissed her.

The fire burned as they held on to each other. They stayed that way until there were only embers left where Audie had lit the pine brush.

They rode back into town a lot slower than they had ridden out. The sky was turning from blue to black as Audie put his horse back in the stable. He walked with Deirdre until they were a few yards from Tabor's Tavern.

"That's where I stay. There are rooms upstairs."

"Can I walk you up?" Audie asked.

"I don't think so, Audie. Mr. Tabor . . . he doesn't like you. I think he's just upset because you won't play his saloon, but I'm afraid there would be trouble if you came in."

Audie clenched his fists at the thought of Tabor. "I don't mind trouble."

Deirdre smiled. "I can see that about you."

"Can I see you again soon, then? Tomorrow?" Audie asked, trying to keep the calm in his voice.

"Yes."

He kissed her goodbye and walked back to his house.

Maybe Shane was right. It was becoming easier to see himself settling down here.

～

"Oh, she was more than friendly with him. She kissed him right on the mouth. I bet your daddy wouldn't like that at all," Santino teased.

James tried not to show his disgust for the naive man who sat before him. He knew his father had more feeling for an old pair of boots than he did for the girl, but he didn't let on.

Tommy Santino had been somewhat of a disappointment to the Tabors so far. His "inside" knowledge of Soapy's operation was extremely limited. Except for busting an occasional lowlife in Soapy's organization for illegal bootlegging or liquor distribution, the man hadn't given them anything even remotely damaging to the wretch at the top.

"That's useful information, Tommy. I'm glad you reported it to me. How are you doing on our other little venture? Any luck in recruiting one of Soapy's men?"

"I'm thinking about it. Not all those guys are as smart as I am, James. They won't see the benefit to being on this side. I'll find a man who'll do the trick, though. It just takes some thinking is all," Tommy explained.

"Well, make sure you do. We'll need a man to turn if we're going to take that crook down."

～

The ladies of the night came out into the parlor one by one, but the patron didn't see any that were to his liking.

"Who doesn't have at least one squaw in a whorehouse in Colorado?"

"What's your name, sir?" A well-dressed lady who was clearly in charge asked.

"Briggs. Why's that matter?"

"Well, Mr. Briggs. I can assure you we have a variety of jeweled birds here who can tickle any fancy you've got," Jennie Rogers, the madam of the House of Mirrors, informed Briggs.

Briggs wasn't at all pleased with the selection. He lit a cigarette and threw the still-burning match on the floor. Jennie quickly extinguished it with her high-heeled shoe. She wasn't the kind of woman to tolerate rudeness in her brothel. There were two men in the next room who were a whistle away from throwing him out on his ass.

"Either pick from what we've got, or you can go out in the alley and pull your own pud," Jennie said without the lovely that was in her voice before.

"I don't think I'll let a bitch like you talk to me like that," Briggs said as he moved slowly toward her.

Her line had been crossed. Briggs had almost reached the madam when the men she had on standby responded to her signal. The two burly protectors burst into the room and manhandled him out into the streets. He fought back with all he had, but it only earned him a severe beating when they had him out of the house.

Once they'd thrown him out in the street, the biggest of the two guards knocked him to the ground with a punch to the nose. He went for an Arkansas Toothpick that was tucked in his left boot, but the man saw his hand reach down and knew what that move meant. He stomped on Briggs's hand until he could hear the stomach-churning crack of bone.

Briggs was curled up on the ground, holding his mangled appendage when the other man joined in. They began kicking him in the ribs, chest, and face until he didn't have the strength to deflect the blows with his one good hand anymore.

He was a bloody mess when they got done with him. He laid there for the better part of half an hour before he gathered the strength to get up and walk away. There were witnesses to the beating, but no one would dare say a word or even help the man. Jennie Rogers's House of Mirrors was protected by Soapy Smith.

That was trouble nobody wanted.

CHAPTER 40

Deirdre was in an exceptionally good mood Monday morning when she got to work. She had picked a handful of wildflowers and placed them in a cup on her desk. She was humming a tune she'd heard the DeVine Devils play when she was interrupted by Horace screaming at her to come in his office.

"Deirdre! Get in here right now, girl!" he commanded.

She timidly did his bidding.

"Come in and shut the door."

James Tabor was sitting in one of the leather seats facing Horace's desk.

"Who were you with yesterday?" Horace interrogated.

"No one, Mr. Tabor. I spent the day looking at dresses on Main Street."

"Lying bitch!" He slammed his hand on the desk. "Tell me who you were with or I'll have your ass working cock in the back alley like you were when I found you!"

Deirdre began to cry softly.

"I was with Audie DeVine," she confessed.

"I save you from the lowly things in this world, and you return to it like a dog to their vomit."

"He's not what you think he is, Mr.—"

"What do you know about what he is?" Horace interrupted. "Your judgment of a man is as worthless as a puddle of pig shit."

Deirdre kept crying. James sat there enjoying the scene.

Horace softened dramatically. He came around the desk and pulled a chair up uncomfortably close to the one Deirdre sat in.

"Deirdre, Deirdre. What am I going to do with you, girl? Don't I take care of you? Don't you have what you need here? It hurts me that you would go looking for affection from another man, Deirdre, especially one as vulgar as that singing hedonist. Don't I take care of you?"

Deirdre continued crying but nodded her head in agreement.

"Yes. You know I do, and I'm the only one who ever has. Even your lowlife father loved the bottle more than you." Horace often brought up her father, despicably trying to convince her that she was the kind of woman who was disposable, even to family.

Horace stood. He held out his arms for Deirdre to come to him. She hesitated, but finally stood up and let him hug her. She kept her arms at her side.

"Oh, Deirdre. I'd die if I lost you. That's why it makes me so angry to see you with him," Horace lied.

James almost laughed out loud.

"Now, we're going to make this right, don't you worry. Maybe we can turn this to our favor. Maybe you could help us figure out some things about him, about him and that wretched band of scoundrels he has. If we could get them playing in our saloon . . . Well, you know we've been losing so much money since him and his boys have been over at Soapy Smith's. Does this man like you, Deirdre? Do you have him in your charm?"

Deirdre didn't like to think of Audie in that way. She loved him already. The thought of trying to manipulate him was sickening to her.

"I don't know," she said.

"Don't lie to me, girl! I know the effect you can have on a man." Horace shook her as he spat the words at her. "Find out what it would take to make him leave Soapy. Now, that shouldn't be hard, should it?" Horace's voice had wilted back down to a soothing tone again.

She looked at him and saw him for the evil he was. She nodded her head as she forced a smile at him, hiding her disgust.

Horace grinned and hugged her tightly one more time.

"Good. You're a good girl, Deirdre. I'll always be here to watch out for you." His stare penetrated her as he said those last words.

"You can go now."

She turned and walked out the door.

"He was that murderous type, Soapy. If there's one thing a woman learns in my line of work, it's how to read a man. This fellow is gonna come back around looking for blood. Give me extra men or just go kill the son of a bitch, 'cause this sort of thing is bad for business! I need you to nip it in the bud, Soapy!"

Jennie was still an attractive woman. Forty-six years and the stress of her brothel business hadn't taken that away from her. Her red hair matched the fire in her demeanor.

She had a special relationship with Soapy. Rumor was he loved her, but she had been married twice and refused to do so again. Whether that was true or not, he protected her business without taking any of the profit, and her business was very profitable. Soapy and some of his top men were allowed to sample the merchandise when they wanted, but no money exchanged hands.

The House of Mirrors was the most upstanding whorehouse in all of Colorado. They paid the cops and imported beautiful woman from places far away. Thus, they avoided any trouble with protective fathers or brothers trying to rescue their own.

The girls were treated well and not overworked. Most only had a four-day workweek. They wore the finest clothes. They drank foreign wine and dined on good meats and cheeses. With the exception of a few being won over by the local church, the girls didn't leave and didn't want to.

Jennie's gilded ladies weren't cheap, though. This kept the clientele at a level where there were very few problems and disruptions. Most of the men were businessmen or successful cattlemen. A lot of the men had wives and families, and discretion was important. Even the miners who had hit a payload and had money burning a hole in their pocket were an easy lot to handle. These kinds of men didn't want to cause a scene.

That's why yesterday's incident was so disturbing. Jennie wanted to make sure it didn't happen again.

"What was this guy's name?" Soapy asked.

"Briggs. That's all I got. Rough-lookin' fellow. Stood straight like he might have been a soldier or something. I don't know. Just take care of it."

"Alright, Jennie. I'll make sure he learns his lesson, if he ain't already."

Jennie turned and left without another word.

Audie was outside waiting to see Soapy. When the door to Soapy's office flung open, he barely got out of the way before it slammed into the wall next to him. A red-headed, angry-looking woman gave him a hard look and walked toward the door leading out to the street.

Soapy motioned Audie in. He entered and closed the door behind him.

Audie grinned at Soapy.

"Man, you've sure got a way with the ladies, Soapy," he prodded.

Soapy smirked. "That's Jennie Rogers. Runs the brothel called the House of Mirrors. Respectable place. Anyway, some fellow came in upset 'cause they didn't have any red meat in there. It got a little out of hand, and he got his ass thrown out in the street. She thinks he might come back."

"What do you mean 'red meat'?"

"You know, Indians. A squaw. She said he was a soldier. Probably developed a taste for it in the Indian wars or something."

Audie felt an old anger creeping up in him.

"Anyways, I'm gonna have to find this prick and put the fear of God in him or give her a couple extra men. I should just kill the perverted bastard and put him out of his misery."

"Kill him."

Soapy laughed out loud. "You violent bastard!" He continued laughing as he talked. "I love it!"

Audie laughed along, though he didn't find any of it funny.

"What was the name of this soldier?" Audie asked, wondering if he might find him before Soapy did.

"Briggs or something. Why, you want a piece of him?"

Audie felt his heart start pounding and blood rush to his face. He didn't hear Soapy's question.

Briggs was the name of the man who had killed his father. He could still hear his grandfather Mac spit it out on his deathbed.

"You alright, Audie? You look like you're about to bust."

Audie got up to go. "Yeah. Yeah, I'm fine."

"You don't look so fine. What'd you come in here for, anyway?" Soapy asked.

Audie composed himself. "I wanted to tell you Tabor sent a man to try and hire me away from you. Not muscle, just some suit. Offered twice what you're paying."

"What'd you tell him?" Soapy asked.

"I said I'd rather screw a pig."

Soapy smiled. "Good man. Good man."

Audie turned and left. Soapy was surprised he hadn't tried to play the Tabor offer for a raise.

The truth was, Audie had every intention of asking Soapy for more money. He'd been thinking of building a home just a little piece outside of the hustle and bustle of Denver. He'd been thinking of a dark-haired angel and how he could see himself coming home to her every night. Until he heard that name.

Briggs.

Now that was all he could think about.

~

It was around noon on Monday afternoon when Audie walked down Blake Street, oblivious to the crowds of people staring at him as he went. His mind was lost in thought. He leaned up against a worn post for a moment in the shade, outside of Burton's Storage and Commission. A young boy of about five came up to him and tugged on his coat.

"Hi" was all the lad offered.

Audie looked down at the boy and stared. He saw an image of himself at that age, before the wolves of this world ripped the innocence from him. He remembered wrestling with Shane in the front yard under the bur oak, Azariah in his rocking chair on the porch of their boyhood home. He could see his mama hanging clothes out on the line and heard her singing softly an old church song that he'd long since forgotten most of the words to.

"Wilt thou cast a sinner out
  Who humbly comes to thee?
  No, my God, I cannot doubt
  Thy mercy is for me."

The sweetness of his mother's voice swayed his soul to a gentle place, pulling him out of his darkness for a moment.

He was jerked back into reality when the boy yanked on his coat again. He reached in his pocket and pulled out a penny, handed it to the boy, and told him to go buy a peppermint, then started walking down the dusty street again.

Briggs took up residence in his mind again and pushed any goodness he'd been thinking of clear out.

~

"All's I'm saying is Tabor's looking for a man on the inside over there at Soapy's. There's a good piece of change for a man who could bring us useful information 'bout his operation. I know Soapy hasn't been the kindest to you, Arny. And you'd be setting yourself up for a job when Tabor takes that prick down someday soon. I always respected you, and I just wanna see you get your due is all."

Tommy Santino laid it on Arny pretty thick. This was as good a chance as any to recruit a man to spy on Soapy. He knew he couldn't ask just anyone on Soapy's payroll, because this kind of thing could get you killed quick.

"Yeah, if Soapy catches me, it's curtains for my guinea ass."

"Soapy ain't gonna catch you, Arny. You ain't gonna talk to a soul about it but me. Now how's he gonna know?" Tommy persuaded.

Arny picked up the glass of whiskey in front of him and slammed it back hard. He winced slightly at the burn.

"Screw it, right? I'm in."

Tommy ordered another round for his newly acquired partner.

CHAPTER 41

Thomas was outside digging up thistle weeds that had grown up around the house. He enjoyed this kind of mindless labor at home when he wasn't off on an assignment. It was mid-August now, and thistles were popping up everywhere around the place.

He wasn't surprised when the postal rider rode up with a letter from the Pinkerton Agency. He'd been expecting termination or at least a reprimand for coming up empty in Wichita long before today.

But he was wrong; instead, he received a new assignment. They wanted him to escort a package from Andrew Carnegie, a Scottish business magnate who had made himself rich here in the States.

Still, Thomas knew this was a punishment of sorts from the agency. He hadn't delivered on his last two assignments, and so he was being demoted to "guard" some package traveling by train. There was no real excitement or accomplishment in these sorts of jobs, just a paycheck.

He was to meet another agent in the City of Kansas in three days to take possession of the package. There was no information about the contents, but he understood the letter to say he was traveling alone, so he figured it was small enough to keep on his person. Otherwise, there would have been at least two agents. A man has to leave the room he's in sometimes.

He would take the package to Golden, Colorado, and wait for instructions there.

He had seen this happen to some of the senior agents before. When the brass at the agency thought you were past your prime, they began to put you out to pasture. It was a win-win for the agency, really. They could tell the client they would have a senior agent on their job and keep that agent around a little longer before they had to get rid of him altogether. Most of the time the agent quit before the agency had to fire him.

Thomas finished with the weeds and headed inside.

Deirdre worked the rest of the day without the lightness that had been in her step earlier. When it was time to go, she rushed out the door without a goodbye to anyone. She headed toward her room on Larimer Street. She didn't wave at familiar people like she normally did or stop at the bakery for a slice of rye bread. All she wanted was to be home, away from the cruel world in which she couldn't seem to win.

She spotted Audie walking her way as she came up Holladay Street. She pulled the hat she was wearing down to hide her face, trying to keep from being seen as she walked passed him.

"Deirdre," he said as she walked by.

She continued walking, hoping he would think he was mistaken and keep going the other direction.

He didn't. He turned and followed after her. When he reached her, he put his hand on her shoulder.

"Deirdre, where are you going so fast?" he asked as she turned to face him.

"I've got to go, Audie. I can't talk right now," she said as she walked the other way again, releasing his hand from her shoulder.

He could tell she was about to cry.

"Wait! What's wrong, Deirdre? Where are you going?"

Deirdre kept walking and had no reply to his questions.

Audie stood in the street watching her walk off.

What the hell was that all about? he thought.

He turned to go, perplexed by the situation. This day had come with a fist right to his gut.

When Audie returned home that night, Shane and Moses were at the table in the kitchen playing a card game called Brag. Since Moses was morally opposed to gambling, they were betting with pebbles that Moses had picked up along the pathway to the saloon. Moses was winning.

"Damn it, Moses! If I didn't know better, I'd think you were cheating! How the hell are you drawing high pair every dad gum time?" Shane protested.

Moses just smiled and pulled the pile of rocks lying in the middle of the table toward him.

"Where's Smyth?" Audie asked.

"Where do you think he is?" Shane answered.

Audie sank into a chair in the sitting room next to the kitchen.

Shane began shuffling the cards and jokingly eyeing Moses like he was gunning for him. Moses kept smiling and staring at him while he arranged his rocks in perfect rows in front of him.

"Briggs is here." Audie cut the air with his words.

"What?" Shane asked.

He remembered the name, but it took a second to register.

"Briggs. The son of a bitch who raided our camp. The bastard who's the reason our father is dead. He's here in Denver."

Moses' smile turned to worry. He had secretly hoped the life of luxury here in Denver had smothered the killer in Audie and Shane.

Shane got up and walked into the sitting room.

"How do you know?"

"He got the shit kicked out of him at a whorehouse of Soapy's last night. Came in looking for a squaw and got his ass hairs up when they didn't have one. Said he was a soldier."

Shane's blood began to boil as hot as Audie's. "Where is he?"

"I don't know. We'll have to find him. That should be easy, given the beating Soapy said he took."

"That's too bad. I would love a fresh canvas to work with," Shane said.

"And another thing . . . Soapy's thinking about killing him."

"I'll kill Soapy before I let him have the pleasure."

Audie spoke no further on it. He and Shane rose and headed for the door to go find Soapy.

Thomas sat at the dinner table that night with Adalina, more willing to tell her of his letter than he had been with previous ones.

"I got a letter today from the agency."

"I know. I saw the rider through the window," she said softly.

Thomas eyed her affectionately. Her gentle spirit was one reason he loved her.

"Well, they want me to take a package to a man in Golden, Colorado, by train. A rich man by the name of Carnegie needs something delivered. There's no real work to it. Golden is just a small piece from Denver. I know you've always wanted to ride on a train, Addy. I want to take you first class. We'll eat fine meals and sleep in a luxurious bed. We can stay in Denver for a spell before we head back. I hear it has one of the best theaters in America."

"Oh, Thomas, I don't know. Who's going to take care of the place?"

"I knew you would worry about that," Thomas said with a smile. "I rode up to talk to Kitch and Mabel this afternoon. I offered them two extra calves this year if they'd look after the place while we're gone. He said it'd be a godsend."

Adalina shook her head slightly, still hesitant to accept.

"Addy, let me show you part of the world before we're too old to see it. You deserve it, sweetheart. This place will be fine."

She looked at Thomas for a bit. She could tell he wanted this badly for her.

"Alright. As long as we don't stay away too long."

He stood up and walked behind Adalina, bending over to wrap his arms around her. He kissed her on the cheek and squeezed her softly.

"Then it's done. I get to show my beautiful wife to the world. I'll have more work fighting men off of you than I will delivering the package," he flirted.

Adalina smiled. Maybe this would be a good distraction from the other things weighing on her mind.

"Two visits in one day from the great Audie DeVine! And you brought your brother, to boot! To what do I owe the pleasure?"

Shane and Audie sat in the two red-leather chairs facing Soapy's desk.

"I need your men to leave while we talk," Audie informed Soapy.

Soapy stared at Audie for some time, trying to decide if there was any danger in this. He liked Audie, but he trusted no one.

"Sal, Tony, go wait outside for a bit."

"But, Boss, I don't—"

"Outside," Soapy said with more conviction.

As they left, the two guards gave Audie and Shane a long look to let them know they didn't like the situation.

"We need a favor, Soapy, and we need your discretion along with it," Audie started.

Soapy lit a cigarette. "I'm listening."

"Briggs, the one who was causing trouble at your friend's whorehouse—"

"Jennie would prefer brothel," Soapy interrupted.

"The one who caused trouble at the brothel. I don't want you killing him."

"Why not?"

"'Cause we're going to."

Soapy got up and walked around to the other side of the desk, leaning on it as he took a long draw off his cigarette. He gave Audie a stout look.

"Why?" Soapy questioned.

"Because he needs killing."

Soapy appraised Audie for a second and then Shane. He could read on them that this deed was about vengeance.

"I can see this is important to you and your brother here, Audie, but I can't have moneymakers like you two getting arrested for murder."

"We won't get arrested," Audie said.

"How do you know?"

"Because we never have before," Shane spoke.

Soapy studied Shane for a minute and knew the words were honest. He pushed off of the desk and walked back around to the other side, smoke trailing over his shoulder.

"Why don't you let one of my men do it? I can promise you they'll get the job done. However you want."

"No," Audie said.

"And you can't tell me what this man did that deserves a six-foot hole?" Soapy tried to pry.

"The less you know, the better."

Soapy smashed the burning end of his cigarette into a giant golden ashtray.

"So what do you need from me? You just want me to stay out of the way?"

"I want you to talk to anyone who met Briggs at the brothel. Give us anything that'll help us find him."

"That's easy. I'll send Tony over there right . . ."

"No, Soapy. I want *you* to talk to them. Nobody else needs to know about this," Audie demanded. He gave Soapy a look that let him know his request was serious.

Soapy revealed another cigarette and pulled in a deep draw of smoke as he lit it.

"Alright. I'll do this for you. But if you get caught, this can't link back to me or Jennie. You understand? You gotta guarantee me that."

Audie shook his head yes. He and Shane both stood.

"Honor among thieves and all that shit, right?" Soapy finished.

"You've got our word."

Soapy shook Shane's hand and then Audie's, and the brothers headed out the door.

Arny, the big Italian man whose nose Audie had broken so many months ago, moved away from the door just as the brothers exited.

As soon as his shift was over that night, he went to find Tommy Santino. Arny assumed his friend would be interested in this new information.

CHAPTER 42

"They're going after some guy named Briggs. They wanna kill him. Wouldn't tell Soapy why."

"Those singers? Really? I knew they could get rowdy, but I never pegged them for stone-cold killers," Tommy surmised.

Arny held his tongue, but he wanted to tell Tommy how stupid he thought he was. That was Tommy's problem. He never could see other people for what they were. He was so worried about being seen as a big shot that he was blind to everything else. Of course the DeVine brothers were killers. Arny had enough sense to know that the first time he met them.

"They're killers. That much I know," was all he gave Tommy.

"Anything else? They didn't give up anything about why they wanna put this guy down?"

"They played their cards close to the vest. Soapy tried, but they wouldn't give it up."

"Alright, Arny. You did good. Let me run this by Tabor. I'll be in touch."

"Whoa. Where's my money? You said I'd get paid, Tommy!"

"And you will, you will. Don't worry, Arny. It's coming. I just got to go see what this is worth to Tabor, is all."

Arny grabbed Tommy by his coat and lifted him about six inches off the ground until they were eye to eye.

"You try to double cross me, you little son of a bitch, and I'll kill you where you stand!"

"Hey! Ain't nobody trying to pull a fast one here! I don't have it on me right now is all!"

Arny held him there a little longer and then set him down. Tommy gave him an ineffective shove as Arny let him go, an attempt to save a little pride.

"I better get paid. I already feel like Soapy has an eye on me. If I go down, you're going too, Tommy," Arny threatened before he turned to leave.

That little altercation just cost Arny half of his reward. Tommy decided he was gonna take a hefty piece of whatever money Tabor gave him for Arny.

~

As promised, Soapy went to Jennie and spoke with her and the two men who'd met Briggs. He walked away with no more information than he had before.

"What I told you's what they know, Audie. There ain't a lot to go on. I can find this guy for you, but I gotta have one of my boys help me. If you can live with that, I'll make it happen."

Audie thought for a second. "I can live with that."

"Give me a couple of days. I'll get you what you want. But you boys better not let this little issue affect your job at the Chicago in the meantime."

Audie assured him they wouldn't and walked out.

~

James Tabor had sent Binkley to retrieve Frederick Briggs after Tommy informed James of the details Arny shared. Binkley was so anxious after he convinced Briggs to come that he went to the mercantile to purchase some laudanum for his nerves.

Briggs had brought his longtime partner, Stephen Waters, along.

"Mr. Briggs, why would this singer have a bone to pick with you? Any reason you can think of?" James Tabor asked.

All of this was news to Briggs.

Waters chuckled. "Ole Briggs here probably poked his mama or something. Hell, Briggs might be the son of a bitch's dad! Wouldn't that be some crazy shit?"

Briggs gave the slightest of smiles at Waters's humor. James was disgusted at the vulgarity of these two men. He hated that these low-quality human beings were even sitting in his office. He preferred not to keep company with men of this caliber.

"I don't know. Everyone's got enemies," Briggs offered.

"Yes, we all do, but this man, Audie, he doesn't seem like a man to be taken lightly. He's very capable of brutality. I'd be careful if you plan on staying in our city here for any length of time," James warned.

"Why is this any concern of yours?" Briggs asked. "What do you care if some kid comes after me?"

"Let's just say this young man isn't a friend to us either. He's a thorn in our side as well. If someone removed that thorn, we would be inclined to celebrate that."

After years of killing Indian women and children, preachers, and whoever else they saw fit, murder wasn't something Briggs and Waters needed to dance around.

"So, what you're saying is you want us to do your dirty work for free?" Waters cut in.

James smiled and held Waters's gaze for a few seconds, but that was all he could stand.

"If you want him dead, we can do that, but that ain't free," Briggs said.

"Well, I can assure you this is not my field of expertise. I'm a lawyer. But I'm going to step out now for a cup of tea and my associate, Mr. Santino here, may want to converse further with you about this matter. I'll leave that up to him."

James rose and put on his coat. He said his goodbyes and walked out, closing the door firmly behind him.

"You boys looking for work?" Tommy asked as he sat in James's chair.

"Always," Briggs answered.

~

"Deirdre, open up! Come on! What did I do to make you so mad at me?"

It was 1:30 a.m., early Thursday morning, and Audie had just finished playing at the Chicago. He was wound up and couldn't sleep.

There were people peeking out of doors, up and down the hall of the second floor of the Pacific House. An older lady in a sleeping gown and housecoat emerged to scold Audie for his interruption of her sleep.

"You should be ashamed of yourself, calling on that young lady in the middle of the night! And for waking us God-fearing folks up doing it!"

"Deirdre! Please, just let me in."

Deidre cracked the door and looked out.

"It's okay, Mrs. Burr. Go back to bed now. I'm sorry for disturbing you."

The old lady gave Audie a stern look and went back in her room. It reminded him of his school days when he would displease his teacher.

"Audie, what are you doing here? It's the middle of night!"

"Just let me in. I need to see you."

Deirdre saw the desperate in his face and stood back, opening the door so he could enter. She gathered her nightgown around her and led him to the kitchen where she lit a small oil lantern. It took a couple of tries for the shaking in her hand. Finally, a warm glow filled the room, and resignedly, she sat at the table. She gestured to the chair next to her, inviting Audie to sit.

He didn't want to sit. He vaguely noticed the cupboards were close to empty and the furniture was minimal, but the place was warm and tidy. He threw his hat on the table, nearly knocking over the candle in his haste.

"What happened? Why am I suddenly the last person you want to see?" Audie asked.

"It's not like that."

"Then what is it? You run from me when I see you on the street, and I haven't heard from you in three days! You haven't even been to a show this week."

"Audie, why can't you just leave it be?" she pleaded. "I'm no good for you. I'm no good for anybody. You can have any girl you want. I don't think—"

"I don't want any other girl, Deirdre. I want you!"

She paused, taking in his words.

"You don't know me, Audie. I'm not what you think I am. I've done some. . . bad things," Deirdre said, looking down at the table. "I'm no prize for a man," she whispered.

"Prize?" Audie said, incredulous. "I'm not trying to win a prize! I just. . . I just want you. God, if you saw my yesterdays, all the people I've. . . hurt. . . I don't care what you've done!" He paused and drew in a deep breath, waiting for her response.

Deirdre was thinking how no man had ever spoken to her like Audie did. They only ever wanted her for physical pleasure, and she only ever thought that was what she deserved. She was accustomed to abusive words and deeds and never allowed herself romance. This was a man who had yet to take her to bed, and he was professing for her a love she'd always dreamed of. It made her both terribly uncomfortable and incredibly desirous.

She sat with her hands in her lap, quietly shaking her head in disagreement. *I don't deserve you,* she thought.

"I love you, Deirdre."

She couldn't respond.

Suddenly, Audie grabbed her arms, drew her up from the chair, and pulled her to his chest. She was shocked at the forcefulness of it, but it wasn't anger. It was passion.

"I love you, Deirdre," he repeated as he held her against him, imploring her to believe him.

Audie could feel every rise and fall of her body when he held her. He hadn't noticed the thin nightgown she wore, the silk so fine it was almost sheer. He'd been too caught up in his words to see the intricate lace against her smooth skin. In the faint light from the lantern, she was again the most beautiful woman he'd ever seen.

Audie gently touched her chin, and Deirdre tilted her head up, hesitantly. She wrapped her arms around his waist and thought maybe this man could offer her...something she never thought she was worthy enough to have.

He kissed her like it was the last kiss they'd ever have. There were no more words the rest of the night. They made love until the sun stole the cover of the darkness away from them.

"Don't go back there, Deirdre. You don't need Tabor anymore. I can take care of you. You can come live with me and the boys till I get us a house."

She laid her head on his chest. The life he spoke of was one she loved seeing herself in.

"I'll buy a plot of land outside of town, and I'll build you a house fit for a queen. I can ride into town to play at night."

He gently pulled her face up so she could look him in the eye.

"I hate this world and everything about it. I fought against it my whole life. You're the first thing I've found that makes me think it's worth living in."

She kissed him softly.

"Okay, Audie," she whispered. In that moment, she felt completely safe.

"Okay? You'll come with me?"

"Yes."

"Ahhh!" Audie let out the breath he was holding in a feigned whoosh of relief, then laughed.

For a little while, he was happy.

~

Adalina tried not to be too giddy about the train ride, but she was like a child with a new toy. Their car was a brand new addition on the Kansas Pacific line. Deep burgundy carpet that looked like it had never been walked on covered their floor. On one end of the room was a chocolate leather sofa with grommets along the back in perfect rows. The cushions were so soft and deep she thought she might not be able to stand back up. On the couch, there were two pillows embroidered with a black-and-gold Kansas Pacific Railroad emblem that looked too fancy to touch. At the other end of the car was a bed with ornate metal posts that Adalina imagined had come from a castle in France. There were four feather-down pillows and a lustfully soft cover that begged her to touch it.

Thomas had received the package from another agent when he met him at the train station. It was a small box, unassuming, about one inch by three inches.

Such a fuss for such a small package, but at least I can keep it in my coat, Thomas thought.

The other agent's name was Billers. Thomas could tell the man was as discouraged by his part in the job as Thomas was.

"How long you been with the agency?" Billers asked.

"Twenty-two years. Long enough not to want to be a delivery boy."

Billers nodded his head in agreement.

"Just seventeen myself. You lasted longer than me. I figure I'll get my walking papers in a month," Billers told Thomas as he left.

~

Adalina was enjoying herself more than he'd seen her in years. It thrilled Thomas to bring her this sort of happiness.

"Tonight we'll take our dinner in the dining car. It'll be the finest meal you've ever eaten, outside of your own cooking, of course," Thomas said.

"Thomas, this is too much! I don't need all of this lavishness."

"Stop complaining, woman!" Thomas said playfully. "Let a man do something nice for his wife."

Adalina took his hand in hers and gave him a look that let him know she loved him. Thomas really was a good man.

"We'll be in Golden in less than three days. I'll deliver this package, and we'll go on to Denver. Now, all I need you to do is get this notion out of your head that you don't deserve this and enjoy it."

She tried her best to do just that.

CHAPTER 43

"Where the hell is Deirdre? I swear that bitch gets more worthless every day!" Tabor shouted to no one in particular.

"She hasn't been here all week, Mr. Tabor, sir. If you'd like I could go over to the Pacific House and check on her," Binkley offered.

"Yes. Go. She'd better be dead or dying," Tabor said.

Things had been calm for a couple of days. The DeVine Devils still played the Chicago every night to a crowd that was insatiable. Soapy couldn't keep enough liquor behind the bar. Deirdre had moved into the Devils' house, so named by the people of Denver.

Soapy was still searching for Briggs.

It was Friday night and the show had gone long. The boys had played two different encores out of necessity. The people who came to the shows were demanding more and more from the DeVine Devils, but it was a demand they could easily meet. The band was comfortable enough playing together that it was second nature to go on for hours. Most nights they played the songs they knew two or three times, but no one ever seemed to mind.

When they finally got the crowd calm enough to let them off the stage, Shane and Smyth decided they would stay and drink for a while. Audie was in a hurry to get home to Deirdre.

Moses was waiting for him outside just behind the saloon. He was sitting on a bench looking up at the stars.

"You boys gettin' better and better, Audie. I swear it's a joy ta my soul ta hear y'all play," he said as he pulled his eyes away from the sky.

The night had a chill in it from the coming fall.

"Thanks, Moses," Audie said as he started to walk toward the house.

He turned back toward Moses after a few steps.

"Ain't you coming?"

"Nah. Not yet. It's such a pretty night. I'm gonna let these stars entertain me a little mo'. You need ta get on back ta that pretty lady ," Moses teased.

"Yes, I do. She's a damn sight more pleasing to be around than you," Audie teased back.

Moses chuckled. "And thank God fo' that."

Audie said goodbye to his friend and headed home.

He opened the door to a darkened house. On late nights like these, Deirdre sometimes went to bed without him. He usually woke her up with a breathy kiss and let her decide how the night would progress. He latched the door behind him and turned to walk in.

The pain in his side came as a surprise, sharp and breathtaking at first. Audie tried to scream when the knife went in, but little sound came out. He fell to his knees and put his hand down over the wound. Blood poured through his fingers.

Audie felt a kick in his chest that knocked him back up against the door. His body hit so hard that a glass pane in the door shattered from the impact.

He heard footsteps and Deirdre's muffled scream.

It was too dark to recognize right away the man who walked over to the lamp and lit the wick inside. The glow revealed his battered face. His left cheek was a swollen, a tight mass, and the white of his right eye was a crimson red. Both eyes were ringed by dark purple.

Briggs. He still wore an army jacket. It had to be him.

To Audie he looked like the lowest form of human one could be as he smiled and sat down on the couch next to Deirdre. She had a rag in her mouth and her hands were tied behind her back.

Briggs's smile faded, and he looked stone-faced at Audie for a long time. Audie made an effort to stay calm, but the pain in his side made him wince with every breath. He realized the soft moaning sound was coming from his own mouth, and he knew he didn't have long before the blood loss made him lose consciousness.

Briggs put his arm around Deirdre and stroked her chin with a knife. She jerked her body away, but he violently pulled her close to him again.

"Leave her alone!" Audie demanded weakly. "She has nothing to do with this!"

"Do I know you?" Briggs asked Audie as if he hadn't heard a word Audie had said.

"You should," Audie answered with as much muscle in his voice as he could.

"Oh, yeah? Why?"

"You killed my father."

"Did I? I killed a lot of fathers. Which one was yours?"

"Azariah DeVine. He was a missionary to the Apache."

"Hmm. I don't remember killing no missionary. You sure it was me?"

Audie was on all fours now, blood soaking his shirt and the left leg of his pants. Briggs enjoyed seeing him suffer.

"Mac. Mac Carson. He told you to raid an Apache village. . ."

Briggs licked his swollen lips and thought for a little while. He kept the bloody knife near Deirdre's throat, the same one he had stabbed

Audie with. She sat frozen next to him, willing herself not to move and not to cry.

"Oh, the preacher! I recollect that now. I didn't kill your daddy, though. That was my friend Waters. He ran a blade through his throat." He laughed and threw a bandaged hand up in the air. "I mean, Waters is a bloody bastard! Always thorough. Don't recall him saying no kid was hangin' around, though. He'll be sad he missed that opportunity."

He chuckled and rose up off of the couch, leaving a trail of Audie's blood across Deirdre's face with the knife as he stood. "So, you got the wrong man, boy! You gonna die, and you didn't even get the right man." He paused. "But he's here in Denver, too. Maybe I should run get him, and he can tell you all about it. How'd that be?"

Briggs cackled like it was the funniest thing he'd ever heard. Killing was about the only thing that ever brought laughter out in the man.

He leaned over and kissed Deirdre on the cheek, then slowly walked over to where Audie knelt.

"Should I just let you die, boy, or put you out of your misery? You want to sit and watch me with your girl here? Come on, boy! What do you want?"

Briggs kicked him in the side where he had stabbed him.

Audie fell over on his other side, and blackness almost overtook him.

"Well, if you won't decide, I'll decide for you," Briggs said as he knelt down beside Audie with the bloodied knife in his hand.

Audie heard a blast and heard a whistle over his head. Deirdre screamed, still muffled. Audie didn't know who the shot came from or if even if he'd been hit. The pain overcame him.

Briggs dropped the knife and slumped over beside Audie, blood pouring from a hole just over his left eye.

Moses dropped his pistol to the floor.

"Moses!" Audie exclaimed as he tried to rise to his knees, but he didn't have the strength.

Moses shakily knelt down to examine Audie. He felt shock trying to claim him, but Deirdre's muffled screams pulled him out of it. He ran over and cut the ropes binding her hands. She slipped the gag from her mouth and ran to Audie.

"Moses! Go get the doctor! Now!" she pleaded.

Moses didn't hesitate and was out the door.

Deidre pressed the rag Briggs had stuffed in her mouth against the wound on Audie's side to stop the flow of blood.

"Come on, Audie. You can't die," she pleaded.

Audie went black.

Tommy saw Moses burst out the front door and sprint up the street. Moses was a good ways down the street, but he heard banging on a door and Moses yelling for Doc Mayer to answer.

The night probably hadn't gone as planned.

Adalina had enjoyed traveling on the train, and much to her surprise, she slept soundly at night when it was chugging along. The distant *chug-a-chug chug* and gentle rocking of the car put her to sleep like a lullaby.

When they arrived in Golden, Thomas went to the postmaster general to check for any wires addressed to him. He did have one waiting, and it told him the man he was directed to meet was a Mr. Timmons. He was to dine with him that evening at Rancher's Restaurant on Washington Avenue.

He rented himself and Adalina a room in the most luxurious hotel Golden had to offer. The feather mattress and pillows and ornately carved wooden baseboards almost made Adalina feel guilty.

"If you will forgive me for not having dinner with you tonight, I promise to be fully devoted to you for the remainder of journey," Thomas vowed when he returned to Adalina. She wore a purple dress with a collar of eyelet lace. He couldn't help thinking how gorgeous she looked in that shade.

"Of course, Thomas. You do what you need to do."

"This hotel offers room service, or you could dine in the restaurant downstairs tonight. Or maybe I could bring you something...whatever you want."

"Thomas, I'm fine. Don't worry. I'll probably have dinner in our room tonight while you're away. I want to read the newspaper. I've never seen a newspaper outside of Missouri. Will you bring me one?"

"Well, alright then. I'll buy you every newspaper Golden has to offer."

He set out to find Adalina what she desired.

~

"Deirdre is living with that pack of hellions now? Son of a bitch!"

Binkley and James sat in the mayor's office and waited patiently as he delivered his tirade.

"Those Devils have screwed me over for the last time! The saloon is going broke because of them, and now they've stolen my. . . my Deirdre."

Losing Deirdre was a matter of pride, not a matter of the heart.

"I think they came here to destroy me. I think the devil himself sent them here to undermine the good work we have done in this city. There will be nothing left if we don't get rid of them."

Tabor stomped around his office, occasionally banging a fist on his desk or a shelf as he spoke.

Binkley shuffled in his chair like hellfire was nipping at his feet. James sat with one leg crossed over the other, as calm as the night when there was no wind.

"Father, I need to talk to you alone," James said.

Binkley sat there oblivious, not realizing both of the men were staring at him, waiting for him to leave.

"Oh! Pardon me! Yes, I. . . I have work to do elsewhere."

He hurriedly gathered himself and rushed for the door.

"That fellow, Briggs," James started when Binkley left, "he attacked the older DeVine brother last night. He wounded Audie gravely, but Briggs was killed. Tommy said Deirdre was there. He heard her screaming."

"Finally, a stroke of luck! So he'll die?" the mayor asked.

"No one knows yet. He's alive now, but evidently it was a severe wound."

"We can use this, son. If we play our cards right, we can use this in our favor."

"Direct your son, Father, and he shall obey."

"Tommy Santino. How valuable is he to you?"

James laughed.

"He's more of a nuisance than a value."

"Well, then he's perfect."

They talked for the rest of the afternoon, sharing ideas about how to rid themselves of the many things that were not useful to them.

"He just now comin' to. If'n you wanna see him," Moses announced to Shane.

Shane walked in the bedroom where his brother lay, afraid of what he was going to see. Audie had never been wounded so badly before.

"Audie?" he asked as he gently pushed the door open.

"Shane," Audie said in a weak voice. "Come in. Me and Deirdre here were just about to start a poker game."

Humor wasn't usually on Audie's radar so it surprised Shane to hear him attempt it.

Deirdre sat on the bed stroking Audie's long black hair down away from his face.

"How are you, brother?" Shane questioned.

"If it wasn't for this hole in my side, I'd be amazing."

"At least you got that son of a bitch."

"I didn't get him."

"He's dead! I saw the coroner haul his ass out of here."

"Moses shot him. He was about to kill me when Moses came."

"Shit."

"Yeah. The sheriff's calling it self-defense. He wouldn't if he knew it'd been a black man who pulled the trigger."

Shane shook his head as Audie recounted details from the night before. Audie grew quiet and then looked at Deirdre.

"Deirdre, can I talk to my brother alone for a bit?" Audie asked.

She leaned in to kiss him on the forehead and left the room, shutting the door behind her.

"I'm going to send Moses away, Shane. I'm going to give him half of the money we've saved and send him away. I want you to go and buy him whatever papers he needs to travel freely. Have Soapy help. He'll know what to do."

"Hell, we should have done that a long time ago, Audie, but he's like family now. I don't want to see Moses go."

"He's a good man, Shane. We're not. He tolerates our ways because we saved him. We need to let that man go find a life he can have some peace in."

Audie's eyes watered, and he stopped talking for a moment.

"I mean, hell, Shane. Being with us just made him do the one thing he swore he'd never do again. He killed another man. If he ever owed a debt to us, it's more than paid."

Shane sat down in the chair next to the bed.

"He won't want to go."

"I know, but I'll make him. I just need you to see to it that those papers are ready in the next few days."

"Okay, Audie."

Audie shifted in the bed and pushed himself to a sitting position. He groaned with the effort, but he wanted Shane to hear the importance of his next words.

"There's something else. Briggs, he raided the camp, but he said he didn't kill our father. He said it was a soldier named Waters and that he's here in Denver, too."

"I'll kill that bastard tonight."

"You're going to have to be smart about this, Shane. If anybody gets wind he's dead, the law will start putting two and two together real quick. Soapy will know where to locate the man. Draw him out somewhere. Put him where no one will find him."

"I can do that."

"I know you can. I just wish I could do it with you."

"You get better, Audie. I'll take care of this."

Shane put his hand on Audie's shoulder for a moment and left. Audie laid back and fell into a deep sleep.

CHAPTER 44

Adalina sat in her hotel room reading the paper on the plush bed. She could hear faint conversation and laughter on the street below, but only enough to pull her from concentration briefly.

She had ordered a vegetable stew and cornbread for her dinner and a glass of wine, all of which was quite enjoyable.

Thomas had bought her three papers: *the Denver Daily Times, the Denver Daily Tribune,* and the *Rocky Mountain News Daily*. They were all yesterday's editions, but the stories were new to her just the same.

She was halfway through the *Denver Daily Tribune* when she saw the headline "DeVine Devils Possess the Soul of Denver."

She took in a deep breath at the sight of her sons.

There was a photo with the article of Audie, Shane, and Smyth. She ran her fingers slowly across her sons' faces.

Even standing room was in short supply last night at the Chicago as the DeVine Devils launched into their opening number. When Audie DeVine, the band's lead singer and guitarist, walked out on the stage, the crowd's roar became so aggressive that the walls of the saloon shook like a stampede of cattle was running through town.

What happened next was a scene from a southern Pentecostal church. Audie raised his hands high in the air to hush the hordes of people, and the crowd went dead silent.

As he broke into their standard song, "Hard Times Come Again No More," a cappella, it was as if the room held its breath. When the other two members of the band joined in, the place erupted in a cheer so loud that it might have been heard in California.

The article went on for three more paragraphs, praising the DeVine Devils for their showmanship.

Adalina pulled out the necklace she had taken from the Pinkerton box and held it in her hands as she prayed for her sons.

Moses opened the door after the second knock to see Soapy and two of his men standing outside.

"How is he?" Soapy questioned.

"He asleep now. But the doc say he gonna make it. Y'all come in."

Soapy stepped inside, but his men waited out by the door.

"Soapy, this is Deirdre. She a friend of Audie's."

Soapy and Deirdre exchanged greetings quickly, as Soapy had intentions to talk to Audie.

"I wanna see him," Soapy said as he made his way toward the closed door he assumed was Audie's room. He was genuinely concerned about his friend.

"He's resting right now, if you want to come back later," she tried to persuade.

Soapy either didn't hear or didn't care what she was saying. He went in the room where Audie lay and closed the door.

He walked over and sat in the chair next to Audie's bed.

"You should've let me take care of this, Audie."

Audie slowly opened his eyes to see Soapy right above his face.

"Hello, Soapy."

"There's another fellow who was traveling with the Briggs guy. He tried to make it out of town this morning. I figured you and your brother would want to talk to him before he left, so he's at my office."

Audie stared at Soapy trying to figure him out.

"Why do you care, Soapy?"

Audie's question offended him.

"Hey! Can't a guy look out for his friends?"

Audie could see he'd hurt Soapy's feelings.

"I didn't mean anything by it. I was just wondering why you would care about a vendetta Shane and I have when you've got enough on your plate."

"Because I know who you are."

Audie closed his eyes and tried to smile.

"No, you don't."

"Yeah. I know who you are. *You're me.* You're the son of a bitch that some son of a bitch burned the heart out of. They did something so bad, so evil to you that now the devil himself couldn't scare you. And every outlaw and law dog both would turn coward if they saw who you really are."

Audie looked at him for a minute and could almost see flames in his eyes.

"You rest up. Don't worry about the Chicago. We'll close for remodeling or some shit till you're better. And I'll kill this cunt Waters myself."

"No. Find Shane. Bring Waters here. Let Shane do it here."

"Audie, just let me take care of it. I'll make the son of a—"

"No! Shane will do it." Audie spoke as loudly as he could.

Soapy could tell this was big to Audie.

"Alright. It'll have to be after hours, but I'll bring him tonight."

Audie reached out a hand to Soapy. Soapy grabbed it firmly and shook it, then exited the room.

～

"I ain't never killed no dame before. You's guys are swinging below the belt here. I mean, I can do it, but this is gonna cost you a piece more than my average pay. You know. . . something like this has gotta be worth fifty bucks, at least," Santino bargained.

Just like always, James Tabor was amazed at how low Tommy Santino's expectations were. Besides, he didn't plan on Santino being able to collect his compensation for this anyway.

"Make it sixty dollars. You deserve it, Tommy," James encouraged. "Just make sure it's discreet."

James stood and reached across the desk to shake Tommy's hand.

"Don't worry, James," Tommy coaxed. "Discreet is my middle name."

James didn't know which he hated worse: Tommy's utter blindness to his own nature or the fact that Tommy called him by his first name.

When Soapy returned to his office, Shane was waiting for him.

"I need to talk to you, Soapy."

"I know. I just came from seeing your brother. Come in."

Shane followed Soapy and his men into the gambling den, past the poker players trying their best to hide the excitement and fear they held with each new hand.

Arny and the other guard, whom they called Southie, followed Soapy, too. They had been the two who went with him to the DeVine house.

When they entered the office and shut the door, Shane wasted no time in asking for what he needed.

"I need traveling papers for Moses, and I need to know where a bastard named Waters is. He was traveling with Briggs."

Soapy sat at his desk and calmly lit a cigarette.

"The papers will take me a couple of days."

"Fine. And Waters?"

"I can give you that right now if you want. Follow me."

Soapy rose from his desk and opened the door to a small closet behind him. Inside was Waters, hands tied and gagged, with dried blood covering most of the left side of his face.

He stared up at the two men in the doorway, wondering what was about to happen next.

Shane instinctively stepped toward the closet with purpose, but Soapy closed the door before he got there.

"You can't have him just yet, though. Audie wants me to bring him around tonight. He wants to watch you do it." Soapy said.

He stared at Arny for an uncomfortable moment before he spoke again.

"But if you want something to tide you over, I can give you Arny here."

Everyone turned to Arny when Soapy spoke. The other guard, Southie, turned to face Arny. Southie pulled a pistol out of a shoulder holster and aimed it at Arny.

"Wha…what's this about, Boss?" Arny stuttered.

But he knew before he asked the question. He just didn't know whether Tommy had backstabbed him or if Soapy had flat figured him out.

Shane was confused.

"Tsk, tsk, tsk," Soapy sounded off while shaking his finger at Arny. "Oh, you know what it's about. Let's not make this more dramatic than it has to be, ya fat prick."

Arny dropped the dumbfounded routine. He knew how this ended.

"How'd ya know?" Arny asked.

Soapy laughed.

"Come on, Arny. You been looking to shank me for a while now. You think I'm blind? I just can't figure one thing. Who'd you tell? How'd you get to Briggs?"

So Tommy hadn't double-crossed him.

Shane began to put things together now.

"Tommy Santino," Arny confessed.

"That tiny, rat-hearted snake. I should have killed that bastard the second he went to Tabor. I didn't think he was worth it."

"Yeah, Soapy. I could kill him. You could give me another chance, Boss. I'd do whatever. I'd sweep the floors or take out the trash or. . . Come on, Soapy! We go back too far for you to kill me!"

Arny started crying as he ended his plea.

Soapy walked over to Arny. He reached up and put his cigarette out on Arny's face. Arny recoiled in pain but never moved to retaliate.

"You're right, you son of a bitch! We do go way back. And you stabbed me in the back for that worthless sack of shit, Tabor. Don't beg me for your life! Be a man!"

Soapy smacked Arny with his backhand and forehand over and over as Arny whimpered. It was more degrading than painful. A perfect circular blister was forming on his cheek from Soapy's ring. Arny instinctually tried to raise his hands to deflect the blows but kept them down below his face, out of fear.

Soapy reached in Arny's coat, took out his pistol, then threw it to Southie.

"You screwed up bad this time, Arny. There ain't no coming back from this one. But it's Shane's brother here who got the heat for it. That bastard almost killed Audie. I'm gonna let him be your judge and jury. These DeVine brothers, they're mean, though. You might wish I'd just—"

Shane moved to Arny so fast it almost didn't seem human. He pulled a knife from his waistband in each hand. He rose up, knives level with Arny's throat, his arms crossed in an X, and swiped the blades across Arny's thick neck, one from the left and one from the right. Blood fountained out in bursts, in time with his slowing heart-beat, and became weaker with every spray.

Arny reflexively pulled his hands up to his throat to stop the blood, but it was too late. The gashes were so wide his hands couldn't cover them, and it looked as if his neck couldn't hold his head up. He went to his knees and then flat on the floor. Facedown, he shook slightly for a moment and then breathed his last.

"Damn it, Shane! I was gonna have you take him out back. You ruined my carpet!" Soapy said, no mention of the man who was lying dead on his office floor.

Shane grabbed a handkerchief from an end table nearby and wiped the blood off of his face. Sprays of crimson still covered his neck and torso.

"Bring that son of a bitch in the closet to the house tonight." Shane turned around and left without another word.

Soapy just smiled. He liked the savagery in Audie and Shane.

When Thomas arrived back at the hotel room after delivering the package, Adalina greeted him at the door. She looked like a child about to take her first pony ride.

He kissed her when he walked in the door, and she kissed him back, but pulled away quickly with excitement.

"The boys are here!" Adalina blurted out.

"What?"

"Shane and Audie! They are playing music at a saloon in Denver!"

"That's. . . that's great, Adalina! What luck!"

"We should leave for Denver first thing in the morning. We can take a coach ride for twenty cents. I'm so excited, Thomas!"

Thomas hugged her and agreed to go. He was happy that Adalina would see her sons again, but he had hoped to spend this time with his wife uninterrupted.

He did his best not to show his disappointment.

CHAPTER 45

It was three o'clock in the morning, and Soapy and his man Southie were making their way through the Chicago and down the high-fenced trail that led to the boys' back door. Southie had Waters over his shoulder, hogtied and gagged to muffle any noises that might rouse a nearby resident.

Moses was fast asleep in his room in the back of the house, and Smyth had bedded down with a woman he'd met while out drinking that night.

Deirdre was asleep beside Audie, who was wide-awake, listening for the arrival of the men.

When Southie and Soapy arrived with Waters, Shane met them at the door. They walked in, and Southie threw Waters down hard on the floor.

"You want we should stick around? You gonna need help with disposing of this piece of shit?"

"No. I have it covered."

Earlier that day, Shane had retrieved his gelding from the stable and rode about a mile outside of town. It had taken him a couple of hours to dig the grave, but he'd hidden the hole behind a thicket of brush just past a grouping of ominous boulders.

"There's a hole already waiting for him," Shane informed Soapy.

"Alright." Soapy lit a cigarette and took a deep draw. "You boys have fun. I need you to get this out of your system so we can get back to business at the Chicago." He flicked the ash on Waters.

"As soon as Audie gets better, we'll be kicking this town's ass again, Soapy. Don't worry about it."

"I'm not worried. I just like it when everything is running smooth. We'll talk to you later."

Southie and Soapy exited the front door, and Shane locked it behind them. He strode back to where Waters lay on the floor mouthing something unintelligible through the gag. Shane silenced him with a kick to the gut and headed down the hall to wake Audie.

Audie had heard the men come in and was at the door of the bedroom with his boots on when Shane opened it. He was struggling to pull a shirt over his head.

"Audie! What are you doing? You don't need to be walking by yourself," Shane whispered to keep from waking Deirdre.

"I'm fine," Audie said as he pushed past Shane to find Waters.

"Let's take him out of town. I don't want Deirdre or Moses to be privy to this."

"Audie, you just got gut-stuck a couple days ago! We can do it here. Let's just keep the gag in."

"No!" Audie demanded. He gritted his teeth. "I want to hear him hurt."

Shane knew when he couldn't argue with his brother. He hit Waters in the jaw hard enough to daze him, then picked up the limp man and carried him outside.

Audie was weak, but he managed to clamber up onto the horse with Shane's help. He let out a quiet grunt of pain as he sat in the saddle.

Shane tied a rope around Waters's already bound feet and climbed on the horse behind Audie. Waters protested as they started dragging him down the street, but he couldn't be heard through the gag as they trotted out of town.

Something had stirred Deirdre awake. She felt around in the darkness and realized Audie wasn't there. She rose instantly, calling for him. When he didn't answer, she made her way down the hall, and movement in the front window caught her eye. Peering out, Deirdre saw Audie and Shane riding away and dragging a body behind a horse.

After a short trip, Shane slowed down and steered his horse into a cluster of chokecherry bushes, past the boulders. The unripened fruit stained Waters's clothing, and the branches whacked at him as if he were an intruder.

They stopped between two ragged Douglas fir trees. Shane dismounted first and then helped Audie down.

Waters saw the hole in the ground and realized it was for him. He was coughing and choking from all the dust he'd inhaled on the ride over, and his shirt was torn in the back, exposing a patch of raw, red skin mingled with dirt, leaves and tiny stones. Shane cut the gag off of his mouth, nicking Waters's unshaven face. He wasn't gentle.

Audie grabbed a canteen off of Shane's horse and offered it to Waters. Waters looked up untrustingly.

"Do you want a drink or not?" Audie demanded.

"Yes. Yes, I want a drink," Waters rasped.

"Cut his feet loose," Audie said to Shane.

Shane looked at his brother and tried to understand what he was thinking. He reached down and cut the ropes around the captive's ankles.

Audie poured water on Waters's face, spilling a good bit in his nose and choking him a little in the process. He was famished so he tried to drink it anyway.

"Who the hell are y'all?" Waters shouted after he recovered from coughing.

Audie leaned on one of the firs for support.

"Don't you recognize us, Waters? Hell, you made us."

Waters narrowed his eyes at Audie for a second and then Shane, trying to decipher the cryptic answer Audie had given him.

"Look, I think you two got me confused with some other son of a bitch. I ain't got no beef with the two of you."

"You ever seen us play? At the Chicago?" Audie asked.

"Yeah, man. Y'all are good. Hell, I went a few times."

"My father gave me that guitar. He taught me to play it. His name was Azariah, and he was a missionary to the Apache out in Arizona territory. A little camp right off the Gila River. Does that ring any bells?"

"Shit, man. I was in the army, for God's sake. I saw a lot of Indian camps. What's that got to do with you and me?"

It frustrated Audie that he didn't remember. He reached out and smacked Waters with the back of his hand.

"Think, you Billy Yank bastard! Look at my face and think!"

Audie stumbled a little from weakness, and Shane grabbed his arm to stabilize him.

In that moment, when Audie had rage on his face, Waters remembered the preacher. He saw Azariah laying there dying before he had run the knife through his throat.

God brought me here! Waters heard the preacher say. They both saw it on Waters's face.

"You're. . . you two are the preacher's kids." Waters stared at them for a few seconds, realization sinking in. After a moment, he started laughing.

"Ah, man. Of all the things that I thought would do me in, damn sure didn't figure on it being no preacher's kid."

Audie couldn't stand the sound of the man laughing. He lunged at him and bit the side of Waters's face, leaving a two-inch piece of flesh dangling from his cheekbone when Shane pulled him off.

Waters put his hand up to the wound and howled in agony as the blood dripped through his fingers.

"You heathen bastard! You bit half my face off!"

Waters hobbled to his feet to rush at Audie, but Shane kicked his legs out from under him as he stood up, pitching him forward face-first into the ground.

"Fight me fair, you son of a bitch! Fight me fair, and we'll see who ends up in that hole down there!" Waters challenged.

"You want a fair fight? Did you kill those women and children in a fair fight? Did you stab my father in a fair fight? Untie his hands!" Audie barked at Shane.

"Audie, let's just—"

"No! He wants a fair fight! Untie him!"

Shane reluctantly went over and cut the ropes around Waters's wrists. Waters stood up with his back to a Douglas fir and squared off, waiting for an attack.

"You try to run, and my brother here will kill you before you make the second step. If you beat me, you walk. Throw him a blade!"

"Audie, come on! You're in no shape to fight. You can barely stand!"

"Give him a knife!" Audie yelled.

Waters assessed the situation for a minute, weighing his options. Shane threw a knife to Waters right between his legs, so close to his balls that he thought he felt the whirr of the blade. The knife stuck in the tree behind him. He reached around and retrieved it, never taking his eyes off of the brothers. The accuracy of Shane's knife swayed him from any thought of escape.

Waters chuckled again. He noticed the bloodstain on the side of Audie's coat.

"Looks like Briggs already did half the job for me. Alright, you singin' son of a bitch, I'll give you what you want."

Waters slow-stepped toward Audie, knife in hand, ready for battle. Audie tossed his own knife from his right hand to his left and back again.

Waters stepped in quickly and swung the Indian dagger at Audie's wounded left side. Audie sidestepped, barely dodging the knife's blade. He brought his knife down and made a sizable gash on the top of Waters's right forearm, stumbling forward as he did. Waters winced and dropped his knife, but reached down with his left hand and picked it up.

"Just finish it, Audie!" Shane screamed as he reached for one of his own knives. He knew Audie could beat Waters, but he feared one more knife hole in Audie would be his last.

Audie righted himself and motioned for Waters to come at him again.

Waters knew the situation didn't bode well for him. He went for broke and dove for Audie.

There were three feet between the two men when Waters jumped at him. Audie tried to shift to the right, but Waters's left hand caught him, sending him flying to the ground.

Waters lost the knife in the process, though.

Audie's world spun for a second when he hit. The pain in his side turned to numbness and stole his equilibrium for a moment.

Waters tried to jump on top of him, pushing his hands away as he did. He could tell Audie was weak and knew if he could get on top it would be over.

As Waters leaned over him, Audie reached up and grabbed his face with both hands, sticking his thumb into Waters's left eye socket. He pushed it in till all three heard the wet popping sound of the eyeball bursting.

Waters screamed and brought his hands up to his face.

Audie mustered up all the energy he could and pushed the screaming man off of him. He stood and looked down at Waters, who was kneeling on the ground cradling his wounded face in his hands. He kicked him in the head and sent him dazed, back to the ground. Audie dropped to his knees and wavered for a bit, close to losing consciousness himself. He lifted his knife up in the air with both hands and came down with it, landing the blade right in Waters's throat.

The gurgling sound of Waters's last breath ushered Audie into blackness.

~

Adalina and Thomas arrived in Denver late morning the next day. She was so excited to see her sons again that she had the door to the coach open before it had even stopped in front of the Chicago. Adalina was through the swinging doors of the saloon by the time Thomas paid the driver for his services.

When she entered, there was no one to be found in the main room, but she could hear movement coming from somewhere in the back. It was the first time Adalina had set foot in a saloon.

"Hello. Is anyone available?" she called out to whomever could hear her.

A surly-looking man with a rather pronounced mustache came out from a room behind the bar.

"We're closed, lady. You need to move along now."

Thomas entered the saloon.

"I'm sorry to bother you, sir. I'm looking for Audie and Shane DeVine. Do you know where I might find them?" Adalina asked in a polite voice.

The bartender let out a sour chuckle.

"You and every other girl in this town. Go home. They've got enough tail chasing them without one who's getting long in the tooth."

Thomas walked toward the man, clinching his fist as he did, readying himself to teach the man a lesson for disrespecting Adalina.

"I'm their mother," Adalina said with enough grit in her voice to make Thomas turn to look at her. He'd never heard that tone from her.

The bartender straightened his posture and put his hands up as if in surrender. "Oh. Pardon me, ma'am. My apologies. Y'all follow me."

He led them to the back door of the saloon that opened to the walkway leading to Audie and Shane's house.

"Y'all just follow this path. At the other end is the door to their house. Again, I'm sorry for my language, ma'am. Serving roughians every night sure has put the dickens in my tongue. If y'all need anything at all, please just ask for me. My name's Sammy, and I'm the manager here."

Audie and Shane had a reputation of intolerance toward those who got on their bad side. Sammy hoped they wouldn't find out he'd been so foul with their mother or he feared he'd end up in rough shape.

Thomas gave the man a look as he walked past him that let him know how unappreciative he was of the man's lack of discretion.

They made their way down the path to the back door of the house. Adalina could barely contain herself as they knocked on the door. They heard movement inside, but no one came to answer. She knocked again, louder.

Finally, Smyth opened the door, shirtless, hungover, and chomping annoyingly on an apple.

"Can I help y'all? How'd you get back here?" Smyth inquired.

"Are Audie and Shane here?" Adalina asked.

"Who's asking?"

Smyth looked at Thomas and realized he'd seen the man before.

"Hey, you're that Pink from Wichita. I remember you. You married — Oh, shit! You're Audie and Shane's mama!"

Adalina and Thomas stood there silently as he put it all together.

"Y'all come in. How'd you get here so quick? I thought y'all lived in Missouri." Smyth continued to engage them in conversation.

Adalina and Thomas were confused by Smyth. They both noticed a dark stain on the wood floor as they entered the house but stepped around it and said nothing.

"We were in Golden and heard the boys were playing here so we came up. You're Smyth, right? The fiddle player?" Thomas asked.

"Aw, man. I'm sorry. Where are my manners?" Smyth set down the apple and stuck out his hand to Thomas and then Adalina.

"Yes. Smyth. Smyth Hoxie. Honored to meet you, ma'am. Y'all have a seat. Let me go tell Deirdre and Shane you're here."

"Deirdre?" Adalina questioned, but Smyth was already peeping inside the bedroom door whispering to someone.

Shane emerged from the bedroom, shutting the door quietly behind him.

"Mama!"

He walked over and gave her a long, full hug, and Adalina held him as close as if he were still an infant.

"It's good to see you, Mama."

"I missed you, Shane. It's good to see you, too."

Thomas and Smyth stood there silent.

"Where is Audie?" Adalina asked.

"You don't know?" Shane asked.

"Know what?"

Shane hesitated.

"Audie's not in good shape, Mama. We don't know—"

Just then Moses came walking in from the back.

"Ms. Adalina, Missa Thomas. Good ta see you folks."

Moses didn't have the same disposition Adalina had remembered. Somehow he looked. . . harder.

"Hello, Moses. Good to see you, too," Thomas said.

Adalina was trying to take it all in.

"What do you mean, not in good shape? Where is he?"

Shane led his mother back to the bedroom where Audie was. Deirdre was holding his hand in one of hers and stroking the backside of it with the other. She turned and stood when she saw the others come in.

"Hello," she said tiredly, weary from sitting up with Audie.

Adalina went to the side of the bed opposite of Deirdre and looked at her oldest son lying unconscious. She began to cry softly. Thomas went to her and laid a comforting hand on her shoulder.

"What happened?"

Deirdre gave Shane an angry look and waited for him to explain to Adalina. She blamed him for Audie's condition.

"There was a fight. Audie took a knife in his side. He lost a lot of blood. The doc says all we can do is wait it out now."

"Who was the fight with?" Thomas inquired.

Shane struggled to find words that wouldn't give them away.

"An intruder. Here. A man named Briggs ambushed Audie inside. He had Deirdre here tied up."

"Where's this Briggs man now?" Thomas asked.

"Audie shot him."

Moses overheard the conversation from outside the bedroom. The lie Shane was telling tugged at his conscience even harder than before.

Adalina put her face in her hands and cried. Thomas moved to hold her.

Adalina spent the better part of the day right by Audie's side, watching him and silently praying for her son to recover. Deirdre and the others left the room to give her time alone with her son.

In the sitting room outside, everyone was getting acquainted with Thomas.

"Deirdre, are you and Audie to be married?" Thomas inquired.

"Yes. Audie has been talking of building us a house just outside of town."

She smiled timidly as she spoke, exposing herself to Thomas. In that moment, he could see the sweet and broken in this girl. He knew why Audie loved her.

"That's nice, Deirdre. I choose to believe that house will still be built," he comforted.

She could tell by his look that he meant those words.

Moses came in with bags full of steak and potatoes for everyone. As they sat at the table divvying up portions, Deirdre walked to the bedroom to offer Adalina some food.

"I brought you something to eat, Mrs. Thorntree."

Adalina opened her eyes from prayer and looked up at the girl in the doorway.

"Thank you, honey."

"Would you like me to leave it here? Or you can come eat with everyone and I'll sit with Audie."

Adalina could tell this woman wanted time with her son. She didn't want to leave, but she surrendered her position as guardian for the time being.

CHAPTER 46

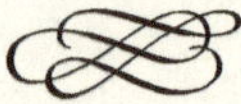

It had been almost three full days of hoping and praying when Audie finally awoke. Deirdre was with him when he came to.

"Audie!" she whispered excitedly when she saw his eyes open.

He smiled at the woman he loved. The smile took most of the strength he had, and he had to shut his eyes for a bit longer before he could speak.

"How long was I out?"

"You've been sleeping for three days now," Deirdre said as she wiped the tears from her eyes on the back of her sleeve.

"I dreamed we lived in a little house somewhere I'd never been. It was a place where we were happy."

"That sounds so nice, Audie."

He closed his eyes to see if he could conjure the memory of it again.

"It was a small house, made of stone and wood. There was a bur oak in the front yard like there was at my father's house, with a swing from a low limb. And there were children, Deirdre. A little boy and a little girl."

He smiled.

"They looked like you. They were sweet like you."

She laughed as she let the tears run down her face. She stroked the stubble that had grown on his cheeks.

"I like this place," she said.

"There was a river in the distance, blue like the water in the Colorado River, but this place wasn't desert, Deirdre. It was green like Missouri. I worked the land and you tended the house. We were. . . just. . . people. We were just people, and we were happy."

He closed his eyes again to rest and didn't wake for another few hours.

When he came to the second time, Shane and Adalina were in the room with Deirdre.

"Mama?"

"Yes, Audie," Adalina said. "I'm right here."

"Mama and Thomas were in Golden on a trip and heard we were here, Audie, so they came up to see us."

"Well, Mama, your timing is a little off. You should have waited a couple of weeks so we could paint the town together."

Everyone chuckled.

"Now, you hush up, Audie," Adalina scolded gently. "I think my timing is perfect. Sweet Deirdre needed a little sleep. She was up day and night with you."

Deirdre kissed Audie on the forehead, then excused herself. She knew Adalina would want some time with her sons alone.

"You boys sure have made a name for yourself in the world."

"We didn't set out to do that, Mama. It just sort of ended up that way."

Adalina started crying, and Shane reached out and took her hand.

"What happened to you? What became of my little boys? What in God's name happened to you?"

Shane and Audie were silent. Neither knew what to say. Defiance toward the world is an easy thing. Being that way toward a kind and loving mother isn't.

"I know—" Adalina started, but cut herself off.

She reached into her purse and pulled out the necklace with the cross and the feather.

Audie tried unsuccessfully to sit up in bed.

"Where did you get that?" he asked.

Adalina cried softly. "Thomas. It was evidence found during a case he was working on."

Her words came out in whispered gasps of sorrow and pain. She tried to keep her voice down.

"Your father did not raise two murderers! What did those godforsaken heathens do to you?"

"Soldiers killed Father, Mama. That had nothing to do with the Apache," Shane defended.

"It had everything to do with them!"

"It's not so simple," Audie offered.

Just then Thomas came in the door. He had heard Adalina crying and came to check on her.

She clutched the necklace so he couldn't see.

"Is everything alright, Addy?" Thomas asked, trying to figure the room.

"Yes. I just got worked up because I'm grateful Audie is doing better," she said and then sniffled.

"Okay. I'm right outside if you need me." He closed the door behind him.

"Does Thomas know?" Audie quietly asked after he left.

"No. And I pray he doesn't find out."

Audie took the necklace from his mother and held it near his heart before he fell back to sleep, and Shane and Adalina left the room to let him rest for a while.

The next morning when Audie woke, he felt some of his strength come back to him. Deirdre was by the bed, as usual, and he smiled to see her next to him.

"Hey, good looking," she said when she noticed him awake.

"Nothing looks as good as what I'm seeing right now," he said as he stared at Deirdre.

She bent down and kissed his lips.

"I'm starving. Would you mind getting me a bite to eat?"

"Of course!" Deirdre said and then left to do just that.

She hurried through the door, and as she did, Moses peeked in to see Audie awake.

"Hello, my friend. Come in," Audie persuaded.

Moses stepped into the room and sat in the chair Deirdre had occupied.

"Good to see you, Moses. I feel like it's been a while."

"Glad ta see ya on the rise, Audie."

"Did Shane give you the papers?"

"Yes. Thank ya fo' that."

"I'm sorry for the other night, Moses. I'm sorry you had to. . . do what you did."

Audie saw the pain in Moses' eyes before he looked away.

"Had ta be done. Just wish I wasn't the one who had ta do it."

"You're a good man, Moses. Don't let this world and the things it makes us do make you believe otherwise. You killed the man who was responsible for my father's death. You killed the man who would've killed me."

Audie saw that his words didn't do much too ease Moses's conscience.

"You need to leave, Moses. Take half of what we saved and go somewhere far away from us."

Surprised, Moses looked at Audie.

"Half my ass, Audie. I ain't done no amount a' work ta account fo' that."

"Moses, don't make me argue with you on this. We've got more than enough. You go make yourself a life worth living somewhere. Hell, go back to Wichita to that Beatrice lady. She sure seemed upset when we left. I don't care what you do, just go find the peace you deserve. The peace you won't ever find taking care of Shane and me."

"But I can't jus' leave while you down like this, Audie."

"I'll be better in a week, and I've got more than enough people to look after me here."

Moses hung his head. He didn't argue.

"I'm grateful fo' what you an' your brother done fo' me, Audie."

"I'm sorry for what me and my brother did to you."

Tears ran down Moses' face.

"Alright then. Let me do some figurin'. I'll get gone in a few days or so."

"To better places," Audie said.

"Ta betta places," Moses repeated.

Deirdre came back with a bowl of chicken broth and two slices of bread on a tray.

Moses had gone with Thomas and Adalina to get some things from the general store. Shane was still asleep, and Smyth hadn't come home last night.

Audie tried to eat but had lost some of the appetite he had earlier. He was going to miss his friend Moses.

"Audie, I need to ask you something," Deirdre started.

He could tell by her tone this wasn't going to be a talk he wanted to have.

"The other night I watched you and Shane leave. I saw a man being dragged behind you. What was that, Audie? And why would you do whatever dangerous thing that put you in this condition?"

Audie sighed. He was weary from heavy conversation.

"Deirdre, there's things you don't need to know."

"You're wrong, Audie. I need to know things about the man I love." Her soft chestnut eyes pleaded for a revelation.

"Who was that man?"

Audie moaned. "Leave it alone, Deirdre!"

"Who was he?"

"He killed my father!"

"So you killed him?"

"Yes! Him and more like him!"

Audie had hellfire in his eyes, and Deirdre couldn't look at him. He laid there, muscles tensed and mouth clenched shut. He didn't have to say anything else.

She burst into tears and ran out of the bedroom and out of the front door.

"Deirdre! Come back!" Audie shouted, realizing he had gone too far.

But she was off down the street.

Audie fought his weakness and rose up on the side of the bed for the first time in days. He stood, dizzily made his way to the washing bowl in his room, and began to clean himself up.

Deirdre ran until she couldn't run anymore. She stopped and sat on a bench in front of a law office on Lawrence street. A sign above her head creaked in the wind that read "The Law Offices of Wyatt & Lynch."

She had been sitting there lost in all her thoughts for about twenty minutes or so when she heard a familiar voice.

"Deirdre Bellafonte! Haven't seen you in a while."

She turned her head toward a small, finely dressed man walking down the street.

It was Tommy Santino.

"Hello, Tommy."

"How's Audie?"

She studied Santino, trying to see if he was sincere or not.

"Oh hell, Deirdre. I'm just askin'."

"He's fine, thank you," she said coldly.

"Why don't you let me buy you a drink? You look like you could use one."

"It's not even noon yet."

"Coffee then. Come on."

"No. Thank you. I'm in a mood to be alone today."

"Pretty girls like you shouldn't be alone."

She got a shiver from the way he said it.

"No, thank you."

"Okay, then. Suit yourself. Just never seen yous without a man for more than five minutes is all."

"You always were an ass, Tommy."

Deirdre was already fed up with the offerings of this day, and it was only ten thirty in the morning.

"Ah, Deirdre. You've grown brave and vulgar since you've been with those devils over there. You never would have used a tongue like that when you were with Tabor. I guess he kept it too busy for you to talk much."

Deirdre abruptly stood, lifted the front of her dress a couple inches off of the ground, and took off down the street again. Tears welled up in her eyes, and the last thing she wanted was to give Tommy the plea-sure of seeing her cry.

"She's a sweet girl, Audie. I can see why you like her," Adalina said.

"She got him wrapped up, that fo' sure," Moses said as he chuckled.

Adalina and Thomas laughed. They all sat around the big wooden table in the dining room.

"Well, while you fine people sit here discussing my leanings, I think I'll go take a walk and try to find her," Audie announced.

"Audie, you're still too weak to be up and walking! You stay here, and I'll go look for her," Adalina offered.

"I'm fine. I need to stretch my legs. I feel like I'm rotting just lying around this long."

"I'm going with you, then." Adalina said.

He wanted to talk to Deirdre alone, but this was his mother.

"Okay, Mama."

Thomas helped him out of the chair, and he and Adalina went looking for Deirdre.

Deirdre walked around the Denver streets for the rest of the day, past the shops and offices and people oblivious to the cares of others. She thought of her life and the men who had come and gone. Her father had been the first one to break her heart, and it seemed every man after had as well, if they'd even stayed around long enough to.

Audie. Audie was different. He looked at her like she had worth in this world. He touched her like it mattered to him how his fingers felt on her body. He was something new and frightening, but she felt no danger from him. Still, she knew he had a darkness, a darkness like she'd never known. She could sense it when he spoke sometimes, hear it in sounds he made when he was sleeping.

She loved him like she had no other. She wanted him despite the darkness.

She was so wrapped up in her thoughts of what could be that she never saw Tommy waiting for her at the corner of Larimer Street near the stable. He had been quietly following her all day since they'd spoken.

"Hey, Deirdre."

A branding iron hit her in the face before she had time to reply.

Audie and Adalina hadn't gotten far before Audie realized he needed to go back. He was weaker than he thought.

"Why would she stay gone so long, son?" Adalina asked.

"We had a fight this morning. I got angry . . ."

"I imagine you're not very good at losing arguments. Neither was your father."

He leaned on his mother a little harder.

"Sorry. I shouldn't have gone so far," Audie admitted.

"I don't mind. I miss holding my baby."

A stable hand found Deirdre the next morning when he took one of the horses out for a ride. She was tied to a post in the back, and the buzzards were starting to get curious.

Her face was pulp. Blood stained the blue dress almost down to her knees, and there was a knife stuck in her chest holding a note that read, *"the devel's lovar."*

Tommy was apprehended and killed before the sun rose the next day. James Tabor had a plan in place with a deputy sheriff on their payroll named Scovey. The deputy would wait until the job was done and then dispose of Tommy Santino after.

James wanted the imbecile dead anyway. This was just a good excuse for it.

As soon as Tommy had reported his work to James, the deputy was informed. The report stated Tommy was killed for resisting arrest. The truth was that Tommy was shot in the back and buried before any questions could be asked.

The news reached the brothers by noon the next day. Soapy heard it first and was the one to tell Audie.

Audie mourned Deirdre day and night until he went mad under the weight of it. He drank. He started bar fights. Her death was the first thing that happened in his life to make him lose control.

He fell off of the face of the earth and didn't care if he landed on his feet.

Shane began drinking more than he ever had, and since the brothers were no longer playing music, Smyth left, traveling with a tribute band, "The Demons of the DeVine." He hated the cheap imitation, but it was the only way he could play the way he wanted to.

Despite his previous plans, Moses stayed with his friends. He nursed wounds, bailed Audie out of jail sometimes, and made sure they didn't squander every last dime they'd made.

Adalina and Thomas stayed on for a while, but they finally went back to Missouri at the behest of Moses. He knew no mother wanted to see her sons in this condition. He promised her he'd look after them.

The DeVine Devils ceased to be.

CHAPTER 47

T *hirteen months later*

Once Lozen began searching, it had taken her three months to locate Shane's whereabouts. Traveling with a child had its drawbacks when it came to stealth operations, but out of necessity, the Apache had learned to teach their children not to cry. From almost the day of birth, when a child would cry, the mother would pinch the child's nose, forcing them to use their mouth for breathing. After a few days, the child learned and would only whimper slightly instead of crying. It was a training that saved many Apache from a soldier or a warring tribe discovering their hiding place when they were under attack.

Onawa had come along to help tend to the child while Lozen tracked down Shane. She had snuck up to a cluster of men headed to California to pan for gold. Sitting around a campfire that night, the men told tales of the DeVine Devils in the city of Denver.

The child was fourteen months old now.

She had named the child Natan.

Natan DeVine.

∾

Soapy had a key to the back door, so he let himself in. He still owned the house where the DeVine brothers lived. It was ten in the morning, but both brothers were sound asleep. Moses had gone out to knock a little dust off of Audie's Palomino stallion.

Soapy walked into Shane's bedroom and found him sprawled out across the bed with only his socks on, lying on his stomach.

"Get up."

Shane didn't budge. Soapy kicked the bed.

"Get up."

Shane turned his head toward the wall but still showed no signs of consciousness.

Soapy grabbed the mattress and rolled Shane off, pinning him between the bed and the wall.

"Get up," Soapy said with a little more steel in his voice.

"What the hell?" Shane said confused.

He rubbed his eyes to focus and realized Soapy was in the room.

"Shit, Soapy! What the. . . ?"

"I wanna talk to you about a job."

"Ahhh," Shane moaned as he rubbed his eyes.

"Put some clothes on and meet me in the Chicago in five minutes."

Soapy left, leaving Shane with no further information.

∾

Shane entered the back doorway of the Chicago looking too rough for even a saloon. His long hair looked like a bird's nest and his shirt was only half-tucked. His beard was uneven and unkempt. He wore no belt, so his pants hung loose and low around his hips.

"You look like shit, Shane," Soapy said as Shane sat next to him in a booth.

"You can eat a cat's ass, Soapy," Shane retorted as he drank the cup of coffee Soapy had waiting.

"Hey! I'm about the only friend you and your loony brother got left in this town!"

Shane sighed and hung his head like he was the most tired man in the West.

"Alright," Shane surrendered. "What can I do for you?"

"I want you and your brother to start playing again. I want you to get off your asses and do one more show."

Shane shook his head like that was the craziest thing he'd ever heard.

"Audie is. . . well, he ain't right, and we haven't hit a lick in over a year. Besides, Smyth is out playing with some crippled-ass band called the Demons or something and—"

"I've already sent someone for Smyth. He should be here in the next couple of days."

Shane chuckled and shook his head again.

"Damn it, Soapy. So what if Smyth is headed back. Even if I'm game, what about Audie?"

"I'll talk to Audie. I just need to know you're gonna back my play when I do."

Shane studied him for a minute. He could tell Soapy meant business.

"Alright. But you've got your work cut out for you with Audie," Shane said as he looked toward the floor.

"Well, maybe he just needs something to fight against."

Shane looked up at Soapy and could tell the man was holding cards he wasn't showing. He trusted Soapy's intentions, and besides, he didn't have the strength to press him on it right now. He needed beer or to go back to bed.

"There was some Indian lady in here last night asking for you. Sammy said she was hell on legs. Seemed like she'd never been around people before."

Shane stood quickly.

"What else did she say? Where'd she go?"

"Easy, friend! I didn't know you loved the reds so much. She didn't say nothing else, and Sammy played dumb 'cause he didn't know who she was to you. She's probably still around town."

Shane ran out the door, tucking in his shirt as he went.

~

"Brought ya some vittles," Moses said as he entered Audie's bedroom.

Audie was sitting on the side of his bed in a pair of torn and dirty long johns. His beard reached down almost a foot from his face, and his hair was almost to his waist. He looked like a castaway, and his bedroom was his island.

A well-used book, *The Ballade of Truthful Charles*, and a copy of the *King James Bible* were on the nightstand beside his bed. They were the only two things he had truly interacted with in months.

Moses moved the books to the back of the nightstand and placed the plate next to Audie. He turned to leave.

"Moses," Audie said, eyes fixed on nothing in particular on the wall.

"Yeah, Audie?"

"I read the story of Samson last night."

"That's good."

"They cut his eyes out when he lost his strength. But he grew strong again in prison and slew thousands in his death."

"I think the point is he woulda lived longer and done mo' good if he had'a done right."

"I like that story. It was one of my father's favorites, too."

"Well, they a lotta good ones in that book. You keep readin'."

Audie let the conversation die, and Moses left the room.

~

Shane looked for Lozen until noon, trying to figure her thought process as he went. He talked to a couple of bartenders in different saloons who had met her, too, but had no luck finding her.

He reached the western entrance to the city early in the afternoon. He knew this was where she would have entered.

She saw him before he saw her. She had camped outside of the city with Onawa and Natan but was riding back to look for him again.

She was only ten yards away when he turned and saw her trotting up to meet him.

She dismounted, and they ran to each other, embracing like they were each other's last hope in the world. They pulled apart and looked at each other for a moment.

"You look like death, Shane."

"Good to see you too, Lozen."

He kissed her.

"Something is different about you," Shane spoke.

"Ride with me."

They both mounted her stallion, and she rode hard toward Shane's surprise.

When they arrived, Onawa was sitting cross-legged outside of the tent.

Shane wondered why Lozen had brought the old woman with them to Colorado. They got off the horse, and Shane said hello to Onawa.

"He has your eyes," Onawa said to him.

"Who has my eyes?" It was then Shane heard a child's voice from inside the tent.

"Go inside. Meet your son," Lozen said.

Shane felt more afraid in that moment than he had in his whole life. He stood there frozen for a few seconds before he moved his thousand-pound feet to the tent. He pulled back the flap, entered, and let his eyes adjust to the darkness for a moment.

As soon as he could see, he knew the boy sitting in front of him was his own. His own eyes looked back at him. He looked at Lozen and looked back at the boy.

"His name is Natan. Pick him up. Hold your son."

Shane reached down and gently touched the boy like he was the most precious and fragile thing in the world.

Lozen laughed. "You won't break him."

Natan stopped jabbering when Shane picked him up. He studied Shane for a moment, sizing him up.

Lozen smiled.

"He's figuring out if he can win against you in a fight."

"Natan. What a good name," Shane said as he walked with the boy outside into the light. He held Natan out for a full view. Natan smiled at him.

"He likes you already," Onawa offered.

Shane spent the rest of the day getting to know his son.

"Come on in."

Moses opened the door for Soapy. Soapy had heard someone moving around inside and thought he'd knock instead of just enter.

"Moses," Soapy said, tipping his hat to him.

"Have you a seat. You wantin' for Shane? He ain't around right now."

"I wanna talk to Audie."

"Now, Missa Soapy, he ain't much on talkin' these days. I don't know if'n it's a good—"

"Oh, he'll talk. Let me see him."

Moses knew it was a command, not a request. He watched the man make his way back to Audie's room.

Audie was lying on the bed in his long johns reading the Bible when Soapy announced himself.

"Hey, Audie. It's your old pal Soapy. Nice duds. Yous wanna hit the town later?" He got no response from Audie.

"Okay. Listen. Put the Good Book down a second. I got something for ya."

Audie laid his Bible facedown open to the page he was reading and looked up at Soapy.

"It's been a year, Audie. Over a year. I don't wanna be insensitive to your loss here, but come on. You ain't worth a bucket full of skunk piss holed up in this house every day. Lying around in your underwear."

Audie just stared at him blankly.

"Get up, Audie."

Audie didn't move. Soapy walked over and slapped him viciously, spinning Audie's head around.

"Get your ass outta that bed!"

Audie turned to look at him again but didn't rise. Soapy knocked him back against the pillow with a right-handed punch to Audie's cheek.

Audie raised back up with blood running slowly out of the left side of his mouth. This time he had anger in his eyes, but he still didn't get up.

"Geez! What is with you and your brother wanting to stay in bed! I said get up! Get the hell outta that bed, Audie!"

He slapped Audie back and forth across the face until Audie stood and grabbed him and slammed him against the wall.

Moses heard the thud and ran into the room. Soapy was talking but held up one hand behind Audie's back to let Moses know it was alright and to keep his distance.

"Yeah, Audie! Get mad! Hit me! Your girl's dead, Audie! You gonna lie there like a coward and wilt away like a daisy the rest of your life? Hit me!"

Audie picked him up and threw him to floor.

"That's it, Audie! Get mad! Come on!"

Soapy stood, and Audie went for him. Soapy slid sideways and got him in a headlock.

"That's the fire! Yeah! That's it!" Soapy grunted as he held Audie.

Audie slammed his body back, throwing them both against the wall, forcing Soapy to release him.

Soapy sank to the floor. Audie stood over him, fist drawn, but stopped before he threw the punch.

They both breathed hard for a few seconds, until Audie let down his fist. Soapy extended a hand for Audie to help him up, and Audie accepted, pulling him to his feet. Soapy rose and put his hands on his knees, still catching his breath.

"I'm too old for this shit. I shoulda sent one of my boys in here," Soapy chuckled.

Audie shook his head and sat back on the edge of the bed, still slightly winded.

"Now that I know you ain't just a walking corpse no more, let's talk business."

Audie stared at Soapy and shook his head. He took the back of his hand and wiped blood from his lip.

"I don't know whether to kill you or kiss you," Audie said, only half joking.

"Why don't you split the difference and just listen to me a bit," Soapy said as he finally caught his breath.

Soapy started in, telling Audie about his plan to get the DeVine Devils back on the stage for one last grand finale.

It was the ending of the day, and the sun was slowly making its exit beneath the horizon, casting long carnival-like shadows across the terrain. Lozen and Shane were sitting outside the tent watching Natan play with Onawa. He would run as fast as his little legs would take him while she chased. Every so often she would catch him and lift him up toward her, tickling his belly by burying her face in it. Natan would laugh a deep-down belly laugh that would brighten anyone's day.

"He's perfect," Shane said.

"Of course, he is. I gave birth to him."

They both laughed.

"What do you want to do, Lozen?"

She didn't answer.

"You could come live with me and Audie. We could probably get our own place if you wanted. We're not working now, but I could find something to make a living."

"You know that can't happen."

This time he was silent.

"He could stay with our people. You could visit him from time to time," Lozen suggested.

"And wind up dead before he's old enough to wield a bow or knife," he added.

She started to protest but caught herself.

"I don't want him to have to fight," Shane said.

"Fighting is noble. Would you rather him be a coward?"

"I'd rather him not have to make a choice."

Shane tossed a pebble out into the field in front of them. The sun was disappearing now, half consumed by the darkening land.

"Neither of us could give him that life," Lozen said. Her voice broke slightly as she spoke.

Shane looked at her. A tear rushed down her face, then slowed after it had descended the cheekbone. He'd never seen her cry and reached up to wipe it away. Lozen turned her head before he could touch her.

He looked back toward the horizon.

"How did we make something so perfect that we can only hurt it?" Shane asked.

The sun vanished leaving a red glow that barely lit the western sky.

CHAPTER 48

"Mr. Tabor. Soapy Smith is in the foyer. He is requesting a meeting, sir," the new secretary informed.

"Soapy Smith?" Tabor asked no one in particular. He instantly reached for the .44 caliber pistol in the left drawer of his desk.

Soapy came walking through the office door. He wasn't much on waiting or formalities.

"Relax, Tabor. I'm just here to talk. You can put that showstopper shaking in your right hand away."

Tabor held the pistol tight. Soapy rolled his eyes.

"Tabor, if I wanted to kill ya, would I do it this way? Put the piece away!"

Tabor slowly laid the pistol back in the drawer but kept the drawer open.

"Shit! This whole damn town is nuts lately. It's like I'm living in a loony bin!" Soapy complained for the benefit of no one but himself.

"What do you want?"

"I want to make peace with ya, Tabor. You cut me deep taking the DeVine Devils out of commission. I gotta say, I didn't think you had it in ya, killing a dame like that, but damn if ya didn't. Ya got no heart, but that took some balls."

Tabor grinned.

"I have no idea what you're talking about," he said coyly.

"Cut the shit, Tabor. We both know how it went down."

Tabor kept his grin intact.

"What do you want, Mr. Smith? I'm a busy man."

"Look, unlike yous, I'm a man with a heart. Audie and Shane, they're just wasting away to nothing since your cold-blooded murder of that innocent girl. I want you to hire them."

Tabor burst out laughing like he was watching a performance from a king's jester.

"What? Seriously, Mr. Smith. In what world do you think that would ever fly? They'd no sooner work for me than Beelzebub himself. Have you lost your mind?"

"Well, they are called the DeVine Devils, Tabor."

Tabor kept chuckling. "That's rich, Soapy. You're a funny man."

"I'm serious. I want you to hire them. You've got that big military celebration coming up in three weeks honoring all those Billy Yanks who fought in the Indian wars and whatnot. You get the most famous band in this country to play that, to come out of retirement, and I don't have to tell you how that would look to the brass that'll be there."

Tabor's grin was gone. Soapy could tell he was thinking about it.

"What's in this for you?" Tabor interrogated.

"Like I said, I've got a heart. Audie and Shane, they're like brothers to me. It's a great sadness to me to see them not using the gifts they have. They need something big to shake them out of their misery! Playing at the Chicago just won't get them going now. I'm just trying to give them a leg up is all, even if I gotta ask a shit bag like you for help."

Tabor gave Soapy a look of disgust. "Why should I trust you?"

"'Cause there's nothing in it for me. I ain't got no play here other than helping my friends."

Tabor leaned back in his chair and folded his hands together across his stomach. "Well, you've piqued my interest."

"Good. You give it a think, and let's reconvene in a couple of days. I'll bring the boys around."

Soapy stood up, walked to the door to leave, and tipped his hat to the beautiful secretary sitting right outside Tabor's door. She gave him an unpleasant look, out of place on her pretty face.

He turned to Tabor. "A man who's gotta pay for it probably ain't much good at it."

Soapy left the building.

"That is the craziest thing I've ever heard, Soapy. How the hell do you think we'd get away with that?" Shane asked.

"Well, the getting away is on you. I figure it ain't the first time you boys had to hightail it out of some—"

"It's perfect," Audie interrupted.

"What?" Shane exclaimed.

"It's perfect. We couldn't have dreamed of a better way to end it."

"End what?"

Shane couldn't believe what he was hearing.

"Our career. Tell Tabor we'll do it."

"Whoa, Audie! Wait a minute!"

Soapy could see this was between the two brothers now. "Alright. You boys discuss it. You know where to find me when you figure it out."

Soapy let himself out.

"Audie, I ain't doing it. I've got more at stake now."

"What? All the whiskey and whores in this town? You're killing yourself on a drip! Remember Natan? Remember our promise? This is like a gift from God! Soapy doesn't even know what he's giving us!"

"I remember Natan," Shane said. "Lozen named my. . . " he trailed off.

"Huh?"

"Take a ride with me, Audie. I've got something to show you."

They walked to the stable, and Shane led Audie west of town to Lozen's camp.

When Audie and Shane arrived, Lozen was the only one outside the tent.

"Lozen! Good to see you," Audie said, surprised, trying to figure out what was going on. "What are you doing here?"

"Shane hasn't told you?" She looked surprised at Shane.

Shane walked in the tent and came out holding his son.

"Audie, meet Natan DeVine."

Shane held Natan out to Audie, and Audie slowly took him.

Audie held the boy and smiled from ear to ear at him.

"You have a son," he said with a smile as he stared at his brother's child.

"You're an uncle, brother."

Audie laughed. Natan squirmed to get down. Audie put him on the ground, and Natan took off running in circles around them.

"I have to earn trust with him. I can respect that," Audie humored.

He understood why things were different now for Shane.

When Audie and Shane arrived, Lozen was the only one outside the

Smyth arrived in town around six that evening. He was looking road weary and tired by the time he got to the house.

Moses answered the knock.

"Well, look what the cat drug in!" Moses reached out and hugged him. "Come on in."

"It's good to see you, Moses." Smyth smiled at his old companion.

"You lookin' beat, Smyth. You want me ta go getcha a bite ta eat?"

"Naw. Y'all got any whiskey in this house?"

Moses laughed. "Ya know we do. Help yo'self."

Moses held out a hand to the bar on the other side of the dining table. "The boys went out fo' a ride. They oughta be gettin' back fo' too long."

Smyth killed an elbow bender as he waited.

⁓

Audie and Shane got back to the house late that night. It was pitch dark, and they heard music coming from the house before they opened the door.

Smyth was sitting in a chair, his boots propped up on a table, sawing away at his fiddle. There was a bottle sitting on the table with just enough whiskey left in it to say it wasn't empty.

"Well, don't you two look like the south end of a north-bound trail horse."

"Good to see you, too, Smyth," Shane said.

Smyth rose and hugged the brothers, starting with Shane.

"Shew! Damn, Smyth! You'd smell better if you shit your britches," Shane told him.

Smyth chuckled. "It ain't been pretty out playing without y'all. I've played some places the devil might find too disagreeable to drink at."

"Well, if you'll set your stinking ass on the other side of the table, I'll drain a bottle with you. Looks like you already laid waste to that rye." Shane pointed to the near empty bottle.

Audie excused himself. He sat on the steps outside the back door and built a smoke. Just as he lit it, Moses came out to join him.

"What are you still doing up?" Audie asked.

"Well, it ain't by choice. Ain't no man with half his hearin' gonna sleep with Smyth in there playin'. It's good an' all, but not when a man tryin' ta sleep."

Audie stared at Moses for a minute without a word.

. . .

"I wish I'd been a better friend to you, Moses. You're as good of a man as I've ever met. I wish I could have given you whatever it is that makes a man know it's okay to tell someone to be quiet so he can get some damn sleep."

Moses sat on the steps beside him and focused on the ground.

"You gave me a hell of a betta life than the one I was livin'."

They were quiet for a while.

"You know, it's strange. You don't agree with a damn thing me and Shane have done, and if hard-pressed, you'd be the last one to judge us."

Moses looked at Audie. "People ain't as easy as black an' white, Audie. They's good and they's bad in all of us, and you ain't guilty'a nothin' I ain't done."

"Yeah, but you don't enjoy doing it like I do."

"I pray fo' you an' Shane. I believe the Good Lawd gonna take that from you some day."

"Like he took it from Samson?"

"Why you keep talkin' 'bout Samson? What you plannin', Audie?"

"I'm not planning anything, Moses. But I need you to get out of here. No more excuses. Go see that lady in Wichita. Or head east on the train to Eminence. Mama would love to have you around. You'd be safe there."

"This got somethin' ta do with Soapy?"

"Just promise me this time, Moses. Promise you're going to leave. Not many people in my life have I cared about enough to. . . I just need to know you'll be alright. Give me that, Moses."

Moses sighed. "I'm glad ta see you up an' about. I's worried with all that ruckus 'tween you and Soapy, but seems that man knew what he's doin'."

Audie just stared at Moses.

"Alright, Audie. I'll leave in the next couple days."

Audie's face softened. "Maybe we should go have a drink with those two bastards in there making all that racket. Shane's got something he wants to tell you."

They headed back inside to a drunk and one on his way.

~

"I got it all worked out. No one's gonna have any guns on them. It's a theatre show. Why would they need guns? Tabor will be up in the balcony. You a good enough shot to take him from the stage?"

Audie grinned. Soapy understood.

"That's what I figured. Okay, you take that son of a bitch out, and I'll have horses for yous three waiting out back. Easy breezy."

"So you get rid of an enemy and we get to become fugitives?"

"It's up to you, Audie. Don't kill him if you want, but I'm giving you a free shot at the man who killed Deirdre."

"Why wouldn't I just go kill him now and ride off?"

"You wasn't gonna do nothin' till I came and beat some sense into that thick skull of yours the other day."

Audie knew he had a point.

"Lookie, Shane was a lush, and you were wasting away to nothing. If you both wanna die, I ain't gonna stop you. But I sure would love to see that piss you had in you before. That's all I'm saying."

"I'm not arguing with you, Soapy. I love your plan. Believe me when I say it's the show I've always wanted to play. Shane ain't sure yet. When I sort that out, I'll let you know."

"Alright then. Let's do this thing."

"You don't think the law dogs will come after you if we do this and get away?" Audie asked.

"I won't be the one running. Won't be no blood on my hands." Soapy grinned and held up his hands as he spoke.

"Soapy, you're a godsend," Audie said.

Soapy looked taken aback. "Well, that's something I ain't never been called before."

~

"What are you going to do about Natan?" The question cut the smoke in the air between Audie and Shane like a fist.

They were sitting at their kitchen table enjoying a cup of Moses' coffee and a smoke. He had gone to the mercantile for the brothers' shopping one last time before he headed east in a couple of days. Smyth was still in bed sleeping off last night's overindulgences.

"I don't know. I don't want him to have our life."

"God forbid," Audie agreed as he sipped his coffee. He set down his cup and stroked his beard that he had whittled down to a manageable length.

"Moses is leaving in a few days. He's going to Eminence. You know Mama will love having another mouth to feed, and he'll be handy around the house while Thomas is off to work," Audie said.

"That should have happened a long time ago," Shane figured out loud.

"Yeah."

They both sat in silence finishing off their coffee.

"Maybe Natan can go with him," Shane said.

"Go with Moses?" Audie asked.

"Yes."

They didn't speak for a while as each pondered it.

"There wouldn't be a better way to grow up in this godforsaken world. Mama raising him, Moses looking after him. Thomas is a good man, too," Audie said.

"Natan could have the life we were supposed to have." Shane's voice cracked with emotion. The sweet thoughts in his head pushed tears to the corners of his eyes.

"I know, brother. I know. Your son should have that."

"He will have that," Shane said as he wiped the tears away with his thumb and forefinger.

"I'm going to see Lozen. I'll be back this evening."

Audie reached out and grabbed his brother's right shoulder, giving it a firm squeeze. Shane tipped his black leather gambler's hat to his brother and headed out the door.

"I don't give a fiddler's fart whether there's supposed to be guns there or not! I want somebody trained on those Devil brothers in case they get any ideas," Tabor shouted.

"Sir, with all due respect, the DeVine Devils haven't even agreed to do the show yet," Binkley started.

"Binkley, you're as fine of an example as there is of why some men serve and others lead. I will be prepared, you fidgety fopdoodle! Either way! God! Someone should shoot you and put us all out of our misery!"

Binkley tucked tail and left to do his master's bidding.

Shane rode up to the camp while the sun was beating straight down. He had stopped at a restaurant and bought steak and potatoes for Lozen and Onawa and stewed tomatoes with sugar cane for Natan. As he rode up and dismounted, Lozen snuck up behind him and put a knife to his throat.

When he realized it was her, he relaxed and removed her hand.

"Dammit, Lozen. I know your stealth. Why do you always have to prove it to me?"

"To keep you sharp, lily."

Shane rolled his eyes and pulled the food out of his saddlebags. "I brought food for you. I would imagine hare and wild onion has lost your favor by now."

They walked over to where Onawa was sitting, sat down, and began to eat.

"The tomatoes are for Natan. They have cane sugar on them."

Lozen set them aside. "He is asleep for his midday nap."

Onawa and Lozen both ate heartily. It was a welcome change from campfire food.

When they had finished, Onawa got up to give the two some privacy.

"I've made a decision, Lozen, about Natan."

Her dark-brown eyes looked at him, waiting for him to continue.

"Natan should go live with my mother in Missouri. Moses is going there in a few days. He can take him. Mama will look after him like her own. Her husband, Thomas, is a good man, and there's not a better man walking this earth than Moses."

Lozen was silent for a moment, thinking through Shane's plan for their son.

"And I will never see my son again?"

"Of course you could. Whenever you wanted. No one would stop you, Lozen."

She studied Shane's eyes. "The thought of him being raised by white men . . ."

"He's half white, Lozen. That's part of him, too."

She watched a blue jay push off of a hackberry tree, flying east and out of sight. It made her sad.

"I don't know, Shane."

"He'll have a mother. A great one. One who hasn't devoted herself to dying as a warrior."

Lozen gave him a sharp look but softened quickly. She knew he was right.

"It is a fair thing," Onawa interrupted.

Shane and Lozen jerked their heads around to look at her. She was standing five feet behind them, listening to the whole conversation.

"It is a fair thing. You and your brother were raised by Apache. Your son will be raised by the white. Peace may not be found by warring. Peace may be found by coming together."

Lozen wanted to speak, but she had nothing to say in return.

"It is a fair thing," Onawa spoke the third time.

Lozen looked from her to Shane and held his gaze a moment. She slowly nodded her head in agreement. Then she rose and walked off to where the blue jay had flown so no one would see the tears beginning to fall.

Natan never woke while his future was being decided. Shane

waited for another hour till he was awake and played with his son until the sun began to set.

"I need a few more days with him," Lozen said while Shane chased Natan around the tent.

He stopped and faced her. "Of course. We have a couple of weeks. But he and Moses will have to be gone by then."

"Why must they leave then?" she asked.

"Audie and I are playing one last show."

CHAPTER 49

"Sit down, Smyth. I want to talk to you before you get good and drunk tonight."

Audie pulled out a chair from the table and gestured for Smyth to sit and join him.

"What's up, chief?"

"This show, it ain't gonna be like any other."

"Why's that?"

"We're going to kill the audience before we finish."

"Why, hell yeah, we are! We always did!" Smyth said unwittingly.

"No, Smyth. I mean we are going to *kill them. Dead.*" Audie spoke clearly so there was no misunderstanding him.

Smyth could tell Audie was serious. "You mean shoot the bastards? A bunch of Billy Yanks? Hell, that's. . . that's crazy, Audie!"

"It's the only reason we ever played music in the first place, Smyth. So we could kill the bastards who killed our father
, the Billy Yanks," Audie explained.

"Soapy sent for you before I even knew about this show. I don't expect you to have any part of this. There's a good chance we won't make it out of there."

Smyth pondered Audie's words quietly. "All my life I've wanted to be an outlaw. Now here you are, giving me the chance."

"It ain't like you think it is, Smyth. You're likely to get hurt. Or worse. And if you don't, they'll hunt you down till you do."

Smyth stared at Audie as he mulled it over, a grin tugging at the corners of his mouth.

"Ain't a thing in my life been worth a shit except playing with you boys. It's the only thing that ever made me feel alive. If that ain't worth dying for, nothing is."

"Alright then."

"Alright then," Smyth agreed.

They shook hands on it.

"I'm gonna need some shooting lessons," Smyth informed.

"I figured. . ."

~

"Moses, can I bend your ear a second?" Shane asked.

"Why sure."

"I need you to take something to Mama for me when you go."

"Of course, Shane. What is it?"

"My son."

Moses stared at him.

"Lozen had a baby after we met out on the trail coming here. She's camped with him outside of town. We decided it was best for him to be raised in Eminence."

Moses soaked it all in.

"And, Moses, I would consider it an honor if you looked after him like he was your own. I know you never got to be a father, but you'd make a damn fine one."

"You want me an' Miss Adalina ta raise yo' boy?"

"I know it's not perfect. But it's better than anything I could do for him. Lozen. . . she wants to fight, and me, well. . . you're the best man I know, Moses. If my son grew up to be like you. . ."

Shane fought back the pain gathering in the corner of his eyes. Moses reached out and put a hand on his shoulder.

"Do your mama know 'bout this?" he asked gently.

"No. But trust me, she's gonna be happy about it."

Moses reached out with his other hand to shake Shane's.

"It'd be a honor, Shane."

"Then it's settled. We'll book you passage on a train to the City of Kansas. I'll send a wire to Thomas to meet you at the station."

"How the train folk gonna feel 'bout a colored man travelin' with a white child?"

"Don't worry about that, Moses. I'll make sure you don't run into trouble."

Shane went to find Audie.

~

"I'm in."

"I knew you would be." Audie smiled at his brother.

"Natan will go back east with Moses. I need a letter from Tabor to guarantee their safety."

"Well, we can make that part of the deal then."

~

Tabor was finishing up a meeting with a potential partner in a silver mine when Audie and Shane came into his office uninvited.

"I told them you were busy, sir, but they insisted," the receptionist tried to explain.

The man, a Mr. Brussels, took one look at the hellions who had just walked in and didn't bother excusing himself. He made for the door before Tabor had a chance to speak, leaving his top hat behind in his rush.

Tabor went for his pistol in the drawer.

"Whoa, now," Audie coaxed. "We're just here to talk about the show."

Tabor reluctantly closed the drawer.

"You're a little jumpy aren't you, Mayor?" Shane teased.

"People are usually announced before they come in here."

"Sorry. Manners ain't our strong suit."

"We'll do your show for a hundred dollars on both sides."

"Well! That's a steep pile of money," Tabor bluffed. He couldn't care less about the amount. The good folks of Denver were paying for this out of city taxes. His pockets would be no less weighted.

"That and a letter guaranteeing safe passage to Missouri for our friend Moses and my son," Shane added.

"Huh! I didn't know you were a father. It doesn't really fit you."

Shane let the intended dig go by without retaliation.

"I'll do one hundred and fifty paid in full after the show." Tabor bargained just to play the game.

"It's a hundred on both sides or no deal. I know what this is worth to you," Audie reasoned.

"You haven't played a show in a year. It's worth something to you, too."

"We haven't played by choice, Tabor. We can get a job playing anytime we want, and you know it."

Tabor appraised the brothers for a moment, slowly stroking the lapel on his tweed jacket.

"Okay, gentlemen. I can see budging you isn't a thing done easy, if at all. One hundred before and after it is. And I'll write your letter right now to seal the deal. Why is it this man needs this letter? And why is he taking your son to Missouri?"

"Our friend is a black man. He's taking my brother's son to stay with our mother for a while."

"Where is this child's mother?" Tabor pushed.

"That's not your business, Tabor," Shane pushed back.

"Alright. Point taken."

Tabor dipped his pen into the ink bottle and began writing.

"What is Moses' last name? And the name of your child?"

"Moses Cofey. My son's name is Natan DeVine."

"Natan? That's an interesting name."

"It's a family name," Audie explained.

"Okay," Tabor said as he finished writing and stamped the mayor's seal onto the letter. "Here's your friend's protection. Can I consider this an agreement between us?"

"Yes," Audie said. "And the upfront money?"

"I'll have a man deliver it to you in the next couple of days. I don't just keep money like that lying around."

Audie nodded at him.

"Then if there's no more business, I'll see you two gentlemen in . . . twelve days at my theatre. Will you need the facility for rehearsal before?"

"Yes, that would be helpful," Audie said.

"See Shelia on the way out to set up a time. If there's nothing else, then goodbye, gentlemen." Tabor motioned to the new girl sitting where Deirdre used to.

Audie and Shane left the room and made arrangements with the receptionist for rehearsal.

∾

Each day for the next week, the brothers and Smyth rode out past Lozen's camp to practice with pistols and knives. Smyth took to it surprisingly well. His aim was much better than even he expected.

Shane would spend time with Lozen and Natan while Audie helped Smyth with his gun skills.

At night, they rehearsed at the theatre. All three felt a strength in playing together again. They fell into their old rhythm like it had never stopped.

∾

Goodbyes were something every one of them had had experience with, but no amount of experience made these goodbyes any easier.

Lozen, Shane, and Audie all accompanied Moses and Natan to the train station to see them off. Moses had bought Natan a new blue corduroy suit and leather shoes for the trip. He wanted the boy to look fine for his grandmother. He had packed diapers, fruit, and a rattle toy for the child.

Shane took Natan from Moses and hugged the boy tightly one last time. He held him against his chest and cupped the back of his head with his hand.

"Son, you go have a good life. There's a giant bur oak in Mama's front yard. It's great for climbing and swinging and doing all the things that a boy needs to do when he's growing up. You help out around the place and listen to Moses and your grandma. I love you, Natan." He was choking up as he spoke his final words of wisdom to his son.

He handed the boy to Lozen. Tears streamed down her face, and for the first time ever, she didn't care who saw.

"You be strong. You be brave," she spoke to Natan in her maiden tongue.

She held him close and sang to him a song of her people as she rocked him. It was a song that told of the bravery of the Jicarilla Apache. It was a song she hoped he would carry with him.

"Goodbye, my friend. Have a better life in Missouri than you had here," Audie said to Moses.

"Goodbye, Audie. You find some peace fo yo'self. You been a good friend ta me."

They shook hands, and Moses turned to Lozen, Shane, and Natan. Lozen kissed Natan on top of his head and slowly handed him to Moses. The boy began to get upset, but Moses shushed him softly and rocked him slightly until he calmed down. It gave Shane and Lozen a small sense of peace watching him calm their son.

Moses said one last goodbye and climbed on the train with Natan.

They all watched the steel wheels follow the tracks until the train faded completely out of sight.

~

The morning of the show came with no more fanfare than any other day of the DeVine Devils' lives of late. It was a crisp June day, the sweet early bird's song slowly fading away with the sounds of the city coming to life.

The sun rushed through the kitchen window and spilled gently across the table covering half of Audie's hand as he sat gathering himself for the day ahead. The soft heat on his fingers pulled his thoughts away for a moment.

Shane walked in and poured himself a cup of coffee. "You sleep well?" he asked Audie.

"No. But I don't need it. I've been asleep for a year. You?"

"Got a couple hours."

"Good."

"You ready for this?" Shane asked.

"Yes."

"Me too."

Smyth slept for another hour and then joined the brothers.

The boys' request and subsequent agreement to payment before and after the show had set Tabor's mind somewhat at ease, but he was never one to trust anything or anyone fully. He was going over the arrangements for security with Binkley and his son.

"The guard will be dressed as one of the curtain men to the side of the stage. His weapons will be concealed in his coat, and if there is any tomfoolery on the part of the Devils, he will be at the ready to lay waste to them. He's been trained in such matters," James informed his father.

"Son, thank heavens I have you by my side. If I only had Binkley here, I'd be a man consumed by worry."

James nodded at his father.

Binkley left to get lunch for Tabor and his son. He was tired of Tabor treating him like a pissing pot. He kicked a stone at a mare tied off in front of the mercantile, and the horse neighed in response. It gave him a small satisfaction.

When he arrived at the restaurant, he saw Audie sitting at a table waiting on his food.

"You're a nightmarish fear to my boss, the mayor," he blurted out as he walked past him. His frustration at his boss had boiled over.

"What?"

"N-nothing," Binkley stuttered, sick that he had spoken in the first place, and turned to go.

"Wait. Why's he scared? Is he planning on reneging on our deal?" Audie inquired. He straightened up and watched the man intently.

"No. I . . . I . . . I misspoke. Forget I said anything."

"Boy, if he's planning on shady dealings, you should tell me. That's a thing I would remember fondly."

Binkley thought of all the talking down from Tabor, the insults and the name-calling, and mustered up his courage.

"He's going to have a man there, a sharpshooter. If he thinks you're going to try anything unruly, the man has orders to kill y'all on the spot," Binkley spilled out as courageous as he could.

"Where's this man going to be?"

"Side stage. Dressed like a curtain man."

"I won't forget you told me that. I'm in your debt."

Binkley was surprised that this man would treat him with respect. It was a thing he'd had very little of.

CHAPTER 50

The DeVine Devils arrived at Tabor's theatre at four o'clock. The show was at seven, but they wanted to make sure there were no other surprises. Audie had shared with the other two the information he'd gotten from Binkley.

Just as they stepped up to the doors to enter, Soapy came up to them from behind.

"Can I hang out with you vagabonds before the show, or do you have to have a pair of tits to do that?" Soapy joked.

"A pair of tits would help," Shane joked back.

"Ah. Well, I don't blame you. I just wanted to talk to Audie here before yous put on this big show."

Shane and Smyth made their way inside while Audie stayed behind with Soapy.

"You greased up? Ready to roll?"

"I am." Audie nodded.

"It's been a pleasure, friend. You're the only man who ever made me feel like I wasn't a lone wolf in this world. I know we fight for different things. But we got the same kind of fight in us."

"Yes, we do," Audie agreed.

"Alright, you bastard. Get your ass out of here pronto when it's over. I don't want to have to pay for a funeral." He reached out and hugged Audie.

Audie went inside to get ready.

~

The high-ranking officers began to file in and walk down the aisles toward the front. They were all wearing the uniforms of a soldier in those days. Blue coats with shiny, gold metal buttons curving around the front of the jacket. Black embroidery stretched from each gold button to connect to another button to form a three-tier design in like fashion to the next. The men wore matching blue pants, a crisp, black stripe cut down each side—the width of the stripe representing the rank of the officer. They all wore dark-brown, flat-toed boots shined to perfection by an underling, no doubt.

There were badges and emblems on their coats that represented courage and valor and victory. They were the same as Indian scalps to Audie and Shane. What little fear the band had began to dissolve as they watched the men file into the room.

The Tabor Grand Opera House was majestic. Plush carpet padded the floor and the walls of the box seats up in the top. The pews were made of oak and had magnificent carvings on the sides. Chandeliers hung from the ceiling like dangling diamonds high above their heads.

Smyth had brought a pint of rotgut and took his first big swig as he watched their audience seat themselves.

"No drunks tonight, Smyth," Audie said.

"This whiskey ain't getting-drunk whiskey. It's hand-steadying whiskey," Smyth declared.

"Well then, by all means, drink," Shane said.

Smyth took another swallow and put the bottle in his coat.

Audie and Smyth began tuning their instruments. Thirty minutes till showtime.

~

Tabor walked out in front of the curtain and held his hands up to hush the chatter of the crowd. After a couple of minutes, everyone grew quiet and fixed their eyes on him.

"Gentlemen! Officers of this great nation! It is an honor to be able to host you in my theatre tonight! You have done a great work in ridding us, the American people, of the vile and savage infestation of the red man! Many a people in this hallowed land will sleep well tonight with the peace that your sword has brought to us!" There were cheers and applause. Tabor held his hands up again, quieting the clamor.

"To honor you in return, I, Horace Tabor, the mayor of this city, have managed to call out of retirement the most coveted band of musicians in this nation! These men are as famous as any minstrels who have ever entertained an audience in our beloved city and, dare I say, in our wonderful country! Please join me in welcoming the DeVine Devils!"

The crowd was on its feet in an instant.

The boys started the set with "Something Bad This Way Come."

And so the night began.

Maybe it was the darkness in their souls that made them shine. Maybe it was the pain of their past. Maybe it was knowing this would be the last time they would ever deliver. Whatever the motivation, they were flawless. The audience was enraptured before the fight even began.

"We've come here tonight to celebrate! To celebrate the death of murderers, thieves, and scoundrels!"

Audie's words reverberated through the theatre amidst the deep victory yell of the soldiers. It was the end of their last song, but Audie hadn't announced that.

"Does anyone know the story of Samson in the Bible?"

His words were met with half-hearted cheers.

"He was a man given to the lusts of the flesh—wine and women and war. He was a killer. Taken down by a beautiful woman. But in the end, he killed more by his death than he ever did with his life. He brought the Philistine temple down around him and took more of his enemies to the grave than an entire army could!"

The theatre had grown quiet now.

"Tonight, men of war, you are the Philistines. . . and we, we are Samson!"

In a single, smooth motion, Audie slung his guitar around his back and threw a knife at the officer sitting center stage right in front of him.

The curtain man at the side of the stage went for his pistols, but Shane was ready for him and landed a knife in his throat before he unholstered his guns. He never got a shot off.

Those working in the theatre ran out the back door or hid in rooms in the back. Some audience members rushed the stage. Some ran for the door.

Audie ran to meet two of the men coming up the steps to the stage. With his left hand, his ax opened an officer's windpipe, and with his right, he buried a blade deep in the other man's liver. Both men fell and rolled back down the stairs, leaving the wood slick with blood.

Smyth shot three men hurrying toward them. He missed two more.

Shane took four men out of commission with his throwing knives.

Unarmed soldiers began running for the exits. One by one, they fell, slumped to the ground before they could reach safety, each impaled by a single arrow to the chest. Eighteen men stopped dead in their tracks.

Lozen.

Audie fought his way through the remaining officers. He headed for Tabor.

Smyth emptied the four pistols he had hidden on him before he grabbed his fiddle and slammed it into a soldier's face, splintering the instrument and knocking his opponent unconscious.

He never saw the man who put the knife in his back.

Shane watched Smyth go down and ran over, planting a knife in the soldier's skull, but it was too late. He kneeled over his friend's body to check if he was breathing.

Audie had made his way up the stairs to the balcony. There were only dying men on the floor of the theatre now.

When he found Tabor, the mayor was cowering between two rows of seats in the balcony box he'd been watching the show from.

Audie stood over him as he pleaded for his life.

"Please! I can give you money! Anything you want! Please!" Tabor begged.

Audie's icy glare remained on Tabor's terrified face. "Deirdre. Remember her?" Audie calmly questioned.

"Yes! Her death was so unfortunate! I loved her, too!"

"You killed her."

"No! No, I didn't hurt—"

"Don't lie to me!" Audie demanded.

"I didn't. . ."

Audie picked him up by the lapels of his tailor-made coat and punched him solidly in the middle of his face. Tabor's nose started leaking blood like a gusher.

"Please don't kill—"

Audie buried the blade right in Tabor's heart.

Tabor gasped for air as his hands shook and grasped at his chest.

Audie smiled at the look on Tabor's face. It was like looking at an old friend.

Death.

He held Tabor's eyes in his glare until all the life faded from them.

Audie threw him over the balcony, and he hit the seats below with the thud that dead things make.

"Thank you," he heard behind him.

Audie spun around and instantly felt a bullet tear straight through his left side. He reached for the man who shot him but fell to his knees instead.

James Tabor stood there holding a pistol. Smoke from the gun clouded the smirk on his face.

"I thought the bastard would live another twenty years. You've done me a huge service," James confessed.

Audie tried to get up, but he was too weak. The room started spinning

And faded to black.

CHAPTER 51

Three years later

"Thomas, you and Moses are going to work yourself to death in this heat. Come inside and get a drink."

The men were tending to the green beans in the garden. It was June, and the beetles had started munching on the leaves, making it necessary to spend hours picking them off.

"And you, young man, how in the world did you get so filthy? Good Lord! It'll take me a week to get all of that dirt out of those britches!"

Natan came down from the bur oak and ran to get a drink of water from Adalina. He took the cup she had for him and drank gulps so big you could hear the water working its way down his throat.

"Thank you, Gramma!" he shouted as he ran off like lightning to the next adventure his imagination could conjure up.

He was wearing moccasins that had been mysteriously left on his windowsill the week before.

The two older men slowly made their way up to the porch and sat on the steps, barely glimpsing the lightning bolt that ran past them.

"He look like his daddy," Moses offered. "Like you, Miss Adalina."

"He's a smart boy. Pretty soon he's going to start asking hard questions," Thomas said as he took a full tin cup of water from Adalina.

They all watched as Natan made his way up and over the worm fence and toward the creek on the other side.

"He'll ask. And we won't lie to him," Adalina instructed as she watched the only Indian she ever loved run.

They sat in silence for a bit.

"Won't have ta lie. They's plenty a good ta tell about his momma and daddy. Ev'rybody got some dark and some light in 'em. When the boy learn that, he'll understand how this world could make a DeVine Devil."

≈

Heroes and villains are judged mostly by the historian's pen.

≈

Forty-two men died that day in the Tabor Grand Opera House. There were three surviving soldiers who told a tale of the minstrel warriors who laid low the others in attendance that evening.

Shane made it out of Denver that night and was hunted for the next six months by every Pinkerton agent and United States Marshall with the sand to track him. A marshall with the last name Richardson and his seven deputies caught up to him in Kansas as he was riding hard to the east.

He told the marshall about killing Jessie and Jacob Halter, the men who had captured Moses. He confessed to killing a band of soldiers headed west with a shipment of Winchester rifles and to the murder of Harold Setters and Burly Welks in Wichita, Kansas. He said he was responsible for the murders of Briggs and Waters. He told Richardson he'd killed a man named Arny. He told him his whole story—the attack on the Apache, his father's death—every detail. He told him about the trappers and scalpers he and Audie had killed when they were still teenagers.

Shane's only request was that the DeVine Devils' story would be documented so that the world would know why they did what they did.

Richardson had a deputy write down every word of it. But the United States government never released the report.

On the way back to Denver for trial, Shane worked himself loose of his shackles and tried to run in the middle of the night. He was shot in the back by Deputy Jessup Ratcliff.

Shane was laid to rest in a cemetery nearby with only a misshapen stone for a marker on his grave.

Devil was what they carved on the stone.

~

Smyth died that night in the theatre from a knife wound in the back. He was immortalized in a popular novel a few years later titled *Hell-bound Hoxie*. The book was a total fabrication of his involvement in the illegal doings of the DeVine Devils. It greatly exaggerated his skill level with the knife and pistol, but he would have loved every word of it. He had always wanted to be an outlaw.

Of the surviving officers in the theatre that night, two told of an Indian who had shot the arrows that were found in the bloodbath, but it was never substantiated.

Audie was still alive, but barely, when they found him in the balcony that night. The doctor declared he would be dead by morning.

The next day when deputies went to collect the body, it was gone.

~

Seven years after the Opera House attack, James Tabor was found dead in his office chair, a knife stuck in his chest. There was a note pinned to the body that read, "Courtesy of the Devil."

~

In the year 1923, a monk died at a monastery in Missouri, the Basilica of the Immaculate Conception. He went by the name Samson Azariah.

Upon his passing, a note was found on his bedside table that read, "My name is Audie DeVine. I am a man of God who knew the devil's work well."

Placed on top of the note was a worn leather band with a cross and a feather.

The End

ABOUT THE AUTHOR

Kentucky born and bred, Jeremy Spillman moved to Nashville, Tennessee to pursue his dream of success as a songwriter at 24. It would be five years before he landed his first cut by a major label artist and signed a publishing deal. Since then, Jeremy has had songs recorded by Eric Church, Tim McGraw, Keith Urban, LANCO, Tenille Townes, Wade Bowen, Randy Rogers, Trace Adkins, Brandy Clark, Midland, Little Big Town, Reba McEntire, Josh Turner, Brantley Gilbert, Jon Pardi, Chris LeDoux, Luke Bryan and many more.

Spillman lives with his wife and four sons south of Nashville, TN. He considers his role as a father the most important in his life. When he's not writing novels and songs or recording music, Spillman is supporting his sons at football and basketball games and spending time with them at home.

Spillman's debut novel, *The DeVine Devils*, is also available as a full cast audiobook and has an accompanying soundtrack. The music was written by Spillman with Nashville songwriters Randy Montana, Dean Dillon and Clint Ingersoll. The soundtrack was recorded, produced and mixed by Spillman at his home studio.

If you enjoyed this novel, please consider leaving a review at your preferred retailer. It is much appreciated.

MUSIC FROM THE DEVINE DEVILS

The soundtrack from *The DeVine Devils* is available everywhere music is streamed or sold. Scan the QR Code to take you directly to the music.

How to scan the QR code:

1. Open your device's Camera app.
2. Hold your device so that the QR code appears in the Camera app's viewfinder. Your device will automatically recognize the QR code and show a notification.
3. Tap the notification to open the link associated with the QR code.

www.ingramcontent.com/pod-product-compliance
Lightning Source LLC
Chambersburg PA
CBHW031609100726
47898CB00006B/1712